Always Knew It Was You (Pink Hotel Book 2)

Small Town Fake Relationship Romantic Suspense

Summer Hunter

Copyright © 2025 by Summer Hunter

All rights reserved.

No part of this book may be reproduced in any form or by any electronic or mechanical means, including information strage and retrieval systems, without written permission from the author.

This is a work of fiction.
Any names, characters, places, or incidents are products of the author's imagination and used in a fictitious manner. Any resemblance to actual people, places, or events is coincidental or fictional.

Contents

1. CHAPTER ONE — 1
2. CHAPTER TWO — 11
3. CHAPTER THREE — 24
4. CHAPTER FOUR — 34
5. CHAPTER FIVE — 42
6. CHAPTER SIX — 52
7. CHAPTER SEVEN — 64
8. CHAPTER EIGHT — 74
9. CHAPTER NINE — 83
10. CHAPTER TEN — 95
11. CHAPTER ELEVEN — 100
12. CHAPTER TWELVE — 114
13. CHAPTER THIRTEEN — 124

14. CHAPTER FOURTEEN — 134
15. CHAPTER FIFTEEN — 143
16. CHAPTER SIXTEEN — 151
17. CHAPTER SEVENTEEN — 162
18. CHAPTER EIGHTEEN — 171
19. CHAPTER NINETEEN — 179
20. CHAPTER TWENTY — 187
21. CHAPTER TWENTY-ONE — 197
22. CHAPTER TWENTY-TWO — 207
23. CHAPTER TWENTY-THREE — 218
24. CHAPTER TWENTY-FOUR — 229
25. CHAPTER TWENTY-FIVE — 238
26. CHAPTER TWENTY-SIX — 247
27. CHAPTER TWENTY-SEVEN — 260
28. CHAPTER TWENTY-EIGHT — 273
29. CHAPTER TWENTY-NINE — 284
30. CHAPTER THIRTY — 292
31. CHAPTER THIRTY-ONE — 299
32. CHAPTER THIRTY-TWO — 307
33. CHAPTER THIRTY-THREE — 315
34. CHAPTER THIRTY-FOUR — 324
35. CHAPTER THIRTY-FIVE — 332

36.	CHAPTER THIRTY-SIX	339
37.	CHAPTER THIRTY-SEVEN	347
38.	CHAPTER THIRTY-EIGHT	356
39.	CHAPTER THIRTY-NINE	366
40.	CHAPTER FORTY	373
41.	CHAPTER FORTY-ONE	379
42.	CHAPTER FORTY-TWO	387
43.	CHAPTER FORTY-THREE	397
44.	CHAPTER FORTY-FOUR	405
45.	EPILOGUE	414
About the author		422

CHAPTER ONE

Carly

"Oh my gosh, that is the most darling bracelet I have ever seen in my life!"

I glance over at the grandiose exclamation, eyeing the tennis bracelet encircling the brunette's wrist. I'm standing with a group of women near the newly installed French windows overlooking the glistening lake in front of the vast forest.

"Thank you," she responds graciously. "Remy bought it at Boucheron the last time he was in Monaco. Allegedly, it belonged to the Countess of Castiglione herself. Only three of these are in the entire world. It cost Remy a hundred thousand and one of his properties in London, but gosh, isn't it beautiful?"

"It is," the three other women coo and I join them. Internally though, I'm reeling.

I'm lucky there's a mask hiding my expression, and I sip on champagne to cover up my gape. A hundred thousand dollars? Plus a house? For that? Sure it's a nice bracelet, but I'm pretty sure I could get something similar at Nordstrom out in Bayview for a couple hundred dollars. Maybe half that, if it was on sale.

But then again, the women standing beside me are pretty clearly in a whole different financial stratosphere from me. Everyone in this party is.

It's a VIP event, a masquerade ball held in the grand hall of the Pink Hotel, meant to remind of the glory days of the historic hotel. Across the rich brown of the exotic hardwood floors, various guests in suits, gowns and elaborate masks gather in groups to enjoy the first exclusive showing of the hotel and the famed Pink Pearl.

The elite guests drift around the newly renovated Victorian ballroom of the Pink Hotel, some admiring the artwork lining the intricate Windsor-paneled walls. A few others coagulate in groups like the one I'm part of, making low conversation with occasional bursts of laughter. Some are reclined in the vintage Restoration-era armchairs fixed in the corners of the room. Others–thanks to the ample champagne–are clearly enjoying a nice buzz, and are now dancing to the softly lilting classical music coming from the quintet on the raised stage. They're apparently a famous orchestra group, consisting of a piano, saxophone, and a variety of violins. The theme of the evening is *Scarlet Night* and so the orchestra, like most guests, are masked and dressed in satin and silks of reds and blacks, sparkling and shining under the warm golden light of the crystal chandelier. Set high into a blue ceiling, the light fixture resembles a thousand diamonds dripping from the sky.

I feel like I've walked into a scene from *The Great Gatsby* and I'm trying not to feel out of place.

Trying and failing.

"Remy's been working hard these days, and he wanted something to make up for his absence," the brunette bracelet-owner—Cherise she said her name was—continues.

"Aww, how adorable," the blonde one with her hair in an elaborate coiffe says. She never introduced herself, but the other women call her V.

"Your love is so beautiful it makes me sob," the third, dark-haired woman says in a quiet voice. She seems to be the quietest of the group and has neither introduced herself nor has she offered up any information about herself.

"I know!" V says. "I'm so jealous because you literally have the perfect husband."

"The absolute perfect husband," the final woman, Heather, says. "With the perfect family and the perfect life. I can't even be jealous, because you deserve it so much, my friend."

The other two women hum their approval while Cherise beams.

I wonder if I'm the only one who can taste the utter fakery in the atmosphere.

I can't see any of their expressions, thanks to the lacy asymmetric masks sitting on the upper half of their faces, but I definitely know they're being less than honest.

And then they turn that look to me, and I realize that I'm the only one who hasn't said anything yet.

"It's a beautiful bracelet," I admit. *Not a hundred thousand dollars beautiful but beautiful all the same.* It was jeweled squares laced around a simple band. High-carat diamonds probably. It undoubtedly cost a lot to make, thanks to the intricate craftsmanship.

But a hundred thousand...I can imagine a plethora of other things I would do with that money. I wouldn't have to worry about my scholarship. Maybe get my parents out of that slowly dilapidating house. Get my cousin out of jail...even though he wholly deserves to be in there; I can't help the tightness in my gut whenever I think about it.

"Thank you," Cherise says. "And don't think I haven't been eyeing your *Queen's Dynasty* all night."

"My....what?"

Her eyes flash in surprise. "Your necklace? Don't tell me you don't know what it's called?"

My hand drifts up to touch the elaborate ruby gems webbed around my neck. "No?"

My best friend Emma called it a statement necklace when it was handed to me, but never mentioned it had a name. Truthfully, I thought the jewelry was a little much, but it matched with my sleek black dress perfectly. And the dress was a simple silk strapless number that even I had to admit made me look wholly like a million bucks.

But neither were mine.

Both the dress and the necklace belonged to Rachel, Emma's fiance's ex-wife. Rachel is a fashion designer, a pretty prolific one, who recently had a string of successful shows at Paris Fashion Week. She insisted on dressing both Emma and me for the occasion today after she took one look at the outfits we planned to wear.

"Polyester?" she squeaked, her face twisting in dramatic horror. "You were going to wear polyester to a ball?" Her voice cracked at the end, and her tone made me feel like I committed a grievous sin. I shared a look with Emma.

"Yeah?" Emma answered weakly. She glanced down at one of the dresses we'd bought from the boutique in Bayview, the fancy one that smelled like eucalyptus and leather. "Is that bad?"

I didn't think it was bad. Like me, Emma grew

up in the small town of Laketown where everyone was dressed pretty lowkey even for fancy events. Although Emma was about to marry an honest-to-God billionaire, and had bodyguards following her around now, her down-to-earth nature hasn't changed. And I loved her for it.

But Rachel's face reddened and she shuddered nearly catatonically.

"Are you kidding?" She looked between the two of us and then shook her head. "Absolutely not. Come." And then she'd spun on her heel walking away, giving us no choice but to follow.

In the end, Rachel drove us from Emma's house back to the boutique in Bayview. We tried on outfit after outfit, and then when she wasn't satisfied with any of them, she had some dresses flown in from her own collection. Eventually, she decided on my dress and Emma's red flare dress that made her look like an actual princess, especially standing across the hall next to her prince of a fiancé.

Declan is the new owner of the Pink Hotel and is the definition of tall, dark, and handsome. His face is usually set in a straight scowl until he looks down at Emma. Then he would smile and softness would fill his eyes.

Like now.

He's staring down at Emma while she speaks passionately, gesturing with her hands. A few paces away from them, two suited men stand, trying to blend in with the wallpaper. And they do succeed partially, because I barely notice Emma's bodyguards half the time. It's so interesting how inconspicuous two large, threatening men can be.

Almost reluctantly, my gaze is drawn to another man standing next to Declan, a man who I very much should not be looking at but who has held my attention all night. Even in a room full of polished diamonds, he shines the brightest.

I tear my attention away from them and back to my companions.

"Sorry," I say. "I had no clue. It was a gift from a friend."

"Oh…" they all chorus.

"What friend?" V asks. Then she follows my staring path to Emma and one finger delicately unwraps from her champagne glass to point. "Any of the people over there?"

"Both of them actually," I respond. While I wouldn't say Declan and I are friends exactly–it's hard to be friends with a man as intimidating as he is–we're on friendly terms. My cousin had been partially involved in the kidnapping of Declan's daughter a few months ago, but Declan actually reassured me that he didn't hold it against me.

"I know how important you are to Emma," he told me during the fall fair after he'd just proposed to her. "And I want you to know that I value and respect your friendship. Whatever Nate did, doesn't change that."

I was both stunned and relieved to hear it. Maybe that was why he didn't press charges on my cousin, although Nate was still facing state charges. And so was Rick, my former boss and a man who was like a father to Emma. He'd been one of the masterminds behind the whole kidnapping, and that very fact broke Emma's heart.

Regardless, while I wouldn't call Declan my friend, he still ranks pretty high in my book. And Emma…well, she's been my best and only friend since I was ten and she was twelve.

It started when she found me crying behind the church parking lot after my mother made a scene at church. Emma convinced me to come home with her and though I knew my mother would be mad, I went anyway. Emma had always seemed nice and I wanted to be around her and her sweet, funny grandpa, who were such a contrast to my tumultuous family.

Her home was as warm and welcoming as I imagined, and her grandpa made us hot chocolate and then took us fishing later that evening before driving me home. My mom yelled at me some more when I got home, but it was worth it for the brief reprieve at Emma's place.

And it wasn't the last time family drama drove me to seek refuge in her home. Emma always let me stay, no questions asked, and for that I'm forever grateful.

V nods at my response. "Ah. Well, I know the dress can't be from Declan Tudor since we recently discovered his engagement to the cute country girl." I frown at her description as she continues, "So it would have to be Micah."

"You're friends with Micah Landing?" Cherise asks.

"How do you know it's Micah standing next to them? He's wearing a mask," the quiet brunette says.

"Oh, please." V is still staring at Micah, her lips twisting. "I would know that frame anywhere."

I glance back to where Micah stands engaged in a discussion with Declan's father. I've been trying all night not to look at the man because looking at him makes me vaguely breathless. No man has a right to be that good-looking even with a black mask covering half their face. But Micah is.

He's about the same height as Declan, if an inch shorter, and instead of dark hair, he has red hair, combed into curls falling around his face. He's dressed in an all-black suit, with navy-blue trimming on the jacket and an expensive-looking watch casually dancing on his wrist. His hands are in his pocket, his broad shoulders completely at ease, even though I know I'm not the only one staring at him.

Every time I look at him, I notice at least one other person doing the same, usually someone of the female variety. But Micah doesn't seem to notice or care.

He's probably used to being the center of attention.

I've never actually had a conversation with him, but I've overheard him talking to Declan and flirting with Emma's other best friend, Tate, so I figure I have a pretty good read on his personality. Wealthy handsome playboy who is accustomed to having beautiful women throw themselves at him. A man who flirted as easily as he breathed. The kind of man who treated women like used panties and never even thought about them after the night was over.

But, just for the night, he probably makes it worth their while.

"I wouldn't say we're friends," I say as the women finally look back at me. "I've never even had a conversation with the man. I'm more so friends with Declan and Emma."

"Good," V says. "Stay away from Micah if you know what's good for you. I've never met a more arrogant, selfish bastard in my life."

"That's not the tune you were singing last summer in Cabo," Cherise quips with a teasing smile and V's complexion reddens.

"Yeah, and I learned my lesson then," she says.

"Was he that bad?" I ask.

"No, dear," Heather winks. "He was that good."

The women giggle again and V rolls her eyes. To

me, she says, "Micah has more charm than the devil himself and has this way of making you feel like you're the most beautiful woman in the world. He'll show you an amazing time and then completely toss you away at the end. He won't so much as return your calls."

"And he'll ruin you for every other man," the quiet dark-haired one says, and then she catches the blonde's frown. "What? We've all heard the rumors. I'm jealous of you, you know. At least, you got to enjoy the ride. I wish I'd gotten that close."

"Me too," Heather sighs.

"Me three," Cherise says and her companions stare at her in surprise.

"You're married," V says.

"So? I'm married, not blind. And what Remington doesn't know won't kill him."

For some reason, the statement has the women breaking into raucous peals of laughter, which I also join.

I quickly grow weary of the conversation after that, and hold up my empty glass as an excuse to melt away. Emma's still with Declan and I don't want to interrupt their romantic ambiance. It's a night for lovers, a beautiful cool spring evening with red maple trees in full bloom outside and the mingling scent of cologne and perfume surrounding me. As I walk away, my eyes wander around the room, wondering if I should intercept another conversation group or simply observe how the rich and powerful interact with each other.

It's why I agreed to accompany Emma to this party in the first place.

I felt like playing dress up and pretending to be someone else for the night. Tonight, I'm not Carly whose cousin is in jail, whose father is a drunk, and whose mother is a thief. I'm not the girl struggling to retain her scholarship and claw her way out of poverty.

Tonight, I'm the girl in the golden mask, beautiful dress, and the necklace that has an expensive-sounding name. Tonight, I can walk with my spine straight because no one knows who I am. I can pretend I'm one of them, that I take trips to Cabo too. I can pretend that I'm the kind of woman Micah Landing would look at.

I find myself staring at him again and, then, in a startling twist, his eyes meet mine.

As the brilliant green flashes, my body blazes to life. My breath lodges in my throat, heat and desire slamming into me. A smirk curves the side of his lips as though he knows the exact effect he has on me.

Damn it.

Nevertheless, I refuse to give him that satisfaction. I school my features underneath the mask into indifference and deliberately roll my gaze down his body. When I meet his eyes again, I shake my head and turn away.

My stomach still flip-flops once it's done, excited at the challenge I've just given him. I feel like I just laid down a gauntlet.

And now his gaze is burning a hole in my back.

CHAPTER TWO

M ICAH

Athena is on the move again.

"Athena" is what I'm calling the girl in the golden mask that covered nearly her entire face except for red luscious lips that looked like they would bounce back if I bit. Her brown locks flow in waves down to somewhere around her midback, and I think she'll have probably been better off arranging it at the top of her head into some kind of bun. That way it can show off the long line of her neck.

And there would be nothing blocking that nice deep décolletage.

My body hardens as my eyes take it in once more.

The woman's body is all soft curves and the black dress she wears highlights every single bend, from the swelled chest, to the dip of her waist, flaring back out to her hips and down her long legs. She's not all that tall, probably a bit taller than average, but somehow her long limbs make her seem even taller.

They also make me imagine all sorts of dirty things, like those legs wrapping around my waist as I pumped into her. I've been watching her, thinking about it for most of the night.

And that was before she'd pulled that stunt.

Now, hunger is an urgent beat in my gut.

"I hope you know what you're doing, son," the warning voice of Frank Tudor interrupts my observation.

"Only about half the time," I quip.

"I'm referring to this hotel that your father and I have put in your hands. I suspect that maybe you're not seeing the bigger picture here." He gestures around the room at the people currently getting drunk and dancing around the ballrooms. At each side, servers stand with more champagne and a couple of security officers guard the door. Even they're dressed in some kind of Victorian-era clothing. It adds to the theme and probably stokes the air of wonder in the room.

All the guests appear relaxed and very pleased with themselves, likely because they feel special to be invited to such a historic occasion: the reopening of a once-dead hotel that faced enough tragedies to be called haunted, but also reportedly hid many treasures. Discovery of those treasures is now frequently in the headlines of many major news stations. I'm waiting for one guest in particular, the one who can get this damn noose of a hotel off my neck, but he's not here yet.

"This is only the beginning, son," Frank says, stressing the words and laying his other hand on my shoulder as though trying to force the gravity of it on me. "This event was restricted to VIPs only, but I've gotten lots of interest for the true opening of the hotel. The waitlist for that event is hundreds of names long. That one is going to be grander, and better. It will make the news again. The Grand Pearl

Hotel is on the trend to surpass even its former glory."

"I know." Part of the reason for the manic interest in this hotel is because of the discovery of a Pink Pearl. It's a gem so rare that most people didn't even believe in its existence. There is only one in the entire world, located at this hotel, and it's why the Grand Pearl Hotel is often called the Pink Hotel.

There's also apparently a bunch of lore surrounding the Pearl, linking back to two lovers who disappeared from the hotel on the night the Pink Pearl initially went missing. One of the lovers, Madam Something-or-Other, owned a diary that somehow fell into the hands of Declan's precocious daughter, Amelia.

According to Amelia, Madam Something was a socialite who ended up tangling with jewel thieves that were plotting to steal the Pink Pearl. Stuff happened, she started a relationship with one of them, her original fiancé died and yada yada, the Pink Pearl went missing. I don't really care enough to remember the fine details. What's truly amazing is that Amelia and Emma put together hints from that story in order to figure out that there was a pearl-smuggling operation happening right under everyone's nose.

That's right, a thirteen-year-old and a young bartender cracked a case wide open. The cops in Laketown ought to be ashamed of themselves.

In any case, discovery of the Pink Pearl came after news of thieves and pearl smugglers stealing rare rainbow pearls from the lakes around Laketown.

All that scandal has catapulted this tiny town into prominence and suddenly tourists are flocking in, everyone wanting to see the famed Pink Pearl or get a rainbow pearl for themselves.

Declan has the Pink Pearl in his possession but he

has kept it under wraps until today when it will be viewed at the end of the event.

Of course, as part owner of the Pink Hotel, I've already seen the gem a few times and still don't get the hype.

"We're on track to make millions of dollars of profit from this investment in just the first year," Frank continues with that tone he often dons when he's in a lecturing mood. Stern and increasingly annoyed. "This is going to be the hotel of the decade."

"I have no doubt," I say, and even with the half mask, I can see him frown at my glibness. If nothing else, thanks to Declan's aggressive renovation and marketing, the Pink Hotel will likely be a success story.

"So then why are you selling your shares to Ben DuPont?"

My eyes flash open as I stare at him. "How did you...?"

"I know everything." The man is good at hiding his expression, but I get the feeling I've disappointed him. He probably thinks I'm dumb for throwing away this opportunity, and maybe I am.

But I'm still going to do it.

I never wanted to be involved with this hotel in the first place.

I told my father as much a few months ago, when he mentioned that he and Frank Tudor had jointly bought the hotel for their sons to run. A dilapidated hotel in a small town seemed like a dumb investment to me, but I have to admit that the story of the hotel has given it an edge and it's gearing to be a very profitable venture. In just a few months, Declan and his real estate company have renovated the hotel from a crumbling shell of itself to a shining beacon that still manages to maintain its historic flair while having a modern appeal.

While I can understand and appreciate the fact that the Pink Hotel has the potential for expansive growth, I have no intention of being a part of that. For starters, I don't know the first thing about running a hotel and don't care to learn. Plus, as part owner, I'm supposed to stay to facilitate the opening of the hotel and that would mean that I would be trapped in Laketown for at least a few months. As charming as it is, Laketown isn't a place I can stand for that long. They have three, maybe four gas stations total, and one road out of town. There's not a single country club, or yacht club, or a bar that's not a dive bar. Apart from the Pink Hotel, the only acceptable lodging is the Marriott. There's nothing here to do at all.

I would lose my mind in under a week.

And then there's the most important reason I want to sell my shares in the Pink Hotel.

Because with that money, I can finally start up my new business.

My family is worth billions, so I'm typically not hurting for cash. The problem is that most of the money is controlled by my father who has been diligently monitoring my expenses in an attempt to reestablish his authority over me. When he catches wind of the fact that I want to start a new company, he's going to be pissed.

Another one? I can hear his sneer now, as well as his exasperation. *How many businesses do you have to try and fail before you learn that you just don't have the knack for it?*

Even just the thought of his admonition gets me irritated. Especially since he's wrong. Technically, only half of my attempted businesses have failed. The others were successful at first and only failed after I lost interest, sold them, and/or deliberately sabotaged them.

But this new business venture is different. It'll be a success; I can feel it. But convincing my father of that will be impossible, which is why I'm going behind his back to sell my hotel shares for starting capital.

"So you found out," I say, annoyed as my eyes find Athena again. She's resting against a wall, observing once more. I wonder if she knows she looks like a goddess amongst mortals.

"I did. Your father isn't going to like this."

The mention of my father has me stiffening as much as I try to hide it. Thankfully, there's a mask shielding my expression. "What Daddy doesn't know won't kill him." Technically, due to the nature of the contract, Frank Tudor and my dad are the majority stakeholders, with Declan and I being the minority. As such there are certain limitations on us selling our shares to other entities, but DuPont knew a way around it.

Frank and Dad's idea, I know, is for both Declan and me to prove ourselves in order to eventually inherit our parents' shares and be in full control of the Pink Hotel. Declan already did his part by renovating the hotel, much to my annoyance. I wanted him to help me sabotage our parents' deal by obstructing the rebuilding efforts, and I initially thought it would be easy enough to get him on board. After all, Declan also thought the purchase of the Pink Hotel was stupid and he didn't want to stay in Laketown either.

But then he had to go and fall in love with a local and that sent all my plans to shit.

As happy as I am for Declan and his future bride, his decision to go along with our dads' plot has forced me into a difficult position.

My father already told me that it's my turn to prove myself by handling the reopening of the hotel. Except I refuse. I have no interest in running this hotel or being my father's errand boy. So I'm selling my shares. Declan already agreed to buy half, and now the other half is going to Ben. For some reason, Frank eyes me carefully. With black eyes set into the narrow eye holes of a black mask, he looks very menacing and I'm almost intimidated. Except that I've received similar glares from my father, and I've gotten too used to them growing up.

Frank is an interesting man. While not as strict as my father, he's not exactly a bed of roses either. Declan is a workaholic and since he was raised solely by his father, I can only blame Frank for that.

And as an old family friend, Frank occasionally likes to pretend to be my father too. Which is why he's here looking at me in disappointment. "Well, you know I'll have to tell your father."

"Do what you need to do." I try to sound casual about it, even as bitterness curdles in my gut. I'm sure Frank's interference is the reason why DuPont didn't show up today despite us pretty much finalizing everything over the phone. Damn it.

There goes the last man in New York City willing and powerful enough to go against my father. Most of the other men in power are firmly within my father's circle of friends. And the only other person I can think of who has the kind of "fuck you" money and influence to go up against Marcus Landing, is an old acquaintance from school, Toby Leviathan. Problem is, he's a recluse who is extremely hard to reach, and even harder to convince.

"I'm sorry, Micah. But I just can't watch someone I care about throw money away."

"Must be why you're the richest sixty-year-old in America."

He snorts. "Second richest, thanks to your father's recent acquisition."

"Oh yeah. I forgot about that." My father has an

eye for taking failing businesses and turning them profitable and his most recent acquisition just catapulted to a billion-dollar value. "But if it makes you feel better, you look younger and better than he does."

Frank snorts.

"Excuse me," I say and he waves me off as I start walking away. Athena is finally alone and this is my chance. Since my night is already ruined, business-wise, I might as well have some fun. I don't miss the fact that she, like many other women at this party, has been sending looks my way all night. That's pretty normal for me. I'm a good-looking guy if I do say so myself and get looks pretty much anywhere I go.

But currently, Athena is the only woman here who caught my attention from the moment she walked in with that damn curve-hugging dress.

"Who is that?" I asked Declan the second she arrived with a masked woman I instantly recognized as Emma.

Declan followed my gaze and shook his head.

"That is not for you," was all he said sternly, and that piqued my curiosity even more.

Being with a woman like that would be enjoyable enough. But messing with Declan while I'm at it would be a nice bonus too.

So I began watching Athena, keeping tabs on her movement in between my conversations. At one point, Emma left her to go to Declan but Athena didn't seem to mind. She immediately drifted to a group of women, joining their conversation with little effort. She was like a chameleon, purposefully fitting herself into the fold and unconsciously mimicking the stance of the women beside her. Even with the mask, I saw her eyes moving over them, her lips curving as though she could read them like a book and was laughing silently at them.

Just like she's doing now from her position against the wall.

She fascinates me. I wonder if she can read me. I wonder what she'll see.

She seems comfortable alone, but I find myself moving to her anyway. She doesn't look at me when I arrive, merely takes another sip of her drink.

"I have a question to ask," I start and even though she still doesn't look at me, I sense her pulse quickening, her breaths coming slightly faster. She's not as unaffected as she's pretending to be.

"A question?" Her voice is soft and unassuming, with a strange breathless quality to it that doesn't feel rehearsed. I'd love to hear that voice whispering in my ear as I thrust into her.

Easy, Micah. Patience. "Yeah. Why the mask?"

She turns to me then and, behind the mask, I notice that her eyes are golden brown with dark lashes. I want to melt in them. She smells delicious too, a subtle sweet scent that I've never smelled before.

I'm so busy taking her in, I forget all about the question I asked until she answers it.

"It's a masquerade ball," she says, in a tone that implies that I might be an idiot.

I smile. "I didn't ask why you were wearing a mask, just why you chose this one. If you haven't noticed, most of the other women in the room have a half mask that at least gives some hints as to who they are. But yours does not. Which tells me that either you're someone who wants to hide or you're trying very hard to be seen as mysterious."

She blinks slowly.

"Or I could just be frightfully ugly," she says. "The type of ugly that scares children and makes small animals distinctly uncomfortable."

"Like the Phantom of the Opera?"

"That's who I'm channeling. Did you consider that option?"

A smile dances at the corner of her lips and I want to kiss them even more than before. "I guess I didn't."

"Somehow I'm not surprised." She turns away.

"And that's supposed to mean?"

"Just that you strike me as the kind of man who wouldn't consider talking to anyone he thinks might be unattractive."

"And that's your way of saying I'm a shallow asshole."

"Shallow? Maybe. Asshole is a matter of perspective. I don't know you enough to call you an asshole." A smile finally rocks her lips. "Although one of the ladies I was talking to seemed to imply that might be the case."

"Which lady?"

"Somehow I doubt you'd remember her even if I told you."

"And now I'm a manwhore too."

"Do you deny it?" She's full-on amused now, seemingly having fun with this conversation. And I'm having fun too, even if it's at the expense of my reputation.

"Only in the sense that I don't require money for my services."

It takes her a moment to get the joke and she rolls her eyes. "Maybe you're just not good enough to get paid."

"Oh, I doubt your friend told you that," he says. "She wouldn't be calling me an asshole if I wasn't."

That finally gets a laugh out of her, a throaty laugh that makes hunger rush through me. I laugh too, feeling elated and a little buzzed.

It's a good day, all things considered. I sold my hotel shares and found an intriguing woman to entertain me for the night. The only thing that would make it better is to find out what's under that mask.

And under that dress.

"What would you say if I told you that I'm not half the shallow asshole you think I am?"

"I would be disappointed." Her response shocks me as she smirks. "I happen to exclusively fuck shallow assholes."

I gape at her for a second, unable to believe the words that left her mouth. And then my mouth moves again, faster than my brain.

"Well then consider me at your service."

She stares at me and I stare back, eyeing her lips. I lean in and whisper, "Just be careful not to fall in love with me."

"Oh, don't worry," she responds breathily. "There's absolutely no danger of that happening."

Being a part-owner of the Pink Hotel has its perks. For one, it means that I have exclusive access to the newly renovated rooms upstairs.

As I take Athena up the vintage winding staircase and down the velvet-encased hallway, anticipation thrums through me as her small hands grip mine.

We barely get the door for one of the rooms open and closed before she kisses me.

I'm still for a second as her tongue teases the seam of my lips sucking my lower lip in hers. Her hand goes to the back of my neck before traveling into my hair and her body is flush against mine.

Fuck.

She kisses like pure sin.

Our masks are knocked askew as I kiss her back roughly, opening my mouth so her tongue can dance with mine. She tastes like champagne and her supple lips move against mine with a keen desperation that only stokes my desire more.

Her hands travel down my back to grip my ass and I groan.

But she's going too fast. At this rate, it'll be over before it begins.

I wrap my hand around her neck ready to dislodge her lips from mine, when I feel her pulse quicken her body melting at the move.

Hmm. Submissive tendencies. Interesting.

Taking note of that exciting piece of information, I tuck it away to use later.

I pull back to tell her that we need to slow down, but when I do, I notice that her mask is still halfway on her face.

I tear it off needing to know what's beneath. Once her face is revealed though, I start in shock.

"Carly." The word whispers into the air as her dusky

gaze leans forward.

"Yes, Micah," she responds, reaching up to pull off my mask. "It's me."

And then as she kisses me again, all my hesitation due to her identity falls away.

CHAPTER THREE

C ARLY

The second Micah's hand wraps around my neck, my entire body quivers. I'm not sure if it's the shock or the hint of danger that has me faltering, but the desire strumming through my veins doesn't. Instead, it burns hotter, and even after he pulls away, I have to kiss him again because I don't want the sensation to stop.

And then he immediately retakes control of the kiss by catching my tongue between his teeth and holding it there.

"Stay," he whispers against my mouth. Then his lips press against mine with an unhurried intensity that fries my brain a little bit. It's the way he's completely in control, his palm on my pulse, his hand at my waist. He has a light hold around my neck and he's not gripping hard at all, but just the dominance is enough to have me squeezing my thighs together, my breath quickening with anticipation.

This just might be my first time with a dominant partner.

I've had sexual encounters with virtual strangers before. In fact, almost all my encounters end up being of that variety because I don't have time for anything more than no-strings-attached fun. Perhaps that's why I only go for good-looking assholes who I have no hope of forming an emotional connection with. They're easy to predict, show me a good time, and then take off once the night is done. Exactly how I like it. Bonus points if they're not from town.

Micah hits all those notes perfectly. He's a lot more handsome and charming than I'm used to, but he's still too shallow for me to take seriously.

It's why I had no qualms whatsoever about coming up here with him.

I saw the surprise when he took off my mask, the shock that colored his features. I thought he might not know who I am, even without the mask because we haven't spoken to each other, but he certainly knows.

He even whispered my name. And then I saw that hesitation in his eyes as he looked down at me, and knew that he was about to think twice about continuing.

But I didn't want him to stop, which is why I took matters into my own hands, kissing him again.

And now as his lips pluck mine, he gives no doubt as to who is really in control.

"Fuck, you have the sexiest lips I've ever tasted," he whispers and drifts across my cheek to kiss my earlobe. I shiver at the movement, and he goes lower, slowly kissing down my neck, melting any resistance I may have had. His other hand slowly lowers from my waist to cup my ass squeezing it. He groans.

"So fucking soft. I've been looking at you all night, did you know?"

"You were?" I whisper, gasping as he nips the base of my neck. I didn't notice him watching me and pleasure slides through me at the thought.

"I was," he says. "Could see the way you read people. Making predictions. Laughing to yourself. Like a goddess amused by the actions of mere mortals."

I hesitate, shocked at how perceptive he is even though his words make what I did seem far loftier than it actually was. The truth is that I've always been a people-watcher from when I was younger. It was how I noticed at the age of six that my family was different from others and that people treated us differently. My mother said it was because they were jealous while my father insisted that everyone else in town were prudes.

But I knew that wasn't true. Mrs. Peach would give me rides from school all the time. Emma's grandpa sometimes let us eat at his restaurant for free. They wouldn't do that if they were prudes or jealous of us.

Finally, when I was twelve, the veil lifted and I finally understood who my parents were. At that point, I began to keep an eye out for them, and learn to read them for my own survival. One look and I would know if it was going to be a good day or a bad day.

Micah licks my shoulder blade and that thought falls away. His hands move to the front of my dress to wrap around my breast. Without a bra, I feel exactly the moment his thumb rests on my nipple, and a moan shivers out of me.

"That's it." He slowly rubs the nipple until it's an engorged point pushing against the silk. I shiver again and my breath hitches as he catches the point between his fingers, pinching it. "Savor it. Nice and slow."

"Micah." My breath catches in my throat and I bring a shaking hand to his hair.

"Don't rush me," he says. "I want to savor this." He kisses me again with that and his hands move up lightly to push under my bodice, wrapping around my breast expertly. The first feel of his palm on my naked nipple has me jerking even before he strokes it with his thumb. My thighs squeeze together even harder, a rivulet of moisture trickling down my upper thigh. My pants are dampening and all he's done so far is feel me up a little. But it's not just the touch. It's more his aura, his presence that has me on the edge. And then to my shock, he rapidly lets go of my neck and bends to capture my nipple in his mouth.

I cry out as he nips it and my hands fly into his hair, gripping it as he sucks me in. My knees shake from the force of desire that slams into me. His hand finds my left breast and the other hand rustles up my skirt, sliding up my thighs and cupping my sex.

"Fuck, you're wet." He lets my nipple lose with a pop and he straightens. I open my eyes that I didn't realize I closed to meet his stormy gaze, his eyes now a mossy green in their passion. "I want to taste it."

"Huh," I utter dumbly. My brain is having difficulty processing simple words, only realizing what's happening when he sweeps me off my feet and carries me to the couch.

He sits me down and before I know it, he's pushing my dress around my waist and ripping my panties off.

His large hands part my thighs, and he meets my eyes wickedly. "Keep these open."

I nod with a swallow and he leans in, his eyes closing as he breathes me in. At the first lick, my thighs slam around his ears and he gives my inner thigh a warning nip.

'Keep them open, princess, or you'll force me to tie them up."

Oh, just the thought of it, has my pussy clenching on nothing.

"Ah, you like that don't you," he says, still looking at my pussy, laid bare and spread for him. "I can see how much you liked that."

I want to close my legs, and something resembling embarrassment tries to creep in, but there's no space for it because Micah follows up by leaning in to lick my clit.

"Argh," I moan loudly, as he does it again. His finger glides down, parting my folds, and circles the entrance. I grasp the seat below me, my stomach clenching and shaking. It's everything I can do not to push and impale myself on his finger instantly, to rush to the finish. But I hold myself still. I let him take control and earn another lusty lick as well as a murmured, "Good girl."

And then he curls his tongue around my clit in a way that should be impossible but sends delicious bolts of electricity racing up my skin. I fall back and close my eyes and he accompanies it with a hard finger thrust into me.

"Yes!" I gasp and slap my hand over my mouth to muffle the begging as he does it again, and again, his tongue lashing me the whole time.

And then with a moan, he buries his entire face inside me, thrusting faster and faster until my toes curl, my pleas leaking through my fingers.

He adds another finger, and it curls up to hit the button right inside me.

This time, I scream when I shake. And then he does it again all the while lashing my clit with his tongue faster and faster.

My orgasm coils inside me so fast and powerful that I can't breathe. My body arches in the air and before I know it, I'm shouting my explosion.

And then in the blink of an eye, I'm sprawled on the couch and he's on top of me, seizing my lips in another fiery, wet kiss. I taste myself on his lips as his tongue invades my mouth. I suck on his tongue, lust lashing me and creating a whirlwind inside as my thighs wrap around his waist.

As the kiss gets filthier, I release my thighs so I can reach down and loosen his buckle.

It takes me several tries of harried movements to unbuckle and push down his pants. And then once I reach inside…

I can't breathe.

He's so large. I pull away with a gasp and look down, unable to believe it.

And when I look back at his face, his eyes are half-mast staring at my lips, his hips begin to move into my fingers, the skin of his cock rubbing against my pussy.

And then the mushroom tip slides in, spreading me apart.

"Micah," I moan, my fingers falling away to allow him to push deeper. His eyes squeeze shut.

"Shit," he rasps. "I didn't mean to do that." He tries to jerk out of me, but then follows it with an even deeper thrust, breathing shakily. "Fuck, you feel amazing. Tight, and hot…I meant to draw this out longer, but once I felt you come I had to… I needed to—" His head falls forward on my neck. His breath hits my skin in pants. "Fuck."

I bite my lips so hard I draw blood, the tension drawing me tight. I can't take it anymore. He needs to move deeper, or else I'll lose my mind.

I shift experimentally, coaxing him inside and then he releases another moaned expletive.

And he slowly thrusts inside me groaning the entire time.

"Fuck!" he groans as I scream.

He swallows it on his tongue. "You okay?" he gasps and I nod.

"Please," I beg. "More."

He doesn't hold back anymore. He slams into me, harried and as out of control as I've ever seen myself. He keeps kissing me throughout, wet, kisses filled with moaned words into each other's mouths.

And then when he eventually bites my lips, I come, seeing stars.

This time, the orgasm is so intense I nearly black out and I barely hear his grunt as he finds his own release.

We pant into the air for what feels like ages. His body is collapsed on mine, but I don't mind his weight. It's like having a warm heated blanket.

"Shit." It's the first thing he says. "I forgot to use the condom."

"Oh," I realize I forgot it too. "Shit. I didn't even think about that." And I should have, considering how often I do this. I've never had sex with anyone without a condom before. Must show how gone I truly was.

Now I see what V was talking about. Micah Landing really can make a girl lose her mind. And I have a feeling I haven't even scratched the surface.

"I'm clean if you want to know," I say and he nods.

"Me too."

"Then there's nothing to worry about. I'll just take the morning-after pill tomorrow morning."

"Tomorrow morning is good." He grins wickedly, moving inside me again. "Because I plan on doing this all night."

The next day, I head out of the hotel, feeling exhausted but also pleasantly relaxed. I manage to make a clean escape out of the Pink Hotel, since all the guests are either gone or asleep. There's a bus stop about half a mile up from the hotel and I walk there. The air is a bit nippy, my nose reddening from the sting, but I still inhale deeply to enjoy the earthy, floral scent of spring.

I'm wearing my dress from yesterday under my jacket, but it's still too early for most people to be out so I shouldn't get too many funny looks.

I pull out my phone, checking my messages as I walk. The last string of messages was from Emma, beginning after I texted her last night that I had taken off.

And you didn't even tell me? she texted back. *Rude.*

There is an angry face at the end of that, which tells me she wasn't really upset. Then again, Emma rarely ever got upset, even when she should.

Sorry, I text, feeling guilty. *It was kinda impromptu.*

It's alright. I'm off with Declan now too.

Of course, she is. Emma hasn't been far from her fiance's side since their engagement. And I didn't blame her. He clearly adores her and she loves him.

Her next text reads: *If you're going to be late to work*

tomorrow, text Yule or Grandpa and let them know. Okay?

A*lright*. I respond. I work part-time as a server at Emma's grandpa's bar, called the Tiki Bar, which he owns with Rick. Since Rick is in jail now, Emma and her grandfather solely run the place, with Emma as the manager. That technically makes her my boss, but she tries her best not to let me feel like it. Nevertheless, I try to remain professional while at work so as not to take advantage of her kind nature.

Emma's always super understanding whenever I have last minute emergencies–like my father being passed out on the park bench–or even school obligations. And when the Tiki Bar was struggling to break even, she didn't let me go, though she probably should have. Now that tourists are flooding into town and the bar is doing great, she even offered me a raise, which I turned down because I didn't quite think I deserve it yet. Still she insists that the raise will be kicked in anyway by summer, whether I like it or not.

Emma's like the sister I always wanted, and I appreciate her looking out for me. The least I can do for her is not slack off.

So I add in the text, *But I won't be late*.

Anyway, there have been no new texts from Emma since then.

There are no messages from my parents either, and I doubt they even noticed I wasn't home. With nothing else to see, I put my phone away to enjoy the morning breeze.

Last night was amazing.

I must have orgasmed like five times and Micah kept going and kept fucking me, unapologetically insatiable. Even though we didn't have the safest sex, I can't regret it. I will need to stop by the pharmacy to get a Plan B, but I wish I could experience this again.

I wish we had morning sex.

But that thought is exactly why I forced myself to get up and out early this morning. I didn't even want to risk flirting with that temptation right now.

Don't even think about it, I tell myself. *Micah is definitely a one-and-done kind of guy. No need to go get yourself hooked on an asshole.*

About an hour later, I'm back in town center, on my way to home. I decide to stop by the pharmacy to grab the morning-after pill while I'm at it. The door of the pharmacy tinkles and I wave at the kindly elderly pharmacist behind the counter as I walk down the aisle. I pick up the box and then slip my phone out again, to check how much I have in my account.

That's when I see that I received a new email from my college.

I don't think anything of it as I open it. It's probably an alert that a professor just graded an assignment. Or some new reading materials.

But once I see the subject of the mail, the pill box slips out of my hand and drops to the floor.

Scholarship for the coming semester at risk of revocation.

CHAPTER FOUR

MICAH

I yawn and turn over in bed, automatically hitting a stretch as I lie on my back. Then I open my eyes.

I blink at silver-tiled ceilings with elaborate engravings that remind me of a cathedral in Milan. A light fixture descends from the middle of the room, not quite as large as the chandelier in the ballroom but just as intricate with crystals dotting each panel. Sunlight washes in from the French doors leading out to a balcony. The corners of the room hold vases with pink flowers that match the pink velvet walls and give off the scent of lilies.

I'm at the Pink Hotel, I realize and with that, the events of last night start rushing back to me. I instantly sit up in bed, glancing around. My muscles ache when I move, protesting the abuse I put them through last night. But I smile regardless, so fucking sated I don't mind.

That was an insanely enjoyable night. Watching Carly come apart in my arms over and over, writhing in passion, demanding and submissive all at once... a man could easily get addicted to that.

It doesn't take more than a quick look around to realize she's gone. I don't hear the shower running in the bathroom, and there's no one on the veranda. It's likely she just stepped out for a second but probably not. She's gone, with no note, no phone number, nothing.

Disappointment weighs heavy in my gut.

Typically, this would be my preferred scenario. When a woman is gone by the morning of a hookup it means she understands that this is simply a one-night stand. Except in rare cases, she won't get attached and start dreaming of wedding bells and engagement rings. She enjoys the fun for what it is, and then moves on the next day.

And true to her word, Carly seems to be exactly the type.

But I'm disappointed because I wouldn't have minded another round before she left. Or maybe have some breakfast with her. I enjoyed our conversation yesterday before we had sex and would have liked to see more of her easy wit.

Oh well. It's not like I don't know where to find her if I need to. I've only met Carly on a few occasions and even "met" is a strong word for it. On the day Declan proposed to Emma, I saw Carly across the grassy field and was around the general vicinity when she and Emma talked. I knew her name but that was about it. I didn't notice her much beyond the fact that she looked cute and innocent.

And cute and innocent has never been my type.

I prefer worldly women, women who know what they want and go for it. Carly with the pigtails and the overly baggy clothing didn't seem like that type.

But as it turns out, I was wrong. Because she definitely went for what she wanted last night.

My smile widens as I get out of bed, padding naked to the bathroom to wash my face. Then I look at my shoulders noting the red marks from when Carly scratched me as I ate her out the second time. I admire the marks like a badge, wondering if I should wear a vest today to show them off. Maybe I'll show up to where she works. It would be worth it to see the blush spreading on her face.

And then maybe I'll even get to see more than her face.

Who knew her baggy clothes were hiding a body like that?

The ringing phone breaks through my thoughts. I turn around and pad back to the room, retrieving my phone from my pocket. I sigh when I see the caller ID.

The jig is up.

I pick up, anticipating the explosion. "Hello?"

"Are you insane?" my father roars, and I can almost see him bristling behind his office desk at the top of a skyscraper near Central Park.

"It depends on the time of day," I respond mildly. "I'm usually fine in the afternoon, but I'm told that I go rabid at night. Like a vampire."

"This isn't time for your stupid jokes, Micah. Do you have any idea what you just tried to do? Are you trying to ruin me?"

I roll my eyes. "You're so dramatic, Dad. How is selling *my* shares in the hotel going to ruin you? You could sneeze on a hypothetical billion-dollar note and it wouldn't hurt you."

"This hotel isn't just any hotel. It's the Pink Hotel, a hotel that has been on the tip of everyone's tongue for months now. It's advertising itself with how much it has been on the news."

"Yes. It's been advertised as the scene of several crimes. You think that people will want to stay here?"

"Are you kidding me? Of course! The only thing better than a vintage hotel is a vintage hotel with a killer story. Do you know how many people would stay in the Manson house if they could? We've struck literal gold here Micah and spent a fortune polishing it up. And now you want to throw all that away by selling it for a pittance of what it's worth. To Benjamin DuPont of all fucking people."

My dad's voice screeches at the end and I move my ear away from the receiver to rub it.

"I'd hardly call thirty million a pittance."

"It's a pittance compared to what we stand to make in the future. It's less than what we're projected to earn even in the next ten years."

"Aren't you the same person who told me not to put too much stock in projections?"

"Now you choose to listen to me?"

"I always listen to you, Father. Listening and obeying are two different things." I pick up the menu by the bed, wondering what to get from room service. Then I remembered the hotel is not technically operational yet and put it down again. I'll have to go into town for breakfast before I leave.

I wait for the rest of my father's rant. I know from his breathing that the old man is only getting started.

"I truly don't know what your problem is, Micah," he continues. "Here am I offering you a chance on a silver platter and you're throwing it away. It's a chance that many would kill for, the chance at a stable income, at ownership, something you could call your own that will make you millions for a lifetime."

"And who says that's a chance I want?" I say. "Maybe I want something different."

My father is silent for a second and then in a shocked tone he says, "You want to be poor?"

"No," I say. "What I want is freedom, Dad. The freedom of not running this hotel and answering to you and Tudor all the damn time. I want to do what excites me."

"All the things that excite you are stupid."

"To you," I say.

"To everyone who's not a child. Micah, you're thirty-five years old. Don't you think it's time to stop your foolishness and start thinking of taking over the family legacy? I'm not going to be alive forever, you know, and someone will have to take the helm. What I'm offering you here is a chance to get the experience you need to run Landing Holdings. You'll need experience to win over the board of directors and our investors and–"

"Yawn," I say, running my hand through my hair. "Those old crones don't want me on the board and, frankly, I don't want to interact with them any more than I have to. As for the family legacy, that wasn't what I signed up for, and it's not the role you raised me to play. That was supposed to be Tristan's job, no?"

My father reacts like I shot him. "Your brother is dead."

"Precisely. And that's the crux of the problem, isn't it? Because with Tristan gone, you need someone to neatly slot into his place. But I'm not him, Dad. I can't just do the things he did and, even if I could, I don't want to. I want something that's mine, that isn't tainted by his legacy." I want to be Micah, not Tristan's less competent wild card brother. I'm sick of playing a role that I'm not good at, a role that chafes.

And then my father goes for the low blow. "And how is that working out for you? What is it, five failed businesses in ten years? It's an impressive track record if I think about it."

I try not to grit my teeth. "Most businessmen fail before they succeed."

"Not when they have billions of dollars at their disposal."

"Okay, this has been a fun talk Dad, but I have to go have breakfast now."

"I'm not going to let you sell those shares."

"They're my shares to sell," I say.

"Shares that I gifted you," he says. "Shares that I still control. I've already spoken to Ben DuPont and confirmed that the deal is off."

Anger spikes inside me but I know better than to react. My father already thinks I'm a child. I don't want to encourage that notion.

Come on, Micah. Say something pithy and mature.

"You can't fucking do that."

Great, way not to sound like a whining child.

"I can and I did," Dad says simply. "And if you try to sell to anyone else, Tudor and I will strike it down too per our contract. If you insist on acting like a child, I'll treat you like one. And I'm going to save you from yourself and make you a man if it's the last thing I do."

As my father hangs up, I resist the urge to fling my

phone against the wall.

Damn.

One word from my dad and all my well-laid plans have gone to shit. I spent weeks convincing DuPont to buy off my shares.

And now he won't do it, because my father got his panties in a twist.

I don't blame Frank Tudor for telling my father. His friendship with my father predates my existence and so it's only fair that his loyalty lies with him.

And so with that, I'm trapped once again.

Except I'm already thinking of a way out of it. And despite what my father thinks, I'm not lazy or stupid. I'm just someone who gets easily bored and needs a challenge. Working at this hotel won't be a challenge. It will be just one more part of the humdrum of life.

Another thing I do that adds no value to the universe. Another thing I do less well than my brother.

I hate that Tristan died and left me to be the one in charge. That was never supposed to be me. I was the fun brother who was very comfortable in his shadow because it gave me the freedom to do what I want. And now, I'm supposed to play discount Tristan.

And then it hits me.

The only one who can help me out of this predicament.

The only person who can overstep my father, and it isn't my mother who I haven't heard from in almost a year, due to her extended sabbatical to cope with my brother's death.

In a world of sharks, there's always a bigger shark.

I go to the window at Laketown. Quaint streets dusted with petals and leaves from the trees framing them. Slow-moving people talking, laughing, holding hands. All the buildings are red brick or colonial-style architecture. Not a single glass skyrise in sight.

I refuse to be trapped here. I refuse.

CHAPTER FIVE

CARLY

Depression weighs heavy on me that afternoon.

I'm lying on a quilted couch blankly watching Judge Judy reruns as a fan circles lazily above me. It's a cool afternoon and I feel it, even though the thermostat is fully functional. Maybe the chill is from the inside. Maybe I'm just imagining my bones turning to ice.

I glance away from the TV to the pruned Christmas tree by the fireplace. The Christmas lights around it blink hypnotically, but it's not enough to distract me from the tears stinging my eyes. It's already spring but I know that tree is probably not going down till summer. Mrs. Peach is clearly still in the holiday spirit and I hate to be a downer on her good mood. I just didn't know where else to go.

Apart from Emma, Mrs. Peach is the person I'm closest to in the world. She lives down the street, a few houses away from mine, and was the only one in the neighborhood who made a concerted effort to visit our family when I was younger. She was on the church charity committee with my mother and even when mom managed to alienate just about everybody else with her constant lying and anger issues, Mrs. Peach stuck around. That was until mom was banned from the church for stealing from the charity fund.

Still, though she didn't come around after that, Mrs. Peach would always call out when she saw me walking home from school, and invite me in for some cookies. She had a bunch of old detective novels in her bookshelf and I spent most of my childhood reading them or watching TV reruns with her while she made dinner. Sometimes we would talk about books or she would tell me stories of when she was younger. I thought she was probably just lonely since she didn't have any family, but she would also tell me often how fond she was of me, though I wasn't sure why. Maybe she felt sorry for me. Either way, she always made sure I ate something before I got home.

Once in a while, she asked me what I now recognize as probing questions about whether or not my mother was physically abusive to me. Mom wasn't, but I knew if she was, Mrs. Peach would have called CPS. It's why I hid the worst of my mother's later abuse from her, because as volatile as Mom could be, I didn't want to be taken into foster care.

Anyway, since that first day, I pretty much show up at Mrs. Peach's house at least once a week, especially now that she's getting older. I help her with her gardening and occasionally cooking when she'll let me.

Mrs. Peach is in the kitchen now and I hear her clattering around. From the scent of it, she seems to be making one of her famous apple pies, which are usually my favorite, meaning she could probably tell how down I was despite my efforts to hide it. And I can't even bring myself to be excited about the apple pie.

I haven't been excited about anything since I got

that email from the school about losing my scholarship.

The second I was done reading through the email, I dashed out of the pharmacy horror adding a spring to my step. I stood at the side of the road and flagged a cab to take me about thirty minutes out of town to the community college in Bayview.

I read through the email again as we drove, scanning it until I could make sense of it. This was all thanks to my damn calculus class. It was taught by the toughest professor in the school, Dr. Lindon, who took particular pride in handing out bad grades. I tried so hard to stay on top of the class all semester, but that last test had been brutal.

And it just cost me my scholarship.

I need to talk to Lindon, get him to give me another chance. It was the only thought I held onto as I arrived at the campus and ran to his office.

He was stepping out of his office when I arrived, and the minute he saw me, his lips downturned in disapproval.

"If this is about your grade, Miss, I suggest you don't even bother."

"Please." Desperation must have shown on my face, and leaked out of my voice. "Please, sir. Just give me another chance. It's been a tough month for me and–"

"You think I care about any of that?" He raised an eyebrow. "Plenty of people have tough months. You fail a test, you fail a test. And that's all there is to it."

Yes, but it's also kind of ridiculous that a single test is fifty percent of your final grade. That means that every single other assignment I've done almost doesn't even matter.

And what made me feel worse was that he was right

in a way. I was having a bad month but I shouldn't have let that distract me from my goal. I was just so unbelievably disappointed with myself even as I begged, "Please. I'll do extra coursework or something. Anything."

"I'm afraid that's not how I operate." He turned to lock his door behind him. "You'll have to accept the grade or repeat the class in the fall."

It isn't retaking the class I'm worried about. With that grade on my resume, it means that my GPA slipped below 3.8, which means that I am going to lose my scholarship.

And without a scholarship, there is no way I can afford to go to school.

"Oowee." Mrs. Peach comes out of the kitchen now, her short round form waddling across the rug. "You still moping on the couch, dear?"

I nod. "Yeah."

"Well, while you do that, can you stir the stew every few minutes while I go to the bathroom? I just popped a Miralax and don't want it to come out the other end."

"Didn't really need to know that last part, Mrs. P," I say mildly. I've never understood why Mrs. Peach felt the need to share intimate details about her bowel movements, when "I need to use the bathroom" alone would have sufficed. But I don't mind much. She's the only one, apart from Emma, who I can go to when I'm down. She's understanding but doesn't hover and doesn't let me catastrophize either. She just lets me talk things out and work through it at my own pace.

I know what she'll say if I tell her what happened. *"It's not the end of the world, dear. We'll just have to find a way to make you money so you can attend school in the fall."*

Easier said than done in a town like this. While the raise Emma offered is certainly generous by Laketown standards, it would still be months if not years before I'm able to save up enough to pay for the cost of tuition.

With Mrs. Peach gone, I get up and head to the kitchen, still wondering how one single failed test could change the trajectory of my life so totally. Especially when I was so close. I am in my final year, set to graduate soon. I was doing so well in every other class, on track to graduate Magna Cum Laude. A single failed test, and it's like everything I worked for the past few years means nothing.

I've told very few people that I'm in college, mostly because I don't want to bear the weight of any expectations. Not that people expect much of me anyway. As the child of a drunk and a thief, whose cousin was part of a high-profile pearl-smuggling operation, it is good enough to most that I am not a criminal. But that isn't good enough for me. I'm sure some of them think I'll follow in the rest of my family's footsteps, which is why I want to prove them wrong.

But I want to do it quietly so that no one mocks me for my dreams. A dream I've sustained even through shitty weeks of being whispered about because my cousin was inadvertently involved in the deaths of multiple people in town.

That combined with my mother's tantrums and my father's drunkenness was what made it impossible to study for the stupid test.

A flush and I hear the bathroom door open. That's when I realize I've been stirring the soup staring into the air for minutes. Mrs. Peach walks into the kitchen and wipes wet hands on a random rag.

She gives me a sympathetic look. "You ready to talk about it now, hun?"

I nod through the lump in my throat. "I'm losing my scholarship."

"Oh no." She walks forward with her hand over her mouth. "How?"

"I failed a test. The professor is refusing any redos, so even if I ace every other test and assignment in that class, in the couple of weeks before we vacate, I'm still down to get a C in the class. And a C isn't good enough for me to hold onto my scholarship."

"Oh, darling, that's horrible. You can't take out student loans?"

I shake my head. "My mom already destroyed my credit. She got a loan in my name when I was fifteen." I didn't know she had done it until I got sent a letter from a collection agency. I was seventeen when I found out and remember being furious at her.

But Mom, as usual, had no remorse.

"I did it for you," she explained. "You needed school supplies. Where on earth was I supposed to get the money from?"

"You should have told me."

She rolled her eyes completely unrepentant. "Well, I'm telling you now."

I swallow back the memories since they'll only depress me more. In any case, student loans are out of the picture.

Mrs. Peach hugs me and rubs my back and the tears start flowing.

"I can't believe I'm losing my scholarship," I sob, chest tightening. "That means everything was for nothing. Unless I can somehow raise the tuition for the next semester, I'll have to drop out and become the failure everyone thinks I am."

"There there," Mrs. Peach says, sliding her hand over my hair and I inhale her peppermint scent, trying to find comfort in it. A cough interrupts and we both glance at the living room door.

Tate Moon is standing there, looking a little uncomfortable.

I immediately straighten, wiping my face and looking away. Tate isn't the last person I want to catch me crying, but she's certainly not high on the list.

Tate is Emma's other best friend and while that should probably make us friends too, it doesn't, despite us often hanging out together due to Emma. We're not enemies, but we're not friends either. Like Declan, Tate is a little intimidating although in a different way. She's very plainspoken and has no qualms about saying whatever outrageous thing she thinks of. Like the first time we met at Emma's house, she asked me, "Is it true your momma stole donations from the church?"

Emma admonished her then and she apologized instantly, but it didn't stop her asking rude questions on other occasions. One time, upon noting how much time I spent at Emma's place she asked, "Why are you never home? Does your house not have a ton of space?"

And then another time, during Emma's birthday party when I was twelve and she was fourteen, she told me, "You should tell your father to lay off the booze."

And the worst part is that she didn't say any of it in that mocking way that the other kids used to. She said it like she was either genuinely curious or genuinely concerned, but it just made me more quiet and withdrawn whenever I was around her. Consequently, I avoided coming over to Emma's when I knew she was there.

It didn't help that Tate was also gorgeous with her

long, luscious red hair, and she was smart too, earning numerous academic awards in high school. She was valedictorian of her class, went off to a state college and now she's a PT who works with patients at the local hospital and also holds free yoga sessions every Saturday morning.

It's hard not to feel like a failure next to her.

"Sorry," she says. "I should have knocked."

Mrs. Peach sighs. "Yes, but no one knocks in this town. Especially not your generation, who has abandoned all pretense at decency. What do you need, dear?"

"My mom sent me over with these." She gestures to a cooler in her hand. "She hunted it today and thought you might want some."

"Oh, how nice." Mrs. Peach moves away from me to take the cooler and heads to the kitchen. "What is it?"

"Pheasant."

"Lovely. Let me put this in the freezer before it goes bad."

As she leaves, an awkward silence descends with Tate walking closer to me. "You okay?"

"Yeah," I answer quickly. "Yeah, I'm fine. Just having a bad day."

"Do you want to talk about it?"

I shake my head. I don't want to tell beautiful, hyper-capable Tate who graduated her physical therapy program with honors, how I screwed up a test and may not be able to finish college as a result.

"Well, I already heard some of it," she continues. "It's about your tuition for the next semester, right?"

Annoyance interrupts my sadness. I don't want to talk about this with her but I don't have a choice. Avoiding the conversation now would be too rude for the small town that raised me, so I try to keep it simple. "Uh, yeah. I lost my scholarship." I shrug. "But it's not a big deal. Just means I'll have to take a break from school for some time until I can save up enough money to go back."

"Or you could just ask Emma for an advance at work," Tate suggests. "I'm sure she would understand and would love to–"

"No," I say instantly. Emma and her grandpa have done enough to help me already, too much that is. Helping me with a job, giving me a place to stay sometimes for weeks on end. Grandpa is the only reason why I've celebrated my last few birthdays. Ever since he found out that my family doesn't even remember my birthday, he's made it a point every year to throw me a small get together at his house, just me, him, Mrs. Peach, Emma, and Yule, the cook at the Tiki Bar.

And although my cousin was the reason Emma's home got broken into recently, she's never held it against me. She's been so considerate of me all my life. I can't ask her for anything else. "I can't do that."

"Sure you can. Her fiancé is loaded, so you know she's not hurting for cash–"

"I said no," I repeat firmly. "And I appreciate you trying to help but I'd rather do this on my own."

Her eyebrows fly up at my tone. "Okay then."

Suddenly guilt washes through me. "I'm sorry. I shouldn't have snapped, it's just..."

"You're having a bad day." She nods. "It's okay. I don't mind being a target. And trust me my mom is much worse when she's cranky."

She offers me a wry grin, and I smile back weakly.

She's even gracious about my rudeness. The thing about Tate is that she's so damn likable it's hard to hate her. Plus, she's really not a bad person. I'm the petty one for being jealous of her after all these years.

"I don't want to tell Emma" I say. "Let's just keep this between us."

She bites her lower lip, then nods. "Sure. But just for the record, I think you should tell her."

"No."

She shrugs. "Worth a shot."

I shake my head and sigh. I have to figure my way out of this alone.

CHAPTER SIX

MICAH

I whistle as I unlock the crafted bronze door of the Gilded Age mansion, letting myself in through the arched doorway.

The entryway is big enough to fit an apartment on its own and fixed with all the makings of a French chateau, including the wide windows that poured light over the vintage furniture, elaborate moldings and statues accenting each entryway, and a grand fireplace, featuring the quintessential gold leaf design.

The space smells of fresh flowers and citrus, which means it was just cleaned a few seconds ago. I hear voices coming from the next room, the dining room, which also means the old man is already up and kicking this morning.

Good.

His mood is always best after he just woke up, which is why I took an early morning flight from Laketown to New York to catch him in these rare early hours of serenity before the rest of the world pisses him off.

I stride into the dining room and catch my grandfather as he's murmuring to his maid to bring him a cup of cappuccino.

I pause as his head slowly swivels to me and I do a double take.

"Oh, I'm sorry," I say. "I think I must be in the wrong house. I was looking for my grandfather, but I seem to have stumbled into the home of a young, handsome Clint Eastwood. Let me try again."

I make a point of walking back to the front door and then returning. "Huh, it says this is the address. Odd. Did you kill my grandfather and take his place, young handsome Clint Eastwood?'

My grandfather doesn't crack a smile. "Your jokes get less amusing with age."

"No, they don't. And what is it with you and Dad age-shaming me all of a sudden? Thirty-five is not old." I walk around the table and grin at the maid, who's trying to hide her smile. "Hi, Elvira. How is it going?"

"Good morning, Master Micah," she greets.

"No need to be so formal, Elvira. You changed my diapers at one point. Just 'Master' should be fine."

She giggles and rolls her eyes before retreating. I face my grandfather who takes a sip of his orange juice. He always likes to have freshly squeezed fruit juice in the morning before he feeds his caffeine addiction.

"I assume you're out of money," he says.

I lay a hand on my chest. "You wound me, Grandfather. Are you trying to imply that the only reason I would visit you is to pad up my finances?"

"Don't be too offended," my grandfather responds drolly. "It's not special. That's the only reason most people visit me."

The thought has some stray guilt propping up.

Well, I probably haven't been coming over like I should, but that's because I've been so busy trying to undo my father's machinations that I haven't had time to consider much else. Heck, I haven't even partied in weeks. "It's not like that, Grandfather."

"Right." He snorts. "Let me guess. You and your father had a fight and he cut you off again."

"No," I say although his guess is eerily close. "We simply had a small disagreement about this new business I'm starting."

"Another one?"

I wince. "Yes, but this one is different. You remember how much I used to love architecture back in college?"

"I remember you dropped it in your third year to pursue a life of debauchery."

Ouch. "Well, it didn't quite happen like that." There was more to it than that, but it would take too long and expose too many scars to explain.

My grandfather fixes me with a look. "You're about to tell me that you dropped out because your father disapproved. That's more of a childish reason than what I said."

"Dad's disapproval isn't the reason I dropped out." Yes, my dad didn't approve of me studying architecture, just like he didn't approve of it when I said I wanted to be a pilot at age twelve. He saw both as childish dreams I would eventually get over, when I was old and mature enough to see things his way. Plus, he's always felt that my true place was in his company as my brother's right-hand man.

Everything else was a distraction he only let me indulge in because he thought it was a hobby.

But when he saw me start to take architecture seriously in college, with an actual plan to start a company and everything, he got threatened.

He wanted me to drop it. I refused. So he approached it in a roundabout way. We had many arguments about it, arguments that my mother stayed out of, and my brother often mediated and took my side on.

"Leave him alone, Dad," Tristan would say. "Can't you see how badly he wants this?"

But my father didn't relent. Ultimately, it came to a head when I started my company while I was still in college, using my savings and some of my inheritance from my mother's side for it. Dad pretended to give up then. He pretended to even be supportive.

There was a building he wanted to renovate and he convinced me to put my bid on the project.

And then got Tristan to reject it, knowing it would hurt more coming from him than from my dad.

"It's nothing personal, Micah," Tristan said apologetically at the time. "It just wasn't good enough, at least not to the stakeholders."

But I knew my design was good. I poured my heart and soul into it, so I didn't understand why he was saying that. Plus, it hurt.

It was one thing to be told I was talentless by my father. It was another for it to be Tristan, who I looked up to so much.

Only later did I realize that my father put him up to it.

Plus, it wasn't just that. Dad also somehow planted moles in my budding company to report my moves to him. Then he made sure to obstruct those as much as possible. Blocking business deals, leaking scandals... all to make me give up.

And he got his wish.

My father's continued sabotaging efforts crashed the company enough for me to give up on that dream.

And I've been making him pay for it ever since with my blatant life of debauchery.

"Anyway, that's not the point," I say, eager to get this conversation back on track. "The point is now I'm ready and I finally have something I want to do, something I'm good at."

"As opposed to the last ten things that you didn't want to do and were terrible at?"

"Just hear me out, Grandfather, alright? At least give me a chance to convince you."

He stares at me and then takes another sip of his orange juice, which is probably all the allowance I'm getting.

I take a deep breath, steeling myself. I'll have to be honest and just a little vulnerable, which I hate doing but honesty is the only thing that will convince him right now.

"I've always liked architecture, even though Dad disapproves. Always. All those years I've been out of college and wandering around, I haven't been doing nothing. I've been exploring architecture from different countries, and studying design and sustainability. Did you know that biophilic designs have recently been proven to improve health outcomes and increase productivity in the workplace? Did you know that Asian bamboo architecture is seeing a rise in popularity in the West? Did you know how many sample designs I've drawn in that time that will never see the light of day? Because Dad doesn't know and he doesn't care to hear any of that. All he wants me to do is be a good boy and take Tristan's place. But that's not for me."

I swallow back the bitterness, although some of it probably leaks into my voice. I also fight the surge of emotion that always hits when I think about Tristan being gone.

My grandfather's expression doesn't change. Not because he doesn't care. Losing Tristan was as hard for him as anyone else, but he's better at controlling his emotions than all of us combined.

"For now," I continue, "Dad wants me to prove myself by running this hotel in Laketown. It's a hotel with a lot of tragedy and the public is eating it up right now so there's a lot of buzz. But that will probably die off soon. There isn't anything really special about the place and the town itself is boring as all get out. I think it's going to be a massive waste of time, but Dad isn't ready to listen to me and wants to force me to stay there and run it, maybe so he can blame me when it doesn't work out."

My grandfather eyes me shrewdly for a few minutes, with a gaze that used to make me quail when I was younger. It's hard to tell in situations like this, but the old man has a softer heart than he puts off.

I remember how he used to terrify me when I was younger. Until one day, I fell out of a tree and broke my leg. No one else was home except him and Elvira, and he picked me up and packed me into his bed. He ordered me to be silent while he worked, but I still kept crying about the pain while waiting for the doctor. And then my grandfather sighed and came to me. I thought he would tell me to shut up again, but the old man got in bed with me and held me while I sobbed.

That was when I saw that his bark was worse than his bite and that he had a soft spot for me. So I use that to my advantage now. He's the only one who can defy my father. I just have to push the right buttons.

But with time and too much button-pushing, his dials were getting rusty.

Elvira comes out to deliver two cappuccinos while Grandpa deliberates. I shoot her a smile in thanks, and as she leaves, I take a sip from my cappuccino cup.

"When do you think you'll be ready for marriage?"

The question takes me off guard so much that the coffee instantly shoots the wrong way and I spray it out on the table, becoming a coughing blubbering mess. Elvira sends me a wry look, to which I respond with an apologetic wince as she whips out a clean rag from her pocket and begins dabbing at the mess.

"What kind of question is that?" I ask my grandfather after Elvira retreats.

"It's a serious question," he says. "You're nearly forty Micah–"

"Thirty-five."

"And time waits for no one," he says. "You keep running from thing to thing lacking stability, lacking the resolve and drive necessary to push past the hard parts. And I don't blame you for not having those skills. Perhaps your father and mother have spoiled you too much. But at some point, you're going to have to grow up, and having a woman by your side would help with that."

I stare at the old man incredulously. Who knew he was such a romantic?

"It's not like I haven't been looking to settle down, Grandpa," I lie because I have not. "It's just that it's so hard to find a good woman these days."

Because I've wronged them all.

"Good women are not to be found in the crowd that you frolic with," Grandpa says sternly. "You only hang out with riffraff and nobodies who have nothing to lose. Women from good families have the breeding necessary to help you grow and raise good children. That's who you need to be meeting."

"Right," I say even though I wholly disagree. It would be pointless to argue. My grandfather, despite being a generally nice guy, is also a raging classist.

"I can introduce you to some of them. The country club is holding a mixer and a lot of single high-society women will likely be in attendance."

I have a distinct idea of the type of women he's talking about and nearly feel my dick shrivel up and die.

"Ah, no you don't have to do that, sir. Actually, I kind of already have someone I'm seeing."

My grandfather's eyes flash with interest. "Is she from a good family?"

"Yes," I say because if I'm going to lie about my fake girlfriend, I might as well make her the perfect one, right? "A very good family. Things have been getting serious between us so… yeah. Very stable."

His eyes study me and I try to look as innocent as can be.

"I want to meet her."

"What?"

"Since things are getting serious it would only make sense for me to meet her and ensure she's the right woman for you. Choosing the right woman is harder than running a business. So if I see she's the right one, then perhaps I'll have more faith in your decisions. Then you may have my support."

"And that's when he all but told me I had to get married for him to give me the loan," I say. "Can you believe it?"

It's a few days later and I'm back in Laketown lying on Declan's office couch, ranting about my problems. The couch is soft imported wool, smells like a lavender cleaning product, and it's immensely comfortable. I should know since I spend a lot of time here lately, at least whenever I'm in Laketown.

Declan is at his desk reading something on his computer and doesn't respond to the end of my story. I frown.

"Declan, are you even listening to me?"

"Yeah. Unfortunately, you're really hard to tune out."

I smile. "That's only because you care, buddy."

He gives me a sour look and I wink in return.

I'll be honest, the only reason I tolerate the frequent trips to Laketown is because of Declan. Annoying him is quickly becoming my number one source of enjoyment.

Mostly though, I'm here to throw my dad off my scent and trick him into thinking that I'm being compliant with his order. I know he monitors my movement. If I spend enough time in Laketown, he'll think I'm helping Declan with the hotel opening and won't see the next part of my scheme coming.

But a plus of this arrangement is that I get to rant to Declan for hours and he will only throw me out when Emma comes in–although frequently Emma actually wants to listen to my rant. She's nice like that.

Declan isn't as nice, as he has a stick up his ass the size of a baseball bat, but I'm used to his brand of cranky. In a lot of ways, he reminds me of my brother.

I brush away the thought as someone knocks on Declan's door.

"Come in," he says and a large man in a long flannel coat walks in. He spots me and raises an eyebrow. I give him a fake salute before he turns to Declan.

"Erm, boss, there's a problem." Sweat is beaded on the man's forehead and he wipes it off with a handkerchief. *Who the hell sweats in fifty-degree weather?*

But as sweaty as he is, he doesn't take off his coat.

"When is there not a problem, Hal?" Declan sighs. "What is it this time?"

"The plumbing guys fucked up the HVAC in about three or four of the rooms. The walls will have to be broken for them to take care of this."

"Jesus. And why didn't y'all catch on before?"

Did he say 'y'all'? I almost snort. *Someone's adopting his fiancée's twang.*

The man itches his hand, through his long sleeve, staring at the floor self-consciously. "Well, it all seemed fine at first. It wasn't until one of the workers tried to use that bathroom that the problem became... obvious."

Declan rubbed his temple. "We're going to have to redo the entire wall after we fix it."

"Not necessarily."

They both glance at me.

"Just add it to the design."

Declan's eyebrows furrow. "Huh?"

"Industrial pipe decor is all the rage nowadays. Just extend the pipe outward and make it part of the design of the room."

"I'm not sure that would work," Hal says. "I'll have to run it by the architect we have on staff first."

"I doubt your architect has studied extensively the mechanics, history, and psychology of eighteenth-century design, but go for it," I say, turning back to stare at the roof.

They're silent for a second and then Declan says, "Just go ask him." The door closes as Hal leaves.

"You know being arrogant won't endear you to people in this town," Declan points out. "I'm speaking from experience."

"Hmm," I say noncommittally. "Speaking of people in this town, how's Carly?"

I turn to find Declan with a warning eyebrow raised. "In what way?"

I grin. "In the way that I'm inquiring about her general well-being."

"And why are you inquiring now? You never have before."

I've never spent a mind-blowing night with her before. "So I can't ask how your fiancé's friend is doing?"

"Stay away from Carly," Declan says sternly. "She's going through a lot, what with her cousin's jail sentence and all. She doesn't need you adding on to it."

Oh, Declan. You're so naive.

He should know me better by now.

Telling me to stay away from someone is a sure way of pushing me closer to them.

CHAPTER SEVEN

C ARLY

"... and the entire place looked like a slaughterhouse."

I stiffen as the tendrils of the conversation reach me. It seems almost uncanny that I was able to pick it out amidst the din.

It's just after five and the bar is packed with both tourists and locals. It's pretty noisy, even without the country song currently blasting on the speakers. The sound and the greasy scent of burgers and beer are almost oppressive, adding a much-needed heat to the cool atmosphere.

I shouldn't have even heard a word of that conversation. But it's always easier to hear bad news and for some reason, I've always been able to sense when people are talking about me or my family. It's like a cruel sixth sense and I hate it because I would much rather be oblivious to the gossip. But I can't help but listen.

I can't physically escape it either as I wait for the elderly man at the opposite table to find his credit card. The words from the table behind me drift to me and it soon proves that they're talking about exactly what I feared they might be.

"That's insane. A shoot-out, from a smuggling ring? Who knew that sort of thing could happen in a town like this??"

"No place is safe," the first voice says. "We're not as bad as the city, thank God, but we got our own share of riffraff. Like that Nate Huntley fella. Turns out he was involved with the smugglers but even before that I knew that boy was no good from the start. Always stealing from us hardworking folk. And now look. He's probably going to rot in prison where he belongs. They're probably going to charge him with all the deaths from the shoot-out.

"They'll charge Rick too," his companion adds. "I didn't see that one coming. He seemed like such a good man, always willing to help me out with cash here and there. Come to find out that he got the cash from smuggling and, thanks to him, a whole bunch of people are dead."

Bile rises in my throat as another one says, "I thought it was only three of them that died."

"The whole lot of them should have died. Everyone involved was a criminal. Who goes around kidnapping little girls? God only knows what they would have done to the poor young thing if her father hadn't gotten there in time. That Declan Tudor has more balls than I thought. He ran in there and saved his daughter and fought off like a dozen of them. Didn't give a damn that they had guns or anything."

"You alright, hon?" The white-haired woman in front of me regards me carefully while her husband slowly pulls out a bunch of gift cards from his wallet one-by-one, shaking his head with each one. The older gentleman mutters to himself as he searches, trying to remember if he even brought the right card. He's already searched through his other wallet and his pockets while I've had to suffer the conversation behind me.

I stiffen at the woman's question and realize that my smile has gotten a little tight at the edges. I try to ease it up, but I'm not sure I succeed. "Yeah, I'm fine, ma'am. Thanks for asking."

"I got it!" her husband suddenly announces, pulling a credit card free and holding it in the air. "I got it, Meryl."

"Thank the Lord." The woman rolls her eyes, but she still smiles affectionately at him as he inserts the card. Then once he's done, she takes the card reader and hands it over to me. "That should do it."

"Thanks." The card reader prints out the receipt and I give it to them, along with their card. Then I head back for the counter but not before I hear, "That entire Huntley family are losers. All of them. We'd be better off running them out of town before they inevitably cause another mess."

Stomach tight, I thankfully reach the counter without further incident. Still, as I go around it, I have to stop and take a few seconds to catch my breath.

Unfortunately, it's right at that time that Emma's grandpa walks out of the kitchen, adjusting his Chinaman's hat on his head.

He takes one look at my face and frowns. "You alright, Lady Fishy?"

Despite feeling like shit, I smile at Grandpa's nickname. He's called me that ever since I was little and told him that I felt sorry for the fishies he was always catching. He teased me and asked if I wanted to be the queen of the fishies, but I said no. I only wanted to be a lady fishy. Thus, the nickname was born.

"Yeah, I'm fine," I tell him.

But despite living with his head in the clouds, Grandpa can provide an annoying perspective sometimes.

"Ah. You heard someone talking trash about your family again, didn't you?"

I shake my head, but he says, "Don't bother lying to me, Carly. I've known you since you were practically at my ankles. You got that look on your face like you're embarrassed, but you shouldn't be. If someone's talking about your family, shake it off, because you're nothing like them. You can't pick the stock you came from, so no need to take on their failures as your own."

"I know that," I tell him. But knowing it and accepting it are two different things. Because I know when other people look at me sometimes, they don't see me as Carly, distinct from my family. Despite a lifetime of clean-cut behavior and hiding my occasional hookups, they look at me like they're just waiting for me to mess up in some way, to maybe hold up a grocery store at gunpoint or pop out a drug dealer's baby or something equally heinous.

"Well, then remember it," Grandpa says and he pats my shoulder. "The same way I'm not gonna beat myself up about what Rick has done, you shouldn't feel responsible about your parents." Pain flashes across Grandpa's face whenever he mentions Rick. The two used to be best friends, as thick as thieves. And now Rick is sitting in jail, refusing visits from everyone, including Grandpa, Emma, and Lou, the owner of the restaurant across the street who Rick had a budding relationship with before he got locked away.

All three are pretty broken up about what happened, but they try to hide it for the most part. For me and Yule though, Rick was more so a friendly employer and so, while we're still sad, we're dealing with it better.

"Alright, I'm going fishing," Grandpa says, shaking off his sudden melancholy. "Y'all got it good here, right?"

"Yup," I say. Emma has hired three more servers and they're all on shift this evening. Plus, Yule has a few assistants now helping him cook the meals.

All these changes happened within the span of a couple of months.

This time last year, we were struggling to get enough customers, but with the reopening of the Pink Hotel and headlines of the recent happenings, Laketown has been flooded with visitors. As one of the only good restaurants in town, the Tiki Bar is now constantly packed. It's overwhelming sometimes, but ever since the new employees got trained, we coordinate seamlessly now.

Therefore, Grandpa doesn't need to be here. "You can take off."

"Alright. See you, Lady Fishy." He whistles as he cuts his way through the crowd, pretty agile for a man who's nearly eighty. He even had a heart attack early last year, but it doesn't seem to have slowed him down even a little bit. He's as agile and active as ever, taking frequent walks in the park and going fishing nearly every evening.

After he's gone, I continue work for the next few hours, trying not to think about the conversation I just heard and trying not to feel like everyone is staring at me. It's probably in my head, I know. It's probably just me being self-conscious. But the discomfort still clings to me all night.

I also try not to think about the college problem, for which I have no solution for now. I'll probably need to get a second job, maybe an accounting internship.

But, although I've applied for a few, none have gotten back to me.

Because you apparently need experience to get experience.

Later that night, as the crowd thins out, I end up manning the drink bar. Emma taught me how to pour a few of our most popular drinks and usually no one orders anything super complicated, which frustrates Emma because she wants to be able to show off the fancy skills that she learned at bartending school. But it's great for nights like tonight when Emma's not around, because it means I pretty much have it handled.

I'm wiping down glasses when a familiar cologne drifts to me followed by a deep voice. "Hello, Athena."

My face shoots up, and a smile spreads to my lips. "You're back." *Did he just call me Athena?*

"Yup." Micah Landing is standing opposite my bar, looking as delicious as always. His hair is damp, his curls shiny. He's dressed today in slacks, a casual polo shirt, and a watch that probably costs more than my parent's entire house. "Flew back this evening to discuss some things with Declan."

"Yeah?" I ask. "Things with the hotel?"

He nods but doesn't elaborate, as his gaze instead traces down my body. "How is it possible that you look even prettier than when I last saw you?"

Anticipation races through my veins at the look in his eyes. "I doubt it. When you last saw me, I was in a five-thousand-dollar dress and just got my makeup done by someone called the Face Reformer." Strange name, I thought, but Rachel assured me that the woman did make up for a bunch of top celebrities. "So I doubt I can beat that, with a black T-shirt and cargo shorts."

Micah smirks and plants his elbows on the counter, leaning forward to whisper. "Actually, when I last saw you, your makeup was long gone and that dress was on the hotel room floor so I don't think either of those things even mattered."

I swallow. My heart is racing and desire is flaying me again making my skin hypersensitive. "Oh?"

"Really," he says. "I can't wait to do it again."

"Who says I'm going to let you?" The challenge slips out breathlessly. "Besides I thought it was a one-night thing."

"One night, two nights, I've never been good at math." He waves a hand. "So what say you we go out tomorrow night? There's a restaurant out in Bayview that's halfway decent. How about I take you out to eat?"

"So you can get in my pants after?"

"No. I can get in your pants anyway. I'm just trying to see you fed."

I laugh and shake my head. I should probably tell him that we don't need to date to mess around. I know what we're doing is strictly casual and I don't need the illusion that he wants something serious with me.

But a meal at a fancy restaurant would be nice.

"Sure," I say. "Although I have to be back home at nine to help my neighbor babysit, so if you do want to have your way with me at some point during the night, we'll have to factor that in."

"Got it." He winks and his eyes drop down to my lips "Can't wait."

Me either.

"Carly."

I jerk and spin around to find Yule staring at me through the serving hatch.

He's giving me a look, and I blush because I don't know how long he's been standing there. Heck, I don't even know how long I've been here. My conversation with Micah seems to have drowned out my environment and I see what V–the woman from the party who hooked up with Micah in the past–meant now. He really can make any woman feel like she's the most important person in the entire world. What a dangerous ability.

"Table nine's been trying to get your attention," Yule says. "I think they want another martini."

"Oh, sure thing," I call, blushing a little as Yule shoots Micah a curious look. Micah salutes him and Yule merely nods as he retreats into his kitchen abode.

"Why did I get the sense he doesn't like me?" Micah asks.

"He's probably annoyed because you're distracting me."

"Ah. That's discrimination then. It's not my fault I'm so distractingly appealing."

I snort and roll my eyes and he leans back.

"I'll let you get back to work and stop being such a distraction. Here, let me get your number before I leave."

"Uh...sure." I rattle it off quickly and then go to attend table nine. It's a group of young, college-age girls who are probably tourists, in town to observe the opening of the hotel.

"That guy you were talking to was so gorgeous," one of them hisses at me as I take their next drink order. "Is he your boyfriend?"

"Uh, no," I say, glancing back to the counter. Micah's

on his way out and throws me another wink as he leaves. It makes at least one of them sigh.

"He's just a friend."

I gape at the statuesque building in front of me, the name of which is embossed in gold letters.

"Juvia?" I turn to Micah in shock. "That's the 'halfway decent' restaurant you were talking about? You got reservations to Juvia?"

Micah shrugs. "What, like it's hard?"

"Uh, yeah. The place is very trendy on social media and they typically have a waitlist that's months out. You've only been in town a single night; how did you get a reservation?"

"I'm Micah Landing," he says as though that explains everything. He settles his hand on my back and leads me to the front door, where a hostess takes his name and then leads us indoors.

Unlike the Tiki Bar, which has that rustic vibe, and smells like hamburgers and fried fish, this place is the epitome of sophistication. Dim lighting, velvet booths, and plants growing through the sleek wooden floors. I've never seen anything like it before. It also has the perfect temperature and a subtle scent I can't put my finger on.

The hostess leads us to a booth on a dais that faces a stage, where a man plays classical music on a piano.

That's when I discover that not only did Micah get a reservation, he got a VIP reservation. Last minute.

I stare at him incredulously as he pulls out my seat. *He must be a bigger deal than I thought.*

"Thank you." As I sit, I take a measured look around the room and suddenly feel weird about my dress. It's the dress that I almost wore to the party, the polyester one that nearly drove Rachel catatonic. And now I see why she didn't want me to wear it.

I feel out of place.

Micah wraps his hand on mine, drawing my attention back to him.

"Hey," he says. "You okay?"

"Yeah," I sigh. "I just wish I knew where we were going sooner. I would have made an effort to look more presentable." *Not that I could afford to get anything nicer than this dress.*

"You look great," he says. "More than great actually." His eyes run down my form again and he bites his lip, making desire coil inside me. He's been throwing me looks like that since he picked me up at Mrs. Peach's house, and it's slowly driving me nuts with lust.

Something is definitely happening tonight.

In the next five minutes, a bottle of wine comes around, and a waiter silently pours two glasses. He places the menu down and then leaves, as I murmur a thank you.

Then I reach for the glass, needing something to help me relax.

"Oh, there's something I wanted to ask you tonight," Micah says, picking up a menu.

"What is it?" I tip the glass into my mouth, the cool, smooth liquid a balm for my parched tongue.

"What do you think about marrying me?"

CHAPTER EIGHT

M ICAH

Wine sprays across the table, hitting me right in the face. The people at the tables surrounding us fall silent.

Luckily, I close my eyes in time, but some of it still gets me in the mouth. Not that I mind too much. It's Carly. She could probably spit straight in my mouth and I wouldn't care.

Now there's an idea we can try later….

Holding that thought, I finally open my eyes to find Carly gaping at me pale-faced. Shock and horror fight for dominance in her expression. I wait for one of them to take hold while I take a napkin and wipe my face clean, trying not to crack up.

"I'm so sorry," she whispers with an almost comical horror in her tone. "I didn't mean to… I can't believe I did that."

"Nah, entirely my fault," I say, somehow managing to keep my face straight. I shouldn't have broken the news to her like that, but the idea just hit me out of nowhere. And I can't lie, I also wanted to surprise her a little, to see what she was like when she got caught off guard.

And, well, I guess I got my wish.

"I really am sorry," she says again in a quieter voice as I dab the liquid from my suit. It won't come out. I already know it's a hopeless case, but I at least want to be able to walk out of here without looking like a two-year-old who hasn't learned how to properly drink from a sippy cup.

"I can get it cleaned for you after."

"That would be pointless. This is cashmere." I wave my hand. "Seriously, don't worry about it. Although, if you're that sorry, then maybe consider saying yes to my little proposition."

"What proposition?"

"To marry me, of course."

Her eyes widen again, and I know if she had more wine in her mouth, it would be spraying through the air again. "Wait, you were serious about that?"

"You think I would risk such a spit take if I wasn't serious?"

Her face flushes and she finally glances around as though realizing we're in public. The restaurant is quiet enough that her antics likely got some attention, and even though almost no one is outwardly staring anymore, quite a few tables are still stealing glances and chuckling. "God, that was embarrassing."

"Nah. It was glorious," I tell her, finally allowing myself to grin. "Ten out of ten accuracy and maximum comic relief with minimum damage. You just made quite a few people's nights. It was the icebreaker they needed to crack the tension. You may have saved a few first dates too, and maybe a few marriages by giving them something else to talk about other than who's sleeping with whose yoga instructor."

"Oh God." She covers her face with one hand. "Of course. The first time I come to a high-class restaurant and I have to make a complete country bumpkin of myself."

I take her other hand from the table, turning it over to trace the lines in the center. She has such soft hands. And while I'm enjoying her embarrassment, I also feel the urge to soothe her worries, and make her comfortable again. "If it makes you feel better, one time I got wasted at a business convention and ended up toppling over a year-long project that was an elaborate twelve-foot model of the Eiffel Tower."

She peeks at me through her fingers. "Really?"

"Yup." The specifics are that it happened a week after my brother's funeral. My father invited me to the business convention because all the important business people were supposed to be there. He wanted me to impress them so that the stakeholders would be okay with me taking my brother's place. It was the first in his long line of acts to force me into the role, while my brother was barely decayed in the ground. I know Dad was grieving him in his own way, but the man could compartmentalize like a pro—grieve but still do his duty, and insist on me doing mine.

But I hated it, hated the role he was forcing me to play. I felt like a misshapen peg that everyone was trying to bang into a clean round whole.

And so, as an act of rebellion, I got drunk before I showed up to the convention so that the shareholders would see how unsuitable I was for the role. Of course, I didn't expect to be that out of control either. I got way too loose, too fast, and blacked out for most of it. I only know what I did thanks to CCTV footage and my dad's later rants.

I didn't drink for weeks after that, and even now, I barely drink at all because of it.

But looking back, it was kind of a funny story.

Carly doesn't need all the backstory, so I just tell her the highlights, about me stumbling around, nearly throwing up on a prime minister's wife, accidentally insulting a liaison to France, and then calling our primary stakeholder a big poopy head.

Carly smiles and eventually laughs as the story unfolds, easing her tension. She has such a pretty laugh. Her nose crinkles a little, her eyes turn into this warm chocolatey color, and her lips downturn, like she's trying her hardest not to give in.

And the sound itself? Throaty, like happiness punching out of her.

"So anyway," I conclude. "The long and short of the story is, Hennesy is the devil's juice and I'm no longer allowed within fifty feet of a Ritz-Carlton. Might also be banned from a few embassies too. You probably need to know that if we're going to be married."

"Why?"

"Why am I banned? Well, I just told you the story of–"

"No." She laughs and holds up her hand to stop my tirade. "I mean why do you want me to marry you?"

"Oh, that. I was wondering when you would get around to asking." Her embarrassment has likely died enough that she's finally ready to confront the question. "It's another pretty long story involving a man called Marcus Landing."

"Your dad?"

"Yes," I say. "How did you know?"

"Because you mentioned in that other story that the ambassador said, 'Marcus, what is the meaning of this,' and I put two and two together."

"Ah." I nod my approval. "Attentive. Good. I like that in a wife."

She rolls her eyes, but she's still smiling so I continue, "My dad wants me to take over his company. Even with the tower-toppling incident, he seems to think that I'm CEO material, despite my hard and honest attempt to show him I'm not."

"So you don't want to take over?"

"Not even a little bit. He's the head of a holding company that manages a bunch of different businesses that are a monopoly in various industries. I think monopolies aren't great for the economic climate to start with, but I don't want to do it mostly because I think his job is incredibly boring. Most of the time, you sit in a room with about thirty old men and deliberate on how to add another trillion dollars to the bazillion you already have. And then you go to a meeting with another old man and try to convince him how you can make *him* another trillion. And then you go to a meeting with a woman and tell her you can make her a trillion too. And so on and so forth until one of you dies. I can't imagine a more drab existence."

Her smile widens. "Well, when you put it like that, it does sound awful."

"It is," I assure her. "Especially for someone like me. I like to travel, see the world, do things, make things. I don't care whether or not my shareholders have the assets to buy another private jet. I want to do something that matters." I'm shocked as the words leave my mouth. I didn't intend to reveal that much, but maybe I've had too much wine tonight and need to pull back. "Anyway, the point is that my father, seeing as he has no other heirs, doesn't give a damn what I want and is trying to manipulate things so I have no choice but to play it his way. And the Pink Hotel is part of it. It's supposed to be my training wheels. I don't want to run the place, but he's making it difficult for me to do anything else. And I'm trying my hardest to show him I won't give into his nefarious schemes."

"By marrying me?"

"No, hold on we haven't gotten to that part yet." I hold my hand up. "Okay, where was I? Oh, so first, I tried to sell my shares of the hotel to an old friend, so that I could use that money to start my own thing. Since Dad controls most of my other accounts, I need one that he can't touch and I need to buy contacts that he can't bribe. But then he blocked the sale of my hotel shares too because he's…well…a poopy head. A very powerful poopy head. No one else will buy the shares from me because no one is going to want to tangle with Marcus Landing on a warpath. No one else except, of course, Marcus' father."

"Your grandfather?"

"Yup. He can help me get out of this and convince my dad to lay off me. Grandfather actually doesn't care who takes over my dad's company. He doesn't see it as his legacy since Dad started it without him, and refused to take over Grandfather's oil business."

"Sounds like you're following in your father's footsteps then," she murmurs, but I don't like the comparison so I continue as though I didn't hear her.

"The thing is, my grandfather is, for whatever reason, deeply concerned about my love life. Don't ask me why, the man had an arranged marriage at eighteen and he and my grandmother hated each other for the entirety of their relationship. They lived in separate houses most of the time, but they never bothered to get a divorce. Nevertheless, he seems to think that marriage is a fantastic idea for me, and that I'm way past the age where I should be married. And he's not going to help me until I agree to make a concerted effort to that end."

"So you want me to play the part of your fake fiancée?" Understanding dawns on her features.

"Ding-ding," I tell her. "I told him I was already seeing someone and that I would bring her over for dinner soon, so I desperately need someone good enough to play the role. I asked a few other people but they... erm, fell through."

I first started the search with my former lovers but they ended up being either completely inappropriate for the role or they still held a torch for me that would make the situation more complicated than it needed to be. And the other people I tried out, the high-society girls that Grandpa liked so much, left me feeling cold and eager to get out of their presence. I don't think I could pretend with them even if I tried my hardest.

When I was flying back to Laketown, I had my assistant looking for actresses to play the part but the problem with that is that my grandfather might hire a PI to look them up and then he would figure out the entire ruse.

It was starting to look hopeless but then just earlier this evening, when I saw Carly in that black dress, the idea hit me.

Carly could do it.

She looks sweet and has that old Hollywood charm about her. When she dresses up, she easily passes for a high-society queen.

Plus, I actually like being around her so it won't be too hard to fake a relationship with her.

"So you just want me to go to dinner with you and your grandfather?" Carly asks, her eyebrow furrowing.

"No, not just that," I tell her. "I'll explain everything more in detail later, but it's going to be a lot of dinners and probably more social events than you think."

"Oh." Apprehension enters her gaze and she bites her lip in brief thought. "Well, it's not like I don't want to help you out, Micah, but it's just that I'm really busy. You know, with work and school, I don't know that I'll have time to even pretend to date you."

Ah, and that's why she's perfect for the role. "Well, I thought it would probably be a big ask, which is why I'm offering a financial incentive."

She pauses and stares at me.

"How does three hundred thousand dollars sound?"

She blinks. And then blinks again. "Are you serious?"

"As a spit take."

She sputters a bunch of choked sounds before she manages to make a full sentence. "You would really offer me that kind of money for pretending to date you?"

"Yeah. Even with my father's antics I still have at least that lying around. I should be able to move it without him noticing."

"I bet that's chicken change to you," she says a little snarky, and I smile.

"Yup."

She shakes her head.

"But seriously," she says. "You're not kidding me, right? This isn't like some prank show, is it? Are cameras going to come out?"

"No," I assure her. "I'm serious. We can even sign a contract to that effect. What do you think?"

She spouts some more words of disbelief for the next few minutes, but by the time the waiter comes back to take our food orders, she says, "Well, I would be stupid to turn that down. Where do I sign?"

I laugh at her eagerness and let her know I'll send her the contract tomorrow. I even tell her that I'll pay if she wants to hire a lawyer to help her look it over, and she beams, radiating excitement the entire night.

It makes the rest of the dinner pleasant. The food is good, the smile doesn't leave her face, and the conversation doesn't end.

And with each second that passes, I want her more and more. I want her glittering eyes staring at me in pure lust. I want her sensual lips under mine. I want her skin between my teeth.

Eventually, I drag my seat closer and reach under the table, touching her thigh.

She looks at me in alarm, which quickly gives way to a moan of desire as I lean over and kiss her neck. "Well, now that we've got that out of the way? How about we have a little fun?"

CHAPTER NINE

CARLY

We don't make it to the car.

It's a testament to how quickly and thoroughly lust takes over because I don't even think anything of it when Micah suddenly spins me around and presses my back against the wall, capturing my lips with his. The taste of wine and lust spreads across my tongue. I get drunk off it, sucking on his tongue, savoring his flavor, the feel of him.

My heart pounds in my ears, waves of lust crashing into me. My brain flatlines. Every single thought is scorched beneath a wave of desire. Every thought except one.

It's not enough.

I need more.

I lift a single leg, through the slit of my dress, wrapping it around his waist as his hips drive deeper into me. Tingles explode all over my skin, sensation focused on his hardness. Memories of his large cock have me gasping into his mouth as I enjoy the heated brand on my pussy. Excitement seeps into my bones.

He's going to fuck me again.

That's already a foregone conclusion. We're going to have explosive sex, right here right now, and the only question is how long we can get it to last. We race toward the peak now, desire shooting up, urging us to go faster. My body longs for the destination even as my mind relishes the journey.

My nipples pucker up, my pussy aches. Need whips me into a frenzy, turning the kiss rougher, wetter, more desperate.

Somewhere in the back of my mind, I recall that we're in a dark alley near the parking lot, between the restaurant and the building next to it that looks like a used car lot. Technically, it's empty right now but it's not private by any stretch of the word. Anyone could walk up and see us, see his lips tearing at mine, my hand tugging his hair desperately as his left hand slowly slides my dress up.

The possibility of getting caught should make me stop.

Instead, it only drives my passion higher. The erotic threat makes us wilder until we're barely taking breaths in between kisses. We're too driven by our need to devour each other.

Micah's lips nip mine and then it's his turn to suck my tongue for a moment before he pulls back. I blink, dazed by the loss of his lip. It takes a second for my vision to focus enough to look into his eyes. They're dark with a half-crazed sheen.

There's a question in them when he growls, "I want you, Carly. So fucking badly."

"I want you too." The words are barely a whisper in the wind before he kisses me again, a short harsh kiss that leads to his kissing down my neck.

With a groan, my head falls back, panted breaths fogging in the air. My heart threatens to beat out of my chest, and I bite back a plea for him to go faster. I don't know if I'll even be able to bear it if he does. His mouth on my neck is already driving me crazy. Each section of skin he licks becomes hypersensitive, even to barest gusts of air. I want to beg him to touch my nipples but that might just send me careening over the edge.

I slowly lose strength in my limbs, as I cling to him. I'm getting drunker off his scent, surrounded by his caresses, his hardness, his hands seeming to touch me endlessly.

As his hand moves under my dress, he mutters about how soft my skin is and how good I feel. Energy ricochets everywhere and I beg him to hurry. Just in case someone comes.

I don't want to stop. The urgency pounds inside me, my pussy pulsing with need. We *can't* stop. I feel so achingly empty, so ready to be filled. It won't wait till we get home or to a hotel. If we have to stop now... I think I might die.

He has to take me now, here against this wall with the wind surrounding us and the moon as our only source of light.

To my delight, Micah seems to be on the same wavelength. He hoists me into the air, pressing me back against the wall as my legs wrap around his waist naturally. He shifts so that he can push his hand between us and cup my pussy through my panties.

Oh yes.

"Fuck, you're already wet," he groans against my skin. "Do you know how sexy you are?"

"Mmmh." I try not to bite my lips too hard as he sucks at a sensitive spot on my neck that makes me shake with pleasure. I've never thought I was particularly sexy or attractive. Just cute. But Micah, with his desperate hands and his filthy words, manages to make me feel like just about the most desirable person on planet Earth.

His other hand is underneath my ass, cupping and squeezing in a deliciously lewd way. I like how he never shies away from taking a handful of me, and working it. My weight is something I've always struggled to accept but Micah's touch makes me forget all about being self-conscious. It's the way he lifts me easily, holds me up, molds my curves, and mutters things like, "*God, you feel so good...*"

Another wave of lust crashes through me at his words. I bite my lip to hold back the moan that threatens.

Then, it gets worse.

Micah's hand finds and rubs my clit over my panties.

"Oh, God." The gasp flies out of me. Desire arcs so sharply that I jolt. My muscles stiffen, awareness centered on his touch. My thighs squeeze tight around him, my heartbeat thundering in my ears.

"Oh, baby..." His voice is pure whiskey. Dark and rich and decadent. The lust already has me leaking onto my panties. But the sound we make when he twists his finger into the fabric turns me on more.

The sound of his finger sliding through my folds is embarrassingly moist. "*So fucking wet.*"

"Yes," I gasp trying to buck against his hand, to encourage him to do more. "I'm wet for you. Please, Micah, make me come."

He doesn't respond, only murmurs something unintelligible as my nerves threaten to break apart.

And then he shifts my panties aside, his finger brushing against my clit.

I release a noisy exhale into the air.

"You're not going to come, baby," he orders, his voice harsh. He sucks my earlobe into his mouth, making me cry out again. "Not until I tell you to."

"Oh, God, Micah." I can only sob at the sheer torture, as he works my swollen nub, his expert fingers applying the perfect amount of pressure. My head digs into the wall behind me. I bite my lip so hard it nearly breaks skin.

Micah thrusts into my pussy hard, with a single finger and I gasp again.

Oh, God.

I'm not going to survive.

I'll die anyway, as tortured desire drags me to the grave.

My nipples are so painfully aroused they chafe underneath my dress. I bring up my hands to rub them but it only makes everything so much worse, my pussy clenching around his finger, creaming for him.

He murmurs his approval, rubbing my clit with his thumb, as he drives a finger into me again, ripping another sob from my throat.

"That's right," he murmurs as my heart threatens to jump out of my chest. "You can touch yourself all you want, baby, but you can't come until I say so." His teeth close around the base of my neck, and the sharp bite of pain makes me exclaim. It enhances the pleasure, even as the proceeding suckling has me melting inside.

I don't know what he's turning me into. I feel like a purely sensate being who can do nothing but feel and give myself over for him to do whatever he wants me to.

And he truly uses me in the best way.

His hand slides down from my clit, pushing two fingers smoothly into my center.

My body hunches over as lust punches through me.

My mind ripples and splits. A part of me yelling to escape his measured, deep thrusts. Another part yearns for more.

I want release. I *need release.*

"Please, Micah," I beg, loudly, lustily. "Please let me come."

He adds another finger and then curves it to hit my G-spot.

A guttural throaty sound escapes from me. My toes curl, my body clenching on his thick digit.

He starts going faster, slamming into me and it feels so good that I can't stand it. My mind is flying apart, but he secures me between his body and the wall so I know there's no danger of falling. I have no clue how he's holding me up this long. I'm not exactly a shrinking daisy, but then I grip his arms and remember how muscular he is. It hides well under the suits he usually wears but the strength in his arms is undeniable.

I shift my hold to his shoulder and start bouncing slowly in the air, on his finger, ever greedy for more. I shut my eyes to savor the feeling of my incoming orgasm driving every other thought from my mind. It's almost there. It rides the base of my spine, skittering along down all my extremities. It grows bigger, pulls tighter. At some point, it's so intense that I bite his shoulder to hold back.

"Yes, fuck," he groans, throwing his head back. "Mark me. Mark me and come for me, baby girl."

That's it. That's all I need. Suddenly without warning, I flood his hand and shout my release into the air.

And that's when I instantly hear voices.

Micah hears them too, because he mutters out a curse and pulls his finger out of me with a wet pop. He hoists me higher and carries me to the parking lot, fumbling his key out of his pocket and unlocking the car as we go.

And once we're in the cool interior of the Porsche, he doesn't stop.

He slides into the car with me in his lap and I can feel the barely bridled energy, waiting to be released. I can feel a hard cock pressing against my pussy.

I shift my panties aside and fumble with his zipper, mindless now, needing to feel him inside me. The location isn't ideal but it's not my first time having car sex. Yes, it can be uncomfortably cramped but I know how to make it work.

And so does Micah, because he pushes the seats all the way back to give him space. Luckily, his rental car has enough headroom that I don't bang my head when he lifts me. Plus, the windows are tinted.

And then finally, I release his cock, watching it rise angrily and proudly from his pants.

I take a second to stare at it in awe.

He looks painfully aroused, I'm surprised he's not a desperate, pleading mess like I am.

His cock is a stiff baton, tip swollen and purple, stalk twitching and quivering as it bounces near his belly button.

Precum has dribbled out the tip and down the stalk. Veins throb at the side.

He only touched me.

All he did was touch me, and he looks just about ready to explode.

Pride merges with passion.

And then, with a curse, Micah drags me forward, arranges me in his lap and drives his cock into me.

"Micah!"

From then on, I can only hold on for the ride.

This coupling isn't like the first time. It's messy and jagged and full of muttered swear words and tongue kisses. A few elbows banging on the car door here and there. Once, my back hits the horn and it goes off. We don't stop. There's no control, no suave moves. All animalistic needs.

And it's glorious.

My body buckles as we rush to the peak. His eyes roll back, pure pleasure in his flushed face. He swears and snarls as desire turns him into an anguished beast.

"Oh, God, I'm coming!" I cry out as my senses splinter again and, almost simultaneously, Micah jerks his own release into me.

I feel it, his hot need spurting inside me and it nearly triggers a second orgasm. But I just don't have it in me.

I sag limply against him and he groans in my hair.

"Jesus," Micah says, clutching me for uncountable seconds after it's done. His hands shake, and he's still panting in my hair.

I try to use the rest of my flagging energy to crawl out of his lap, but his arms tighten around me keeping me in place.

"That was insane," he breathes.

"Yeah," I whisper, resting back on him. That last orgasm seems to have sucked the last bit of strength out of me and I'm in a pleasant fog, ready to fall asleep right here on his chest. Especially with the way his hand begins running through my hair at regular intervals, his heartbeat racing under my ear.

And then in an instant, as if just realizing what he was doing, he lets his hand drop and says, "I need to get you home, don't I?"

"Yeah," I recognize the words for what they are, a need to detach. Still, when I attempt to climb off his lap for the second time, he holds on to my thigh for a second and his hand almost seems reluctant to release me. Which is crazy because he's the one making it clear that this moment of intimacy is over.

Not that I mind much. I'm used to fun meaningless sex, and I know how to keep myself from falling too deeply. I also know that a man holding you and kissing you and sometimes even telling you he loves you after mind-blowing sex means nothing. It's all just hormones.

I straighten my dress and take off my damp panties, as I get into my seat. Out of the corner of my eye, I catch sight of him tucking his cock back into his pants, with a wet patch in front. God, even soft he's still majestic, long and thick. I want him in my mouth and make a mental note to do that the next time we hook up. If there is a next time.

When I glance up, he's looking at me, something dark in his gaze.

"What?" I ask, and he shakes his head.

"Nothing." Then he reaches over and slips my seat belt over my body. While he's at it, his arm brushes against my thigh and triggers aftershocks inside my pussy.

Down girl. Maybe next time.

The ride back to my neighborhood is cozy and quiet. I relax in the seat, languishing in the feel of a luxury car gliding smoothly along the roads. I've never been a car girl, never known the difference between one or another, but I have to admit there's something just nice about coasting in a smooth car with comfortable leather seats that feel like they could melt the stress right out of you.

Suddenly, my phone rings loud enough to cut through the comfortable silence.

My eyes pop open and I reach for my purse, which had slipped from my shoulders unceremoniously in our little tumble. I'm glad I didn't somehow lose it when we were hooking up at the restaurant because I didn't even have the presence of mind to search for it before I left.

I fish the phone out of the bag, ready to answer automatically, until I see the unknown number.

Unknown but very familiar.

Whoever is calling is doing so from the Laketown jailhouse.

I swallow, all my relaxation dissipating as tension coils in my muscles. There are three people who it could be.

It could be my dad, arrested for public drunkenness or belligerently starting a fight with a bartender.

My mother, arrested for swiping someone's wallet or trying to box a church lady.

Or Nate.

Somehow, somehow, I know in my bones that it's that last one.

And talking to Nate is worse than the other two, because it's more painful. On some level, I've managed to detach myself somewhat from my parents and their misdeeds. I still feel I owe them some loyalty because they're my parents but their screwups no longer hurt me as deeply.

But Nate... what he did hurt.

Because I cared about him, and still do care about him. And I know he's not truly a bad person, which is what makes this whole thing worse. I seem to be the only one who still holds onto the notion because admittedly, Nate has done a truly horrible thing.

"You okay?" Micah asks and I realize that I've been staring at the phone for a long time.

"Yeah," I answer and with great difficulty, I hang up the call. "I'm fine."

"Was that your cousin?"

My head whips to him, widening in surprise. *How did he know Nate was my cousin? Did I accidentally say something to him about it?*

"Declan told me all about him," he says.

Of course, I think bitterly, although I can't really blame Declan here.

"It's good that you hung up. You don't need to keep in contact with someone like that."

Rather than make me feel good, his words irritate me. "Someone like what? You don't even know him."

"I don't need to. I know he conspires with kidnappers, thieves, and murderers."

He has a point there, but I don't want to acknowledge it. "He hasn't had an easy life."

"Neither have you and you seem to be better adjusted than he is."

"It's different," I say and then lay my head back. My

post-orgasm bliss is ruined. "I don't want to talk about this anymore."

"Fine by me. But for the record, I want you to stay away from him at least for the duration of our deal."

"What? Why?" I plan on staying away from Nate anyway, but it's one thing to do it and another thing to be told I have to do it.

"Because I don't want anyone finding out that my fiancée is cousins with a potential criminal."

The words immediately strike clean, hitting me in my most exposed insecure place. I stare at him, disbelievingly. I didn't expect that from him, especially when he told me of his colorful past. I should have expected it, but I didn't.

And I hate the way he just made me feel.

"I'm not saying that to make you feel bad," he says, but I don't care. "I'm saying it to help you."

Help me how? I want to scream, but I ignore the urge. I don't want to give him the satisfaction of knowing he got under my skin.

"It's fine," I say tersely, turning back to the window.

It's my fault. I shouldn't have expected him to be different from all the others in Lakeview.

He doesn't owe me anything and this deal of ours won't last long anyway.

And once it's over, I'll be three hundred thousand dollars richer and he'll be thankfully out of my life.

CHAPTER TEN

MICAH

Carly insists I drop her at the end of her street, so no one sees us. She assures me it's safe, but I still wait in my car and watch her until she's inside her home.

Then, I drive away with an unsettled feeling in my stomach.

Carly's mood changed swiftly after our conversation. She was quiet during the second half of the trip, but not the same comfortable silence that she held in the first half. Instead, it felt distant, angry, and like she firmly erected an unspeakable wall between us.

I couldn't figure out why.

Is it because of her cousin?

But surely, she can't be naive enough to think that I was wrong in my assessment of him. Heck, I was there myself when those smugglers were shooting at Declan. I helped fish his body out of the pond; the poor guy almost died.

And while Carly's cousin wasn't among the shooters, he confessed that he was working with the people who did it. Not only that, but he'd broken into Emma's house and ransacked the place, destroying furniture, all in an attempt to steal something from her. Despite everything Emma and her grandfather did for the boy.

As far as I'm concerned, someone like that is beyond redemption, and Carly is better off without him. But she still seems to care about him for whatever reason. She even looked guilty when she hung up the phone.

And I won't lie, that's part of the reason I said what I said, about her not talking to him for the duration of our deal.

I know deep inside she probably knows that she's better off staying away from him, but perhaps she needs someone else to give her the order so she doesn't have to deal with the guilt. She needs it to be someone else's call.

And I have no problem doing it, because I truly don't mind being the bad guy.

What I do mind is the way she looked at me when I said it, like I'd said something hurtful to attack her personally. I can't figure out why she looked at me like that.

It's bothering me.

Why?

I release a sigh and grip the steering wheel, clenching my teeth. Whatever. If she wants to be pissed because I pointed out something that was fairly common sense, then that's her prerogative. I don't even know why I care anyway. What we have is a mild friendship at best, but it's mostly a business deal. And as much as I like Carly, I have no doubt that once our business together is over, I probably won't see her again.

I'll be too busy living my life somewhere far, far away from Laketown.

In a flash, something jumps into the road, and on instinct, I immediately hit the brakes.

"Jesus."

My car comes to a near-instant halt, jerking me forward and then back in my seat as I blink at my windshield. My heart pounds with adrenaline, rushing through me. It takes me a second to make sense of events.

What the fuck did I just hit? A deer? A raccoon?

Turns out, none of the above.

It's a shorter man, leaning on my bumper looking bleary-eyed at me.

"What the fuck?" I get out of the car as the man mumbles to himself.

"You didn't hit me," he drawls drunkenly. "You were supposed to hit me."

I stare at his state, noting his five-o'clock shadow, red eyes, and most prominently, the brown bag with a bottle clutched in his hand. Something about him seems familiar but I can't put my finger on it.

"What are you, fucking nuts?" I ask him, my New York accent thickening. "Get the fuck off my car."

"No," he says stubbornly. He lies on the bumper. "I'm gonna call the cops and tell them you hit me unless you give me five hundred bucks right now."

"Oh, that's your grift?" I laugh darkly. "And what, you think the cops are going to believe you looking like that?"

He glares at me, offended. "What the hell is that supposed to mean?"

"You look like shit. Plus you stink." I approach him and spot his wallet sticking out from his back pocket. I swipe it and open it.

"Hey, that's mine." He lunges at me, but I sidestep him easily and he staggers to the ground. I frown at what I'm seeing.

His ID is in there and it says he's Raymond Huntley.

That's Carly's last name, and Nate's last name too.

Could he be…

"You wouldn't happen to know Carly Huntley would you?"

He squints at me from the ground. "Carly's my daughter."

Shit. She really got the short end of the stick when it comes to family huh?

As I watch the man wobble back to his feet, I can't help but feel really bad for her. And mad that this bastard, who's supposed to be her dad, is here drunkenly trying to pull scams on people, while she works like an honest citizen.

Lord only knows how she's so well-adjusted.

I reach down and pick the man up by the scruff of his shirt, slamming him into the Porsche.

"Hey!"

"I thought this is what you wanted." I smile evilly at the fear that suddenly jumps into his eyes. "I thought you wanted me to manhandle you so you can get money out of me, you scamming bastard."

"Get off me."

"Oh, I will. But first, let me warn you, so you quit making your family's life a living hell. The next time you try something like this with me, I'll run you over. I don't stop for scum like you, and since you want it so badly, I'll put you out of your misery." I lean in and whisper, "And trust me. I have the money and power to get away with it."

I pull back and watch even more fear bleed into his gaze, while I maintain my pleasant smile. "Oh, and that goes for anyone else you try this on. Trust me, I'll know. I got eyes all around this town." It doesn't make sense since I'm a stranger here, but he's likely too drunk to recall much more than a rich maniac threatening him. "If I even hear about you trying this again, you'll hear from me. Got it?"

He swallows and nods rapidly. I release him, throwing him to the ground, feeling nothing but disgust as I watch him scramble to his feet and run away.

Good. Hopefully, that makes things a little easier for Carly.

CHAPTER ELEVEN

CARLY

I'm still pissed at Micah as I climb Mrs. Peach's porch stairs.

More than the anger though, what bothers me is the bitter feeling lingering in my gut, the self-loathing that always plagues me whenever anyone alludes to my family's various crimes. I hate that feeling, hate it so much.

No matter how hard I try, their words feel like a judgment on me too. After all, I grew up with the very people they shun. My parents raised me. If everyone in my family is a screwup, what makes me so different?

Maybe it's only a matter of time before I become a screwup too.

My head hurts as I reach the top step. My mood worsens.

I wish I could erase that last fifteen minutes or so.

The night was going so well until then. Everything else seemed straight out of a fairy tale, from the fancy restaurant to the amazing wine to Micah's company and even his unbelievable deal that would solve all my financial problems right now.

It was all fantastic.

And then Nate called, breaking the illusion.

I was suddenly no longer just an ordinary girl having fun with an ordinary guy.

I was practically trailer trash hooking up with a billionaire.

I wonder if Micah finds the whole concept of our relationship as ridiculous and amusing as I do. I also wonder why I'm sleeping with a guy who thinks badly about my family and me.

I mean he probably thinks I'm easy, considering how effortless it was to get me into bed with him.

"Whatever," I mutter to myself. "It's not like I need his approval anyway."

Before I can grasp the door handle, it swings open on its own. I jump back, startled as my best friend stands at the doorway blinking at me in silence.

"Emma!" I exclaim. I'm not sure who's more surprised, me or her.

"Hey," she says. "I dropped by to talk, but Mrs. Peach said you went on a date. She told me that would be back soon, so I decided to wait."

"Oh. Uh, yeah," I say. And that's when I notice a black Mercedes parked in the driveway, the one I missed because I was too busy brooding. The bodyguards are probably choosing to wait there, to give the girls privacy. I know Emma is starting to chafe under their constant regard, and she's complained to me a few times about just how invasive having bodyguards is.

But Declan won't budge on her having them, until the Pearl case is entirely resolved. Possibly even after.

Emma glances behind me to the other end of the road where Micah's rental Porsche was sitting. I wonder if she saw him drive off.

"Was that Micah who dropped you off?"

Shit. She saw him.

"Uh, yeah," I say, trying to act casual as I attempt to step past her. Emma gives me space so I can enter the empty living room. "Where are Mrs. Peach and Kayla?" Kayla is the six-year-old girl she's babysitting, one of the neighbor's kids.

"In the bedroom. Mrs. Peach is reading her a bedtime story." I hear the door shut behind me as I head to the kitchen. Emma follows. "Amelia was helping too, although I'm pretty sure she just wanted a chance to tell someone about the diary again."

"Amelia's here too?" Declan's daughter is a precocious almost fourteen-year-old, who is always a hoot, with her endless curiosity and conspiracy theories.

"Yup," Emma answers. "We were having a girl's day and decided to drop by."

"Cool."

Emma clears her throat, before she says, "So Micah was the one you went on a date with?"

"Well, I wouldn't call it a date."

"What would you call it then?"

I open the fridge. While the food at the restaurant was good, and the wine was even better, their portion sizes left much to be desired. I'm still hungry hours later, but luckily, Mrs. Peach always has leftovers.

I visually scroll through the items as I mull over how to answer Emma's question.

"We just went to a restaurant to talk. He has a problem that he needs my help to solve."

"Right." Emma doesn't sound like she believes a word I'm saying, and when I straighten with a Tupperware of mashed potatoes and greens, she has an eyebrow raised and a half smile on her face. "You went on to a restaurant with Micah Landing, in that dress, and all you did was talk?"

I shrug, but I can already feel the heat spreading across my face. Damn my pale coloring. I can lie and mask my expression excellently, make my features convincingly bland, but then a random blush will give the whole thing away.

Emma's expression loses all its humor, and she sighs. "Look, babe, I know Micah looks like a dream boat–"

"Don't let your fiancé hear you say that." Declan is famously jealous.

Emma rolls her eyes at my wry comment and continues, "Micah is objectively good-looking, but he's not really… relationship material."

I raise an eyebrow. "What on earth gave you the impression that I wanted a relationship with him?"

"I know you don't date. I also know you have your own set of attachment issues, but I'm worried that dealing with Micah will worsen your view of men and completely shatter whatever shred of romantic inclinations you may have. I mean he's a nice guy, but he's also…"

"A spoiled, irreverent womanizer?" I volunteer when she lets the sentence hang.

"Well… yeah."

I snort, placing the Tupperware on the kitchen counter and retrieve a bottle of water, cracking it open. "Yeah, I already figured out the kind of man Micah is. Don't worry. There's no risk of me getting my heart broken by that guy." At most, Micah irritates and arouses me, but he doesn't trigger me on a deeply emotional level that would suggest an intimate connection. We're fuck buddies. And that's how it's going to remain.

For now…. The threat lingers in my mind longer than it should.

"We're just hooking up while he's in town." I decide to be honest with Emma. "And then when he's gone, I'll forget all about him. You know me, Emma. When have I ever been hung up on a guy?"

Emma still looked doubtful. "I don't know. It's just… I've heard about Micah."

"From Declan?"

"Him and others. Apparently, Micah's pretty well known for leaving a trail of broken hearts behind him, even from, as Rachel would put it, 'smarter women who should know better.'"

"Yeah, well, that's probably because those women aren't used to the disappointment of not getting what they want," I point out. "They probably saw him as a challenge, and when they lost him, the disappointment felt like heartbreak. Versus me, who is very familiar with both disappointment and heartbreak. Micah Landing will not break my heart. That's for sure."

Emma lets out a heavy sigh. "Well, if you're sure. Anyway, that isn't really what I came to talk to you about anyway."

"Oh? And what did you come to talk to me about?" I grab a spoon to start scooping some of the food into a plate and then pop the plate in the microwave. I then return the Tupperware to the fridge and drink some more water, all without Emma saying a single word.

She seems to struggle with whatever she wants to say.

And when she finally speaks, I understand why.

"I spoke to Tate..."

I nearly groan. *Of course. The one thing I ask from that girl is to keep a secret from Emma, and she can't even do that for me.*

To be fair, Tate has never been able to keep a secret even when we were young. I don't know why I expected her to do so now.

I already know where this conversation is going but I'm resentful that I even have to have it, so I don't try to help Emma get the words out at all.

Her lips form shapes as she fights against the awkwardness, and then with a sigh of frustration, she finally blurts out, "You know you can always come to me if you need help. Right?"

"I know. But like I told Tate, this is something I want to handle on my own. And I *can* handle it on my own." *What part of that is so hard for people to understand?*

"But you don't have to," she says. "Look if you need money, I can give you some–"

"No."

"We can call it an advance, a work advance although you don't even have to pay me back, to be honest–"

"We're not doing that."

"We've been friends forever. And if it's more than I can afford, I can just ask Declan–"

"Emma, I already said no!" I finally explode. "Why does no one understand that I don't need help? I don't need anyone!'

There's a moment of silence during which my outbursts sink like a stone between us. Emma reacts like she's been slapped, reeling back and blinking. The flash of hurt on her face makes me feel like the lowest life form on the planet.

Regret instantly fills me.

"I'm sorry," I say, walking close and hugging her. "I'm being a shitty friend, and I'm sorry I went off on you like that. I guess I'm just a bit more sensitive tonight than I thought." Probably because of my cousin's call and Micah's words that stung more than I let on.

And the truth is that I'm not even sure why it hurt so much. It's not like he insulted me outright, and everything he said about my folks is true.

But for some reason, his words continue echoing in my head, digging into me like a vulture picking at a wound.

"No, it's fine," Emma says, as she wraps her arms around me. "You were right to be mad. I'm being the bad friend by not respecting your wishes and trying to insert myself where I don't belong. It's just that... I'm worried about you."

I sigh, allowing some of the tension to leak out of me.

"I know. And I appreciate it, I really do, but I just... I need to do this on my own. Okay?"

Emma nods and pulls back. She finally allows a hesitant smile to spread her cheeks, and her eyes finally regain their mischievous gleam. "So, we gonna crack open that ice cream and talk about the date, or what?"

I smile at her incorrigibility. "Yes to the ice cream, no to talking about the date that wasn't really a date."

"Boo. You're no fun."

"Emma." A new voice interrupts our conversation and I turn to find Amelia, standing at the kitchen archway, blinking her bright eyes. "Oh. Hey, Carly."
"Hi, hi." I wave. "What's up?"

"Nothing. Kayla is asleep and so is Mrs. Peach. They fell asleep in the middle of *Golden Girls*, but with the way Mrs. Peach is snoring, Kayla might not stay asleep for long."

"Oh, don't worry," I say. "Once Kay's down, she sleeps like the dead."

A hint of relief flashes in her face. "Okay, that's good. I really don't want to have to watch another episode or read another bedtime story."

I snort and finally notice what she's holding in her hand, a folder neatly packed with stray sheets of paper. I know what's in the folder, having had numerous conversations with Amelia about it while visiting Emma.

Lately, all the young girl wants to talk about is the disappearance of Madam T, a socialite who stayed at the Pink Hotel about fifty or so years ago.

In a way, Amelia's obsession with Madam T is a good thing. After all, it was her intense perusal of Madam T's diary that led the police to capturing the rainbow pearl smugglers that no one even knew about in the first place.

It's just strange to think that Emma was given the diary years ago by her grandfather, and she only gave it to Amelia when the latter first moved here. It was supposed to be a simple welcoming gift, something to make her visit to Laketown more exciting.

But, within a few months, the little genius used the diary to solve a major crime. Insane.

The diary's now with the police as part of their investigation, but Amelia made photocopies of every page and often carries it around in that folder she's holding. I know that with only the mildest prompting, she'll go into detailed explanation of every theory she has about Madam T's disappearance and what happened with the thieves and how it all links together.

Amelia also, for whatever reason, thinks the original jewel thieves might come back for the Pink Pearl now that it's been found, even though they haven't been seen in fifty years already.

"How's the investigation going?" I ask, nodding toward the folder. Emma throws me a droll look that Amelia doesn't catch because she looks to the ceiling and sighs dramatically.

"I think I've hit a dead end," she says. "I've read the diary cover to cover, looked into all the clues, tried to piece together any information I can find online but still nothing. I still can't figure out where Madam T and Vincent went after they ran away from the hotel."

"Isn't that the magic of it?" I know a little bit about the story of the missing lovers, some of it from what Emma told me and the rest from Amelia. Madam T, the owner of the diary, was a noble socialite who just lost her father. She came to the Pink Hotel with her fiancé to distract herself from her grief. But her fiancé, the cold bastard, was just there to sign business deals and didn't really wanna deal with her. So, he left her alone most of the time to hang out with the other gentlemen at the hotel.

Unbeknownst to either of them, there were jewel thieves in the hotel too, plotting to steal the Pink Pearl. One of them, Vincent, set his sights on Madam T and wanted to use her to get closer to the pearl.

He started sending her love letters, impersonating her fiancé, and she responded to them in kind. Slowly, they fell in love for real and the thief came clean about his deception.

But then Madam T's fiancé found out about everything and all hell broke loose. There was a gun fight, the fiancé got shot, and the three thieves and Madam T were lost to the wind.

And now, many decades later, Amelia is obsessed with finding out what happened to them.

"Maybe we're not meant to know," I say. "Not knowing is part of the fun, don't you think?"

The teen doesn't seem convinced. "Well, I don't like not knowing things. And I won't stop until I get to the bottom of this." She bites her lip in thought for several seconds, and then like flipping a switch, her expression brightens up. "On the bright side, I met this kid on an online forum and he says he'll help me with the investigation. His dad's a cop and so he knows what to look for in a cold case. He gave me all sorts of things to think about too. Wanna hear them?"

Emma and I share a look. Ice cream and conspiracy theories doesn't sound half bad right now.

"Alright." I open the fridge up again to retrieve the tub. "Let's do this."

The next day, a Lamborghini is sitting in the Tiki Bar parking lot.

It's such an odd and funny sight, watching the sleek red car between two rusty trucks, one of which should have been deposited in the junkyard ages ago.

I pause to stare in amazement. And I'm not the only one. A group of teenage boys are staring at the car in awe too. One of them even leans on the hood to take a selfie with it.

Only for him to jump up when the door pops open and Micah emerges.

"Sorry!" the selfie-taker scurries off red-faced as his friends laugh at him.

"No worries," Micah waves them off good-naturedly. Then he faces me.

"Hey there, pretty lady," Micah calls out, taking off his sunglasses in such a smooth move, that my heart skips a beat.

He looks like a movie star.

I can feel other people's gazes on me as I approach him, and it's an interesting sensation. Usually, when people stare at me, it's due to either scorn or pity. But this time, it's clear envy they emanate, as well as curiosity.

Compared to scorn and pity, I have to admit, envy and curiosity feel kinda nice.

"What happened to the Porsche?" I ask as I walk around to the passenger side. Micah follows me to pull open the door.

"Wasn't my style," he says as I climb in. "Too bulky. I actually wanted this in the first place, but some senator's son was in town and already rented it out."

"Ah," I laughed at his disgruntled expression.

"Luckily, they couldn't afford it for another day, and now I get to play with this baby."

"You know this is my first time in a sports car?" I tell him as he gets in the driver's seat. I stare at the mustard-brown interior and inhale the fresh scent of exotic leather and cologne.

"For real?" he turns to me and then says, "Well then. I'll make sure to make it a ride you won't forget."

The car purrs to life, the sound a pleasant hum that fades into almost nothing. Micah pulls out of the parking lot in a smooth move, and when he reverses to get the turn right, the smart screen in front of him shows our back in exquisite detail.

And then, as the car joins the road, he kicks up the speed in a heart-pounding rush.

"Micah," I warn as my hands clutch the leather seats below me, my heart rate ticking up steadily. The car is a well-oiled machine, too well-oiled, offering no resistance at all as it zooms down the road. I've never gone this fast before. It's a little disconcerting. The roads are mostly empty but still. Once we get on the highway, the world whizzes by even faster and the loss of control scares me.

And also... thrills me.

"Relax," Micah says. "I got you."

He takes one hand off the wheel and folds it over the hand that's clutching the seat. He turns it over, making me hold his hand tightly instead.

The ride continues at the same stomach-dropping speed, switching lanes and slowing only for red lights.

After a while, I start to relax.

Maybe because it's so clear that Micah is in complete control here. Maybe it's the steady rhythm or the solid feel of the vehicle, or the cologne-scented seats. Or maybe it's Micah's touch. Either way, my muscles start to unknot and before I know it, I'm just holding Micah's hand rather than squeezing the life out of it as I lean back into the seat.

"See?" Micah says. "Isn't that nice?"

"Mhmmm," I respond. Now that I'm not scared for my life, I can enjoy the smooth navigation and bone-meltingly comfortable seats. Not to mention all the buttons on the dashboard. "Where are we going?"

"Shopping," he says. "I forgot to mention yesterday, but my grandfather is, well, a snob. It's why I lied and told him that you were a high-society girl. Now, you have to look and play the part."

"Ah." I nod. "Like *Pretty Woman*."

"Exactly like *Pretty Woman*." He nods enthusiastically and runs his thumb over my fingers in approval. "What an excellent movie that was."

"I don't know about that. It seemed a little far-fetched to me."

He gives me a look of mock horror. "Blasphemy."

I roll my eyes. "Come on. A wealthy, upper-crust businessman falls in love with a hooker? And what's more, he marries her? Please. That would never happen in real life."

"Yes, it could. Where's your sense of romance?"

"I'm a realist. And in reality, even if he did fall in love with her, he would never claim her in public, much less marry her. She would simply live her life as his hidden mistress."

As we reach a red light, he stares for a long time, thoughtful. "Man, you're jaded."

I shrug. "I prefer the term pragmatic"

"Hmm. We'll put a pin in that discussion for now. But today, we're going to have your *Pretty Woman* shopping montage."

"Alright." I figure if we're going shopping, we're probably headed to Bayview. That's where all the nice boutiques are, and it should take us an hour or so to get there.

I lean back and close my eyes, imagining what I would look like dressed as a high-society girl. Mostly though I'm enjoying the ride and enjoying Micah's hand holding mine.

I don't know that I doze off until someone shakes me awake. "We're here, sleeping beauty."

My eyes blink open and turn to look out the open door to the sunset, behind a jet-black plane.

I blink again. "Where are we?"

"On the airport tarmac."

I stare at him in confusion. "Why?"

He smiles mischievously. "I already told you. We're going shopping."

CHAPTER TWELVE

M ICAH

Carly still seems struck silent with disbelief, and it's an adorable look on her.

The black midsize private jet waits behind us, along with a full eight-person crew that stands beside the descended stairs in welcome.

Carly still hasn't said a word.

I resist the urge to grin triumphantly, although the jet is sadly not mine. While my family does own a private jet, I'm currently banned from using it until I "see reason." Plus, even if I wasn't banned, using the family private jet would make it easier for my dad to spy on me and make it likelier that he would figure out what I was up to.

So instead, I asked an old college friend to borrow his jet.

It cost me a favor and a few thousand dollars, but it's worth it to see the look of absolute awe on Carly's face as she steps out of the car.

"Like it?" I ask.

"Uh-huh." She nods slowly. "Are we really going to ride in that thing?"

"Yup," I respond, amused at her sudden grin.

"Eek! I can't believe it!" She skips a few times and beams with barely bridled excitement. "Little old Carly riding in a private jet. I feel like a Kardashian."

I laugh then, her joy contagious. I'm typically not excited by things like this. I've ridden in private jets enough times that this is nothing special to me anymore, but watching Carly's excitement reminds me of the first time I was brought on one when I was six.

"Shall we?" I ask her, looking forward to seeing her expression at the interior.

"Uh-huh," she says and takes my hand as we walk to the stairs. A sudden gust of sharp wind blows her hair into my face, and I smell her vanilla-scented shampoo. Delicious. It makes me want to grab her close and inhale her, but I resist the urge as we approach the plane.

She greets all the staff as we ascend, and I follow suit even though I almost never do that. Usually, when I'm boarding a private jet ,I'm in a conversation with someone or on my phone. Chatting with the staff isn't something that comes to mind.

But Carly gives them all the whole midwestern, "How y'all doing?" and actually waits for their murmured response before continuing up the stairs. As she enters the jets, her eyes go to the star-studded gold-paneled ceiling, her jaw falling open.

"It's like I'm looking at the stars indoors," she declares.

"Yeah, that's the intended effect," I say.

"It's beautiful."

"Uh-huh." But I'm not looking up. I'm looking at her instead.

I've mostly seen Carly calm and collected, whether amused or vaguely annoyed. The only time she loses that measured control is when she's lost in the throes of passion.

But seeing her like this, filled with childish glee, triggers a whole different sensation within me. I can't help but notice that when she's like this, she glows so beautifully.

My eyes follow her as she starts down the aisle toward the seats on the left.

Customary monogrammed cashmere blankets are folded on the seats and Carly takes one as she sits by the windows. She giggles to herself and then immediately starts fiddling with the seatbelts trying to hook it on.

"You don't have to put that on right now," I tell her, smiling.

"Oh." She blushes. "Sorry. I've never been on a plane before," she admits as I settle beside her. "I always hear people complaining about the legroom, but either it's not as bad as I thought it would be or I'm really short."

"More like this isn't indicative of most planes. Economy class does indeed have shitty legroom." Not that I would know. I've never flown economy in my life.

As we settle down, one of the flight attendants, a blonde with her hair in a carefully coiffed bun at the back of her head strolls to us, her hands folded in front of her.

"Welcome aboard, sir, madam." She gives a perfunctory smile and then continues, "The pilot has indicated we can take off in fifteen minutes. In the meantime, is there anything you would like to eat? Drink? We have champagne and several types of wine, and we can also order directly from the airport if you would like."

When Carly's eyes travel to me, I remain silent, letting her decide.

"Ugh, sure, I guess wine would be okay," she says.

"Eh!" I make the sound of a buzzer, making both women start. "Wrong answer."

"Huh?"

"You don't just ask for wine," I tell her. "That indicates a lack of education on the subject. You have to be more specific."

Carly raises her eyebrow. "But I am uneducated on the subject. Wine is just wine to me."

"Yeah, but you can't show that. Especially not in front of my grandfather." I sigh, anticipating that this is going to be harder than I thought. "Listen, there's several intricacies and subtext behind certain wine options and your choice says about you. If you were indeed a wealthy socialite, this is probably something you would have been taught in any etiquette class or prep school you attended. And so it's something Grandpa's going to expect you to know."

"Okay. So what do I say?"

"Well, it depends. What do you like to drink? Tart, sweet, white, red?"

"I guess sweet and white is fine."

"So a chardonnay?"

"Sure." She turns back to the flight attendant. "I would like a chardonnay, please."

"Eh!" I buzz loudly again. "Wrong choice again. Chardonnay is too common, plebeian even. No respectable high-society lady drinks that, because it's what wannabe's order. Plus, that shit's disgusting. "

The flight attendant snorts and Carly rolls her eyes, clearly starting to get annoyed. "Then why did you even suggest it?"

"That, my dear, is what we call classic misdirection. Or a trick question. You'll have to get used to it because my grandfather is the king of that."

She sighs. "Okay, I'll get used to it later, but for now, can you just tell me what wine to order?"

I think about it. "Get the Montrachet. Not too sweet, and just refined enough to suit the taste buds. Not trendy and most importantly, not disgusting."

She nods and then turns to the flight attendant. "I guess I would like Montrachet please."

"That's not how you say it," I say and nearly see the vein tick at the side of her forehead. "*Montrachet*. You have to sound more dignified, more... snooty. Otherwise, they'll know instantly you're not who you say you are. Certain places may not even serve you if you don't have the right accent. Remember the shopping scene in *Pretty Woman*? When the shop attendants were mean to Julia Roberts and she came back and bought the whole place up as a result?"

"That's not what happened." Carly frowns. "She went shopping elsewhere, then came back and rubbed it in their face."

"Aha!" I point. "So you have watched it! And you must have enjoyed it to remember a detail like that."

"I didn't say I didn't enjoy it, I said it was overrated

and unrealistic."

I scowl. "You're overrated and unrealistic." Not the most mature answer, but I don't like hearing one of my childhood classics maligned like that.

She rolls her eyes this time and then tells the flight attendant. "Ignore him. I think he was dropped too many times on the head as a child. Can I please have the *Montrachet*? And imagine I just said that in the snootiest voice possible."

"Of course, madam." The woman looks like she's trying to hold back a laugh as she turns to me. "Anything else for you, sir?"

"I'll have the same." Although I probably won't have more than a glass because I need to stay focused for the rest of the day. Apart from shopping, there's so much to teach her, so much for her to learn. My young, pretty padawan.

As the flight attendant walks away, I tell Carly, "Alright. Now, it's time to learn how to sit like a high-society lady."

She raises an eyebrow. "Right now? Before the wine?"

"Yes, before the wine." This requires all the focus we can manage. "Now this is one of the most important things you can learn for this ruse to work. You have to sit like British royalty. This one is called the Sussex slant. Let me demonstrate." I shift into position and clear my throat. "You sit up straight, chin up, shoulders back. And then you slide one leg over the other like that. Then you put it to the side."

She snorts and then slaps her hand over her mouth to hide her snicker. "Are you sure about that? That looks wrong."

"Of course, I'm sure." I give her my most dignified snooty look that only makes her snort harder. "I called up a lady I used to date, who was an etiquette teacher. Also watched a few YouTube videos." Not to mention I've been around high-society girls all my life. I've seen them sit like this plenty of times. "Now you try."

She's still grinning as she obeys, but as she tries to get in the position, doubt fills her features. "Yeah, this definitely feels wrong."

"That's because you're twisting your legs together like snakes. Here, do it like this. And make sure you sit up straight!"

She tries but the more she does, the more comical it gets until she finally gives up in fits of laughter. I have to smile too. Maybe I need to get a real high-society girl to teach her. Ironic that I used to avoid them like a plague and now I'm trying to turn Carly into one of them.

We keep trying, although the attempts get sloppier after a few glasses of wine. And then when we finally land in LA, we take a limo to Beverly Hills, and I watch Carly's eyes glow as she takes in the city, the skyscrapers, and the glittering neon lights, the pulsing energy of the city.

And also, the late evening traffic.

"Damn. I forgot how annoying driving through the city was," I say.

"Yeah, that's exactly how I would describe a stretch limo ride in one of the most glamorous cities in the world," Carly quips, glancing at me with twinkling eyes. "Annoying."

I chuckle.

Eventually, we end up on Rodeo Drive, walking down the stretch of stores, with Carly subtly pointing out some fellow stretch-walkers carrying absurdly tiny dogs. We laugh at it together, but then she pulls to a stop near our destination, when a boy of about ten in ratty clothes approaches tentatively.

"E-Excuse me," he stammers, twisting his fingers in his hands. "D-do you have any change to spare?"

She stares at him for a few seconds, in horror and pity. I can see her heart melting and then she reaches into her pocket emptying out a few twenties from it.

"You got anything?" she asks me and I shake my head. She's about to hand him the cash she dug up but I reach out and snag her wrists.

She frowns at me. "What?"

I shake my head again subtly, not wanting to get into it in front of the boy. But Carly is stubborn.

"Let go." She attempts to tug her hand out of my hold, but I don't release it.

"Don't do it," I tell her. "It's a ruse."

"What are you even talking about?"

Before I can explain, the boy gets visibly nervous and darts away.

"Hey!" Carly calls after him but he doesn't look back. "Great, now you scared him."

"Good," I say, receiving an outraged look. "It's a scam, Carly. Usually anyways. The parents set the kids up to go and beg on their behalf because everyone is far more eager to help homeless kids than adults."

"It doesn't matter," she argues back. "He was clearly hungry or at least in need of help."

"There are a lot of initiatives here that can reach out and help people like him. Donate to them instead."

"And what makes you think those are any less corrupt than the boy's parents? You know that up to seventy percent of money given to charities end up in the CEO's pockets?"

"That's probably not entirely true or at least it's largely dependent on the charity. Just do your research when donating or better yet, set up your own charity and help people like him."

Carly makes a face.

"What?" I say.

"Nothing. You said 'people like him' twice and you just... you say it so carelessly."

"How else was I supposed to say it?"

She sighs and shakes her head. "Never mind."

I want to press the issue but I don't have to. I already know she thinks I'm a callous bastard. And maybe I am, but at least on this issue I'm pretty sure I'm right. I used to give cash to kids like that too all the time, whenever I saw them around LA. But after learning the truth, and actually catching one of the parents in the act of coaching their daughter, I got disgusted by the exploitation of the children and I just couldn't feed into it anymore.

But Carly doesn't care. In her eyes, I'm just a selfish, rich asshole who hates poor kids. It's a little frustrating that she's not even trying to see my side here.

She's still annoyed as we head inside, but when we get to a store on the first floor her annoyance retreats behind wonder. The store looks like it's made entirely of glass and white crystals.

"It looks just like in *Pretty Woman*," Carly gasps.

"It's better," I tell her as we step inside, instantly assailed by the soothing scent of eucalyptus and rosy perfumes.

One of the attendants instantly recognizes me and makes a beeline in my direction. "Welcome back, sir!"

"Glad to be back," I tell her. "My fiancée is looking for a few items for a bunch of events we'll be attending. Think you can help her?"

"Of course," she says and then gently but firmly guides Carly behind a shelf of designer bags, to look at fabrics and clothes.

Carly throws me an apprehensive look as she goes but she doesn't protest. I wink in response.

Once she's gone, I approach the jewelry counter, mildly looking through a few pieces and chatting with the other attendant as I wait. Time passes as I make a few selections, and I get lost in thoughts of Carly draped in only jewelry.

Suddenly, I hear from behind me, "How do I look?"

I turn to look at Carly to give a measured response …. and every semblance of diction flees my mind as I nearly swallow my tongue.

CHAPTER THIRTEEN

CARLY

Micah's stunned jaw-drop was gratifying at first, but now it's starting to disconcert me.

He's been staring at me wordlessly for what feels like hours even though it's probably just seconds. His emerald-colored eyes continuously crawl down the length of the silky red dress to the heels on my feet, and then they crawl back up just as slowly.

When he reaches the point where the fabric clings to the swell of my hips, he licks his lips. Like someone just offered him a tempting feast.

I'm wearing a simple floor-length gown with a boat-neck Audrey Hepburn bodice, form-fitting skirt except for a slight mermaid flair, and gemstones in a flamelike pattern from the hem of the dress up to the knee.

Does it look bad? Or do I look so good that he's

struck him speechless?

Something tells me it's the latter.

As evidenced by his stare when his eyes finally reach mine.

The green is glowing, his gaze scorching hot.

Heat explodes through my entire body in response, quickening my pulse, and awakening lust that had been simmering till now. Anticipation races through me. I'm immediately struck by the memories of that night together in the alley parking lot and then in his car.

I want that. Want him again.

I exhale to rid myself of the lustful thought and I think I hear the growl echo in his chest.

"So…" The attendant's loud voice breaks the silence. She looks between the two of us, clearly oblivious to the sexual tension thickening the air. "Do you like it? Or do we try on more?"

"I like it," Micah finally responds, his voice deeper than it was before. "But let's try more. More like this. But also more… different." Contrary to his usual eloquence, his words are now short and clipped as though he has to make an effort to get them out, to have them make sense.

As though he's just barely winning against the desire stealing his sanity.

"Alright." The attendant, instantly seeing dollar signs, immediately heads to the other side of the store, selecting more outfits, hanging on a rack. "We'll have to get a few of these tailor-made to fit your gorgeous figure, and that can all be done and shipped to your address within a few days."

"Oh?" I make a mental note to have it shipped to Micah instead. I shudder to think of what my mom would do if these were to show up at my doorstep.

"Yes, of course," she continues. "We also have a few pieces from the new haute couture collections. These haven't officially hit the shelves or the runway yet, so they're still samples, but we get ahead of the waitlist due to our long and illustrious history with various designers. For example, this Vivienne Westwood." She takes the dress off the hanger, adds it to the pile in her arms, and then points. "Chanel." She takes that one too. "And of course, the lovely St. Laurent."

"Um…" As the pile grows, I start to get worried. It's going to be a lot trying all that on. Also, it's all starting to get very… expensive. I've never bought a designer piece in my entire life but I at least know how much stuff like that costs. And I doubt that anything hanging over her elbow is under a thousand dollars.

As she continues to add to that number, I figure we're quickly edging toward fifty grand easily.

I glance at Micah expecting him to put a stop to it at any moment now, but he's distracted staring at the jewelry in the pristine glass display cases in front of the store. He's talking to the other attendant, pointing and having her bring something out.

He's buying me jewelry too? Oh, this is too much. We're going to blow a hundred thousand dollars on shopping if we're not careful.

But before I can protest, the friendly woman blocks my view with her blinding smile, hooks her arms through mine, and says, "Let's try on these before we get some more."

With a weak smile, I succumb to peer pressure and let her drag me away again.

I don't make it through the whole pile. After trying on the first dozen pieces, I'm exhausted. Not only from trying it on but from the discourse that ensues after. The attendant, Lacey, is very thorough and attentive, and wants to discuss how I feel in the dress, how movable it is, if I want to adjust or loosen anything, if I want more detailing, what shoes will complement the dress…

On the one hand, it's almost touching to be treated with such consideration. Most of my experience shopping at higher-end stores–not this high end, obviously, but higher than Marshall's–as a curvier woman is that a lot of things don't fit me quite right. But for some reason, this woman has a lot of things in my size and is very conscientious about how they fit. I don't know how Micah found this store, but it's really a godsend and if I ever become a billionaire, I know where to shop.

However, it's also exhausting having so much attention on me.

After about an hour passes, I finally step out of the dressing room for hopefully the last time and say, "Micah I think we have enough–holy moly, what are you doing?"

There are gift boxes lined up in stacks on the counter, nearly reaching the ceiling. Micah gives me an innocent look. "What?"

"Did you buy all that?"

He glances at the pile consideringly and then turns to me and says, "Yeah."

"For me?"

"Yup. With one or two matching pieces for myself, so we can wear them together."

I shake my head, utterly stunned. "How did you even find that many things to buy?"

"Well, it's easy. I saw this one bangle and I really liked it and wasn't sure whether to get it in gold or silver. I mean you're pretty neutral-toned, but I think silver looks best on you. Nevertheless, you really can't beat gold for quality so I just got the bracelet in both. And then they had one with diamond stud detailing so I bought that too. And then there were matching earrings. And a necklace that would also go well with it." He shrugs. "It all kind of spiraled from there."

How on earth does it spiral from that into what looks to be about fifty pieces of jewelry?

"Okay, we'll... discuss that later. I think I've tried on enough dresses."

"Good." He glances at the attendant behind me. "Make the necessary adjustments and send them all to my condo. The address is on file."

"Micah, I truly don't need all of them."

"You don't like them?" he says. "Alright. We can keep looking if you want. I know a few other stores we can try too."

"No, I don't want to keep looking." I may never want to try on another piece of clothing for the rest of my life. "The dresses are fine. I just don't need that many."

Micah gives me a look. "You realize we'll be attending more than just a few events together, right? And you won't be allowed to repeat outfits with them."

"Yes, but..." I glance at the woman who's still standing there eyeing us hopefully. After she's caught, she immediately moves back behind the counter, to give us some privacy.

I move closer to whisper, "Micah, that's a lot of stuff. A lot of very expensive stuff."

Micah simply gives me a bemused expression. "Just who do you think you're talking to right now?"

"Yeah, yeah, I know you're a billionaire, but it's just...

I'm not used to owning this much stuff. What if I lose it?"

"It's yours. You can lose it if you want."

I frown. "You mean I keep it after our deal?"

"Yeah." Micah seems even more bemused, with a touch of offense. "What, did you think I was going to take it back?"

"Well…"

"Okay, now I'm feeling a little insulted. Babe, it's a gift. All this is a gift. You can take it, lose it, keep it, toss it away, donate it, wipe your ass with it… whatever you want. It's all yours to do with as you wish."

I stare at him, fighting the urge to protest. Deep inside, I know I'm probably overreacting. Micah is a wealthy billionaire from a very affluent family, and spending money like this is probably nothing to him.

But that little girl who insists on not needing anyone, the one who's trying to make it on her own to prove everyone wrong, is rejecting this with everything inside me.

Micah seems to understand because his expression becomes softer. "You don't get a lot of gifts, do you?"

It's not said in a mean way. In fact, it's said in the nicest way possible but somehow that hint of pity strikes a sensitive part of me and makes me jump on the defensive.

"I receive plenty of gifts," I say tersely, and it's true. I've spent too many birthdays with loved ones, receiving thoughtful handcrafted jewelry or paintings from Emma, my own fishing pole from Grandpa, and books from Mrs. Peach. They may not be as expensive, sure, but those are the gifts that truly matter, not overpriced dresses. "But I'm sorry, I don't know if I can accept this from you."

"Why not?"

"We barely know each other. And once our deal is over, I won't even know what to do with them."

"Sell them."

"That's too much money on top of everything else you're already giving me. I'm sorry, I can't."

Micah watches me closely. His gaze feels so perceptive that I duck my head to avoid it. It feels too much like he can see through me.

"We can just go shopping whenever we need a new outfit," I say. "After all, we're not sure how long this is going to last."

Micah pouts. "But then I may not even get to see you try it on. And I haven't seen you in these either."

"Micah…"

"Please." His voice is suddenly serious, surprising my eyebrows into my scalp. "Please. I really, *really* want to see you in these dresses."

Micah strikes me as the kind of guy who doesn't use the "p word" a lot. Especially with that expression, so lacking his normal brand of humor. He's dead serious now. And I don't know how to deal with it.

It makes me falter. It makes my heart stumble in a way that scares me and I have to tear my gaze away.

"Fine," I say.

"You'll try it on for me?" He walks closer surrounding me with his scent, bringing his body flush against mine.

"Sure." I can't look at his eyes. Not with him so close. Not only is his scent spiking the desire inside me, but my heart is reacting dangerously.

Especially when he leans down and kisses my forehead. "Good girl."

Shit. The words send my heartbeat into overdrive.

And I don't understand why, this weird reaction to him.

As we drive home, it's not just me that's lost in my thoughts. Micah is also quieter than usual. Per his insistence, I'm still wearing one of the dresses I got from the store, the red one that I tried on first. Micah stared at me when I wore it again, his look telling me everything I needed to know.

The atmosphere is tense with thoughts and unspent desire. I feel the urge to break the silence, at least to distract myself.

"How did you find this store anyway?" I ask. "Frankly, I didn't even know mainstream designers make samples in my size."

"They don't when you're a regular person," he says. "When you have the means and the contacts, you can get anything you want in any size you want. The owner of the store is a millionaire so she gets the samples in whatever size she wants."

"Ah. So that's how you discovered it? Through the owner?"

"Nope. I dated a woman once and this was her favorite store."

"Really? How nice." There's an odd note in my voice. I guess I don't like hearing about the girls he dates.

"Jealous?" he teases.

"No," I say, with the same odd note and he laughs.

"I don't even remember her name if it makes you feel

better. Just that she brought me here a few times to shop."

It really doesn't. Because pretty soon I'll be the girl whose name he doesn't remember too.

More tumultuous feelings arise at that realization and they last even as Micah takes me up to his penthouse in Bel Air.

It's at the top of a luxury hotel and when we arrive, I greet the elderly doorman with a friendly smile and he grins back and then winks at Micah. "Owee. I know you do well with the ladies, Mr. Landing, but you really got a smokeshow tonight. If I were twenty years younger, I would try to steal her from you."

"You would have gotten a black eye for your trouble. Don't stare too hard at my woman, Patrick," Micah teases.

Patrick chuckles. "Or what? You're going to kick an old man's ass, boss?"

"No, I'm going to call your wife and let her do it for me."

I blush at the man's compliments, and his hearty laughter follows us to the elevators.

When we get up to the topmost floor, Micah enters a code into the keypad, letting me into the large, art deco living room and then I have a sudden thought.

In times of confusion, turn it back to what you know.

Sex.

Once we get into the house I don't waste time. I kiss him, deeply.

And promptly find my back pressed against the wall.

Micah groans into my mouth as he swallows the kiss, his tongue sliding against mine. His hand clutches the back of my hair, a note of desperation in his touch that tells me he's been thinking about this as long as I have.

That he's wanted to do this all day too.

I fling my mind to the wind and wrap my arms around his neck. Once again, I cease to care about anyone or anything else. Just the taste of him, like wine and sin. The scent of him, strong, solid, and spicy. The feel of him, hard and relentless.

He picks me up and I wrap my legs around his waist. It's crazy how easily he carries me. He walks with me too, a few steps until, suddenly, my back is against a plush couch.

His arms grip my thighs, forcing them open, ripping off my panties.

And then with a dragged-out curse, his lips are suddenly on my pussy.

CHAPTER FOURTEEN

MICAH

As I get lost in the exhilarating scent of Carly's musk, I come to a troubling realization.

There's a huge difference between having sex and having sex with Carly.

The former is a fun activity that usually gets my mind off my stress and I sometimes remember it fondly for days after.

The second thing though is an all-consuming experience that takes over my senses while it's happening and the effects linger for days after.

I feel it's mark even now, as I eat her out, her taste sliding down my tongue like the finest liquors, the best ambrosia, the most addictive drug I've ever ingested. It makes all the voices in my mind shut down, awareness of my environment fades and everything that's not her becomes irrelevant.

All I care about is her. Her thighs around my ears, forming ocean sounds. Her cries echoing around me, a decadent soundtrack and her sultry movement against my tongue driving me into a world of bliss.

As I bury my tongue deeper into her hole, I open my eyes half-mast and stare at her engorged clit. So fucking pretty and pink and pulsing for me. Greed pumps headily through me. I want to devour her, all of her, all at once. That need battles another even more powerful urge to take my time and make this last as long as possible, to give her the highest, sublime pleasure. To have her screaming and begging for more.

Because the faces she makes when she's kept on the precipice... God, the sounds... I need to hear them. It's becoming an addiction at this point. I love hearing it, love the way she cries for me, the way her entire body scrabbles for the pleasure.

Carly writhes in the silk dress on my couch like a siren, driving me crazy. Melting for me. Aching for me. Her eyes are dark with want for me.

"Please," she confesses in that throaty voice of hers, her thighs squeezing around my head, her voice hoarse. "More."

With difficulty, I detach my mouth from her pussy and rise above her, wrapping my hand lightly, experimentally around her neck. I watch her, study her response, and wait for her to swallow as I lean down to whisper into her ear, "Give me a safe word. Something you can remember."

"What?"

I nip her shoulder, unable to stop myself from tasting her skin as I whisper, "A safe word, for when it gets too intense."

She's quiet for a single second. Then, "Banana."

I pull back. "Can you remember 'banana'?"

Her eyes blink a little the desire receding slightly and then returning full force as she understands the meaning of my words and why she would need a safe word. A shaky noisy exhale follows. She swallows tightly and nods.

"Say it."

"Banana," she repeats.

"Good girl." I reward her by working her clit slowly. Her eyes roll back in her head, which falls over the edge of the couch. A strangled moan leaves her mouth and she gyrates her hips into my touch. "I'm going to ask you again. Just to make sure you really remember it."

"Oh my God, Micah."

"Mmm, I love it when you say my name like that. It makes me want to do filthy things to you." I strum her clit one more time and then slide my finger down toward her soaked hole, pushing ever so slightly into the silky warmth.

Once I feel it, the urgency rages back to life, full force, so much so that I have to grit my teeth to hold back.

I want to fuck you so hard that you black out. I push into her slowly, ignoring her sobbing pleas for me to go faster. *Want to get you so high that you can't even think, much less speak. I want your fingers to score my shoulder and your scream to render me deaf. I want you to cry out for me until your voice is hoarse. I want to possess you, my Athena, make you mine.*

All the while I tease her, my cock is throbbing harder than a motherfucker, precum staining my pants. My free hand grips the couch, shaking with the need to hold back.

Fuck, I've never been this hard in my life and I've

only barely touched her.

What the hell is going on?

It's not just the BDSM aspect driving me wild because I've explored this darker side with women before.

I'm not a pain kind of guy. Light spanking and such is fine, but my thing is really getting inside my partner's head and edging them out until they weep. It's what I do to Carly now, strumming my finger back and forth over her clit, as she begs me, leaning down to take her lips in mine. She moves helplessly into my touch and I feel powerful. I've reduced her to a pleading mess.

While exploring my dominant side has always been fun for me, I've never felt such a strong need to control and maximize someone else's pleasure before. It's like I don't matter anymore. All that matters is her and her satisfaction.

I almost lose myself in the kiss but then pull back, snagging her nipples between my teeth, giving her the edge of a bite, and watching her response.

Carly moans for me, her pussy squeezing around my fingers.

And then, when I feel her on the verge of coming, I pull back.

"Oh, God, Micah," she whimpers. Her arms reach for me.

I avoid them, chuckling. "Do I have to tie you up?" I want to. But then that would require me to step away from her, and I'm not sure I can manage that even for one second. Still, I tease her with the possibility, loving the way it makes her shake her head tightly. "I could have your hands above your head, with your legs splayed wide for me. You wouldn't be able to move or do anything but take whatever I give you."

"Oh shit." I can tell from the way she squirms that the idea turns her on even more. And fuck it turns me on too. As much as I try to ignore it, my cock is screaming in demand, lust flooding through every nerve in my body. She's so fucking gorgeous. So responsive. Her eyes are dark pools of desire now, her hair fanned out over her head. She's a goddess, beckoning me to slake my lust.

But if I do, she'll possess me.

It's almost like she's the one that holds the true power here.

Doesn't she? My inner voice mocks. Look at you. All turned on and eager to serve her every whim. You're trying so hard to make this amazing for her, that you're ignoring your own desires.

Even though I want her mouth on me more than I want to live.

I close my eyes, the image whipping through my mind, distracting me from my goal. It almost becomes too much at a point. I almost say fuck it, and rip my clothes off so I can sink into her soaking wet heat, and lose my mind in her once again.

But no.

I tear my eyes open, taking in her flushed face, her swollen lips, and her nipples puckered underneath the silk.

I can't give in. That loss of control would be uncharacteristic for me, and it would symbolize something that I'm not willing to examine too closely.

I have to prove to myself that this is just a game. We're just playing a game and having fun and that's all it is.

So I take my time, finger-fucking her slowly again, groaning as the desire becomes too much to bear. To prove a point, I leaned down to nip her lips. Her entire body curves up the second I move, trembling, begging for my touch and I nearly lose it then. *Oh, my gorgeous needy Athena. I fucking love seeing you like this for me.*

It makes me feel like the most powerful man in the world to watch her eyes, usually so full of sensibility and jadedness, now fade away to wide-eyed passion.

But as our lips meet again, my control cracks.

I try to keep the kiss light and teasing but the allure is too strong, and before I know it, I'm devouring her. Her taste floods me. My need takes over. My mind shuts down as passion pounds through me. I can't help it. My fingers clench on the couch below her as I eat at her lips, feeling my mind drift farther and farther away.

This might be a game, but I'm not the leader here. I'm just as lost as she is.

"Fuck." I rip my lips away from her to gasp in the air. I don't know what the fuck is going on with me. I'm usually so suave, so smooth, but tonight I feel like a bumbling idiot for whatever reason.

"What's wrong?" Her voice is husky, half desire, half concern.

I shake my head, not meeting her eyes while I give her the truth. "I can't... I'm trying to edge you out and make this good for you but I don't know if I can." It's embarrassing to admit to performance issues at this stage in the game but I push forward. "It has never happened to me before, but I think if I don't get inside you in the next three seconds, I'm going to explode."

"Yeah, that's fine." Her words are a desperate whisper as her hands go to undo my belt. "We can do the other stuff later. Let's just fuck for now.

"But..." The words cut off in a groan at the feel of

her hands on my cock. A full-body shudder runs through my body. I snatch her wrist before she can do more damage. "I need... fuck... I *need* to make this good for you."

"Micah, if it was any better, I think I would pass out." I meet her eyes and see the honest red-hot sultry desire stoked in them. "Please. Fuck me."

I can't hold back anymore. My fingers grip her dress and with a rip, it's off and on the floor. She has a second to gasp before I consume her lips again, our tongues dueling in time with our racing hearts.

Her legs fall open and her arms clutch me as I find her center. The second I feel the suckling warmth, I nearly ejaculate there and then. I need to pull back and breathe and groan into the couch to keep myself from shooting off like a horny teenager. And even after nearly a full minute of that, while I work her clit, the second I push into her again, it only takes me an embarrassingly low number of strokes until I'm screaming my release, pumping it into her.

Luckily, she announces her orgasms too, as I collapse on top of her, more drained than I can ever remember being in my life.

"Jesus." My breath is tight, and my pulse is still a little too quick. "Fuck me. That has never happened before."

"Really?" At least I'm satisfied from the knowledge that she sounds just as breathless as me.

"Really." I pull back to watch her deliciously disheveled face, which does funny things to my insides. And then I do something I've also never done after sex before. I lean down and kiss her, sweetly. "Thank you."

When I pull back, she blinks stunned. Then she grins. "You're welcome."

I feel something growing inside me the longer I stare

at her, and the alarm bells start ringing. This is going too far. It's time to detach.

Despite my weakness, I immediately stand from the couch and then stare at the clothes in tatters on the floor. Her red dress is no more.

"Shame," I murmur. But I can always just buy a new one. I zip up my pants as I pad to the cabinet in the corner, select a blanket, and return to throw it over her shivering body. I watch her eyes close and she snuggles under it.

"I'll order some food," I tell her.

"Mmm," she murmurs. "I'll just take a quick nap before we have to leave."

"Leave? Where are we going?"

One eye opens. "I assume you're taking me home?"

"Yes, but not today."

Both eyes open this time and she frowns at me. "What do you mean not today?"

"Oh, I didn't mention? We have a gala tomorrow evening here in LA. We'll be attending it together."

"That's…" She struggles to sit up, clutching the blanket in front of her. "You should have told me that earlier. You can't just spring that on me at the last minute. I have things to do tomorrow, Micah. School and work."

I shrug. "Well, I didn't think it would be a big deal."

"Didn't think my school and work would be a big deal?" She sounds insulted. "Micah, that's my life! It might not seem like much to you, but it means everything to me. You can't just fly me halfway around the country at the last minute and jeopardize my education as a result. You have to tell me these things ahead of time."

I wait till she's done, let a beat of silence pass, and then say, "My bad. You want me to add on an extra thousand dollars as compensation?"

Carly laughs darkly. "Of course, you would throw money at the problem. I knew it was only a matter of time before you shoved your wealth in my face." She glares at me. "Why is it every time we have sex, you have to remind me of what an ass you are?"

Because if not, I might be tempted to let that blissful feeling take over and turn into something else. I chuckle, lean in, and tweak her nose. "Maybe to prove that you would still like me anyway."

CHAPTER FIFTEEN

CARLY

The next few hours are spent solving the mess that Micah has put me in while doing my best to ignore his presence.

I head to his bedroom to be away from him for a while, just until I calm down.

Because I have to calm down. As much as I want to wallow in my anger and sulk for the rest of this trip, I can't afford to not do my part.

Micah has given me a way to solve my financial problems, and maybe even build a life away from my family. I'm not going to let anything get in the way of it, not even my pride.

Besides, it's probably good that Micah is behaving like this, and showing me who he really is. The sex we just had was intense. It wasn't like the other two times when it was just us having fun. This was…

more. I can't put my finger on exactly how, but it was unlike any other sexual encounter I've ever had. And paired up with an entire day spent with him buying me things and making me laugh, it was scarily easy to forget that all this was an elaborate ruse.

So his immediately being an asshole after sex allows me to maintain perspective and re-erect the much-needed emotional distance between us. I remind myself that Micah isn't my boyfriend. He's not even really my friend. He's my business partner-slash-hook-up buddy. That's it.

Realizing that makes it easier to let go of my anger. I only hold on to the lesson I learned today, a lesson I'm very familiar with thanks to my family.

Don't trust anyone else to care about your personal goals or ambitions. Expect most people, especially Micah, to act on their whims without consideration of how it would affect anyone but themselves.

The only exceptions to those rules are goodhearted people like Mrs. Peach, Emma, and her grandfather.

Definitely not someone like Micah Landing.

I don't think Micah is intentionally malicious, but he's selfish at heart and seems to lack the ability to see things from any perspective except his own.

I could tell from the second he told me the story about his dad and painted the older man in such a wholly villainous light. Not to say that his dad is perfect, but he at least seems to care about Micah's future and Micah didn't see that as a good thing.

I guess I'm not the best judge of parents though. I didn't have the best example, so my assessment is likely skewed in that regard. I mean, the very fact that Micah's father seems to care whether he's alive or dead puts him leagues ahead of my folks.

But that's all beside the point. The thing is, I decide to let go of my bitterness because it's essentially pointless to be angry at Micah. I need to accept who he is and behave accordingly.

So, I immediately email Emma, telling her that I'm out of town and won't be able to cover my shift tomorrow. Emma is, of course, overly understanding and tells me not to worry about it, but I email Yule too, so he can make sure I'm added to the roster on my day off. And then, I email my professors to let them know I'll be unable to attend tomorrow's classes. Luckily only one of the classes has mandatory attendance and I'm currently doing well in it, and have a great rapport with the professor. She emails me back instantly, informing me that she won't mark my absence against me, but adding that I shouldn't make a habit of it. I send her a message assuring her I won't.

With that done, I return to the living room, where Micah is receiving a brown paper bag from a delivery man and placing it on the table, where two glasses of wine already sit.

"Done with what you need to do?" he asks.

"Yeah," I respond, then gesture to the bag in his hand. "What's that?"

"Chinese food. Emma told me that was your favorite."

"You asked Emma what my favorite food was?"

"Yeah. Right after she threatened to cut off my balls if I ever hurt you."

My eyes flare open and then I sigh. I should have known. Even though I got her to back down on the tuition, it was probably too much to ask Emma to stay out of my relationship with Micah completely.

Micah doesn't look bothered by her involvement though. On the contrary, he grins. "She explained it in detail too. Told me she watched a video on quartering bulls and she knew her way around garden shears. And then right after that, she told me about your particular fondness for soup dumplings. I got a bunch today."

I shake my head, allowing a weak smile. "Thanks. For the dumplings that is. I was afraid you would order disgusting rich people food to test my taste buds."

"I thought about it, but I think maybe I've tortured you enough." He places the bag on the table, no longer looking at me when he adds, "Besides, I also wanted to apologize."

That shocks me. "You did?"

"Yeah. I should have asked you if you had plans tomorrow, and I meant to, but it kind of slipped my mind." He sends me an apologetic look. "I also didn't think to ask what you wanted the money for either. It's for college?"

The words are a peace offering, an invitation for me to share my story with him. But a part of me can't forget what he said.

"Maybe to prove that you would still like me anyway."

Ass. He's likely right because despite his asshole nature I still can't stay mad at him. Still, he doesn't have to rub it in my face.

I should have known he would gloat and throw money in my face eventually. The rich and powerful can't help it sometimes, and he probably felt the need to show me the gap between our socioeconomic statuses after losing control so thoroughly in bed.

I smile at the memory. Well, at least that's one win for me. He looked so disheveled after we had sex, discombobulated and confused by his own loss of control.

I made him like that.

Little old Carly Huntley reduced the great Micah

Landing to a one-minute man.

It's probably why he was so acerbic after because he felt the need to reestablish his superiority. Whatever. I don't care. I'll suffer through all his attitude just to get the pot of gold at the end of the rainbow.

Even go to a stupid party full of elite snobs who will probably look down their nose at me.

In any case, I can't let myself forget who Micah is, nor can I forget he's playing a game. And I have to hold my cards to my chest too.

"It's okay," I say to end that conversation. "So now what? More sitting lessons?"

He hesitates, appearing a little taken aback by my abruptness before he answers. "Yup. And we're also going to talk about conversation starters, and what to not do at tomorrow's gala."

I sigh. It sounds like it's going to be a long night.

And the following day is a whirlwind of activity as well. Breakfast is at an upscale country club where he teaches me proper table etiquette. Then after, we visit a woman who teaches me how to walk and wave like the queen. It doesn't sound like much, but there's a whole lot of things to remember.

And then comes the moment of truth.

The night of the governor's gala.

"Don't be nervous," he tells me as the limo pulls into the front of a hotel. There's a legit red carpet rolled out with limos lining up at each side, releasing their inhabitants. Elegantly dressed patrons step out in suits and long sparkly dresses. One by one they laugh and go around to meet each other, showing off outfits and jewelry with enough dazzle to rival the stars.

And they're all dressed tastefully too. Not too much

skin, nor too much bling. Everything is done exactly right.

I'm suddenly grateful for Micah's stylist who put together my outfit for the day. I wouldn't have felt confident walking out otherwise.

"Shall we?" Micah says as the two valets open our limo doors.

I inhale deeply. "Here goes nothing."

The Silver Dais Hotel exudes luxury, a neoclassical building stretching high into the sky, with a grand entrance bordered by large stone columns. Numerous stairs lead up to the sweeping arches and each has intricate detailing on the sandstone. As we slowly ascend, I try to remember all my lessons all at once, so I don't make a fool of myself.

"Micah!" a woman screams from afar, and before I can examine where the voice is coming from, I'm hit by a gust of wind and Arabian-scented perfumes as a short woman jumps into Micah's arms.

The strawberry blonde woman hugging Micah wears a shorter, pretty A-line dress with a sweetheart neckline. As she steps back, I take in the intricate detailing at the hem. "I didn't know you were coming!"

"I didn't know I was coming either, short stuff," Micah laughingly responds as she pouts.

"You know I hate it when you call me that."

"I know. That's why I do it."

I feel slightly out of place, but then Micah wraps his arm around my waist again, physically and metaphorically dragging me back into the conversation. "Sweetie, this is Ally, an old friend from boarding school. Ally, this is my fiancée, Carlette."

I nearly snicker at the name. Micah thought that

Carlette sounded a lot fancier, and while I agree, it also has a ridiculous ring to it.

"Just Carly is fine," I tell the woman. "Only my enemies call me Carlette."

The woman gapes at us for a full ten seconds. "Shut up. You're getting married?"

"It seems so."

"Oh, God. Jamie isn't going to believe this. Jameson, get over here! Micah is getting married."

Jameson happens to be a larger bear of a man, who's also Ally's husband. He's a lot quieter than his wife but smiles pleasantly as she chatters along, telling me all about Micah's past misdeeds in every single relationship he's ever had.

"Seriously," she says. "I never thought he would keep a steady girlfriend much less get married. How on earth did this happen?"

I shrug. "I'm not sure myself. The whole thing feels a little bit like a whirlwind."

Micah smiles. "Sweetie, don't do that. You'll make my friends think you don't actually want to marry me." There's a warning sharpness in his voice.

"I do," I respond. "It's just... hearing all about your past does give me pause." I figure that to sell this story as well as possible, I have to act as realistic as possible. And any reasonable woman will likely have reservations after hearing all those stories.

And his friends don't even attempt to defend him.

As Micah raises an eyebrow, Jameson says, "She's smart."

"No kidding." His wife echoes. "I like her."

I grin. "I think I like you too."

"Yay!" Ally laces her arm through mine and continues on the story as I try to maintain my stiff, elegant walk. Thankfully, we soon get to the top of the staircase and enter a grand ballroom that puts the Pink Hotel to shame. Seriously. One wall seems to be solely dedicated to intricate glasswork, there are large windows covered by silk damask curtains, and the white marbled floors sparkle under the crystal chandelier.

The minute we get to the foyer, I make a beeline to the bathroom. I'm not sure if it's the nerves or the dress I'm wearing but I suddenly really need to pee.

I turn a corner following the signs when I hear the sounds of commotion.

"Are you kidding me? Just what kind of trash do they have working here, huh?"

In a near-empty hallway, a shorter balding man in a suit is screaming at what looks to be a server, with a tray and broken glass at her feet. "Do you have any idea how much this costs?"

"I'm sorry, sir!" She wrings her hands, seemingly distraught.

"Sorry? Sorry! You think sorry is going to fix this mess." He has a mildly European-sounding accent. "You stupid, stupid girl."

And then he does something shockingly infuriating. He draws his hand back as though to hit her.

I immediately step out into the hallway. "Don't you fucking dare touch her."

CHAPTER SIXTEEN

M ICAH

The second Carly is out of earshot, Ally delivers a swift, painful thwack to my arm.

"Ow." I grasp my arm, feigning pain. "That hurt, Ally."

Her eyes glitter menacingly. "I'm going to hurt you a lot worse if you don't tell me what's going on here. Who is that?"

"I already told you. She's my fiancée," I tease. "Or were you not listening?"

She narrows her eyes suspiciously, but I merely waggle my eyebrows in response.

I didn't necessarily expect to meet Ally at this party, but it's a good thing I did. No one knows how to spread gossip better than good old Ally Wilcox nee Petrova.

Her family is old money, and they move in pretty much the same circles as my grandfather, so news will get back to him in no time.

"I *was* paying attention," Ally responds, "but I've also known you since we were practically in diapers. There is no way Micah Landing, the whore of the seven seas, is getting married. Not without some serious intervention. Right, Jamie?"

Jameson nods, and his wife uses it as a confidence boost. She crosses her arms over her chest.

"Look, what's going on? Is this a scheme of yours? Is she an actress you hired?"

"You think I would go as far as to propose to someone for a scheme?"

Her face shows her slight doubt but she shakes it off. "I mean that seems more believable than you getting married. I thought hell would freeze over before that happened."

I shrug. "Well, I'm not going to pretend like it was entirely my choice.'

"Aha! I knew there was a catch."

I grin. "My grandfather and I had 'the talk.' He thinks it's time for me to settle down and... I can't help but agree with him. I'm nearly forty, and not getting any younger. The whole party boy lifestyle is getting old, and I don't want to be the single fifty-year-old still chasing his youth at the club."

"Ah." She nods sagely. "So this is some kind of arranged marriage situation."

"Not at all," I say. "I like Carly. We've known each other for a few years already and we meet up whenever I travel. It's always a fun time with her. Now I'm not going to say that we're a match made in heaven or anything, but I like her more than I've ever liked anyone else I've been with." I pause on that thought, realizing that it's not a total lie. I try to recall any woman who has affected me as much as Carly, someone who I enjoy spending time with as much as I do with her, and I can't. No one even compares. Odd, considering I've only known Carly a short while.

I shake my head. "Anyway, she ticks all the boxes so far. So why not marry her?"

Ally and Jameson share a look, before turning back to me.

"You don't love her?" Jameson sounds almost saddened by the news.

I shrug. "Between you and me, I'm not sure I'm capable of love. And you know in our circles, love marriages like yours are hard to come by." Jameson and Ally's relationship is a rare occurrence in high society. They were best friends turned high school sweethearts, with Jameson having held a torch for her most of his life. Ally finally returned his affection somewhere around the 11th grade after Jameson shot up several inches and grew respectable facial hair. They've been in love and inseparable ever since.

But I don't expect to find anything like that with anyone else I know.

Most people in our circles marry for mutual benefit and to forge powerful connections. That's it.

"So who is she?" Ally says. "To win your grandpa's approval, she can't be any ordinary socialite, right?"

"Oh no. I'm not falling for that." I shake my head. "As far as everyone is concerned, Carly is just a normal girl. A downright nobody, in fact."

"Bullshit." I've laid enough seeds that Ally's eyes are now glittering with curiosity. "Oh, come on. Tell us. You know I can keep a secret."

Oh, Ally, my dear, you absolutely cannot.

I sigh for dramatic effect. "I really can't go into it, Ally. It's not my secret to tell."

"But we won't tell anyone. And I'm not going to leave you alone until I hear the secret. You know how much of a pest I can be when I want to. Right, Jamie?"

Jamie murmurs something that's somehow both an affectionate assent and a fervent denial.

I inhale deeply and pretend like she's backed me into a corner. "Fine. I'll tell you one thing but you have to promise that this doesn't leave here. It's just between the three of us.

"Of course." Eagerness glows in her expression. "We can keep a secret. Right, Jamie?"

Jamie simply throws her an amused look that she misses, because she's entirely focused on me and this hot new piece of gossip I'm about to share with her.

"Carly is…" I pretend to struggle with the words. "Look, her family is really important. European royalty, but kept highly under wraps due to the circumstances of her birth. That's all I can say without giving everything away, and Carly would kill me if even this much got out. They're all extremely private people."

"Oh, don't worry about it, my lips are sealed." Her eyes track behind me to where Carly must have gone. "So she's royalty huh? No wonder."

"What do you mean?" I ask, curious.

Ally shakes her head but then admits. "She has the look of it. Also has this guardedness about her, like she's constantly on the lookout or something. Holds herself a little stiff too, but isn't prissy and doesn't speak like she thinks she's better than anyone. Just cautious. Must be her family upbringing."

"Right." I follow her gaze. Ally has no idea how on the money she is with that description. I've also noticed the same thing about Carly, that apart from the moments when we're having sex, she has this wall up most of the time. Sometimes it's more subtle and she hides it behind jokes and eye rolls. Other times, like tonight, it's more apparent.

And from what little I know about her family, I have no doubt that it's their fault she's so guarded. She grew up knowing she couldn't trust them to watch out for her, and so she's always had to watch out for herself. Probably had to protect herself from them too.

The thought of little Carly watching her father stumble home drunk, or seeing her cousin dragged off to jail makes me irrationally furious.

I guess that's one thing I can do for her before this is over. Make sure she has enough money to be self-sufficient and able to cut her family off for good.

Yeah, it may not be my business, but I'm making it my business. I want her away from them, one way or another.

She's not going to like it though.

"I better make sure my bride-to-be hasn't gone in the wrong direction," I say. Mostly though, I'm concerned that all this has been too overwhelming for Carly and she's hyperventilating in the bathroom. She seemed okay walking in here. Regal in fact. She held up well despite all the eyes on her.

But I think maybe she got more attention than she bargained.

That old Hollywood look of hers and that dress caressing her curves made her hard to ignore. It's definitely been distracting me as we walked in here, that and her subtle perfume.

The thing we have to be careful of though is cameras. I can't risk her getting photographed, or someone might be able to do a little bit of digging and find out the truth about her origins. Sure, Carly doesn't have social media and Laketown is pretty isolated, but still. Someone might recognize her and risk this whole thing.

I brought her to this party to be seen, but not exactly remembered. She's supposed to be the enigma that disappears at the end of the night. Micah Landing's mysterious new woman. That's what the gossip should say.

And to that end, we only need to spend maybe half an hour here before we go.

As I leave Ally and Jamie and head to the side of the hallway, voices immediately begin to drift to me. The male one reaches me first, angry and tremulous.

"Who the hell do you think you are to interfere? You don't even have a clue what's going on here, do you?"

"I don't care what's going on here. You don't hit people or harass them for what was clearly a mistake."

The second voice is Carly's, and I frown as I get closer and the man's voice rises threateningly.

"Listen, woman. Do you have any idea who I am? You're lucky I'm being nice now, but you better get out of here before I ruin your *fucking* life."

"No problem. I'll get out of your hair. But she's coming with me."

When I turn the corner, I finally see the woman that Carly's talking about, a server that seems to be throwing Carly alarmed looks from her cowering position against the wall. Below her is broken glass and I put two and two together to figure out what happened here. The man looming over the server has a stain on his Tom Ford suit, and wrath stamped on his face.

He's much larger than the server, and larger than Carly too, although most of his weight is distributed in his belly. He doesn't seem to see me arrive, too focused on glaring at Carly, so I lean against the wall to observe.

"She made a mistake," Carly says slowly as though she's explaining something to a child. "It happens. But you trying to hit her because of it is completely unacceptable."

The man gives a bitter laugh. "Oh really? And who the fuck are you to tell me what I can or cannot do? That woman got wine on my ten-thousand-dollar jacket."

Carly runs her eyes over his clothes disinterestedly. "It'll come out. Probably."

Ha. I almost snort at that.

The man's face turns red with apoplectic rage.

"I'll give you an address. You can send the bill there," Carly continues and I'm further impressed. She's doing a very good impression of a casual, unaffected socialite who has money to burn. She's a better actress than I thought.

"The stain won't come out, moron," he says. "This is prime silk. A Zegna."

"Oh, is that it? Then get a new jacket and send that bill to me."

Oooh. She's having fun playing with my money.

I don't mind at all. It's actually kind of hot to watch her like this. I find her audaciousness sexy, and I want to watch her throw more money at the problem.

But then the asshole takes a step toward her, snapping me out of my revery as an alarm shoots through me. Fury too as I realize he's trying to get close enough to hit her.

"Touch her and die." The words growl out of my mouth, and all three people turn around to stare at me.

"I'm serious," I say and even though I try to talk casually, my voice has dropped into a deadly register and my fists are clenched at my side. "You lay one finger on her and I will kill you."

The man hesitates, fear flashing across his face, mixing in with the anger. He swallows, breathing hard through his nostrils, sizing me up.

And then, his sense probably returns as he mutters, "I don't fucking need this," before stalking off, trembling with anger.

I make a note to myself to find out who that man is and make a point to ruin *his* life. For trying to hit a woman, and then trying to hit *my* woman. And for calling her a moron on top of it.

"You okay?" I ask Carly, who's staring at me now, her boldness turning bashful.

"Yeah," she answers. "Sorry, I didn't mean to cause a scene."

"No biggie. I'm the only one who saw it. Plus, it was fun to watch until the end."

She nods and looks back at the server, who is now kneeling hastily picking up the broken glass from the floor.

"Hey," Carly calls her attention softly. "Are you doing okay? He didn't hurt you, did he?"

She seems surprised that Carly is addressing her and then nods. "No, he didn't hurt me. Although, he'll probably get me fired after this."

"That won't happen," I say to her and she turns to me. "I can assure you of it." I know the owner of this hotel and can pretty much ensure that she keeps her job. "What's your name?"

"Clara," she says. "Clara Romano."

I nod and say, "You won't be losing your job, Clara Romano."

She swallows and offers me a small smile. "Thank you."

Carly tries to help the woman pick up the pieces of glass, but she waves Carly off insistently, then rushes off before we can say anything else. After, Carly finally uses the bathroom. Then we head back to the party.

The grand ballroom is already full by this point with people swarming around the dance floor, talking in groups, or waltzing to the orchestra on stage. Goody bags sit to the side, meant for the guests upon leaving. Servers glide about with drinks on their trays, eagle-eyed and searching for beckoning guests.

Carly stiffens as she takes it all in, and her expression begins to look distinctly uncomfortable.

"Relax," I say. "We're just going to mingle a little, have a little wine, and then we leave."

"For how long?"

"Maybe ten, thirty minutes. Here..." I snag two wine glasses from a passing server's tray and hand one of them to her. "Have some wine. Relax."

She downs that glass in a few seconds flat and then finishes off my glass too. Only then does she begin to visibly ease up. We find Jamie and Ally again and spend most of the time talking to them with Jamie and Carly being mostly quietly attentive, and Ally and me doing most of the talking.

In any case, thirty minutes pass pretty quickly and before we know it, we're saying our goodbyes and stepping out through the back to avoid the paparazzi.

"Ah," she says as she turns her face to the sky, a gentle breeze ruffling her hair, and surrounding me in the smell of pine. "Freedom at last."

I laugh. "It wasn't that bad."

"No, it wasn't." She sounds surprised to admit. "It was kind of fun. And your friends aren't as snobby as I thought they would be. But it is nice to be out." She finally turns to the goody bag in her hand. "I wonder what's in here."

"Probably jewelry." That's usually the types of goodies we get. "Something basic. Maybe a Cartier bracelet, or a Rolex."

"That's basic to you?" She says in amazement, pulling out the box. Turns out I'm right. It is a Rolex.

She opens up the box and analyzes it.

"How much do you think this costs?" she asks.

"This isn't a super expensive model. Maybe twenty thousand. Why?"

She stares at me. "Can we go to a pawnshop? I think I saw one on the way here and it might still be open."

"Why?"

"Because I can think of a few things I want more than a watch."

I shake my head. "Yeah, but you're going to get lowballed at a pawnshop. Better to resell it online."

She shakes her head. "No. It has to be done today."

"What do you need the money for?" I cock my head. "If you need it urgently, I can just send it to you."

"No. This is something I have to do myself and I have to do it today."

After a few more minutes of back and forth, during which Carly stubbornly sticks to her guns, we take the limo to a pawnshop that Carly saw, and fortunately for her, it is open. Carly isn't a bad haggler and manages to sell the watch for close to its original price of eighteen thousand. And then she directs us to a twenty-four-hour grocery store next, in order to buy canned food of all things.

She refuses to explain to me what they're for. And by the time, I realize what she's doing it's already too late.

"There's a food bank around the corner, walking distance," she says when we step out of the store, with both arms full of grocery bags. She has a smile that shines brighter than the moon. "Let's go."

CHAPTER SEVENTEEN

C ARLY

Micah grows quiet as we head to the food bank, carrying several bags of canned beans, corn, and a bunch of other goodies. They only cost a few hundred dollars and I'll donate the rest of the money I got from the pawnshop in the morning before we leave. But I want to do this tonight, and don't want to be dissuaded.

Even with Micah accompanying me silently, his disapproval thick in the air.

I'm not sure why he's not saying anything. I thought he would try harder to argue against what I'm doing now or claim that I shouldn't be doing it in a dress that cost thousands of dollars. I thought he would at least mention the risk of getting robbed. It's something I thought about myself, but the food bank is close enough that I'm not super worried. Besides, we seem to be in a safe neighborhood.

Still, I expected Micah to argue. But he remains thoughtfully quiet instead, and quietly judgmental.

Finally, I can't tolerate the silence anymore, so I turn around to find that he's watching me as he walks, his perusing expression highlighted by the moon.

"What?" I ask.

"Nothing." But there's a mocking smile at the corner of his lips, revealing that his "nothing" isn't nothing.

"Just say it," I say. "You think I'm stupid for doing this, don't you?"

"Not stupid. Just unexpectedly naive."

I glare at him. I'm grown enough to understand that naive is just a nice word for stupid. Either way, I don't appreciate it.

"What do you have against charity anyway?" I ask.

"I have nothing against charity. Last I checked, you were the one who said that charities only use their money to pad their CEO's pocket."

I blush at the reminder. "Uh-huh. And I was wrong."

I researched it last night after he went to sleep and found that he was right. A lot of charities did use most of their donations directly to help the needy. I just assumed they didn't because of what I heard my mother say. She used to denigrate NGOs in the past, particularly every time our church hosted its annual charity drive. Whenever I suggested we ask them for help, my mother would say, "Charities aren't for us. They just use people like us to collect more money to give to their big bosses."

And I just took what she said at face value after watching them turn her away a few times. That's my fault for believing my mother, a well-known liar. I should have known that if a charity didn't want to help her, then she probably did something to deserve it.

Last night, I also extensively researched Last Hope Food Bank, where we're headed right now. They're very open online posting on their website how much they receive in donations and also giving a detailed breakdown of exactly what that money is used for. Everything I've read about them, including reviews, suggests that they're one of the better food banks in the city. Luckily, they also have a repository outside their office, where we can leave the canned food and anyone in need can access it twenty-four-seven.

But on the way there, we happen upon groups of people sleeping on the streets, curled into walls to fit underneath the building's awning. Sympathy twinges in my heart. One of them meets my eyes and I pause, then squat and lower some cans of beans for him. I don't say anything else, and he simply nods as I leave.

Another thing I used to hate about asking for help was the stares I got. I hated the pitying look that people used to give me, how it robbed me of dignity. So I don't stop and gawk and I don't wait for any acknowledgement. I just place the cans and go.

As I move, I place more cans along the way. Some of the sleeping are awoken by the clatter and jerk back from me, and others just stare off. A few mutter out a thanks as I walk away. The response doesn't matter. I keep the same routine until I've given everyone at least half a dozen cans of food.

"You keep that up, you're not going to have enough by the time we get to the food bank," Micah says as we turn the corner. He says it in a wry tone and once again, his total detachment irritates me.

He makes no secret that he doesn't care about any of this, and thinks what I'm doing is stupid. But of course, he doesn't. He's probably never had to beg or visit a food bank in his life.

I resolve to ignore him at first, but eventually, as we get close to our destination, my indignation builds until I can't hold it back.

"I don't know what your problem is," I finally say turning on him.

He raises an eyebrow. "My problem?"

"Yeah. Aren't rich people supposed to at least pretend to be nice and care about the less fortunate? Did you see that party we were just at? The gift bags? The hosts spent more on hors d'oeuvres than some people might make their entire lives."

"And that's supposed to be my fault?"

"No, of course not. But it wouldn't kill you to at least give something back. Show some empathy, damn it. Care about someone else other than yourself."

He's silent for a few seconds, pinning me with a look. "You think that's what this is? You think I lack empathy?"

I raise a challenging eyebrow. "Don't you? You don't seem to care about anyone else, and you actively get mad when you see me trying to help people."

He laughs, loud and long. "You think what you're doing is helping people? By what? Spending time buying cans of beans?" He chuckles again, shaking his head. "What's the point of doing this when you know nothing is going to change? None of this matters. You'll give cans of beans today and then what? What will they get tomorrow? Because you know they'll still be hungry and homeless tomorrow. And the day after that and the day after that too. You won't make a difference because the system is built against positive change. There will always be people suffering because there *has* to be. And that number will only grow because more and more cities are built to be unlivable by the common population. You see, the rich like comfort, opulence, and mega-mansions. And cities like the rich. So forget about sustainable buildings and rent control. The cost of living will continue to skyrocket and there will only be more and more homeless people until eventually humanity eats itself." His eyes glitter. "I didn't create the game, darling. I'm only playing it."

I blink. That was not at all the answer I expected. I expected him to laugh and say something flippant, not to be unexpectedly profound.

It sounds like he has thought about this problem in depth.

And he doesn't stop there, eyes blazing as he continues, "In the grand scheme of things, giving someone a few cans of beans doesn't even matter. I know it doesn't matter. And secretly you know it doesn't matter too, besides making you feel better for a few hours. So let's not stand here and pretend any of it makes a difference. I don't have the stomach for that much hypocrisy."

I'm quiet for a second, some of my ire dissipating in the face of what he's saying. He's right of course. But in a funny way, he's also being short-sighted.

"Do you think it matters to them?" I ask quietly, watching his eyes glitter. "The people we just gave the beans to, do you think it mattered? Or would they rather we just walked by pretending that we didn't see them?"

His mouth closes, jaw clenching as he looks back in the direction that we just came from. His expression shifts slightly as though he's struggling with himself.

"No," he finally answers. "I think it mattered to them."

I nod. "And that's all I need to know. So what if it makes me a hypocrite? I'd rather be a hypocrite for at least trying to do something good than accept that I can't make a change so do nothing. Sure, I'm not going to change the world. But I don't think I have to. I think it's okay if I just change one night, for one person. Or a couple of people. Or just do something nice, no matter how small it is. Sometimes that has to be enough."

The air whistles after my speech and I pull Micah's jacket tighter around me. He gave it to me in the grocery store and it smells like him. I enjoy the strong scent as he ponders on what I said.

He's thinking about it deeply; I can see it in his face. I give him a few seconds to consider it, and then finally, he grants me a weak smile. "I guess you're right."

I smile back too. As we continue to the food bank, I realize that I may have just unlocked a facet of his personality. Perhaps he's not as callous as I once thought. He's not Prince Charming by any means and he's probably never going to be a super kind and affectionate person.

But perhaps his lack of consideration doesn't necessarily indicate a lack of care.

Or maybe I'm just being delusional for trying to see the good in him again.

The food bank is closed by the time we get there, so we put the food in a collecting receptacle and leave. Micah takes hold of my hand and we walk back to the limo, the silence now filled with a different, familiar warmth.

"You seem to have really done your research about homelessness, huh?" I inquire.

He runs his thumb across the back of my hand. "Yeah. It was part of a project I once proposed that my brother seemed interested in."

"Your brother?"

"Yeah. Tristan told me he wanted to run for office in

New York someday. I told him if he won, we could do something about the housing problem. Like a joint venture."

"That was nice." It makes me see him in a whole new light. "But..."

He sighs. "But Dad wanted him to take over the family business and so he did." His eyebrows ruffle and he sighs. "And I guess he let his political dreams die there. He was never good at resisting Dad. I thought eventually he would snap out of it but he never did. He lived for that man until the day he died."

Bitterness leaks out of Micah's tone and I squeeze his hand. I also make a note to be careful when asking questions about his brother. Seems to still be a sore topic.

When we finally get back into the car, Micah pulls me close, wraps his hand in my hair, and kisses me, murmuring against my lips, "Finally. I've been thinking about that all night."

❦ ⋅⋅ ✦ ⋅⋅ ❦

The next day, after we fly back and Micah drops me off at Mrs. Peach's home, I feel a little like Cinderella after the clock strikes midnight. All the fancy clothes are gone, and so are the fancy buildings and people. I'm back to my regular life.

And it isn't a bad life at all.

It's just that, as I walk back to my house, I realize that my regular life is especially loud and chaotic.

"You cheating bastard!" I can hear my mother screaming from outside the house. "I'm going to kill you if you come near me!"

"I didn't cheat on you, harpy!" my father yells back and sounds of crashing echo. "But I should have!"

I exhale. I'm so tempted to leave them to it and go somewhere else, but the last time I did, my father ended up in the hospital and it was on me to take care of that bill.

So I climb the porch stairs and open the door, in time to see a lamp go flying. My father crouches to avoid the projectile and the ceramic crashes onto the wall.

"Mom!" I yell. "Stop."

She ignores me. "You drunk imbecile. Good for nothing. You ruin everything. You ruined my life!"

"You ruined your own life, Imogen."

Mom picks up another lamp to throw, and I rush to stand in front of her, grabbing her wrist.

"Let me go, Carly!"

"No," I say. "I saw Officer Jensen riding around the neighborhood. He hears a commotion like this and he's going to come right over. Do you want to spend another night in jail?"

That finally reaches through the rage and she reluctantly drops her hand, her dark angry eyes turning to me.

"Where have you been?" she says in an accusatory voice.

"I was sleeping over at Emma's," I lie. "I had to work a late shift and didn't want to wake you guys."

Emma doesn't talk to my parents, so it's an easy lie to get away with. Besides, my mother doesn't even care to confirm the story. She simply glares at my father for the last time, before storming upstairs.

I stare at him too, at his haggard looks and his red eyes. I shake my head and go upstairs too to get ready for work.

At work, I'm still feeling the whiplash of returning to Laketown. It's just been a stark difference from the past few days that it's almost like I have a hangover. But I ignore my feelings and just keep moving and working. When I take a break, I notice a text on my phone from an unknown number. But I already know who it is.

Call me back. It's serious.

I stare at the text Nate sent, apprehension and guilt tangling in my gut. It spreads through my mind, peppering it with questions.

Should I call him back? I probably shouldn't. How did he even text me from jail? You know what, I don't even want to know.

I battle with myself for minutes, but before I can decide, another call comes in. From Micah.

"Bad news," he says. "My grandfather wants to meet you next weekend."

CHAPTER EIGHTEEN

MICAH

The call from my grandfather comes sooner than I expect.

I'm on my way back to the hotel from dropping Carly off when my phone starts ringing again. I glance down at the caller ID flashing on the dashboard screen as I drive, raising an eyebrow in surprise.

I answer with the click of a button. "Yes, my dear old man?"

"I'm told that you're seeing someone." My grandfather of course gets straight to the point without bothering with formalities. "A European princess?"

Damn, Ally. You move fast. Not even a day?

"Who told you that?" I ask.

"Is it true?"

"No. At least for the purposes of this conversation, it's not true."

"You're lying."

"Why would I lie about that? Her family is wealthy, yes, but they're not royalty."

"And who is this family of hers?"

"That I can't tell you."

He huffs his disdain. "Then you leave me no choice but to find out for myself."

"Grandfather, please." I try to strike the right balance of annoyance and pleading in my tone. "This is the first woman that I've found in a long time that I actually like. We're taking it slow for now and I don't want to scare her off by having my grandfather investigate her. Please don't ruin this for me."

He grows quiet as he considers my request. I hope the act was enough to sell it.

"Why is she so secretive about her upbringing?" he asks next. "That makes me suspicious of her intentions."

I hesitate for a few seconds before I answer. "It's because she's an illegitimate child. She's not *really* royalty, in the sense that she's distant enough to never have to worry about taking the throne or attending any royal events. But according to what I heard, her father is a noble. So is her mother. They were both married to different people and had an affair with each other. They gave her away pretty quickly to hide the affair but they kept in touch with her and her adoptive parents from when she was quite young. They've also given her proper etiquette and training from when she was young and plan to eventually introduce her to their respective families, after all their children are adults."

I wait for my grandfather to digest that while feeling

the first tendril of nerves in my stomach. *Was that a good story? Is he going to buy it?*

To be very honest, the story itself is kind of a risk. I know my grandfather specifically wanted me to marry a high-class woman from a stable family unit, but there's no way he was going to accept me keeping Carly's ancestry a secret without a really good excuse for it. At this point, I'm just hoping that he'll settle for Carly being blueblooded and well-trained.

"I've met her parents," I continue. "Kind of by coincidence actually. So I know the story is legit. And I really, *really* like her. She's smart, cultured, funny. She… calms me. I don't know what it is, but I think this might be the one."

Okay, dial it back a little. I don't think the great Mark Landing will believe I'm in love at this point, not when he saw me partying it up in Turks and Caicos only months ago.

Still, I have to convince him that I'm somewhat serious. So I add, "What you said to me at our last meeting… I was thinking about it and I think she might be the one I marry."

My grandfather scoffs and murmurs something unintelligible. My nerves multiply. Did he catch on? Did I say too much? Not enough?

What's he going to say next?

"I need to meet her," he orders. "Invite her over for brunch next weekend at The Vineyard."

"Um…" Relief mixes with a different type of dread. On one hand, I'm happy that he seems to accept my story at face value. On the other hand, Carly's nowhere near prepared enough to meet with my grandfather. She needs at least another three weeks of training. I never expected him to want to meet with her this early.

"I don't know about that," I say. "She's still a bit skittish and I don't want to rush her into something–"

"If she's not even willing to meet your family, then she's not ready to marry you." He cuts me off. "And you're too old to play around."

Oh, come on, again? I'm only thirty-five!

"I have to meet this woman, Micah. I've grown to have little faith in your taste in women. If you like this girl so much, there's a chance she might be a complete disaster. I can't let your relationship continue until I know she's not."

"Gee, thanks for the vote of confidence," I say wryly. I quickly scroll through a bunch of excuses in my head, but I know that none of them will be enough to get me out of this mess. And they may raise more alarm bells for gramps.

"Fine," I answer as I turn into my hotel. "Sunday brunch, it is."

After I get back to my hotel room, I take a quick shower, make some business calls, and then call Carly to warn her about the recent development.

"Wow," she says after I explain it to her. "That was fast."

"Yup. I'm as shocked as you are. I thought I'd have to drag you to at least a few more events before he took notice. But he wants to meet you now and there's nothing I can do about it." I pinch the bridge of my nose, sensing her nervous silence at the other end of the line. "Listen, it will be fine. He's not that bad, truly, it's just that you need to get some more practice in before we go see him."

I hear her inhale a nervous breath, but her voice is steady when she says, "Alright. I'm ready. What do I need to do?"

Atta girl. "What days do you have work and school?"

She rattles off her schedule and I note it in my phone. Apart from a few virtual business meetings, I'm not really doing much in town so I have a bunch of free time to work around her schedule.

And that's what we do.

We meet up mostly in the evenings between school and her restaurant shifts, and I tutor her on etiquette, European royal lore, and everything there is to know about my grandfather. We work on a few of her quirks, and enhance her diction and articulation, and I try to coach her on everything that I think my grandfather will be on the lookout for. It's a lot of information to take in, but she does a good job of remembering the important stuff.

The dresses we bought in LA arrive later that week after their adjustments have been made. Carly tries them in my hotel room as we attempt to figure out which would be best for brunch.

That's when it gets real hard not to get distracted.

And I do mean extremely hard.

"How does this look?" She comes out in an A-line lacy white dress that covers up any cleavage and looks like something my grandma would wear to the chapel. Except on Carly, it gives a different vibe. It glides over her curves, unable to *not* show them off. She just has a body that would look good in anything, the kind that makes any outfit she dons instantly seductive.

And now I'm hard as a rock, fighting the urge to drag her into my lap and fuck her six ways to Sunday.

No time, I struggle to remind myself. *We have no time for that right now.*

But God, I really wish we did.

I tell myself we'll have time after brunch. After the meeting with my grandfather, we have the rest of the day in New York to spend together. I'll have her all to myself with no one to stop me from totally devouring her.

Heck, I'll ask her to take a few days off work just so we can fool around. And I'm going to take my time with it too, and make sure that I get to taste every single piece of her without rushing to the finish like last time.

The memory of that premature ending is still embarrassing to this day.

But I'm ready to potentially embarrass myself again, because my addiction to her has me by the throat and it's not ready to let go.

Finally, after days of planning, it's the day of the brunch.

We fly to New York early in the morning, and Carly sleeps for most of the plane ride. Upon landing, we lodge at a hotel in Long Island where she gets dressed. And then we take a drive down to Old Westbury.

Brunch is at The Vineyard, a sprawling garden restaurant that oozes class. It has an outdoor seating area, attached to a romantic French villa, and its terrace is decorated with lush shrubbery, colorful flowers, and strong trees.

I find my grandfather sitting in the corner reading a magazine, face unsmiling as usual. I approach, with an arm around Carly's waist.

Here goes nothing.

"If it isn't the handsome, polished Mark Landing in the flesh," I greet with a smile as his gaze flicks up from his business journal.

"You're late," is all he says in return.

He eyes Carly, who to her benefit holds his gaze

pretty steadily.

She also holds her hand out to shake his. "I'm Carlette Stonewall. It's nice to meet you, sir."

He nods as though it's a given and takes her hand. "Any relation to the Stonewalls of Massachusetts?"

"I don't think so. My parents grew up in Virginia."

My grandfather nods, but his face shows little of his emotions. "I hope you had a good flight."

I pull out Carly's seat for her and she takes it elegantly before she answers. "Yes. The view driving down here was unbelievable."

"Is it your first time?"

"In Long Island? Yes. Usually, when I'm in New York I stick to Manhattan."

Mark sighs. "Yes, well, the city used to be lovely too, until the damn politicians started flooding our streets with the homeless junkies and riffraff."

Carly visibly stiffens.

Ah, shit. I forgot to warn her that my grandfather was also staunchly anti-homeless.

She meets my eyes, and I send her a silent plea. *Come on, Carly, just this once ignore it. Be cool.*

She takes a deep breath and smiles, but it's tight. "Yes, well. I suppose there's nothing we can do about that now."

Mark harrumphs in response. "So what do you do Carly?"

"I'm in college. Currently studying accounting."

"That's a good career. Do you plan on working after you get married?"

Aha. This was a question I coached her extensively on. And she answers it perfectly.

"It would depend. I do like to stay busy, but in my experience, kids are best raised by stay-at-home mothers. Of course, I could always help my husband's business, but raising a family is what comes first."

My grandfather offers her a smile and I nearly crow in victory. *Nailed it.*

"You seem to understand the importance of the family unit. Many young women don't."

"Yes," Carly says with a forlorn look that plays up her background. "In my opinion, family is everything."

Oh, that was gold, Carly. Way to go.

My grandfather seems to buy it nodding, sagely. "I'm glad you think so. Which is why you should know something about Micah's family before you decide to continue. You should know that he has tainted blood."

I freeze. I throw my grandfather a horrified look.

He wouldn't.

Oh, God, please tell me he wouldn't.

But Mark seems to be testing both of us, and Carly throws me a surprised look as he drops a bomb on us. "Did Micah not tell you that he was adopted?"

CHAPTER NINETEEN

CARLY

The announcement stuns me silent.

It's all I can do to keep from gaping like a fish, but I restrain the urge because Micah already warned me that his grandfather finds over-expressiveness to be uncouth and unladylike.

Something tells me this man finds a lot of normal behavior uncouth and unladylike but that's beside the point.

I'm supposed to be on my best behavior here.

But the reveal nearly breaks my decorum.

Especially when I see Micah's expression and it feels like something reaches into my chest and squeezes.

He looks like someone slapped him across the face.

He's full-on gaping incredulously at his grandfather, in a way that suggests he never expected the older man to share that piece of information. His eyes are shocked and hurt. He even makes a choking sound.

And Mark Landing regards him with a stern glittery gaze that seems almost like a dare. As if to say, "Yes, I said it. And what are you going to do about it?"

Suddenly I'm filled with outrage.

I know all about parents picking on their children and poking at their insecurities to amuse themselves. My mother used to do it all the time. Every time she wanted to establish some power over me or simply use me as an emotional punching bag for whatever slight she'd received, she would come to my room and start provoking me with insults. Fatso. Ugly. Those were the usual culprits, juvenile but effective.

And after she left, I would always sit there and cry and wonder what I did to deserve it.

She would also have that same vindictive gleam that I see in Micah's grandfather's eyes now. And Micah might not see it, and might think his grandfather "isn't that bad," but it's his affection for the older man that blinds him.

I see Mark Landing for what he is though—a mean old classist bully.

"Tainted?" The word slides out of my mouth, hard as steel. "You think his blood is tainted because he was adopted?"

His grandfather raises his eyebrows. "You don't look surprised. So he told you?"

"No, he didn't. But he wouldn't need to. It wouldn't have mattered to me anyway and I would never call him 'tainted' because of it."

The man takes a sip of his coffee. "Maybe, but your

parents might if they find out the truth about his parentage."

"Grandfather," Micah's voice is different. I've never heard him like this before. Hoarse. A little shaky. Restrained. "Enough."

But the man keeps going. He doesn't even spare Micah a glance as he continues talking to me. "My daughter-in-law used to do a lot of charity work in inner cities. At first, I encouraged it, because that kind of publicity was good for the family name. Plus, it kept her mind off her endless miscarriages.

"And then one day, she went to a foster care center where a sick one-year-old boy was brought in. He was the son of one of those riffraff that sleep on the city streets and his parents couldn't afford to take care of him anymore, so they'd left him on the doorsteps."

"Grandfather," Micah begs again. He doesn't like this story. He doesn't want him to tell it.

But the man continues as though Micah never spoke. "For whatever reason, my daughter-in-law decided to take him in. Maybe it was because she had just found out she couldn't have any more children, or maybe she was just too religious and saw Micah as some kind of sign. She always did pray for another son. Or perhaps it was because her first son wanted a brother. In any case, Micah was soon adopted, and we've raised him as a Landing all his life. And he is a Landing in everything but blood, understand that. But to be fair to you, I also want you to know that you will be getting a Landing with tainted blood."

"That's bullshit." The words explode out of me, shocking Micah's grandfather into a wide-eyed stare. "It doesn't matter who his parents are, his blood isn't tainted and you don't get to say that to him. You think you're better than him because you're a Landing by blood? How do you even know?

Who says your mother didn't get knocked up by some two-bit asshole boyfriend of hers and just passed you off as your father's kid."

The shock explodes all over the old man's expression.

"Carly," Micah says, but I'm too heated to stop.

"Blood doesn't make you better than him. It doesn't make him tainted either. I'm sure you think you're very nice people and pat yourselves on the back for adopting a poor, sick child, but it doesn't count if you're going to throw it in his face every chance you get. It isn't his fault that his parents couldn't afford to keep him, nor is it his fault that they were drug addicts or whatever you think they were. And while we're on the topic, why do you assume they were bad people simply because they were homeless? It would be one thing if they were abusive to him, but you didn't mention anything about it. Tons of people are homeless not for any faults of their own, but that's because so many cities are run by selfish, egomaniacs like you who can only think about bloodlines and power while everyone else rots underneath their feet. And for you to complain about homelessness as though it wasn't partially the fault of people like you is frankly *laughably* hypocritical–"

"Carly!" Micah barks this time, loud enough to alert the people at the next table. "Enough."

I finally turn to watch his eyes glittering in anger.

"We're leaving." His chair scrapes across the terrazzo, and he takes my hand.

"Yes, that's probably for the best," his grandfather says tightly as Micah practically drags me out of my seat, and marches me out to the car. We get in and, he doesn't say anything, simply turns it on and starts to drive.

I'm silent too, seething at what just happened.

What an odious old man.

It's good we left. I didn't know how I was going to endure and stomach a meal while listening to all that bullshit about homeless people from a man who'd probably never struggled in his life. Not to mention what he called his own grandson. Unbelievable. No wonder Micah is the way he is.

I'm surprised he didn't turn out worse actually.

I'm so worked up I can't even think straight. God, it's a good thing this relationship is fake, because I can't imagine how insufferable it would be to have to join that family and listen to that bullshit more than once.

As we finally get back to the hotel, Micah passes the car key to the valet without a word and storms up the entrance steps. We take the elevator up with the same stony silence. He doesn't take my hand again as we head down the halls to our hotel room.

Finally, as he closes the door, he turns on me.

"Why the fuck did you do that?"

"Do what?"

"Say all that shit to my grandfather?"

I blink. "You mean when I defended you?

"I didn't ask you to defend me," he shouts. "All you had to do was play the role. Smile, agree with whatever the fuck he says, and be the sweet blueblooded granddaughter-in-law. Was that so hard?"

"Are you kidding me?" I yell back. "Are you actually mad at me right now?"

"Yes! Because of you, I might have just lost the only chance at getting out of my father's trap!"

"Because of…" I laugh incredulously. "Oh, grow up,

you jerk. You crazy asshole, your grandfather was probably never going to give you that loan. He's toying with you, don't you see that? He enjoys kicking you around. You talk all this big talk about how you hate that your dad is trying to control you and yet your grandfather is doing the same thing and you're somehow okay with that?"

"Who said I was okay with it? I was handling it. I don't need you to defend me like I'm a little boy."

"Noted! I'd be crazy to ever defend you again." I head to the door, only for him to snatch my arm and pull me right back.

"Where are you going?" he asks heatedly.

"Anywhere but around you." The words hiss out of my mouth as I stare at his glittering eyes. It fills me with such wrath.

Oh, I hate him so much. I can't believe I tried to stick up for him, can't believe that I thought he was hurt by that "tainted blood" comment. Scratch that, he *was* hurt by the comment. And now he's trying to take that hurt out on me.

But I'm no one's fucking punching bag.

"I don't need this," I tell him. "I have a bunch of shit going on in my life, serious shit. I don't need to be here playing this game with you."

"And yet here you are." His voice is quieter now, menacingly so, yet somehow also sultry. A different kind of heat is starting to pulse between us.

Shit.

It's always so annoying how quickly anger can turn to lust.

I start struggling to get out of his hold even as my body betrays me.

"Let go."

"You drive me crazy," he says, as though I didn't speak. "Absolutely crazy. What am I going to do with you, Carly Huntley?"

He sounds like he's talking more to himself as he pulls me closer, his breath passing over my lips.

"Don't you dare—" I snarl. But he does.

He seals it with a kiss.

I wish I could say that I fought him. And to be fair, I bite his lip at first, punishing him for his audacity. He jerks back for a second.

Only to smile and kiss me again.

Crazy jerk.

Maybe it's the smile that did it, or maybe I'm crazy too. Because I kiss him back.

Asshole.

I rip his shirt off savagely, driven by a primal need to possess him. I don't know what comes over me. A second ago, I hated him. I still hate him.

But for some reason, I can't get enough of him.

Maybe it's because as his lips devour mine, as his taste floods my mouth, I can't forget the look on his face. That shattered, hurt look when his grandfather called his blood tainted, the way his eyes avoided mine for just a second as though he had something to be ashamed of.

He has nothing to be ashamed of, except for the fact that he's an asshole. But even that isn't enough to stop me from kissing him.

His lips bruise mine in their passion, but I give back as good as I get. As his hands grasp my ass, I lift my leg and curve it around his ass, pushing his throbbing cock against my pussy. We both groan at the sensation bolting through us. He thrusts hard and I close my eyes and nearly sob, a violent ache centered in my pussy now.

"Carly." He whispers my name against my skin and then pulls back for a poignant second. His dark emerald eyes gleam, a question in their depths. I know what this is. He's giving me a chance to put a stop to this, to pull away.

To tell him to get lost.

And that's what I absolutely should do.

Right after I'm done fucking his brains out.

I grasp his hair and pull his lips back to mine.

CHAPTER TWENTY

MICAH

I'm losing my mind.

And it's all her fault.

Carly rips her mouth away from mine and then her tongue on my pulse sends it skittering. A moan melts out of my mouth as my head drops back. She's not soft or gentle with either. She nips and bites as she suckles my neck, her nails scoring my shoulders.

She leaves no hint as to the fact that she wants me. Badly.

How can she still want me? I capture her lips again, nipping ferociously at my hunger, pulling it back into mine. I kiss her hard and long until pressure builds in my chest. No chance to breathe here. No chance to escape.

She knows what a fraud I am now. Knows the entire

disgusting backstory. And yet she's still here, consuming me like I'm her favorite meal.

The feeling, the emotion piercing through me is indescribable.

Yet, I shove it away, focusing on the lust instead.

I decide she's enjoying herself far too fucking much.

After that stunt she pulled, she needs a little punishment with her pleasure. And something tells me she just might enjoy that punishment too.

I pick her up and spin her around, carrying her into the bedroom. She holds on for dear life, attacking every piece of my skin with her mouth, and her hands while I try to maintain my sanity enough to find the fucking bedroom that is right in front of me. I grit my teeth when her tongue locates my nipple. As she surrounds it with wet heat, my cock jerks and weeps from need.

I ignore it, forcing thoughts of my own desire from my mind. If I focus on that right now, I'm going to lose it. Better I focus on her, and what she needs.

The minute I walk through the doors, I toss her onto the bed. She releases a sharp breath as she bounces on the mattress, and I grab her legs, tugging her closer. Her eyes meet mine, questioning, desiring. Her hands reach for me again, trying to pull me back, to use me to sate that ferocious need raging in her eyes.

And God almighty, there's nothing I want more than to be the object that slakes her lust.

Except maybe to be the one to stoke it even higher.

I bend over her to grasp both her wrists and hold them above her head. Then I single-handedly undo and tug off my belt, maintaining eye contact the whole time. Intensity blazes from her gaze, and it only gets worse when she realizes what I intend to do. As I begin to wrap the belt around her wrist, her mouth falls open, and breaths pass quickly through her lips in short pants.

It gets worse when I tie her bound hands to the metal rungs of the headboard.

Then, I slide my hands down her arms, watching the goosebumps break out over her skin, admiring her soft shivers at my touch.

So beautiful. Such a tigress, but at the same time a soft pussy cat.

She swallows as she watches me, waiting, wanting.

"Do you remember what the safe word is?" I whisper.

Her mouth falls open again and only a single breath passes. At first, I think that means she doesn't remember. But then she finally admits in a voice tight and airy, "Banana."

"Good." I grin wickedly, as I admit to her, "I'm going to torture you now, Carly. Put you through sheer misery. I'm going to make you cry and feel like you're on the brink of insanity. I'm going to edge you until every part of your skin feels like an exposed nerve. I'll take you to the peak and force you back and take you there again. And until you say that word, I'm not going to stop. Understood?"

Her pants get faster, her chest rising and falling desperately. She nods frantically. The rise and fall of her chest brings my attention to her nipples, puckered against the fabric.

That looks like a great place to start.

I can't fucking wait.

I lower my head and let the tip of my tongue just barely graze the point pushing against the fabric. She gasps, shoulders shaking as she drives upward but then I pull back and meet her gaze again.

"If you move..." I say, spanking her ever so slightly on her pussy. It's a pat more than anything, not even enough to sting but the gasp she lets out is explosive, hinting as to how much she loved that.

I lift the skirt of her dress, revealing her silky panties, soaked in the middle, with a hint of a protrusion at the top.

"Oh, baby." The groan rips out of my chest. "You have the prettiest pussy in the world."

I almost lose control of my breathing then. Even covered with panties, it's a thing of beauty so seductive it beckons me.

I fight to look away but I can't.

"It tastes even better," she whispers in a breathy voice. Her legs open wider in invitation, her thighs trembling with the strength of her desire. Shit, she knows just what buttons to push.

She knows how much I crave her taste.

And God knows I want to take her up on the offer. I want to bury my face into her pussy and drink in her honey until I can no longer think straight or even breathe.

But then I don't want this to end so quickly.

The point of this is to teach her a lesson, before giving her sublime pleasure.

"You were supposed to do something today," I tell her, shifting back into position. I stare hard at her nipples. They seems to respond to my gaze, growing even more engorged. "Something you promised me you could do. And yet you failed."

"I was–" Her breathing pauses as I lift a finger, skimming over the top. She bites out a moan, but she manages to resist pushing her breast into my touch this time. "I was trying to help."

"Did you think I needed help?" I continue smoothly, circling over her nipple, watching the agony scatter her breathing patterns and make her toes curl. "Did I look like I needed protection?"

It takes a while for her to answer, for her brain to work.

"No," she finally manages in a strained voice.

"No?" I meet her eyes, telling her what I want. "Who are you talking to right now?"

She seems to get it almost immediately. Swallowing with her flushed face, and hazy eyes, she says, "No, sir."

Oh fuck, that almost made me come right there.

I want her to say it again, and then I want to come on her face, on her skin, on her tongue.

I want her to come all over me too.

"Good girl." I lean down and replace the finger with my tongue, savoring her broken cry as I trace circles around her nipple. I add a little more pressure as I go along, wanting to reward her and myself for good behavior. And then finally, I draw the point in between my teeth and roll it.

At the same time, I slide my hands over her panties, rubbing around her clit, feeling my cock ache with need as she mewls for me.

"Please!" The plea burst out of her lips. My mind splinters and my cock aches from hearing it. "Please."

I force myself to laugh even though I want to beg too. I'm dying to give her release. My cock is a rod of pain aching for her sweet warmth.

But I'm going to torture the both of us some more before we get to the end.

"This is only the beginning," I tell her. "And you're going to beg me a lot more than that by the time I'm done."

And it's true.

She does beg a lot more times than that.

But the torture never stops.

Time fades to nothing, as I continue the light, teasing touches, the almost kisses, taking her closer and closer to the edge, before patting her on the pussy and watching her entire body jerk and shake. Right as she's on the precipice of an orgasm, I let her go, holding back for a few minutes until she calms down.

Only to start all over again. Over and over. Driving us both wild. We become sensitive creatures, no longer able to use words. We breathe into each other's mouths when we kiss, and we communicate only through moans and eye contact.

We lose pieces of ourselves to each other. She becomes my slave bending to my every touch. I become her slave, denying myself for her pleasure.

And then finally, after what feels like hours, I slide my finger into her pussy, and bite my lips as a rush of pure bliss hits me like a drug.

She's fucking soaked.

I can't help but explore, thrusting my finger inside, making her cry out and move into my hand. She shakes like she's on the verge of coming but I pull out and watch her sob and beg. Then I take her lips in a violent kiss as her body arcs and tries to find mine, tortured by her own need.

Yet I deny it. The same way I deny her release.

I do it again and again, back and forth, push and pull. I laugh madly, resisting every voice screaming in my head to just fucking take her already!

Until I rub her clit for the thousandth time and pull back too late. A small mini orgasm ricochets through her body. I groan as I watch her purr and hiss, her eyes squeezed shut with the pleasure so intense it probably feels like pain.

Then I finally give into the urge to kiss her again, fireworks exploding in my mind as I drive my fingers inside her, extending the orgasms, and making her shout loud enough to bring the walls down around us.

"Yes!" she screams. "Oh, Micah, fucking yes! It's so fucking good!"

The first orgasm doesn't stop. It bleeds into the second, as I keep thrusting into her pussy. She screams loud enough to wake the dead.

I love it.

I keep her going.

Her essence pools all over my fingers, making a mess of the both of us. It seems to go on forever.

And then, as though her body gives up, she finally slumps in the bed.

The only indication that she hasn't passed out is that her eyes are still open, unseeing, cloudy with need.

Only then, do I finally take my own pleasure.

Or I take whatever the fuck this is because it no longer even feels like just pleasure anymore. At this point, my cock is red and angry and feels on the verge of a painful explosion. I've ignored it for so long, disconnected it from my mind, that plugging back in feels like waves of biting heat rushing through my body. An urgent need to release pulses in my brain. My hands shake when I put my cock to her pussy.

Sweet slicks down my back as I push. Pain and pleasure scorch my mind, my cock growing impossibly harder.

I might die from this, I realize incredulously. *This might be how I go.*

But I can't stop. Her limbs shakily wrap around my waist. She bites her lips and moans, words garbled.

"Oh, God." An animalistic groan escapes from me. I'm not going to last. I barely know how to breathe.

Please, God, let me take this slow. Let me not embarrass myself again.

But the minute I seat all the way in, she gasps, her pussy ripples around me in a silent orgasm. And so I let the madness completely consume my mind.

"Hey, hot stuff."

I barely glanced at the woman who followed me onto the empty yacht deck. It's a week later and I'm in Cannes, watching the sunset over vast oceans while the party goes on behind me. I'm supposed to be joining in. But instead, I'm over here enjoying the scent of the salt and sea, feeling the wind on my face.

Carly flew back to Laketown without me, and I flew straight here.

I've been ignoring everyone's calls ever since. My grandfather. My father. They've probably reached out to my mom too, even though she hasn't spoken to anyone since her sabbatical started. The radio silence from the woman who raised me used to bother me, but I don't resent it anymore.

I understand her completely.

I don't feel like talking to anyone right now either. I didn't even want to party but I needed a distraction. Cannes has always been that for me.

But it's not doing its job today. After a few hours of pretending I can't stomach it anymore. Because it's not adequately distracting me from the fact that the one person I do want to hear from hasn't sent a word to me.

Carly hasn't spoken to me since that day. Even after we had sex, and she fell asleep in my arms, I woke up later to find her putting her clothes on silently before requesting that she wants to go back home. We left New York City in strained silence and since then... nothing.

And it's driving me insane.

How does she detach so easily? How could we have sex that intense and she just leave like it's nothing to her?

What's driving me even more insane is that I can't figure out why I care so much. The deal was a bust. My grandfather will never approve of her now. I should forget all about her and maybe think about someone else I can use to convince my grandfather.

But instead, all week my mind has been filled with fucking Carly Huntley.

"Hey, are you even listening to me?"

I turn and consider the woman. I don't recognize her but she's pretty enough. Tall, svelte. Blonde. Of course, my grandfather would never approve of her for marriage, but she's a good candidate for a few hours of distraction.

But even as I have the thought, my body does not rise to the occasion. Some disgust even echoes in my mind.

Nothing about me wants to be with this woman today. I don't want to be with anyone else right now either.

And I cannot for the life of me figure out why.

"Sorry," I tell her. "I'm afraid I'm not good company today."

"Are you sure?" She crosses her arms underneath her chest, in a way that shows off her perfectly perky breasts. They really are nice. It would be great if my body gave a fuck.

"Yes," I sigh and turn back to the ocean. "I'm sure."

CHAPTER TWENTY-ONE

CARLY

"Son of a bitch!"

The words explode out of my mouth as pain arcs across my palm and up my entire hand. I immediately yank said hand away from the hot pan handle and dash over to the sink. My other hand fumbles with the tap and a second later, cold water gushes out. I shove my hand underneath, biting my lip as the water slashed over the burn.

The door behind me opens and closes and Yule calls out, "What happened?"

"Nothing," I say. "I just burned myself."

He doesn't say anything else, just steps in beside me to analyze the damage. He sees the red spot on my palm and puts two and two together. "You tried to grab the pot without using the rag, didn't you?"

I don't say anything. I don't have to, as his frown deepens.

"Damn it, Carly, I warned you." His usual easygoing drawl now takes on a scolding tone. "You've been distracted all damn morning. I told you that if you had something serious on your mind you could just go home for the day."

"Except I can't just go home, Yule." Apart from the fact that I've already taken off way more days than I should, I don't want to go home. Going home would just give me more time to sit around and do nothing but think about my problems. And lately, those problems just seem to pile up more and more.

Going home would also mean having no distraction to keep from thinking about Micah.

Except I'm thinking about him at work anyway, which is why I got burned, damn it.

"I'll grab the first aid kit," Yule says.

"It's fine. I'm not bleeding or anything, and it will probably just bruise."

Yule silences my protests with a dirty look and goes off to grab the first aid kit anyway. I sigh and shut my eyes, letting my head drop forward and feeling the dissatisfaction roll through me.

Why the hell can't I stop thinking about that jerk?

Ever since I came back to Laketown practically bristling with rage, Micah Landing has continuously polluted my thoughts. My feelings oscillate between anger, hurt, and worst of all a strange longing that makes me hate myself just a little. I cannot believe a part of me still misses him. How can I yearn for someone who treated me like he did? Who yelled at me for defending him, who treated me like I was disposable?

I thought we were at least friends, but he clearly

didn't want my input or interference with his life. He probably only saw me as a tool that was supposed to keep my mouth shut and play my role.

I mean, that's what he essentially said back at the hotel.

Every time I remember that, and also that scene with his grandfather, it makes me furious all over again. I'm mad at myself for interjecting, and mad at Micah's grandfather for being a bully. I'm also mad at Micah for being blind to it.

But even with my anger, a part of me still can't forget Micah's look when the older man cut him at the knees, how hurt he appeared that someone he trusted ripped off his mask and exposed his vulnerability so casually. Like it was nothing.

I truly can't blame Micah for being defensive because he probably felt so betrayed.

And that's the thing that makes it hard for me to totally dismiss him as an irredeemable jerk. Because I always stupidly scramble to find the good in everyone and treat people with consideration they don't often afford me. I've been like that since I was a child, and even as an adult, I've found myself excusing my parents' abusive behavior on more than one occasion.

But I know I can't keep accepting that kind of treatment. Especially not from Micah. It's not healthy for me to make excuses for him to the detriment of myself. Even if he was hurt by his grandfather, what does it matter? It still doesn't give him the right to treat me like he did. To yell at me. To completely refuse to see my side of things.

I allow the memories to stoke my anger, justifying my ire.

And then, ultimately, those thoughts lead to what happened after.

The sex that I'm scared to even think about, even though the memories still visit me at night.

And whenever I dream about it, I wake up wet and aching and furious.

I never should have slept with him again.

It was bad enough that I craved him before, but that afternoon... he awakened something deep inside me, something raw, a deep-seated need that I'm scared no one will ever fulfill again,

That's ridiculous. I blow out a breath. *And melodramatic.*

So what if I had mind-blowing sex with him, big deal. I'm sure I can find someone else to have mind-blowing sex with. Heck, there are a few numbers in my phone that I can probably call for some out-of-town, no-strings-attached fun.

Both body and mind fight against that though, warning me that sleeping with anyone else right now would be a mistake. None of them can hold a candle to Micah and I'll only leave disappointed.

But that's just for now though. It's only because Micah was so recent and is still so fresh in my mind. I guarantee later on, I can find a man who's better in bed than Micah Landing.

And if not, well, too bad.

Great sex isn't everything and it certainly isn't worth my pride. I'm not about to turn into one of those women who cling to him and beg for his attention after he's already made it clear he doesn't want to be with them anymore.

I'm used to disappointment, I remind myself. *What's one more to add?*

I shut off the tap and await Yule's return. I refuse to think about Micah Landing anymore this afternoon.

I don't have time for that. I need to focus on what I'm going to do about my college tuition. That is problem number one right now.

On the bright side, I heard back from an accounting firm in Bayview and they offered me an internship. But the proposed salary won't be enough to pay my tuition. Plus, I would need to stop working at the Tiki Bar to take the job, and also worry about the commute, since it's in Bayview.

Typically, I'm only in Bayview twice a week for class and even that's tough. Five days a week will be killer.

Unless I get an apartment in Bayview, which I currently can't afford either.

And even if I could... would I leave?

Bayview is only a town over but it might as well be another world. It's more city than Laketown, larger population, and everything is shinier and more modern.

On one hand, it might be nice to get out of Laketown for some time. I've been in this town my entire life, and I've never gotten a chance to explore what life in other places is like. Being with Micah is the first time I've ever traveled out of state, and just that experience was more intoxicating than I ever thought it would be.

And hell, there really is a whole world out there. There's an entire glittering and vibrant existence outside of Laketown. Just a taste of it, makes me want to see more.

And as much as I'm mad right now, I'm grateful to Micah for showing me at least that.

But even with that, I'm not sure I'm ready to leave Laketown long-term yet. So many things keep me tethered here. I don't know anything about the outside world, and I wouldn't have anyone in Bayview. The added cost of getting an apartment is also another turnoff. Plus, there's my family. They might kill each other without me here.

And speaking of family…

That thought leads me to the next thing troubling my mind. The text from Nate.

That in particular has been eating at me no matter how much I try to ignore it. It's constantly nudging at my brain, plaguing me with guilt I shouldn't feel.

And an infernal curiosity too.

I can't help but wonder what it is he wants.

Maybe there really is some danger that he wants to warn me about. But then why not just do it over text? Why do I have to go see him in person?

More than likely, this is some ploy to get me to visit.

But I should at least go. He's being held without bail and he might be sentenced soon. I should at least see him, even if it's just to say goodbye.

Pain pierces my chest, but I restrain the tears as I hear Yule's footsteps coming back to the kitchen. Tomorrow, I tell myself. Tomorrow I'll go see him.

The next day begins with a surprise.

I wake up to an email alert concerning a transfer of money into my checking account.

I stare down at my phone, wondering if I'm still dreaming.

One hundred and fifty thousand dollars received into my account.

I blink away the sleep from my eyes peering at the amount again. And then it comes rushing back to me. That's half the amount that Micah said he would pay me. He told me on the plane that I would receive the first half after successfully meeting with his grandfather and the rest once this whole thing was over. And even though the meeting was a disaster, I guess he's still keeping his word.

But rather than delight me, the gesture makes me irrationally furious. Because how dare he?

Is he sending me money out of pity? Or is he buying my silence? Either way, I'm angry that he would just send me anything without even a word of an apology for how shitty he treated me. Does he think that's all it takes? That all he has to do when he fucks up is throw money at the problem?

Well, not with me, asshole.

And so, although it hurts and I really could use that money for a lot, I immediately get into contact with my bank, to start the process of reversing the money back into whatever account sent it.

Because I'm not taking that bullshit.

Once I'm done, I finally get dressed and head downstairs. My first stop this morning is the Bayview Penitentiary, where Nate is being held before his trial. Thankfully, neither my mother nor father are at home, so I have a quiet breakfast by myself before I leave.

The Bayview Penitentiary is one U-shaped building with dull grey walls and a fluorescent light over the entrance that never stops blinking. The air is oppressive and heavy, and the interior smells stale, like sweaty bodies and hopelessness. The minute I walk into the dark lobby, I'm assailed by the echoing clang of metal doors and shuffling footsteps. I head over to the counter to sign in, and they lead me into a vast waiting room with concrete walls and large windows that allow light to pour in.

I sit and wait nervously as they retrieve my cousin. And then he comes out and takes the seat.

We stare at each other in silence for several seconds.

"Hey, Carly," he says. "You look good."

"You don't." Nate was considered good-looking before all this happened, but he seems to have aged several years in just a few months. He's painfully thin now, pale skin a stark contrast to his overgrown dark hair. His eyes have bags underneath them and collarbones jut out of his skin. He looks like he hasn't slept or eaten much.

Emotion washes through me. It hurts me to see him like this. For all his faults, Nate has always been the only one in our family who actively cared about me. He would babysit me sometimes, and when I was really hungry, I could call him and he would bring food over. I would later find out most of that food was stolen but still. I don't even blame him for his pilfering ways. At least my parents bothered to feed us most of the time. His mother was usually high out of her mind and his dad was nowhere to be found.

He had to learn from a young age to take care of himself.

Which is why he's now twenty years old and being held on trial for theft, accessory to kidnapping, and accessory to murder.

"So how have you been?" he asks, trying to look laid-back as always. He even attempts a smile as though that would help with the gauntness.

I sigh, steeling my heart. "Why did you call me here, Nate?"

"You're still mad at me."

I roll my eyes. "Of course, I'm still mad at you. And more than that, I'm disappointed. I thought... you promised me you wouldn't do that stuff again. And like an idiot, I believed you."

To his credit, my cousin looked chagrined.

Once, when I was fifteen, Nate made me lie to the cops on his behalf. I swore to the police that he was with me while he'd been out carjacking, and I lied because he promised me he would never do anything like that again. I cried after, feeling so guilty, and made Nate swear to me that he would go on the straight and narrow from then on.

And for a while, I thought he was keeping to the promise. I defended him to anyone who talked badly about him and told them that he had changed.

Only to once again be made the fool.

"Nate, I'm not having a great day, so just tell me what you want to talk to me about. You said I might be in danger?"

"Yeah, yeah." His hands fiddled on the table. "But I don't think you are."

"What?"

"I don't know I..." His eyes shift around the whole room before they come back to me again. "Have you noticed anyone watching you? Received any strange calls?"

'What are you talking about, Nate?"

"If not, then it's fine," he says. "Just forget about it. You shouldn't know. But if you see anyone, especially an old man with a burn scar on his face and neck, then go to the police. No, not the police that's too dangerous... Declan–"

"Are you messing with me right now?" I say. "Because that's not even remotely funny."

He smiles. "I missed you, Carls."

The nickname and the affectionate gaze are like a punch in the gut.

I can't do this. Unshed tears push at the back of my eyes.

I hate seeing him like this. I hate that this is how his story ends. That I couldn't somehow prevent this from happening.

And I hate that I feel that deep down, he's still the kind Nate I've always known.

I have to go before I break down again. The chairs scrape against the floor as I push back and get to my feet.

"Goodbye, Nate," I croak and hightail it out of there.

CHAPTER TWENTY-TWO

M ICAH

She blocked me.

I stare down at my green text, which was marked as neither sent nor delivered, and laugh in disbelief.

I'm sitting on the private plane heading back to New York after one of the shittiest vacations I've had in a while. I filled my time with mindless day parties, anxiety-riddled nights, and afternoons where my thoughts wandered in circles with no fixed destination and no epiphany to be had.

Plus, the one time I decided to go to the beach, it rained.

Just a miserable set of weeks.

And then finally, *finally*, I allowed my pride to bend enough to text Carly again. Nothing much, just to reach out and see if she's doing okay.

Only to find that the text doesn't get delivered.

After trying two more times, I conclude that I'm blocked. Which is hilarious.

I've been blocked by women before, so it's not my first rodeo. But usually, I get unblocked within a few hours after they realize I'm not the guy who's going to go chasing after them, and I will more than likely move on without a single thought.

But something tells me Carly isn't that quick to forgive.

And it's already been a few days and she hasn't unblocked me.

I catch myself checking practically every day now, sending her "hi" texts like an obsessive fucker. And maybe I am obsessed. After all, she's all I can fucking think about for whatever reason. Even at that yacht party, surrounded by mind-altering drugs and gorgeous women and just about everything a man like me could ask for, promising a night to remember.

I partook in none of that.

Instead, I sat in the corner with wine and sulked after a woman like… like Declan of all people.

I couldn't even tell you what happened at the party except for the fact that I spent most of the time brooding and thinking about Carly.

Getting pissed because she ruined my plans.

Feeling guilty because I yelled at her.

Feeling ashamed and angry that she now knows my darkest secret and I didn't get the chance to even prepare her for the reveal.

Not that she looked like she needed preparation. She seemed to take it in stride after getting over the initial shock. But still. I didn't want her to know. Not like that.

The dirtier part of my mind also keeps bringing me back to that hotel room, where I drove her insane with passion, where she was limp and listlessly looking at me, where I lost myself to her again.

And beyond that, I just fucking miss her company. And I think that's the worst part of it all. I miss her.

But I'm assuming, to her, this is the end of our agreement and thus our relationship. It should be the end anyway.

But the thought of not seeing her again makes me antsy and miserable.

You shouldn't be thinking about this.

I look away from my phone and stare out at the endless blue-and-white sky, noting the lights in the far distance below. *You should be preparing for the meeting with your grandfather right now.*

Gramps texted me a few days ago, saying he wanted to meet up. I almost ignored his text, still mad at the foul stunt he pulled.

But I decided not to be a child about this. He's likely expecting me to be pissy and avoidant, but I'm not going to give him the satisfaction of being right.

Besides, I still need his help.

And so I gave it a day or two to text him back, then got on the jet headed to New York immediately.

And now I'm realizing that even just being on the plane reminds me of Carly and her first private jet ride. The way her eyes glittered as she took in the interior, the way her hands gripped the chair on the descent and her lips curled upward in excitement.

I sigh. *Focus, Micah, Focus.*

I don't know what Grandfather has planned for me today, but I need to prepare myself for another surprise. Best case scenario, it's going to be a lecture about me learning discernment and how to pick the right woman. Hopefully, it ends there. And hopefully, Carly's outburst didn't have him looking too deeply into her past, unraveling the secrets we've so painstakingly crafted.

However, I happen to have a contingency plan for that too. Still, I would rather not have to use it.

I tap my finger on my brandy glass as the pilot announces our initial descent. The skyrises that litter the ground soon grow rapidly in size. I remember my conversation with Carly about those and the housing plan my brother and I had for NYC. I intended to take Carly to New York next, showing her Broadway and a bunch of other interesting places. I was looking forward to seeing what expression she would make then. I wanted to see her marvel and delight again. There's something addictive about watching her eyes glow in wonder.

I've never really been able to see the beauty in the luxury I have so far, but I could see it there in her eyes. And through her, I could feel that childish innocent awe again, could soak it all in.

Oh well. I assume a nonchalant shrug to no one. I guess that won't happen anymore. Since she blocked me and everything.

The wheels touch the ground and the plane experiences a slight jump. We're in New York.

Okay. Here goes nothing.

I hear voices when I enter my grandfather's mansion, and they're coming from the balcony across the expansive living room. As I walk toward it, I nod at Elvira who is fluffing one of the pillows on the vintage chairs. She sends me a fond smile in return.

As I get closer to the sliding French doors of the balcony, I realize that my grandfather is talking to a young woman I've never seen before.

I open the door and they both turn to me. The woman has blonde hair that is arranged at the top of her head in the most complicated pattern I've ever seen. She also has a pleasant enough face, and a laid-back casual style, wearing a button-down cardigan, vintage jeans, and Chanel espadrilles. She sends me a friendly smile when I walk in and I return it automatically.

"Hey, Gramps," I say turning to my grandfather who looks to be in a good mood. "Sorry to interrupt you two, but I thought we had a meeting scheduled today."

"Yes," he responds, "and you're late."

"My bad. But to be fair, you should be used to it by now. Do you want me to return after you're done with Ms..."

"Wentworth," she responds in a lightly accented voice. "We met at the Governor's charity ball if you remember."

"Oh yeah, that's right." I don't remember but it would be rude to say so. "How have you been?"

"Good."

"Great. I'll just leave you two to it then–"

"No, Micah," my grandfather says. "The meeting is not with me and you. It's with you and Ms. Wentworth."

I raise an eyebrow. "Oh. Okay. Why?"

My grandfather sighs as though I'm being willfully obtuse and Ms. Wentworth's smile widens.

"Actually," she says, picking up her bag. Also Chanel. "I do need to use the little lady's room. If you could direct me…"

"Sure." I step out of her way as she rises. "Just down the hall and to your left."

"Thank you." She shoots me a look from underneath her eyelashes as she walks past me, leaving the scent of lilies in her wake. I give her a polite smile in return and once she's gone, I turn to my grandfather.

"Okay. You want to tell me why she's here?"

My grandfather stares at me unblinkingly for a few seconds before reaching for his glass of orange juice. "Ms. Cara Wentworth comes from extremely fine stock."

Fine stock? I almost ask. *Like she's a cow?*

But his words confirm my suspicions.

He brought Cara Wentworth here to audition for the fiancé role. The old man is so predictable sometimes.

And it's strange how much "Cara" sounds like "Carly." I wonder if that played a part in his decision.

I know my grandfather is ridiculous enough to think that the similarity will work in her favor. I can see him sitting in his study, with a cup of coffee in hand thinking, *Well, since Micah appears to like women with names starting in C-A-R, how about that Ms. Cara Wentworth?*

I terminate the amusing thought and focus on the issue at hand. What to do next.

On the one hand, it makes it easy for me.

I can say yes to starting something with Cara, comply for long enough, and then once Grandpa gives me the loan, I'll make up whatever excuse to break up with her, or do something that will drive her to break up with me.

But even just the idea of pretending to date another woman is wholly unappetizing.

I mean, if it's just dates it might be one thing, but I'll probably have to sleep with her at some point to sell it. I can already tell my body wants no part of that. For the first time in my life, I'm not sure I would even be able to get it up.

Strange as it is, I only want Carly.

I can't tell Grandpa that though, at least not until I can convince him to give Carly another chance.

I don't know if I can, but I'm going to try. "Listen to what happened at brunch the other day..."

"I don't want to talk about it." He waves a hand dismissively but he doesn't look angry, which is a good thing. "It's not like I had lofty expectations anyway, Micah. I've always known that your taste in women is lacking, so I expected whoever you brought to have some flaw. But I didn't quite expect her to be a hellion."

Well, you were deliberately provoking her. I immediately want to jump into her defense.

But I hold back, so as not to make it worse.

"Right," I say, gritting my teeth at the end. "But you see the thing is, Carly is having a tough time right now with her family and I think what you said might have triggered–"

"That's not important. A woman who cannot control her temper is a liability to you." He gestures to the chair. "Now sit. Cara will return soon."

I sigh and seeing no choice, I obey him. He's not going to listen to me right now, but I can probably try again after Cara leaves.

So I sit there as Cara returns and I initiate a conversation about our last meeting at this gala, refreshing my memory on who exactly she is. My grandfather interjects once in a while, but then he eventually walks away to leave Cara and me to talk between ourselves. And to be fair, it's not a bad conversation. She's very articulate, cultured, with a great sense of humor too. Not to mention now that I've had time to look at her, she's not just pleasant-looking. She's pretty. Some would even describe her as gorgeous.

So yes, I spend most of my afternoon talking to a gorgeous, amiable woman who would probably be some guy's dream woman.

But I'm completely bored out of my mind.

There's no instant connection like what I had with Carly, no banter, no underlying sexual tension. I don't find myself drawn to her mystique or curious about the way her mind works. I don't find myself looking forward to the next words out of her mouth either.

It's all forced on my end, feigning interest and playing a part.

There's no way I can do this for months on end. Nope, not happening.

No one else will do.

I need to get Carly back.

I touch down in Michigan around four p.m. and am met with the setting sun and a golden Lambo from the rental agency. My agent seems to have made good note of my tastes and has the car waiting for me on the tarmac.

Going back to Laketown elicits a strange mixture of emotion. On one hand, there's that resentment that always arises whenever I'm here, reminding me that my father intended this place to be my prison for however many years. I can also feel the boredom start to seep in when I imagine spending my days here. Passing by mundane grocery stores and the intermittent bars punctuated by long stretches of greenery only solidifies that feeling. The town still looks drab and unexciting, and eerily quiet most of the time, offering nothing at all to occupy my mind.

Nothing that is except Carly.

And just the very fact that I'm going to see her again fills me with a humming exhilaration that adds just a little more color to the scene.

Suddenly, the spring flowers that line my path look a little brighter. The gentle air feels fresher when I put the top down. I can almost smell the lakes and the light lilac of Carly's shampoo. I pass by the restaurant we ate at for our first date and feel nostalgic, remembering kissing her, making her laugh, her incredible spit take. Something hums in the atmosphere, a feverish anticipation that invades me. A longing. A need.

It makes me think that maybe it's not so bad that I'll need to stay for a few days, just in case my father sends someone down to check if I'm doing what I'm supposed to be doing.

Speaking of my father, I wonder how long until he calls and asks me about progress on the hotel. Declan has agreed to cover me so far, but he won't do it forever. I'll either have to take the mantle or find someone to do it for me.

It makes the hours-long drive down to Laketown as

pleasant as possible, as I think about what I'm going to tell Carly to get her back.

I could try being my usual charming self times three but I have a feeling that's not going to work. Neither will offering her gifts or money. That might make her madder actually.

Hmm, it's a tough problem to solve.

I decide to first head over to Declan's to ask for his advice. Usually, he would be the last person to go to for relationship advice, but he's known Carly longer than me and perhaps he can consult Emma on what to do. I would ask Emma myself, but she sounded serious on the phone about what she would do if I ever hurt Carly, and what I did seemed like a ball-cutting offense. Declan can play mediator and ask her on my behalf.

So once I pass by the *Welcome to Laketown* sign, I take the scenic route along the backroads, surrounded by trees with the barest hints of their spring bloom. The road to the Pink Hotel is a long, winding path that seems to go on forever, but eventually, the pink-painted Grand Pearl Hotel appears at the end of the road.

There are construction workers still on site, making the finishing touches. I nod at them as I park and walk around the back to Declan's office.

But before I get there something stops me in my tracks. It damn near sucker punches me in the face.

It's Carly, sitting on the porch next to another man.

She's smiling at him and he's smiling back at her. Holding her wrist as she pushes him laughing. They seem to be play-fighting and Carly looks to be enjoying herself very much. Definitely not sitting around moping like I've been.

She squeals out another trilling laugh as he grabs her by the shoulder, pulling her close.

That tinkling sound echoes in my ear and has a possessive rage flushing out every other thought.

Only one thing remains in my mind:

He's going to die.

CHAPTER TWENTY-THREE

C ARLY

"You okay, Carls?"

I turn around and squint against the sunlight to identify the broad, stocky man standing behind me. Robbie Wilkins. He once pushed me off a swing in middle school and I twisted my ankle in the process. And then after his mom tanned his hide for that, he had to help me carry my school bag to and from the bus stop every day until my ankle healed.

We became friendly-ish after that, or about as friendly as a hormonal teenage boy can be with a girl who his mother warned him was off limits due to her terrible family.

He now works in construction and was on the team

that renovated the Pink Hotel. I guess they're still working on it today.

I grin at him. "Yeah, I'm good. Just thinking." *It seems like all I do lately is think.*

It's been about three weeks since I last spoke to Micah, and I'm now sitting out on the porch of the Pink Hotel, waiting for Emma to finish her discussion with Declan so we can head to her house and finally have the talk.

Yes, the talk I've dreaded for weeks, but I don't see any way out of it now. I'm going to swallow my pride and ask my best friend for money.

I'll specify it's a loan and insist we draw up a contract mandating that I'll pay her back.

Then, I'm going to save like mad and make sure every spare penny goes toward paying the debt.

I still hate that I have to do this, but I don't have a choice now. I have to ask so I can finish school.

I'm not going to let my pride destroy my only chance at a future.

But the situation is making me depressed still.

I was staring off, thinking about how to approach it when Robbie showed up behind me.

He steps down onto the base and sits beside me.

"Want to talk about whatever's bugging you?" he asks.

I raise an eyebrow. "*You* want to talk about feelings?"

"God no." He gives me a mock horrified look. "But I figure if it's something practical you need help with, like a pipe leak or something, then I gotcha."

I laugh and shake my head. "Nah, it's nothing like

that. I just... I don't know." I sigh. It's hard to describe my feelings, but I push to get it out for whatever reason. "I don't know what to do anymore. I feel like I keep trying and trying and life keeps finding new ways to knock me down. To the point that I'm scared of trying anymore. You know?

He blinks at me and says plainly, "Nope. That kinda talk is way above my pay grade."

For some reason that makes me snort and I shove him. This leads to him shoving me back and I try to tackle his head under my armpit to give him a noogie like when we were kids, but he laughingly traps my wrists and my shoulders in a bear hug that I can't escape from.

A loudly cleared throat interrupts our battle.

I shift my head and then gape at a familiar form, silhouetted against the sunset.

Micah.

My heart stops and then gallops away like a horse.

As he moves closer, I meet his glittering eyes.

His emerald gaze gleams with an almost feline grace as he hovers over us.

Elation and annoyance hit me in even waves, and I try to stop my heart from beating erratically at his presence.

He's back?

Damn it, why is he here? Why now?

I mean logically it makes sense why he's here. It's partially his hotel after all. But still. I didn't think he would be back so soon, since he's mentioned a few times how much he dislikes Laketown.

I wish he would have stayed away for at least a few

more weeks.

I almost started to convince myself to forget him. To forget about how green his eyes are, and the way his hair curls over his face. I almost stopped thinking about his smile filled with mischief, his seductively plump lower lip, his wicked gaze, and his tall, built form, always impeccably dressed in something that makes him look like a million bucks.

I told myself constantly that I exaggerated how handsome he was and how breathless he made me feel.

But staring at him now, I can't convince myself of that lie anymore. I was only trying to gaslight myself into forgetting him.

Because even unsmiling and looking vaguely threatening, Micah is as delicious and earth-shatteringly dazzling as ever.

It takes me a second to realize he's no longer looking at me. His eyes shift to Robbie with a predatory gleam, which looks even scarier when he flashes his teeth in a mocking smile.

"Who is this?" he says, his tone artificially upbeat. "New boyfriend?"

"Who are you?" Robbie asks blankly. He gets to his feet, still holding my hand. "I don't think I've ever seen you before. If you're new in town, the Pink Hotel's not open for guests yet. You should try the Marriott."

"Right." Micah doesn't look like he paid any attention to anything Robbie said because as he talked, his eyes were trained solely on the grip Robbie has on my wrist. And Micah keeps staring at it, long after Robbie is done talking, long enough for the atmosphere to turn awkward.

"Are you going to let go of her or what?" he says finally.

Robbie frowns at him. "What's it to you?"

"What it is to me is that you should let her go. Or you're going to find your teeth on the ground."

My jaw drops. I can't believe he just said that. Did he just threaten Robbie?

Robbie's face reddens.

"Oh yeah, pretty boy?" He glares at Micah, sizing him up. They're both about the same height and weight probably, but there's just something dangerous about Micah right now.

I decide this has gone way too far. I pull my hand out of Robbie's grip and hold both hands out to ward off the violence I can sense coming.

"Calm down, both of you," I say. "Micah, if you want to see Declan, he's meeting with Emma right now."

"I need to talk to you."

I cross my hands over my chest. "Okay. So talk."

"Alone." He shoots Robbie another hard look and says, "Scram, you."

Rage twists Robbie's expression.

"Oh, that's it, you preppy motherfucker." He snarls and snatches Micah by the front of his shirt. But then Micah moves faster than I've ever seen anyone move, grabbing Robbie's wrist, stepping out, and then throwing him over his shoulder.

Robbie crashes hard onto the floor on his back and rears forward in pain.

"Fuck," he explodes.

"Micah!" I gasp in horror, grabbing his arm to drag him away from Robbie. "What do you think you're doing?"

"You touch her again, and I'm going to break that arm." Micah is still holding Robbie's wrist and he twists it, leading the other man to howl again. "Got it?"

"Micah, let him go right this instant."

Micah spares me a glance and I glare at him sternly. At first, it looks like he won't oblige, that stubborn anger holding on firmly.

But then he suddenly schools his features into an implacable mask and releases Robbie, stepping back.

"You crazy asshole," Robbie says, stumbling back to his feet. "Come on, Carly. Let's get out of here and call the cops."

"She's not going anywhere with you."

"She's not staying here with you either, you jerk. You must be out of your mind. Heck, you could have broken my spine with that bullshit. Carly, get away from him, he's clearly unhinged."

Both men turn to stare at me waiting for my decision.

I hesitate for a moment, biting my lip as I come to a reluctant decision.

"Robbie, can you give me a second?" I tell him. "I actually do need to talk to Micah about something."

Robbie seems unsure, as Micah shoots him a triumphant look.

"Are you sure?"

I nod. "Unfortunately."

He gives Micah another threatening look, which Micah returns with a droll look of his own before Robbie walks off.

"What the hell was that?" I turn on Micah the second Robbie is far enough away still shooting Micah dirty looks. "How dare you just come up here and attack my friend?"

"Friend?" Micah's eyebrow cocks sardonically. "He wasn't looking at you in a very friendly way."

I roll my eyes. "Really? We've known each other since we were kids, and I'm pretty sure I'm better at reading him than you are. Robbie and I have no interest in each other. The only reason you can't see that is because you're having a jealous fit."

"Jealous?" He even laughs while he says it like it's the most ridiculous thing he's ever heard. "I don't get jealous."

Is he for real right now? He just came up and attacked someone for no reason, but he's not going to admit that he did it out of jealousy?

Of course not, because that giant ego of his won't let him. He's Micah Landing and there is no way the great Micah Landing would ever be jealous over little old Carly Huntley.

I glower at him. "What do you want, Micah?"

"Like I said, I came to talk to you. Before I saw that bastard pawing at you."

Frustration jumps out of me. "He *wasn't* pawing at me."

"Yes, he was, and it's crazy that you don't see it."

"Oh, so now I'm crazy." My voice is loud enough to probably be heard by the workers inside the hotel but, frankly, I don't care anymore. For the first time in a long time, I don't care if I'm making a scene, or proving people right. I don't care about keeping my head down to make up for my family's reputation.

Since Micah thinks I'm crazy anyway, why not show

him crazy?

"You're the insane one," I tell him, practically hollering. "You yell at me for defending you in front of your grandfather then you take me back to your hotel and fuck the shit out of me and then you fly me back in your private jet and don't speak to me for weeks. Now you're back here assaulting my friends and acting like a jealous husband! Is that not the definition of insanity?"

"I wasn't jealous."

"Right," I scoff, because of course that would be the part he picks up on. "If you can't even be honest with yourself, that already tells me how the rest of this conversation is going to go. Have a nice life, Micah."

"Carly." He grabs my arm as I attempt to walk away. I try to wrench out of his grasp as hard as I can, only to end up nearly losing my balance in the process. He catches me when I stumble and draws me close. Suddenly his scent hits me.

I almost moan from how good he smells.

"Easy there." His voice is practically a whisper in my ears, soothing, making my pores more sensitive to the wind. Desire instantly flares, but I push away from him, angrier than I can ever remember being.

"Don't touch me, asshole."

"I won't." He puts his hand up in the air and stares at me with some contrition finally trickling into his expression. "Look, Carly, I didn't come here to fight with you."

"Then what on earth are you here for?"

"I came to apologize," he says, shocking me. "Both for how I acted with my grandfather and... for now. You were right. I was... bothered by seeing you with that guy."

I blink. I didn't expect him to admit it that fast or at all for that matter. And now the part of me still itching to fight feels frustrated that it can't yell at him anymore.

But I'm still mad. "Well, if you're done apologizing, then get lost."

"Carly..."

"What?" I raise my eyebrow. "You thought you would come here and say you're sorry and I would forgive you just like that?"

"Yeah." A small smile crooks his lips. "I mean isn't that how apologies work?"

I don't smile back. "You're kidding me."

"Carly, you don't know how much it's taking out of me to even be here. How much I have to bury my pride—"

"I don't give a rat's ass about your pride. What about *my* pride? What about the fact that I tried to do something nice and you threw it in my face, you jerk?"

"Not that I'm not enjoying this soap opera..." A new voice interrupts and we both turn to find Declan and Emma staring at us with a great deal of interest, along with a handful of construction workers behind them. I recognize a few of them like One-Eyed Mark Piedmont and Hal Rojas. Hal, despite looking like the strong silent type, is one of the biggest gossips in town.

"But can you save the pillow talk for later?" Declan continues. "The two of you are distracting my workers."

"Also, Carly," Emma points out, "your phone has been ringing for a while now."

I glance back at my tote bag vibrating on the porch.

I didn't even hear it. All that yelling and the blood pounding in my ears made it impossible to. Sanity only returned once Emma pointed out the ringing of the phone, and my anger recedes as I take a deep breath.

Then I reach for my bag and fumble with it, feeling self-conscious as I pull my phone. The heat fills my face as I finally realize what just happened. What those people heard me say. With Hal, news is going to make it around town by tomorrow.

Oh, God, this is going to be a disaster.

"Hello?" I say as I pick up the phone.

"Took you long enough to answer," my mother snarls. "Get to the hospital now."

"Why? What happened?"

"It's your father. He got attacked last night and beat up by a bunch of thugs. He's in a bad state."

"What?"

"I'm not going to repeat myself. Just get here." She hangs up.

I stare at the phone, my ears ringing unable to believe what I just heard.

"Carly?" I glance over at Emma who called my name, concern shining in her eyes.

"What's wrong?" Micah asks.

"Someone attacked my dad," I say softly, still in shock. "'I have to go to the hospital."

"I'll drive you."

"No," I say. He's the last person I want to be around right now.

"Come on," Micah cajoles. "It's faster than taking the bus."

Shit, that's right. Emma and I took the bus here because she refused to drive the new car that Declan got her. She says it's so shiny she's scared of wrecking it. The only other person I can ask for a ride right now is Declan, but I don't want to pull him from his work.

I struggle with the thought.

"I can drive you," Declan offers but I shake my head. It's nice for him to offer but I don't want to make a nuisance of myself.

I glare at Micah. "No, it's fine. He'll take me."

CHAPTER TWENTY-FOUR

MICAH

Carly sits in stony silence beside me as we navigate back down the hill. She hasn't said a single word since she got into the car, resolutely staring out the window and pretending like I don't exist.

Not that I blame her. Now that she put my actions into perspective, I've been a grade-A ass to her this whole time.

I yelled at her for sticking up for me.

Then had sex with her and coldly flew her out like she was a hooker.

Then I show up without warning and assault a guy who I'm still not convinced is just a friend.

Still, I can't even believe I did all that. Especially that last part. It was like something else came over me, some green-eyed demon. I rarely cause a scene like that when I'm sober. And I never do so out of jealousy.

I don't get jealous. Ever.

But when I saw that man holding her, with her smiling up at him and the bastard smiling right back down at her as though he had every right to... I can't lie. I saw red for several seconds and it blinded me. My mind blanked. Rationality ceased to exist.

All I know is that I wanted to punch his face in so he could never smile at her again.

Which is an unhinged thought to have, admittedly. More than that, it's scary that I almost acted on it.

Sure, the idiot attacked first, but I took it a little too far, and probably would have kept going and snapped his wrist if not for Carly calling me out on my bullshit.

And she did it in front of all those people too. I nearly chuckle. I didn't expect that from her either. I might not mind causing a scene, but I know Carly does.

Over the weeks we've known each other, I've gleaned how private and low-key she usually is and can only imagine how mortified she's feeling right now.

My amusement dies when I sneak a look at her. She's not finding it very funny. And this whole fiasco is my fault.

I screwed up. On so many levels.

I stare at the open road, and wonder how to fix the mess I made.

"I'm sorry," I say even though the word feels too inadequate. I try to inject more of my sincerity into my tone. "I mean it. For how I acted with my grandfather... I... When he said what he said, I didn't know how to react. I thought it had ruined everything.

And then I did ruin everything. But at the same time, I didn't want you to feel sorry for me, and I acted like an ass because it's my defense mechanism and..." I sigh because this is coming out all wrong, an endless jumble of words I can't put together right. What's happening to me? I'm usually more eloquent than this. "Is this making any sense to you?"

"What do you want, Micah?" she says, steel-toned. "I know you don't want to talk to me just to apologize to me, so tell me what you really want."

Guilt slices through me. She read me accurately again. I didn't come all the way here just for an apology even though I should have. I came because I want her back.

But now that I'm faced with the truth of what I did, I almost don't have the guts to even ask that of her. Maybe I should let the idea of using her for the ruse die. I can't use her if it's going to hurt her, and putting her in my Grandfather's path will do at least that.

"I don't want anything," I say instead. "Just for you to forgive me."

"You could have done that on the phone."

"I tried. You had me blocked."

"Oh," she says. She probably forgot that she did it too.

"You also sent back the money that my accountant sent you." The man informed me on the way here that the deposit had been reversed.

She shrugs. "Well, I assumed since our deal was done, then there was no need for you to pay me anymore."

"You thought wrong," I say. "Even if our deal is done, you still fulfilled your part. You're at least entitled to that money. More than that, in fact. I want you to have it."

She doesn't seem pleased with the concession. Instead, she eyes me suspiciously.

Why?" she asks. "Is this your way of trying to buy me back?"

"No, Carly." She really does think lowly of me. And the worst part about it is how close she comes to being right. "This is my way of saying that the money is yours. We had a deal and you did your part. I'm the one who screwed up. So even if you take that money and tell me to get lost again, it would still be yours. I'll accept your wishes without any problem."

It'll be a tough pill to swallow. I would hate to pretend-date any other woman, and also losing Carly proved painful in general.

But I'll do it if that's truly what she wants.

I can feel her staring at me.

"Why?" she asks again, quietly this time. "Why are you doing this?'

I should probably say something meaningful right now, something profound and charming that would win her back and make her forgive me for all my stupid mistakes. Something suave and smooth, something typical of the quintessential sweet-talker himself.

"Damned if I know," I answer honestly instead.

She snorts and turns back to stare out the window.

We arrive at the hospital in due time, pulling in front of a white several-story concrete building with rusted iron stair railings. Carly rushes out ahead of me as I park the car, and by the time I catch up, she's marching in through the sliding entrance doors the inner air slightly warmer than the outdoors.

Like most hospitals, there's a septic scent in the air, the murmur of endless chatter, the consistent beeps of machines, and the occasional droning of the call system above us.

Carly's steps are clipped and agitated, and her hand grips the strap of her bouncing tote bag slung across her shoulders. She strides down the hallway through the emergency entrance, approaching the nurse's desk with a determined look on her face.

"Hey, Gracie," she says to the pleasantly plump elderly woman who was in the process of reaching for something on the other side of the aisle.

Gracie smiles kindly at Carly. "Hey, Carly. Are you here for your dad?"

"I was told he was brought in."

"Yup. He's in Room 5 down the hall. Someone kicked his ass and practically left him for dead right on a park bench. It must have happened sometime during the night too, because Officer Jensen only found him while doing his morning patrols."

"Jesus," Carly whispers in horror and Gracie nods her sympathy. Then she shifts her attention to me, her eyes flaring with that familiar gleam I see in many women's faces.

I wink in return. "How's it going?"

"Well, hello, handsome," she croons. "I think I've seen you around here before. The night of the shooting. You brought Declan and Emma to the hospital, right?"

"Yeah, I was there," I say. I remember plenty of things about that day. Driving into town to look for Declan and hearing that he'd gone alone to save his daughter from pearl smuggling kidnappers. He wasn't back yet and Emma was nearly in a panic, so I went with her to rescue him.

We got there in enough time to find Amelia making her way out of the forest herself. While Emma and Monty, the bodyguard, went off to find Declan, I carried Amelia back to the car, protecting her.

And then the gunfire started.

After that, the details get a little foggy. The adrenaline kicked in and all I remember is flashes of images: Declan getting dragged out by Monty and Emma, sporting a nasty gunshot wound, trying to get him to the hospital along with his daughter crying in the back seat and Declan threatening to lose consciousness.

Everything after that and until Declan was declared stable was a fog. I was just operating on autopilot at that point. It's the first time I've ever seen anyone close to death since my brother. The trauma of that night doesn't necessarily haunt me anymore, but I've been less enthusiastic about going to hospitals since then.

So it's very likely that I did meet this woman that night and just don't remember her. Of course, I'll never tell a lady that though.

So I wink at her and say, "You know, I felt we had met before too, but I thought it was only in my dreams."

It has the desired effect. The woman snorts and says, "Boy, stop blowing smoke up my ass."

Carly cringes a little and then rolls her eyes before heading away to hospital room five.

"We'll talk," I tell the nurse, and she chortles as I follow Carly.

"You really can't help yourself, can you?" Carly mutters.

"Nope," I say and she shakes her head. "And you have to admit that was a good one to come up with on the fly."

"No, it wasn't." But I can almost see the hint of a smile at the corner of her lips.

Oh yeah, I'm getting her to smile again. We're getting there.

And then she draws the curtains open and the smile disappears entirely.

There are four people in the room, all looking at Carly. Well three of them are. The one in the bed, Carly's dad, is currently unconscious, with tubes going in and out of his mouth, a bruised cheek, and swollen eyes.

A dark-haired woman who looks like a thinner, more severe-faced version of Carly is sitting beside him holding his hand. Opposite them is another shorter woman and then a man who appears more annoyed than concerned.

"Took you long enough." The sitting woman talks to Carly first. "I told you your father was in the hospital and it took you almost an hour to get here."

"Sorry, Mom. I was all the way at the Pink Hotel across town." She approaches the bed tentatively. "How is he? Gracie said he got beat up by someone."

"Yeah. Probably borrowed money from the wrong person for booze and didn't pay back," the man grouched.

Carly's mother nods.

"Stupid fucker. I told him drinking would be the death of him."

"And it's gonna be the death of me too! How on earth am I going to pay that hospital bill? Your bastard brother should have just stayed home like I told him to and none of this would have happened."

As they spoke the other woman had her eyes trained on me. Unlike with Gracie, I feel zero inclination to joke around with this lady or even smile at her. So I just blankly stare back at her.

"Who are you?" she finally asks.

Carly turns and gestures to me. "This is Micah," she says. "My—"

"Boyfriend," I don't know what causes me to say it but the minute I do, Carly's eyes pop open beyond belief and she gapes at me.

Still, I maintain composure. "I'm Carly's boyfriend."

There's a second of shocked silence and then everyone starts talking at once.

"You are?"

"Carly's never had a boyfriend. I'm her aunt, I would know."

"You're way too good-looking to be her boyfriend."

That last sentence makes me frown at the speaker: Carly's mom of all people.

And you're way too heartless to be her mother dances on my tongue but I refrain from saying it. I already know how sensitive Carly is about her family.

Instead, I attempt to smooth it over with humor. "If you ask me, I'm the one punching way above my league."

"Yeah right," Carly's mother snorts like I just said a joke and my dislike for the woman deepens.

"I'm serious. Carly's a beautiful woman and smart. Smarter than I ever was and more driven too, putting herself through college. I got my whole tuition paid when I was her age and I still dropped out."

"We'll see if she finishes," the other woman, Carly's

aunt, adds and I instantly dislike her too.

"You look familiar," the man, probably Carly's uncle, says. "I feel I've seen you on TV or something before. Are you a singer?"

"No," I say but it only makes the man peer at me with even more suspicion.

"He's Declan's friend, Uncle Allan," Carly says, and suddenly their eyes all light in interest.

"Declan Tudor? The billionaire?" Allan says. And then they look at me with renewed interest, eyes tracking my clothes.

"Carly's boyfriend," her mother murmurs. The frown is gone from her face, and there's a new respect in her eyes as she looks at me. I recognize it for what it is.

And I hate it.

Carly on the other hand looks mortified.

Especially when her mother turns to her and says, "How are we going to pay for this, Carly?"

There was enough suggestion in her tone to make me frown. There are three adults in the room. Why is it on her?

But Carly doesn't complain. She simply swallows and says, "It's fine. I'll figure it out."

CHAPTER TWENTY-FIVE

C ARLY

I don't take a full breath until I step out of the room, closing the curtains behind me.

I hear Micah step out too but I don't look at him yet. I can't. There's too much turmoil going on inside and I feel like, if I look at him, it might all come pouring out.

I walk down the hallway slowly and hear his footsteps follow me. I don't stop until I'm outside and down the stairs, heading across the parking lot.

Finally, I get to his car, lean against it and inhale deeply, then exhale.

It doesn't do much to ease the pressure inside of me. Somehow, it makes it worse.

I'm just so fucking exhausted.

I turn back to Micah, who is standing a few feet away, watching me steadily. Waiting. I don't know what for. But I don't want him here. Or at least I'm not supposed to want him here.

I try to recover some of the anger I felt toward him earlier today, but I don't even have the energy to do that. I'm tired of being mad. I'm tired of feeling like life is unfair and everything is against me. I'm so tired of being tired.

Micah walks closer to me and I don't stop him as he takes my wrist and tugs me to his body.

"Let me go," I murmur weakly into his chest but he just shushes me, wrapping his arms around my back.

"It's okay," he says. "You can let go."

I don't want to, but I can feel the emotion hiccupping into my throat. My chest tightens, tears stinging the back of my eyes. I don't want to cry. I'm so sick of crying. But it flows down my cheeks anyway, silently, as I clench my fists stubbornly attempting to hold them back. Then I grip his shirt too, inhaling him, crackling sobs piercing out of my throat. The breath that I couldn't get out, forces its way out of me in an explosive hacking sound and then the dam breaks and it's all rushing forward.

"Why?" I rasp harshly. "Why, why, why the fuck does this keep happening?"

I don't know what's going on anymore. I feel cursed, like life is determined to teach me a lesson. But I don't know what that lesson is. Is it that I'm not supposed to have nice things? Everything is just meant to go wrong? Am I supposed to stop trying?

"I'm sorry." Micah's nose rubs in my hair and his arms tighten around me. Right now, it feels like they're the only thing holding me together. "I'm so sorry."

He sounds so genuinely sad. Why? It's not like he

gives a damn about my family and it's not like he cares about me either.

It's probably just a part of his game, I think, but it doesn't stop me from clinging to him either, holding him close, using him as an outlet to let out all the emotions and stress of the past few weeks.

And then, finally, as the sobs subside, the tightness in my chest eases, and I'm surprised to find that I feel a little better than I did just minutes ago.

I finally let go of him and make a move to step out of his hold but he takes a few seconds to release me.

I avoid his eyes wiping my face.

"Sorry about that," I say.

"Don't apologize." When I finally risk a glance at his face, it's to find his expression soft. Not pitying, but gentle. "I didn't mind at all."

I nod. "In any case, I'm fine now. I have to go back in there to figure out the hospital bills and everything, but I'm pretty sure Emma's picking me up when I'm done so don't feel like you have to stick around."

"Why?"

I don't understand the question so I cock my head. "Why what?"

"Why is it on you to figure out the hospital bills? Does no one else in your family work?"

My spine immediately straightens, as I get on the defensive.

"Remember how you yelled at me for scolding your grandfather?" I say.

He smirks. "You mean the thing I just apologized for?"

"Yeah, well, I'm not going to apologize for what I say to you if you say anything bad about my folks. They may be trashy and rude, but they're my trashy and rude, if you know what I mean."

His expression is admiring, but also holds a tinge of frustration.

"You're incredible, you know that?"

I'm stunned because I don't expect him to say that. "I am?"

He nods. Then he takes my hand. "Come with me for a second. I want to show you something."

"I already told you I can't. I have to–"

"I'll take care of the bills."

I shake my head. "No Micah, I can't let you–"

"I already did," he says. "Dropped my card off with Gracie on the way out and told her to charge whatever insurance doesn't pay for."

I gape. "No, you didn't."

"No, but now I'm going to." He leans down so we're nose to nose. "You can't stop me from taking care of my fake girlfriend."

That drags a smile onto my face, but I step back. I still don't trust this sudden kindness. "I don't want you to pay for it though. And you shouldn't have told them you were my boyfriend. My family... they're kind of like vultures. If they feel like you have something to offer them, they'll take and take and take and pick you clean until there's nothing left."

He snorts. "I'd like to see them try. Fortunately, I have a lot of money to blow through." He reaches out and tucks a strand of hair behind my ear. "I may not like your parents and I may think that they're deadweight dragging you down, but for the very fact that you care for them, means I have to care for them too."

I frown. "Why? Why do you have to?"

He shrugs. "I'm not sure. Believe it or not, I actually don't know what's going on here either, or why I came back running to you when it would have probably been better to move on. All I know is that here I am. Because I have to be. Because I missed you more than I've ever missed anyone in my life."

My emotions tremble again, and a breath gets stuck in my throat.

I believe him. Maybe I shouldn't but I do.

There's no disguising the honesty in his eyes, the faintly confused but bemused expression as he speaks about something he can't entirely describe.

But something I can totally relate to as well.

And perhaps that's the thing that helps to melt away the last of my anger.

"Come with me," he says. "You're not doing them any good here and I want to give you a massage."

I give him a look. "Really?

"Just a massage," he assures me with a wicked smile. "I got a new massage bed brought to my room at the Marriot and I want you to try it out. I think it would help you with all your stress. Of course, if you want to jump my bones at any point during, I'm not going to push you off."

"Yeah right." I roll my eyes at his chuckle and weigh my options.

What to do now.

I could go back into the hospital but I'm not sure that would be the best idea. My mom's in a mood and seems like she's itching for a fight. Plus, they'll all grill me about Micah and I'm not ready for that yet.

Alternatively, I could go home or to the Tiki Bar, but I'm not on shift today and I'll just sit around and be bored. There's nothing else for me to do either. Mrs. Peach is out with her friends and Emma is with Declan, and I really don't want to be alone right now.

Something internally warns me that I'm about to make the wrong choice, but I still sigh and give in. "Fine. But no funny business."

"Scout's honor."

"You were never a boy scout, were you?"

He grins mischievously.

Nevertheless, we return to Micah's hotel suite and I walk in, admiring the understated elegance of the room. It's not much compared to the hotel room we got in New York and it's not even close to Micah's penthouse. But it's nice and spacious, with taupe and brown accents, tasteful paintings hung up on the wall, and the faint scent of lavender lingering in the air.

It also has a massage bed smack dab in the living room.

Micah gestures to it with an elaborate flourish.

"Feel free to lay down," he says. "We can do it clothed, but I'll tell you that it's far more effective if you're nude."

"Yeah, in your dreams," I murmur and he laughs again.

I climb onto the massage bed with his assistance, following his directions to lie flat on my back.

He turns a button and then twists a dial and the bed

begins vibrating at a low hum, kneading my muscles lightly.

"Mmm." I moan as it digs into some of the kinks in my back.

"Feel good?"

"Uh huh." My voice comes out watery and he chuckles. My eyes slide closed as I enjoy the gentle drumming on my back. He turns it up a notch, and the pressure and release grows even more intense. At some point, I feel him lift my hand in his and begin to massage it with strong strokes from the palm out.

It doesn't take long for the addictive effects to seep in. Suddenly, I'm relaxed and languid more than I've ever felt before. I suddenly feel lips brush against my forehead and my eyes open lazily to meet Micah's darkened gaze.

"I thought you said it was just going to be a massage," I whisper even as desire thickens my voice.

He notices and grins at me. "I lied."

Large hands slide up my thighs and I shiver.

Micah keeps the touch light, teasing, but already my body is starting to respond. My pussy begins its familiar pulse. My clit starts to throb. The relaxation is turning into a languorous heat, that slowly climbs the more he touches me.

And then he starts to softly kiss the back of my thighs. His soft lips nip worshipfully on my skin, teasing, and then finally his tongue comes into play.

His finger cups my pussy at the same time. I feel the pressure even over my pants and I squirm.

As his thumb finds my clit, pleasure rockets through my body, forcing a moan out of my mouth.

I can feel his smile as he continues up my thigh with

his other hand. He barely holds my waist, and I'm already turning over for him, my whole body aching and far too sensitive for the fabric resting on it. I lift my hip so that he can tug my pants down more easily. I said I wouldn't do this. I should be ashamed that I'm giving in so easily, but there'll be time for shame later.

Right now, I want rapture.

At first, I'm scared he's going to continue the teasing but he doesn't. As though drawn by invisible hands, his face plunges downward and he presses his nose against my panties, inhaling deeply.

"God…" he hisses like he just had a hit of his favorite drug. "I missed that."

"I missed you too," I moan as I slide my fingers into his hair. Maybe I'm not supposed to do that. Maybe I'm supposed to play the submissive role again. But right now, neither of us cares.

I'm too turned on for that it's been too long.

"Please," I tell him, both loving and hating that he makes me beg. Luckily, he doesn't need to be asked twice. His finger hooks on my panties, slide them to the side, and his tongue is suddenly, rudely on my clit.

"Oh God."

My head falls back, digging into the pillow. My body arches in the air. It's a fucking star show in my body, all my synapses firing off at the same time. I tremble and sob from the force of the passion driving me, from the sheer magnitude of lust that makes me writhe against his face.

His tongue is everywhere all at once. He doesn't give me a single reprieve eating like a starved man. A soprano sings in my ear as my mind slowly disintegrates. And then I look down at him…

It makes everything worse.

I've never seen anyone eat my pussy with that look on their face before. That look of absolute devotion, sated and hungry at the same time. His eyes are fogged over with bliss before they shut. His nose digs into me along with his lips. As though he needs this more than he needs his next breath.

I need it too.

He cups his hands underneath my ass, driving me closer to his face. I writhe and ride his face with abandon, garbled words escaping me.

"Micah!" Suddenly without warning, I'm coming all over his face, all my reservations in tatters on the floor.

CHAPTER TWENTY-SIX

M ICAH

Getting my hands on Carly's soft body is a miracle and I don't intend to take it for granted again.

As the taste of her lingers on my tongue, my hunger kicks back into overdrive.

As if she didn't just come all over my face.

I want to lick her furiously until she does it again. And then I want to turn her around, bend her over the damn massage bed and fuck her brains out.

But, gentleman that I am, I resist the urge.

Believe it or not, fucking Carly is not what I brought her here for. I came to help her relax, and what we just did was part of it. But I don't plan on taking advantage and taking it further, not until she's sure about me again. And if I go mad in the process then so be it. Small price to pay.

Just seeing her sated form, her chest rising and falling, is enough, and though it tempts me beyond my goodwill, I refuse to give in.

Instead, I squat beside her, smiling as she tries to catch her breath and one eye finally peels open.

"So," I grin, "Do you forgive me now? For real?"

She brings out a hand and weakly shoves me. "Don't ask me things like that when I can't even remember my own name." But there's a smile on her face when she says it that tells me everything I need to know.

I catch her hand and kiss the back of it, silently thanking her for her forgiveness. Her gaze slides lazily down my body, to the erection pushing against the front of my pants.

"Do you want me to return the favor?" she asks, a sultry note in her voice.

I'm about to say no when she licks her lips. Suddenly my core clenches violently and my brain is assailed with images of her on her knees, her tongue teasing my cock into a frenzy before swallowing down, the tip hitting the back of her throat.

Fuck, I want that. I want it so bad.

I bite off the groan that threatens to tear out my chest.

"No, thanks," I force myself to say and she must see how much of a struggle it is because she giggles.

"Are you sure about that?"

No. "Yup." I stand and dust my hands over my pants like a damn boy scout. "I'm good to go."

She shakes her head again, amusement gleaming in her eyes.

"Suit yourself." She throws her hands over her head

and stretches her entire body like a kitten, making her shirt ride up even higher.

Fuck me.

I get a full frontal and it's not like I haven't seen her naked before, but each time it's like an amazing discovery. This time, she invokes the imagery of a lounging goddess, satisfied after indulging in a lustful frenzy.

I take a mental snapshot, knowing full well that this is the image I'm going to pull up when I'm jerking off later in the shower.

Carly stares up at the ceiling and after a few seconds, she sighs. I can see her worries, the ones I've tried so hard to get rid of, returning to her gaze. I wish there was a way to stop it, or at least stave it off for longer.

"What are you doing tomorrow?" I ask, mostly to distract her. "I thought we could grab brunch or something at a restaurant."

She shakes her head. "No. Tomorrow is a church picnic out in St. Mary's, and I already told Mrs. Peach that I would help her with her cookie stand. She can't make it but Hal and I will be there."

"Ah. I see."

"Will you be coming?"

"To the church picnic?" I shrug. "I dunno if I can. I'm not religious and I don't remember my Hail Mary's too well."

"It's not a Catholic church. It's episcopal I think," she says. "And I'm not religious either. The picnic is after church and it's mostly just a small get-together for everyone in town. Like a town fair, but more low-key."

"Ah, I see." I thought church would be more relevant

here, but small towns seem to participate in selective religiousness as much as cities do. Not that I mind.

I was never religious growing up. My mom was a religious woman though and she took it *very* seriously. To the point where she's been on a religious sabbatical since my brother died, and self-imposed strict rules indicating that none of us contact her while she's gone. Maybe it's her way of dealing with her grief, but also something, a nagging voice tells me it's because she's angry at me and regrets adopting me.

"You don't have to come if you don't want to."

"Huh?" I break out of my thoughts to refocus on Carly.

"I said you don't have to think too hard about it. You don't have to come. I don't mind."

"Oh." She must have misread my expression and probably thought that I was intensely wondering whether to go to the picnic or not. She thought that was why I was frowning.

"That's not what I was thinking about," I assure her. "But yeah, I can come to the picnic."

"It's fine. Seriously, Micah. You don't have to."

I cock my head.

And even though she says she doesn't mind me not accompanying her to this picnic, the way she averts her gaze after a few seconds tells me she does. It also alerts me that there's more to her questioning than she's revealing.

"Do you *not* want me to come?" I ask.

She thinks about it, then shrugs. "I mean, it doesn't matter to me one way or the other."

"You sure about that? Because it kinda sounds to me like you asked me on a date and now you're trying to back out of it."

"It wasn't a date! You know what? Never mind. Forget I said anything."

"No, no, no," I laugh. "You can't take it back now. You asked me out, Carly. And if my fake girlfriend wants me to go to a church picnic with her then guess what I'm doing? Going to the damn church picnic."

"I'm not your fake girlfriend anymore."

"Doesn't matter. I'm coming. Now what exactly does one wear to a church picnic?" I sigh feeling like slapping my forehead. "And here I thought I wouldn't have anything to go to. I left all the good stuff in France. Shit, even my Valentinos."

"No, no, no, you can't wear anything like that." She waved her hands emphatically. "Regular clothes only. Nothing too fancy. We're in Laketown, after all."

I raise an eyebrow. "Yeah, but… it's a church event. I can't just wear jeans and a T-shirt."

"Why not? That's pretty much what Emma's grandpa wears. And Poppy Moon wears hunting gear everywhere, so you won't stick out like a sore thumb for being too casual." She bites her lip in uncertainty. "But on second thought, maybe you shouldn't go with me."

"Why not? I can do casual." I already have in mind what I'm going to wear. Ralph Lauren polo shirt, and Cuccinelli leisure-fit linen pants. Maybe Gucci loafers. Not fancy at all, very mainstream and I wore that outfit at least twice before, which makes it very casual as a matter of fact.

She offers a tiny, hesitant smile. "No, that's not it… I mean, you can go to the picnic, it's just that I'm not so sure you want to show up with me.'

"Why not?"

"Well, as you might have guessed, my family isn't exactly well-liked in this town. And for a pretty good reason, to be fair. If you show up to the picnic with me, people will think we're dating."

"And?"

"And... it might affect your reputation. They might think there's something wrong with you for slumming it with me."

I immediately scowl. *Slumming it*? That's how she describes our relationship?

She thinks that I somehow see her as inferior and I'm only tolerating her presence for what... sex?

God. I hate everyone who's ever intentionally or unintentionally made her feel that way. Probably began with those damn parents of hers. Her words speak to some deep-seated insecurities that I'll need to help her deal with later. But it will probably take a more sensitive touch than I have right now.

"Besides," she continues as I try to control the anger induced by listening to her talk about herself like that. "If we go together that might signal to my family that we're actually in a serious relationship. Like I said, those guys are vultures. And there's more of them that you haven't met yet. The second they know about you though, they'll descend and start asking for favors, as if it's your responsibility to take care of the whole brood." She sighs and closes her eyes. "It gets pretty annoying. You'd basically have to be an asshole if you want to get them off you."

I tut. "It's funny how you think I care about any of that, either my reputation or being an asshole to your family. Just FYI, I didn't care about my reputation when I was a teenager surrounded by elite snobs trained with sharp tongues and the ability to verbally slice you off at the ankles if they thought they were somehow better than you. I certainly don't care now that I'm in a town with strangers, most of whom I don't give a damn about. No offense."

Carly merely smiles as I continue.

"And as for the second thing, your parents aren't the first pair of opportunistic vultures I've met. Trust me when I say I know very well how to handle them." Of course, it would be easier to handle if Carly would agree to simply detach herself from them, but I don't see that happening anytime soon.

"You paid for their medical bills," she says quietly.

"Yes, but that's only to save you from having to do it," I say. "I don't know why it was on you in the first place, seeing as how there were three other adults in the room."

Carly shakes her head. "My mom hasn't worked since I was in high school. She kept getting fired from her jobs for either stealing or starting fights with her boss and eventually no one in town would hire her again. Dad collects disability from a back injury he had and he's still getting some retirement but it's not enough. Uncle Allan is on parole for assaulting someone and that limits his income too and his wife's a holistic pet masseuse, so she doesn't really get much in terms of financial compensation."

Jesus. No wonder Carly worked so hard. They all relied on her. A bunch of losers and users all of them.

But I don't want to say anything that offends Carly, so I simply say, "I see. In any case, I'll figure out how to handle your family."

Carly opens her mouth like she wants to argue some more against me coming. But then I interrupt her by asking, "On a separate but related topic, what are *you* wearing for this picnic? I brought all the dresses from LA for you to choose from."

She groans. "Nope. Can't wear any of that. You should sell them and get your money back."

"I can't sell them, they're tailored to your specific, *exquisitely rare* body type." I waggle my eyebrows making her snort and roll her eyes. "And even if I could, I'm not going to because I bought them for you. I only want to see those dresses on you."

I think I see her gaze soften slightly, but she still maintains, "I can't wear such things in Laketown."

"Who says? Every town needs a beauty queen, and I have yet to see one as beautiful as you."

She chuckles again. "You are just on a roll today with the compliments."

"Yeah." I grin and then bend over, to brush my lips against her. "But you make it so easy."

The town picnic is both exactly what I thought it would be and not at all what I expected.

It's held out on the lawn of a small, brown building with a modest cross on top of it. Tents are set up over green grass, each holding different delicacies whose scents mingle in the air. My mouth waters as the smell of warm chocolate chip cookies and brownies assail me, and I'm happy to find that we're moving in that direction. I also spot a few tents holding arts and crafts, and even motor parts, which is strange to have at a picnic.

Apparently, this church "picnic" event is held to raise money for the church fund and so they accept sales of pretty much everything. Also, everything's a little overpriced, for Laketown that is, although it would be considered underpriced anywhere else. The smells of fair food, giggles of children running around, cool wind on the fresh grass, and petals falling around us added a homey ambiance to the picnic.

The lawn is far from crowded. Only about thirty or so people were milling about and from the way they called out, they all knew each other. All that's to be expected.

What I don't expect is to enjoy myself as much as I do.

It's partially because of the dress. Carly and I find a compromise, which really means I manage to bully her into wearing one of the dresses we got in LA. It's a simple Givenchy A-line mid-length dress in mustard yellow with an off-shoulder sleeve. Hermes sandals and a matching yellow Hermes scarf tie the whole look together, accentuating her delicate feet and graceful neck.

Carly looks like the goddess of the sun wearing it, and every time I look at her, I just have to smile.

But she's still a little anxious and when we're close to our destination booth, she pauses, "I feel like people are staring at me.

"Of course they are," I tell her. "You look gorgeous." Most of the people we passed by threw admiring glances at her. Someone even tells her when Carly goes over to the cookie stand. Even the man in a lounge chair behind the counter we're heading to squints his one good eye at her, and says, "That's a real pretty dress, Carls."

"Thanks, Mark." She blushes and continues walking. "Do you need any help?"

"Nah. I got it. But you can hang around if you want to." Mark immediately eyes me. "This your fella?"

"No, he's just a friend."

I cock an eyebrow. Oh, that's what we were going to

play it? Just friends?

She sends me a pleading look and I smirk.

Alright then. We can be just friends for now.

"I'm Micah. Carly's *friend*." I offer the other man a handshake.

The man holds my gaze for a split second before he takes it. "Nice to meet you. The folks here call me One-Eyed Mark. On account of me only having one working eye." The other eye was looking in a completely different direction and didn't blink. Probably a prosthetic.

"How appropriate," I say, not knowing how else to comment on it.

He nods. "Y'all can pull up a chair from over there and sit with me. Boy, have I got news for you Carly."

And then for the next hour or so, as Carly mans the table, Mark and I talk about everything under the sun. He tells me about what happened at last year's picnic, and how Pastor Allan's chicken fighting ring got blown open by the sheriff. He tells me that Macy and her husband are divorcing because she caught him with their daughter's male gym coach. He also tells me that there's a betting pool for when Poppy Moon and Grandpa Crane start dating.

It's right around the third story that it hits me. One-eyed Mark is a huge gossip.

Lucky for him, I'm a gossip monger. I love hearing stories about people I don't know and I enjoy seeing Mark's eye twinkle whenever I ask, "And then what happened?"

A few more people tell Carly how pretty she looks when they stop by our booth. She always blushes and says thanks in that shy manner. I think Carly may be exaggerating how scorned she is in this town because I don't notice much animosity directed at her either.

And then when Emma and Declan show up to set up their booth, Emma's jaw drops as she looks at Carly.

"Oh my God, " she says. "You look so pretty!"

Carly blushes. "It's the dress. It sucks me in all the right places."

"That's not it." Emma isn't willing to let Carly put herself down either "You look radiant, Carls. I'm serious."

She blushes even deeper. "Thank you."

"Told you." I wrap my arm around her waist and shift her closer. Of course, that has Emma's and Declan's gazes instantly dropping to my arm and then they share a knowing look like one of them just won a bet.

Declan then looks at me with amused eyes. "What are *you* doing here? I thought you wouldn't be caught dead at one of these things."

I shrug. "Well, it's not so bad. I figured I might as well come. If I'm going to be stuck in this town for however many months, I should get used to participating in its... is that lady wearing fatigues?

They both turn. "Yup. That's Poppy Moon. You should meet her. Poppy, Tate, over here!"

The petite, fierce-faced, red-haired lady with the fatigues walks to us, along with her pretty daughter who looks just like her.

The younger one, Tate I'm guessing, hugs Emma first and asks, "Where's your grandfather?"

"I don't know. He went fishing with Amelia this morning and they haven't been back."

"Huh. I should have known he'd try to dodge his responsibility." Poppy's eyes turn even sharper as she narrows them. "He owes me fifty bucks."

"They had a bet," Tate explains. "And Mom refuses to let it go."

"What bet?"

"Don't ask." Tate finally throws Carly a tentative smile. "Hey, Carly. You look amazing today."

"Thanks. So do you." Carly says it in a similarly awkward tone and it's followed by a few seconds of awkward silence.

I glance at Poppy who is peering at me owlishly.

"Cool gun," I say gesturing to the one strapped to her thigh.

She shrugs. "It's nothing special. Just my .44 mag. But I got a scope on it so I can blow your head off from a mile away."

"Oh, um..." I'm mildly confused, not knowing if she was referring to my head specifically or just heads in general. Either way, best not to get on her bad side. "Good to know. I didn't even think pistols could have scopes."

"Of course you didn't," Poppy scoffs. "You're a city boy." She shakes her head at the sky. "As if we needed more city boys in this town."

"That was directed at me, wasn't it?" Declan smirks.

"If the shoe fits..."

"If it makes you feel better, my dad and I used to hunt deer once upon a time," I tell Poppy. "But we stopped because I felt bad for the deer."

"That's 'cause you were raised soft. In the wild, you wouldn't have felt bad for the bear. You would have accepted that that's the natural course of nature."

"Yes, but we don't live in the wild, Mom. We live in a civilized society, and there's really no reason for us to be killing things to eat them anymore."

"Oh, don't start with your vegan nonsense, Tate Marie. I'll kill whatever I damn well please. God intends it that way and no city-boy pansy is going to convince me different."

"Sorry," Tate immediately apologizes on her mother's behalf. "Mom thinks everyone who doesn't eat meat is a pansy. And she has wild conspiracies about God's purpose for living beings."

"What a coincidence." I smile. "So does mine. Except my mom thinks that we were put on this earth to suffer and only in suffering can we find absolution."

Everyone looks at me, as though they can't decide if I said something profound or profoundly stupid.

"Or something like that, I wasn't paying attention."

We all laugh, and the small talk continues, trading banter among ready friends.

But I sense a change in Carly at some point. It's like she gets quieter and quieter. Saying less.

And then finally, she says, "Hey, guys, sorry, I need a minute. I'll be back."

And without further explanation, she turns to walk away.

I'm not the only one who watches her leave. Emma frowns. "Is she okay?"

"I don't know." I keep my eyes on Carly's retreating form, noticing she's heading for the exit. "But I'm going to find out."

CHAPTER TWENTY-SEVEN

Carly

I avoid Micah's regard when I walk away, even though I feel his gaze on my back. I don't want him to look into my eyes. I'm scared he'll see the thoughts running through my mind, nasty thoughts that don't deserve to see the light of day.

Thoughts I never thought I would have about another woman, much less someone I consider a friend.

Well, maybe not a friend, but at least an acquaintance and not an enemy.

And those thoughts originate from somewhere deep inside, a malevolent envy that I've felt probably my whole life.

And I hate that I feel that way, hate that I'm getting

possessive and jealous over a man who's not mine and will probably not even remember my face when he leaves. I hate that I was thinking of pulling him away from a conversation he was enjoying, just so he and Tate couldn't continue their banter. So that he wouldn't realize how much prettier, smarter, and better she is than me.

But he probably already sees it. Anyone with eyes and a working brain can see it.

And that's what makes it hurt worse.

Luckily, I think I hid my feelings pretty well. I treated Tate with the same friendliness as always, but I was hoping that she and her mom wouldn't linger. Seeing her joking around with Micah, with her long legs and beautiful smile and luscious red hair... I felt like a drab fat little mouse in comparison. And watching Micah smile back at her, made it so much worse.

He's going to leave you for her. The thought consistently pounds against my skull, and it's not an entirely irrational one. After all, Micah promised no loyalty to me and he would be well within his rights to exercise other options.

I bet Tate would make a better fake girlfriend than me. Heck, she could even be his real girlfriend eventually. They fit well. Tate's smart, accomplished, and bold. I bet she wouldn't have goofed up with his grandfather. She would have handled that situation with more finesse and found a way to defend Micah without pissing off his family.

Something I couldn't do.

I just need to go home. Hal seems to have the cookie stand under control, and Kayla's mom will be coming later to help. Emma has Tate to hang out with, and Declan and Micah can have their manly talk. I doubt anyone would miss me if I were gone.

My thoughts are interrupted when someone from

behind grabs my wrist.

I already know it's Micah, even before he spins me around to pin me with a look.

His eyes scan my face and he frowns. "What's wrong?"

"Nothing," I say. "I guess... I don't know. I got tired. I have a headache and I want to go home."

"Why didn't you say anything?" He tucks my hair behind my ear.

"I didn't want to interrupt y'all's conversation. But you can stay, I don't mind."

His eyes continue to search for a clue in my features that would hint at the cause of my mood switch.

"You're really not going to tell me?" He let his hand rest on my waist and the orange glow of the sun gives his emerald eyes a fiery glint. His scent is strong, gaze, soft, beseeching, lingering on my lips as my breath catches.

I can't do this with him right now. Not here. I'm not confident I won't cry.

"I'll tell you later."

"Are you sure?"

I nod. I can't talk about my feelings to Micah when they're still fresh. But maybe later I can turn it into a joke. Tell him I was just PMS-ing and we'll laugh at how ridiculous my hormonal brain is.

Or maybe, hopefully, later will never come, because Micah would have forgotten all about the questions he has and we'll move on from it without incident.

Micah places a soft kiss on my forehead and the move is so tender I blink back tears.

Shit, I really need to get out of here.

Luckily, he doesn't stop me from leaving. Instead, he takes my hand and walks out with me, letting me have my silence while still being a steady rock at my side.

I can't help myself. I hold his hand tight.

As much as I hate to admit it, I'm glad he followed me out. His presence is comforting and it helps soothe my emotionality.

We continue strolling down the pavement, smelling the grass, listening to the birds chirping, and watching the shimmering lake in the distance.

"This is nice," Micah says. "You know you could build a great country club with a view like that. Buy a few yachts and rent them out. That would be a fantastic experience to offer tourists."

"Yeah, but build it with what money? That would require investment and no one here has it. I bet most of the people in Laketown don't know what a country club is."

"Hmm. You're right. I'll talk to Declan, and see if he wants to do a joint venture with me."

I send him an amused look. "You realize doing something like that will make you have to stay in Laketown longer than you intend to right?"

He sighs. "Neither my grandfather nor dad are budging, so it looks like I'm already going to be staying a while. Like I said, I might as well do something with that time."

"So you've given up on leaving? You'll stay in Laketown?" I don't want to evaluate the quick flutter of my heart at the thought.

"No," he says, facing me. "Just putting a pause on my dreams until I figure out what my next steps are with my firm."

I swallow the sinking feeling and nod. "Do you have the architecture firm already set up or is that what you need the money from your grandpa for?"

"Yup, more or less. I technically started the firm back in college, but we disbanded after my father's sabotage. But there was always an unspoken agreement that we could come back together eventually. We just need an initial investment and a few big projects to solidify our name. And we're working on both those things. We're courting a huge real estate mogul who wants to build a string of shopping malls. He's impressed by my ideas but he's not going to give me the contract unless we look like we have our shit together. And that's where the money comes in."

"Wow," I say. I can see the clear passion on his face whenever he talks about his architectural dream.

It's so interesting to see because as a rich kid from a wealthy family, he technically doesn't *need* to do anything else for the rest of his life. He can just rely on his family's money. And for a while there, I thought that was all he was doing.

Despite everything he told me, I never really noticed this driven side of him before. And it's admirable, especially given his circumstances.

I'm driven because I'm trying to escape poverty and make something of myself.

He's doing it simply because he wants to.

We walk a little more and I spot a boat coasting close to the shore with two familiar people climbing aboard. I smile.

"Speaking of yachts, if you want someone to help pilot them, I know the perfect person."

"Emma's grandpa?" He guesses because I'm staring in that direction.

"Yup. That old man loves the water so much that I think he might have been a pirate in his past life. "

Micah chuckles and Grandpa Crane catches sight of me.

"Is that my Lady Fishy?" he calls out, his voice echoing across the field. I lift my hand and wave.

"Lady Fishy?" Micah murmurs.

"An old nickname. I'll explain later." I head over to where Grandpa and Amelia are sitting on a small fishing boat, aware that Micah is following me. Grandpa adjusts his trademark Chinaman's hat to shield his face from the sun. Amelia is wearing a similar, albeit smaller, hat.

Grandpa peers at Micah first. "Hey, I know you. You're that Mark fella that was at Declan's engagement party."

"Micah," Amelia and Micah correct simultaneously and then look at each other. Micah grins and attempts to snatch the hat off her head while she scowls and fights him off. I suppose the two of them are well acquainted. I remember Emma told me that Micah helped Amelia escape the forest when she was kidnapped. And with Micah and Declan working together, they've probably met more times than that.

"Hey, Amelia," I greet. "What are you guys up to?"

"Grandpa says he's going to show me Burgstone Wharf, and he'll tell me the story of the Burned Man."

"Burned Man?"

"Oh, I never told you that story?" Grandpa Crane's eyes glitter with excitement under the brim of his Chinaman's hat.

I shake my head. To be fair, he could have told me the story but he tells so many of them, that they kind of start to blur into each other after a while.

"Oh, it's a good one. Get in the boat, the two of you can join us and I'll catch you up to speed."

"Oh, I'm not sure about that, Grandpa." I share a look with an amused Micah. "We're just coming back from the picnic, and I'm sure Micah has work to do."

"Nonsense. You don't work after a picnic; a picnic is an excuse for a lazy day. And it's a Sunday too. No one is supposed to be working on the Lord's day."

"Um..." I try to find another excuse but I already suspect it will be futile.

The only thing Grandpa loves more than fishing is telling one of his elaborate and unrealistically epic stories, and he just found two more semi-willing victims.

So Micah and I climb onto Grandpa's boat and shift our weight around so as to make it as well-balanced as possible. This means that I'm sitting next to Grandpa and Amelia is sitting on the other end next to Micah.

She gives him a funny look and then turns it on me. "Are you two dating now?"

"Um, no," I say quickly, side-eyeing Grandpa. "We're just friends.

"That's what Emma and my dad used to say when they were dating."

Shoot. "Yeah, but we really are just friends. Right, Micah?"

But Micah, the little devil, only winks conspiratorially at Amelia who makes a face.

"Gross. Everyone's dating now. Pretty soon this town will be filled with gross couples and you'll all be popping out crying little babies."

Micah laughs at that. Grandpa says, "Love is a beautiful thing, Amelia. You shouldn't find it gross."

"It's not a beautiful thing. Mysteries are beautiful. Like the one you're going to tell me."

That's all the prompting he needs as he pushes us off the shore. "Alright. Let's get ready for the ride."

As the boat sways and surges at a steady pace, Grandpa begins his story. "It was a warm and stormy night. Sometime in summer. And it was practically hailing. I'm talking about the kind of rain that makes you feel like the world is ending. Just big fat drops pelting..."

"We get it, Grandpa," Amelia says, sounding very much like Emma in that moment. "No offense, but can we get to the meat of the story."

"Patience is a virtue, my dear." Grandpa smiles at her indulgently. "Anyway, just to continue setting the scene. This was nearly two decades ago. The hotel fire had happened just a few weeks before, and most of the Pink Hotel had burned to ashes. I lost my little boy and his wife." Grandpa swallows thickly, a sad smile on his face. "But of course, my grief was nothing compared to little Emma's. She cried nearly every day and asked if there was a way we could get them back. And then she watched this fairy-tale movie on TV– I forget the name–but it had her convinced that if she went to the hotel and said a magic spell, it would bring them back. Of course, I tried to dissuade her, but even back then, my Emma was very stubborn when she put her mind to something. So I had no choice but to take her, to see for herself."

The boat's now entering a tunnel, where the lake continues out on the other side. "Of course, neither of us accounted for the rain. And when we were about half a mile away, it started pouring. I had to jet to make it in so we didn't get too soaked. You would have thought I was in high school again." His eyes twinkle at the memory. "Although to be honest, I wasn't much of a jock in high school. I could have been, had I not torn my Achilles in freshman year…"

"Grandpa…"

"Sorry, sorry. Anyway, where was I? Oh yes. We dashed into the hotel to protect ourselves from the storm, but when we arrived, there were already wet footsteps on the floor. Meaning that someone had gotten there right before us. Now, I thought they might still be there, so I called out and no one answered. It was a little spooky. And then, suddenly, when we walked across the hall, someone ran down the stairs and out the door. I only got a glimpse of him but he had white hair and a huge burn scar on his face and a little on his neck."

"Wait, what?" I jerk to attention. "A man with a burn scar on his neck and face?"

"Yes." Grandpa seems delighted by my enthusiasm. "And I swear on the almighty, Carly, I've never seen that man before and never saw him since. I think maybe he could have even been a ghost. I thought he was a ghost. Until recently, I saw him for the second time."

Anxiety tightens my stomach and my spine laces straight. "Where?"

"It was a few days ago, in the alley behind Lou's. A few of the guys and I were over at Lou's playing poker but I needed to take a leak and the bathroom was choked up. So I went out back to do my business and there he was coming out. Our eyes met and he took off running again."

"Strange," Micah murmurs.

No. It's more than strange. Internally I'm freaking out a little.

I tune out the rest of the conversation as my mind whirls around one thing. The man with the burn scar. Just like the guy Nate described to me.

I thought my cousin was just messing around. Trying to scare me into coming to visit him more often.

But what Grandpa Crane is saying...

No. There can be more than one person with a burn scar on their arm and face. It may be a coincidence.

Or it may not.

But I don't know what to think right now.

As Grandpa continues the elaborate story that somehow includes him beating everyone at the bar at pool, my mind remains on what he just told me. Even after getting assaulted by a flying fish, much to the mirth of everyone else on board, I still can't forget it.

And unluckily, Micah also hasn't forgotten about our conversation. When we get back into our hotel room about an hour later, he closes the door behind me and summarily sweeps me off my feet.

"Micah!" I yell, shocked. My legs kick in protest but he carries me with relative ease over to the couch and sits with me on his lap. "Do you want to tell me what was bothering you now?"

"You didn't have to carry me, you know?"

"Didn't have to. But wanted to. Now tell me. What happened at the picnic?"

I blow out a breath staring up at the ceiling. I don't want to talk about this. I *really* don't want to talk about it, but knowing Micah, he's not going to let this go. So I have no choice but to try and explain it as maturely as possible.

"It was nothing," I say. "I just thought, since you and Tate were hitting it off, maybe it was just time to make my exit."

I say it as effortlessly as I can, as though the bad thoughts weren't eating me inside. I'm hoping he won't dig deeper but that's clearly too much to hope for.

"Hitting it off?" He sounds confused at first, and then his eyes flare in understanding. "Wait, you mean like flirting?"

I try to imitate a casual shrug, but I don't quite think I land it. "I mean, that's what it looked like. I thought maybe you wanted to... anyway, I didn't want to be a third wheel so I gave you your space."

Micah makes a choking sputtering sound. The look on his face is a combination of shocked and wounded, and he stares at me like I said something so insanely crazy.

"You thought I was flirting with your friend in front of you?"

I try another shrug. Once again, I think I miss the mark. "I mean there's nothing wrong with it. We're not exclusive or anything."

"Yes we damn sure are," he snaps, shocking me. "Let's not lie to ourselves. For as long as this fling lasts neither of us is fucking anybody other than each other. And if I see you with that *friend* of yours, touching all over you again, I'm gonna snap his wrist for good this time."

I snort at the impassioned look on his face. "Okay, Don Corleone. I get it."

It takes a second, but amusement finally appears on his features, and his anger retreats.

He sighs. "Maybe it's my fault for not discussing it before, but I thought it was understood that we're exclusive. And even if we weren't, I'm not that much of a heel that I would flirt with your friend in front of you. Come on, that's tacky as hell."

He looks so offended that I would even think such a thing that I have to believe him. Now that I think about it, my view of that scene was probably already colored by my feelings of inadequacy and jealousy toward Tate.

And now that I realize it, I can't help but be ashamed. I duck my head. "Yeah, you're right. I was probably just PMS-ing."

He smirks. "Yeah. Same way I was PMS-ing when I hit your friend Bobby."

"Robbie."

"Whatever."

I smirk at the dark jealousy in his voice. He's still mad about that conversation with Robbie. It's unbelievable, but also unbelievably vindicating.

And because of that, I find myself admitting, "It's just that, with Tate, there's something between us that I can't explain. Maybe it's because we've known each other most of our lives and we're both friends with Emma. But I can't help but compare myself to her, and I fall short every time." There. The words are out. I also feel the need to clarify that Tate's not at fault here. "She's never done anything to explicitly stoke the jealousy though. She's always been nice and thoughtful, but for some reason, I can't help but be jealous of her."

Micah takes a few thoughtful seconds. And I start to feel a bit more embarrassed. And then he says, "I think I know what you mean."

"You do?"

"Yeah." He smiles. "My brother and I went to the same private school, and everyone always compared me to him. I think that's standard when it comes to having an older brother, but Tristan was also just better than me in every way. Smarter. Kinder. Calmer."

"Was he a ladies' man too?" I tease softly, and he shakes his head.

"Nah. That was the worst part though. He was decent with the ladies, but he never actually made an effort. It was like he didn't have to. Girls just gravitated toward him and even some of my hookups would probably have preferred to be with him. All the smart girls liked him, wanted to be with him, but they only wanted to fuck me. And they weren't shy about letting me know who they thought the better brother was."

It's my turn to stay quiet for a few seconds, sympathy blooming in my chest. "I'm sorry. That must have sucked."

"It did. I almost hated him for a bit there, but it was hard to. He was just so *nice*. And super understanding. Really, the best brother." He sighs. "Sometimes I can't believe he's gone."

His loss magnifies in the air and I wrap my hands around his neck, burying my face in his chest. I let him have a few more seconds before he says, "Anyway, that's probably why I'm the way I am with women. Maybe it's a deep insecurity stemming from my brother."

I can sense the forced levity in his tone, so I pull back and quip, "Maybe. Or maybe you're just a horn dog."

He winks. "That too."

We both laugh and it's like a weight lifts from the whole room.

We spend most of the night trading stories about our childhood and our insecurities. And then at some point, I fall asleep in his lap and feel him carrying me to bed.

It's a bizarre night, but it's one of the best I've had in a while.

CHAPTER TWENTY-EIGHT

M ICAH

The next day, Declan sends me an early text to "meet him in the office for vital business matters."

Yes, that's actually how he phrases it because the anal man can't simply text someone, "Hey, come over and let's talk." Or even just call. I mean he knows I'm better with phone calls than texting, so a call would be the best way to reach me. But he probably thinks calling would indicate some kind of friendship between us and God forbid he ever admit such a thing.

I smirk as I reread the message, shaking my head. After all that time we've spent together and all we've been through including him literally bleeding on me, Declan doesn't seem ready to accept our friendship yet.

Oh well. I'm not in a hurry. I'll wear him down eventually.

After replying to his text with a cheery "okey dokey," I turn over to watch Carly, still fast asleep in bed. Her hair is all mussed around her face and her mouth is slightly open, a trail of drool streaking her cheek. She didn't wipe her mascara off yesterday and it leaked down her eyes, giving her the look of a goth chick going through a bad breakup. One hand is thrown over half her face, and the other clutches the blanket, as though someone's going to steal it from her. As if she's not the worst blanket hog in the entire world.

I shake my head, feeling a smile slowly spread my lips.

She's a mess. A vibrant, crazy, gorgeous mess.

I keep watching her for even more seconds, reaching over to draw her hair back over so I can take in even more of her features. I can't believe what she told me yesterday about her being jealous of Tate Moon. I mean I guess I can believe it since I saw the way her mood changed when I talked to Tate, but I can't believe that (A) she would think that I would flirt with another woman in front of her (elderly nurses don't count), and (B) she actually thought Tate was better than her.

How on earth does Carly not see how gorgeous and amazing she is?

Who did such a number on her that she can't even see her own worth?

Moreover, I thought I made it clear how crazy I am about her, and how hard it is to even notice anyone else when she's around. It's something I've pondered and tried to wrap my head around, but I can't, so I've simply just accepted that she's captivated me. And yeah, Tate is pretty, I suppose, and her mother is fascinatingly terrifying, but none of them have held my interest even half as much as Carly does. None of them form distinct images that pop up in my head often, of her eyes sparking with ire, or when her lips get that sarcastic quirk to them. Or when she says something witty or rolls her eyes at one of my antics.

I don't know how to describe the feeling Carly gives me. It's not just the lust, and I don't just like her. I feel... more myself when I'm with her. She's comfortable, like a warm blanket by the fireplace. Like I can relax and not worry about being the Micah Landing everyone else expects me to be.

I don't have to be the replacement for my brother like my dad expects.

Or a true blueblood like my grandfather wants.

Or the good Christian child my mother always wanted.

And I don't have to be the life of the party either. Most of my friends expect that side of me, and while it's fun sometimes, it's exhausting.

But with her, I can just be Micah. Last night proved it. When we opened up to each other, baring our vulnerability, I somehow didn't feel the need to hold back. I wanted her to see all of me, even the childish parts of me that made me feel small. And I think she wanted the same in reverse. There was nothing she could have said last night that would have made me see her as any less. And maybe she felt the same way about me.

I don't know. But I didn't want the night to end.

And I hope this fling lasts for a good while, because I'd like to explore this "fun" for as long as possible. Of course, until I inevitably get bored of it, at which point we'll go our separate ways, no harm no foul.

I see her eyes squeeze shut, and her eyebrows furrow, as though preternaturally detecting that she's being watched.

I take advantage of that to lay a soft kiss on her lips. "Rise and shine sleeping beauty."

"Ugh..." she groans, one eye opening and squinting up at me. "Oh, I hate you. You look so nice and put together when you wake up and I look like the witch who gave snow white the apple."

I chuckle. "Well, technically that witch was also a beautiful queen so... I guess I see the resemblance."

"Are you trying to butter me up by saying I look both like a witch and like a queen?"

"The dichotomy of woman."

She levels a weak punch at my arm and I laugh as I catch her fist, once again pressing it against my lips.

"What are you up to today?" I ask her.

"School." She stretches as she replies. "I have to be there at nine a.m. Speaking of which, what time is it?"

I check the clock on the other side of the bed. "Eight-thirty."

She freezes, then instantly bolts up in bed. "You're kidding."

"Nope." And she confirms for herself when her eyes meet the hands of the clock. That sends her careening over as she tumbles out of bed to grab her jeans.

"Oh my gosh, why didn't you wake me up? I'm going to be late. Oh, God, and it just had to be Kennedy's class that I'm going to be late for. I know he's just dying to mark me absent and destroy my perfect attendance. Seriously, Micah, you should have woken me up."

"I didn't know what time your class was." I shrug. "Plus, you looked so beautiful when you were sleeping, I was entranced by your spell."

That earns me an oh-so-delightful eye roll as she runs around getting ready, gathering her hair in a bun at the top of her head, brushing her teeth, washing her face, pulling on clothes.

Meanwhile, I head over to the kitchen area and make her some coffee (lots of cream like she likes it), and also order a breakfast sandwich over the phone to be quickly wrapped and brought up.

"Hey." She pokes her head out of the bathroom and holds up my shirt. "Can I borrow this? I don't want to wear my shirt. It smells like fish."

"Knock yourself out," I say and she goes back in. It only takes her a few minutes to get ready and by that time, the sandwich has arrived and I also have her coffee in a monogrammed hotel mug ready to go for her. I would have put it in a Stanley cup or a thermos if I had one, but alas, I have to make do.

I hand it to her when we finally get into the car, and that's when she realizes what I'm holding in my hand.

"You ordered that for me?"

"Yup," I say. "And made the coffee too. Breakfast is the most important meal of the day as my grandmother used to say. Of course, she also lived on a steady diet of coffee and cigars. She was more of a do-as-I-say-not-as-I-do kind of woman."

Her eyes soften as she takes it and says a tad shyly. "Thank you."

"No problem."

Throughout the drive, Carly keeps sipping her coffee and eating her sandwich, throwing me grateful looks as though I gave her a kidney rather than overpriced hotel breakfast food. I mean I don't mind her gratitude, but the fact she's gushing so much over so little means that she's very much not used to people doing stuff like that for her, at least not the men she dates.

"None of your former boyfriends ever got you food?" I inquire as I overtake a jeep on the highway.

She snorts so hard she nearly spills her coffee. "What boyfriend?"

"You've never had a boyfriend?"

"Nah." She shakes her head. "I was always too busy to date, and then there was my family to think about. Everyone in town knew who they were, and parents warned their little boys to stay away from me."

"And they all did?" In my experience, teenage boys weren't so good at taking their parents' advice.

"Not all of them. But the ones who didn't were only interested in hookups so that was all we did.

I gape at her. "Seriously?"

She nods.

I turn back to the wheel, indignant. I feel a violent surge of anger toward all those boys who used her like that. I mean, yeah, I know teenage boys can be stupid but… still.

"Relax," she giggles. "It wasn't like that. I was also just interested in hooking up. Most of them were either dumb jocks or they were out-of-towners who I'd never see again, which is good because I didn't want to get a reputation.

Ah, yes. Small towns and the ever-important reputation.

I'm still mad at them though, and at their parents and everyone else in this damn town who made her bear scorn for things that weren't her fault. Jeez, no wonder she had low self-esteem.

And all those jackasses took advantage of it. "Assholes."

She gives me an amused look. "Really? You're that bothered by it?"

"Of course."

"Isn't that exactly what you used to do to the women you dated?"

"No," I deny instantly. "I never rejected them for their background."

Carly sent me an amused, yet disbelieving look.

"I didn't," I say. "It's only recently, thanks to my grandpa's whole ultimatum, that I even paid attention to such things. I never cared about who their parents were or where they were from."

"So why did you reject them?"

I hesitate, trying to think of it. "I don't know. It just never felt... right."

She eyes me for a few more seconds, then sips her coffee and turns away.

But the more I look at it, the more I realize that I was callous in my treatment of those women the same way those men were callous in their treatment of Carly.

Up until Carly, I only had extremely casual relationships. As much as I tried to go for women who knew the score and only wanted something casual from me in return, I knew that quite a few of them inevitably ended up catching some kind of feelings for me. And I wouldn't always move on when they did. Sometimes I would string them along simply because I was bored, or because the sex was good and I didn't want to bother with the whole breakup drama. And then when I had my feelings, I would simply disappear from their lives.

And then it hits me, the uncomfortable, ugly truth. I'm not just as bad as those men. I'm worse.

And though Carly pretends like she doesn't care, some part of it must sting.

It's not often I'm ashamed of my actions, but shame peppers my thoughts even after I drop Carly off from school.

I head back to Laketown for the meeting with Declan, only for him to postpone it to the afternoon so he can spend time with his daughter. I don't mind. I get that his daughter comes first.

I decide to get breakfast at a restaurant opposite the Tiki Bar called My Fair Lady Steakhouse. They're offering a breakfast buffet and it doesn't smell half bad. The place has a rustic, old bed-and-breakfast vibe mixed with log cabin charm. The smell of sizzling bacon and rich coffee colors the air, and my mouth waters.

Conversations buzz around me as I walk to the front, where a tall, curvy woman with sad eyes stares at me from behind the counter.

I smile at her, but she doesn't smile back. And I guess I do it for a tad too long because her frown deepens.

"What do you want?" she says.

"Well, some food would be nice," I quip but she still doesn't crack a smile.

"You the owner?" I ask because she gives off an aura of command.

She nods and simply gestures down the line, looking away dismissively.

As I go down the line, a rounder, kindly older woman in front of me, leans in to whisper, "You'll have to forgive, Lou. She's having a bad few months and her boyfriend just got locked up."

"Really?"

She nods, but she doesn't say anything more.

After I'm done grabbing some bacon, eggs, steak, and a coffee, I search around for somewhere to sit. Though the venue is packed, I manage to find an empty table where I can spend time with my own thoughts, and guilt, alone.

Or at least alone for the first few minutes of my meal. Before I finish up, Poppy and the kindly woman from before walk up to my table.

Poppy sits without any invitation, but the older woman asks, "Young man, can you please pull that out for me?"

"Sure thing." Not sure what this is about, but I get up and help her into a seat.

"Good." She sighs as she settles. "I gotta wait for my antacids to kick in or I'm going to be farting up a storm on my way out of here."

"Ah." Instantly, I know who the woman is. "You must be Mrs. Peach."

Carly told me about her and her tendency to mention her stomach issues even in polite company.

"That I am. My Carly told you about me, didn't she? Of course, she did." She answers her own question, her smile widening. "You know, I heard you attended the picnic with my Carly yesterday. I hope you don't mind me being a nosy Nelly, but that little girl is like a daughter to me and I don't want her hurt. So I want to make sure you have only the purest intentions toward her. You picking up what I'm putting down?"

I take a sip of my coffee and say, "I think so."

"You better know so," Poppy says, giving me a hard look. "I've seen your type before, city boys looking to schlub it with a small-town girl and then taking off when they get her pregnant or worse. If you think you can do that to Carly, you've got another think coming. I've got a little friend here that I can introduce to your caboose anytime you fuck up. So don't fuck up. You got it?"

I raise an eyebrow at the thinly veiled threat. "I got it. My caboose likes to be intact, so I won't fuck up. Look, I'm not trying to hurt Carly. We're not..." I don't want to tell these women we're just sleeping together because I have a feeling Poppy might plug me with a warning shot if I do. So I say, "Everything's still new and we're not really sure what this is yet. But I assure you I'm being as honest and fair to her as I can be. And don't ever say that schlubbing thing about her again. Nothing schlubby about Carly." That last part comes out in a harder tone than I expected, and I can tell it surprises the women.

Poppy peers at me. "You know what folks around here say about her right?"

"Yeah," I meet the older woman's gaze head-on. "And I don't give a damn. Stupid people are stupid people. They can think whatever they want. Carly is an amazing woman and I'm proud to be dating her." I shrug.

The two women share a long look and then Mrs. Peach turns back to me with a glint in her eyes. She beams. "When you're done eating, you should come with us, Mitch."

"It's Micah," I correct smoothly. "And where to?"

"To St. Jude. It's bible study today."

"Oh, erm..." I murmur a little awkwardly. "You should know I'm not really religious."

Her smile only widens. "It's alright. Jesus doesn't mind."

CHAPTER TWENTY-NINE

CARLY

Once I get out of class, I think of calling Micah to come pick me up, but I stop myself.

Why do I need to call him when I can get myself back to Laketown just as well without him? Why am I relying on him for a ride now? As a matter of fact, why did I rely on him to get me up on time and bring me here in the first place?

I should have taken a cab or an Uber or something, even though those were practically impossible to come by in Laketown. Still, I should have figured something out myself so that I didn't have to owe him any favors. So I don't rely on him.

Because eventually he's going to leave and then what am I going to do?

I shake my head.

No. I can't start relying on Micah. He's already told me multiple times that he's not a reliable person and when someone tells you who they are, believe them. Even when they start doing things like giving me massages and making me coffee. And paying my dad's hospital bills. And cuddling with me at night, and making me feel better about myself and my negative emotions. Even when he sometimes looks at me like he feels something... something deeper....

I can't believe it.

I have to take him at face value and not even let myself think about anything beyond that.

Micah Landing is not a forever guy. He's simply around for a good time and soon he'll be gone. I need to come to terms with it.

And even if he did want something serious with me–and that's a big if born only from the most delusional of minds–what's the end goal here? He clearly doesn't want to stay in Laketown for more than a few months and as much as I want to, I can't leave. Not yet.

So even on that fundamental level, we wouldn't work. Not to mention bigger incompatibilities, our families and such.

There are so many reasons why this can't work, why we can't take each other seriously. So I guess in that way we're on the same page.

I smirk and then head to the bus station, waiting for the bus that'll take me down to Laketown. While there, I finally open up my messages to see that Micah texted me twice, one of them to say, "Headed to church with Mrs. Peach and Poppy."

I frown at that. He told me he had a meeting with Declan that morning. *How on earth did he end up with Mrs. Peach? And why church?*

I thought you said you weren't religious, I text back.

The answer comes almost instantly. *I told her that too. She said Jesus doesn't care.*

I snort. That does sound like something Mrs. Peach would say.

You need me to come pick you up? he texts next.

No, I'm fine. I'll come meet you at church. I'm curious to see what Mrs. Peach has him doing over there, and the sight of Micah with the old ladies bent over their Bibles or leading a prayer sends me into peals of laughter.

But, lo and behold, what I find is even funnier.

Micah isn't necessarily in the church itself. Rather, he's in the church parking lot, surrounded by rose bushes and wearing sweatpants, an eighties bright pink top and a matching headband.

He's also practicing yoga along with a dozen other elderly people, who are all separated by mats as they face off against Tate who is leading the class.

"Alright, guys, now I want you to get into the downward dog, and just inhale," Tate says.

"What on earth?" I look behind me and see Declan approaching also with a puzzled look on his face. He looks at me in question. I shrug.

"I have no idea. I just got here."

Declan turns back to Micah. "We're supposed to meet for a late lunch. He told me to pick him up here, but I had no idea this was why."

And Micah clearly enjoys surprising us, because, in the middle of his downward dog, he turns and gives us both a wave and a wink.

And Micah really seems into it too, executing the stretch perfectly and then turning to tell Mrs. Henderson beside him, "No, my love, you have to extend your back a little more. Just a little. Engage your core."

"I'm gonna pop a hip if I do that."

"No, you won't. Let me show you." He stands and then goes to her, his hand hovering over his body. "May I?"

"Please," she sends him a flirtatious smile, which he returns with a wink of his own.

Micah then gently positions her body into a better pose that takes the weight off her lower body. He also puts his hand on her stomach and asks her to inhale and hold the strength there so she can find her balance. He then makes micro-adjustments to her posture so she neither overextends nor rounds out her back. It takes Mrs. Henderson a few tries but she finally gets it. Micah's so gentle and patient in his guidance that even Poppy looks impressed. Her eyes meet mine over their heads, and she gives me a little nod and a thumbs up.

And then, when Mrs. Henderson is more stable, Micah gets back into his pose, closes his eyes, and transitions into a child's pose.

"That's right," he says to the class. "Feel the stretch."

"I'm feeling something alright. And it's 'embarrassed.'" Old Man Shoreton snarls, his hands shaking in an attempt to hold the pose.

"Embarrassment is just shame leaving your body," Micah says, which makes the old man snort and half the class laugh.

It continues like that for another few minutes until Tate finally calls out, "And that's the last move guys. Good job. You guys really did great today."

"Yeah, that's thanks to your pansy assistant over there," Shoreton responds with a theatrical whisper, jabbing his head in Micah's direction though everyone already knows who he's talking about.

Micah doesn't take offense. "I resemble that remark," he says as he bounces to his feet, jogging over to meet me and Declan bright-eyed.

"Hey, guys. What do you think?"

Declan looks too discombobulated to even speak.

I shake my head and snort at his clothes. "What's with the getup?"

He glances down at himself. "Oh, this old thing? It was all they had in the church lost and found. Mrs. Peach wouldn't let me go home and change before yoga. She seemed to think that I wouldn't come back."

"Right.

"And how did you end up getting dragged into the yoga session anyway?" Declan asks.

"It's a long story," Micah sighs dramatically. "But basically, what happened is that during bible study, Mrs. Peach was telling me about her waist problem, and then I go, 'You know what would help with that? Yoga.' She tells me that Tate will be having a yoga session in the afternoon, but she's too embarrassed to go because she'll be the oldest one there. And I told her that it was nonsense and that she should go and rock her stuff, and in between trying to encourage her, I somehow got wrapped in it. She was saying that she wouldn't go unless I did and well... I ended up here."

Declan sends that puzzled look to me as though to say, "What do you even see in this dweeb?"

I, on the other hand, am trying my best not to laugh. And that's when I get that warm tingling feeling in my chest.

That feeling gives me pause and wipes the smile

right off my face.

Oh no.

I think I know what that is.

Because while I like suave, sexy Micah, and dominant Micah, and heck even arrogant Micah…

Goofy Micah, the one in the pink headband, the one who escorts old ladies to yoga. That man is my kryptonite.

And that's when I know I'm in serious trouble.

I look away from him and immediately catch Tate's eyes. She's standing a little away from the crowd, near the back of the parking lot. I get the feeling she's been waiting to talk to me for some time and now that we're looking at each other, she beckons me over.

"Give me a second, guys," I say to the two men before I walk to her.

I barely get there before she begins talking.

"Hey, I just wanted to apologize," she starts. "You know with me telling Emma about your problem. You were right, it's not my place to interfere and even though it came from a place of genuine care, I shouldn't have butted my nose into something that wasn't my business."

I blink at her.

"Well, thank you for saying that," I respond. And since she's being honest, I decide to be honest right back. "I can't lie, I was really pissed when you did that."

"Yeah, I know." She gives me a wry look. "Try as you might, Carly, you're not very good at hiding your emotions. Which is how I also know you don't really like me very much. No, don't deny it." She holds up her hand when I try to protest. "I've known for a while. Even Emma knows. She thinks it's because of all those shitty questions I asked when we were younger. I know now how uncomfortable they made you. I'm sorry about that. I didn't mean it that way; I just don't think before things come out of my mouth sometimes."

I sigh. This isn't where or how I wanted to have this conversation, but it's a conversation we need to have. Tate is doing her part. I need to do mine too.

I stare Tate in the eyes, feeling like I'm seeing her for the first time. And I want her to see me too.

"I don't dislike you, Tate," I tell her. "Honest. I was just always ferociously jealous of you."

Her perfectly arched eyebrows climb up her forehead. "*Jealous* of me?"

"Well, duh. Half the girls in our class were, maybe except Emma because she has a heart of gold. Have you seen yourself? You're gorgeous. Accomplished. Smart. And you don't take shit from anyone. I wanted to be you but hard as I might try, I couldn't do it."

Tate remains wide-eyed for the better part of a minute.

And she bursts into loud peals of laughter, which attracts the attention of some of the elderly leaving the lot.

"Jealous?" she says in a much lower tone. "*You* were jealous of *me*?"

"Of course."

"Oh, Carly. I was jealous of you too."

"Really?" I frown. Now that made no sense. "Why would you be?"

She shakes her head. "I guess you don't see yourself

as you are either. Carly, I've always admired your strength and how driven you are. How you hold your head up high despite your disaster of a family. How hard you work to take care of them still and make a name for yourself. How you stand up to them while still loving them. That's a balance I've never found with my mom and she's not quite as bad. And, Carly, you... I've never seen anyone more driven and kinder than you. Even to people who don't deserve it."

I stand there staring at her. I truly don't know what to say. This wasn't at all how I expected today to go, and this talk has even veered off the cliff as well.

Tate Moon was jealous of me, Carly Huntley.

It sounds so ridiculous, I can't even imagine it.

But Tate stands there, looking slightly unsure, as though she just bared a deep insecurity of hers.

I can't hold back anymore.

Suddenly, I burst out laughing.

The best part is that Tate does too.

CHAPTER THIRTY

M ICAH

Carly's in a great mood when we head back to the hotel. I guess her talk with Tate must have been good, because she laughs at all my jokes in the car, even the really stupid ones. And the minute we get into my hotel room and I close the door behind her, she's on me, her lips capturing mine with the fury of pent-up hunger.

Passion erupts throughout my body, sinking my goodwill. My hand grips her waist, and I have to fight every instinct so I can push her away.

"'Wait, Carly." I tear my lips away and her mouth attacks my neck. She nips a sensitive spot and for a second, I forget how to think and breathe and speak. Her teeth score the edge of my skin, biting down slightly before suckling hard enough to leave a hickey.

"Oh, baby." God, she's so hungry for it and it's making

me lose it.

My cock is already at attention, my hips unconsciously seeking the juncture of her thighs. And then her tongue traces down a very sensitive line in my neck and I purr.

I fucking purr for her.

I need to get a hold of myself.

"We need to talk." Somehow the words end up gasping out of my mouth, even though I have no recollection of saying them.

"About what?" Her voice is as hurried as her movement, her fingers shoving underneath my shirt, her palms smoothing over my heated skin.

"Stuff," I tell her hoarsely, not knowing what I'm talking about or how I even managed to get those words out. "We need to talk about stuff."

If you ask me exactly what that stuff is right about now, I have not the slightest idea.

Her kisses make my mind flail, her naughty tongue making a weakling out of me. As she licks my pulse, my knees shake. All the blood rushes from my head down south.

Fuck, fuck, fuck.

I want her pussy in my mouth. I can smell it from here, her desire. I can feel the desperation in her shaky hands as she attempts to tear off my clothes. I want to give her the heat she so desperately seeks, to stoke the fire inside her.

I want to fuck her till we both can't move.

But there's a reason I can't do it. I don't know the reason yet, but I know there is one pushed to the back of my mind by a wave of impossible lust.

But fuck it, I *need* her right now.

More importantly, she needs me.

I pick her up in my arms, seeking to carry her to the closest surface. I don't have the presence of mind to find a bed right now, but as I walk, my ankle hits a side table, and Carly whispers, "Sorry."

That's not enough to stop me though. I keep moving, bumping into things, eyes slightly unseeing due to the sheer force of the desire pumping in my veins. But it's not until I nearly face-plant into a flower vase, that I finally stop and take a breath.

I pause, tense up my whole body, and bury my face in her hair.

Breathe, Micah. Think. Fuck. You're not a fucking randy little teenager led around by your dick. Take a second and think about what you're doing.

So I stand there, in the middle of the God-knows-where, and do breathing exercises like a fucking newb. In. Out. In. Out.

When I come back to myself, it's to find Carly with her shoulders shaking, her face buried in my chest.

It takes me a second to realize what she's doing.

"Are you laughing at me right now?"

"No," she says even though her voice is watery and she snorts too. And when she pulls back actual tears of mirth are rolling down her cheeks. "I'm not laughing at you. I'm laughing at… the situation."

"The situation."

"Yeah. It's funny, isn't it?"

I shake my head but crack a smile. It may not be funny right now, but from the outside looking in, it is kind of a funny situation.

She chuckles a little more wiping the tears out of her eyes, and then she wraps her arms around my neck. "Okay. So are we good now?"

She trails her finger down my chest and gives me a come-hither look. I shut my eyes trying to block out the images she sends storming through my brain.

"Actually, we need to talk about something first."

"What is it?" she asks.

"Carly I... shit, I'm not good at this." I take a deep breath. "I've just... I guess I've just recently realized that I care about you. A crap ton. And I wanted to let you know that before we have sex. This isn't... what we have isn't just regular sex to me. I'm not really sure what it is, but it's not like anything I've ever felt before. I care about you, Carly. I really do. I'm a selfish man by nature so that might rear its ugly head here and there. And this whole might fall apart at any point, because who the fuck even knows what we're doing? But whatever happens, just remember that I do care about you. Okay?" That's what I want to tell her. I wanted to tell her that before we have sex again, so she wouldn't think I was doing the same thing as all those other men, those idiots who used and tossed her aside.

Idiots like I used to be.

She doesn't say anything. She just stares at me for a long time with a fathomless look in her eyes that I can't decipher. Annoyance? Sadness? Pain? Humor? I don't know.

But then she gives me an even more mysterious sad little smile and then cups my face pulling my lips back to hers. This time I don't stop her. I can't even if I wanted to.

We take it slowly this time. I break off the kiss so I can safely navigate us to a bed. And then I lay her down like the princess she is. I take her lips again, teasing her tongue into a gentle unhurried dance. And then I pull back and kiss her closed eyelid, the tip of her nose, and her lips.

I care about you, Carly. I try to instill that thought into every touch and every embrace. *I really*, really *do.*

What happens next isn't the wild and furious sex we usually have. It's the exact type of sex that I would see in movies and roll my eyes at because it was just so unrealistically sappy. I would even call it boring.

But nothing is boring about what's going on here. The two of us are filled with so many emotions, and we try to communicate them with tender touches, and kisses, and sucking, and loving.

Our bodies express everything our mouths can't do properly. We don't stop when we orgasm. We don't even know when the waves rise and fall. All we know is finding pleasure in each other and a mutually assured connection.

A connection is all I can call it now because I don't really know what I feel for her.

But the depth of it scares me.

Declan and I finally have our talk the next morning. It turns out that he's about to make me a job offer.

"My father wants me to restore a series of national buildings back in New York. I want to enlist you as our lead architect on the project. Or if you're ready we can take on your entire firm."

I widen my eyes when he tells me. "Are you serious?"

"Yes," he says. "I wouldn't tell you if I weren't serious.

Are you not interested?"

"No, I am. It's just something of this scale... I mean you realize that I'm just getting the firm off the ground again, right? And you haven't even seen my portfolio."

"Well, I heard you talking about it the other day to Hal and you seemed to know your stuff. Besides, I know you."

"What's that supposed to mean?" Is he going to give me the role just because he knows me? That doesn't sound like Declan.

But it turns out that's not what he meant at all.

"I know you're too arrogant to do something you're not good at and put this much effort into it. It's why you destroy all the businesses that you only had middling success in and those you have no interest in too, just for shits and giggles. Because deep inside, you hate being mediocre at anything. For you to put all your effort into reviving an architecture firm despite the obstacles in your way indicates not only passion but talent." He cocks his head. "Or am I wrong?"

I nearly fall over. I'm surprised that Declan managed to read me so well. Especially since he still doesn't think we're friends.

"No," I tell him. "No, you're not wrong. But Declan I had no idea you were paying such close attention to me. You do care after all."

"The nature of the job means you'll have to do the planning with me in person." He completely ignores my words, moving straight back into business. "Which means you'll need to be in Laketown because I don't plan on leaving my pregnant wife and daughter alone.

"I don't mind staying here for a few more months," I answer quickly, too quickly because Declan gives me a knowing look.

"What?" I say defensively. "It's not forever. Just a few months."

"Right," he snorts. "Be careful. That's what I say too. But Laketown has a way of sinking its teeth into you and making itself your forever home.

CHAPTER THIRTY-ONE

C ARLY

I can't stop smiling and it's becoming a problem.

Yule already caught me doing it twice, smiling at nothing while I was wiping down the counter. After the third time, on his way back to the kitchen, he frowns and asks me, "You doing okay, Carly?"

"Of course," I answer without looking up. "Why?"

"Because you seem exceptionally chipper today. And I haven't seen you looking like that for a while."

I finally glance up and say, "I'm not sure what you're talking about."

Yule raises an eyebrow. "You've had that cat-ate-the-canary grin all morning. What gives?"

"Oh, she ate something alright," Emma calls from her position behind the cocktail bar. She has a shit-eating grin on her face and she winks at Yule conspiratorially. "Or maybe it's the other way round. Maybe something ate her."

"Oh, you hush your mouth, Emma Jane." I giggle as a hot blush fills my face, and Emma snorts her amusement. Meanwhile, Yule looks between us even more confused.

"Alright, either of you want to tell me what's going on here?"

"Nothing's going on," I say. "It's just been a good day." And it was. The Tiki Bar has been busy all day but never too busy. We have enough staff to cover all the tables and no one has dropped or spilled anything today. Plus, all my tables were big tippers and I have several hundred bucks tucked into my jeans.

Now that things have wound down in preparation for the evening rush, what's there not to be happy about?

"Yeah, right." Emma isn't willing to let it go like that. She puts one hand up around her mouth to block my view and then stage-whispers to Yule. "Carly has a boyfriend."

"No, I do not!" I protest like a teenage girl, which makes Emma giggle even more madly, and even Yule cracks a smile. He crosses his arms over his chest and he leans against the counter.

"A boyfriend, huh?" he says teasingly. "And do I know this fella?"

"You don't know him because he doesn't exist. I don't have a boyfriend."

"It's Micah Landing," Emma says, talking over me and Yule's smile turns puzzled.

"I don't think I know that name, Landing. Is he one of the mayor's out-of-wedlock kids?"

"No. He's Declan's friend. You know the one with red hair, tall, handsome. He was at my engagement party.

"Oh, that guy?" Yule's smile instantly turns into a frown. "Carly, no offense, but that guy doesn't seem like the kind of man you make a boyfriend."

"No offense taken, Yule, because you're exactly right. And Micah isn't my boyfriend." I send Emma a pointed look. "We're just hooking up."

"Right," Yule says. "But even then, you gotta be careful. You know how you women are. One second you're just hooking up and the next second you're getting your own heart broken because you start asking all types of questions about 'what are we' and dropping 'L-bombs' here and there, while he was honest with you from the beginning that he just wanted a simple roll in the hay. And now he looks like the asshole for leaving you, and you get angry enough that you justify slashing his brand-new tires that he just got for half off."

We both blink at Yule after his little rant, and Emma tentatively asks, "Erm, you okay, Yule?"

"Yeah. Just an old memory. I'm over it." The irritated flash on his face tells us he's not that over it, but he continues. "Anyway, just be careful. It'll be easy to fall for a pretty face like that and want to believe any lies he tells you, but you gotta remember who he is, and who you are. And he may not even mean to hurt you. It may just be in his DNA. Guys that look like that have been breaking women's hearts since they could walk."

"I will," I assure him and stick my tongue out at Emma who rolls her eyes while still chortling. Everything Yule said I already knew. No matter what Micah tells me, I'm still not deluding myself about the nature of our relationship. It's a short-term fling, a situationship at best. Sure, he might feel "things" for me, but those are directly linked to how much fun we have together and how fuckable he finds me. They're certainly not things that I can even start to mistake as love.

So I know all of that.

But that still doesn't stop me from smiling at inopportune moments during the night, when I think about him again.

Especially when I think about him in that stupid pink shirt doing yoga with the elderly. Or him getting my coffee ready while I rush to school, calmly handing it to me in the car like it's no big deal. Or even just how he looks when he's telling me about his dream to recondition the New York skyline and make housing more sustainable and affordable, or when he tells me jokes about all those stupid things he did in the past.

Now I see why all those women found it so hard to let go once the relationship was done. It wasn't just the mind-blowing sex, although that's certainly part of it too. But the thing that's going to be hardest to let go of is the companionship, the banter, the comfortable routine of hanging with each other every single day and just talking.

Oh, God, slow down, Carly. Yule is right. You really have to be careful here, because you're going toward the deep end.

I pull back from my thoughts and decide not to think about Micah for the rest of the evening.

But it's difficult because I find myself doing so anyway at odd times during the evening rush. Sometimes I'll hear a joke and think, *Micah would probably enjoy that. I should tell him later.* I'll see someone wink and it will remind me of him. It's awful, and If I was in the right presence of mind, I would realize that it's pretty dangerous for me to be thinking this way. But I can't help it.

"Hello." A knock on the table finally gets me out of my reverie and I glance down at the patron in front of me. Oh, God, I zoned out right as I was about to take his order and, now he and his table full of large flannel-wearing men are looking at me like I'm crazy.

"I'm so sorry about that," I apologize instantly. "My mind's kind of a mess today. What did you want to order?"

A leer spreads across the man's face, chasing away his annoyance as his eyes crawl down my body.

"I don't suppose you're on the menu, are you?" he drawls as his friends snicker between themselves. I raise an eyebrow.

"No," I say firmly. "I'm not. But I do recommend the special, Chef Yule's making a mean tomahawk today, and it goes well with the mac and cheese."

"Nah," he says. "Not a huge fan of cheese. But I do like a nice curvy woman that can keep me warm at night. And I'm wondering how much I gotta blow on a meal to get her."

My lip turns. *Ew. Creep.*

"It's not happening," I tell him in a polite but firm voice. The man is pretty huge and I don't want repercussions.

He laughs. "Oh, come on, don't pretend to be all uppity now, Carly? Don't you remember me? And what we had in high school?"

Huh? High school? I peer at the man not trying to recognize him behind his bushy beard and his balding head. But I'm drawing a blank.

"It's me," he says. 'Tiny Tony."

Tiny... the name takes a while to ring a bell and when it does, I almost groan in regret. Of course. He was one of the boys I made out with in my freshman year of high school. But he looks nothing like what he did before. He was short and scrawny at the time, but he had really sweet blue eyes and he seemed nice and harmless enough when he asked me to hook up. Part of the reason I said yes to it is because I knew his family was leaving town the next day and I thought there was a good chance I would never see him again, and he wouldn't have time to go around spreading rumors about me after it was done. It seemed like a good idea at the time.

But now seeing what he's become, I regret it deeply.

Still, he's a customer so I try to be pleasant. I fake a friendly smile. "Hey, Tony. How's it going? Nice to see you back."

"It's going pretty good. Great now that I've seen you." He seems to take our previous fling as an excuse to lean in to whisper, "You still as good with your tongue as I remember?"

My entire being flushes with anger and indignation, especially as his friends laugh meanly.

Before I can stop myself, I snap back, "I don't know. You still as stupid as I remember or did you finally pass eighth-grade math?"

That makes his friends laugh even more, and some anger tightens Tony's features.

But he retains his smile. "Feisty. Good. I like a woman with a little heat. Makes rolling around a lot more interesting."

"I'm not rolling around with you." I snap my notebook close and prepare to make my exit. "And it looks like I'm not taking your order either."

As I turn to head back to the counter, my face burning with anger, he reaches out and snags my wrist, holding me in place.

Irritation and fear pulse inside me. "Let me go."

"Now why are you being like that?" he croons. "I was going to be nice to you but now you're trying to make me the jackass."

You already were a jackass, I think but I don't say it. The fear is louder than the wrath and it's preaching that I take a lot of caution here. Tiny Tony is now a huge man and so are his friends. And he seems like the type to seek retribution.

So I gentle my voice and say, "Look this isn't the time or place. I have other customers."

"Okay, then tell me the time and the place. Where do you live?"

Yeah, like I'm going to give this asshole my address. I open my mouth ready to rattle off a fake address, when suddenly, someone clears his throat.

I look up and my heart drops.

Micah is standing a few feet away from us, near the entrance. And the look on his face is quickly growing from annoyed to dangerous.

"You know there's a lot of things in this town that I'm getting used to," Micah says as he saunters over to us. "How quiet it is. How long deliveries take. The fact there are no organic kumquats in their grocery store." He reaches us and then pins Tony with a look that can only be described as murderous. "But the one thing I can never get used to is random assholes thinking that they can just grab anyone they want. That gets me heated, especially when it's my woman."

Tony's eyes show his surprise and he shares a look with his boys before he sneers. "She's your woman?"

"Yup. So you better take that hand off, or I'll take it off for you. I'm trying to be on best behavior here so I'm giving you a chance to rectify your error.

But if you push me, believe me, you won't like my methods."

"Oh yeah?" Tony laughs like it's funny. "And what are you gonna do, preppy boy?"

Micah doesn't say anything in response. He simply closes his eyes and begins humming quietly.

The other men share a confused look as he does, but only I know what he's doing. He told me before that when he gets really angry, he sometimes has to hum to calm himself down. And that's what he's doing now.

Tony and friends find it funny, but only I know the danger they're in. I've seen Micah fight and I know what he's capable of. But I'm also worried about Micah picking a fight with them. Sure, he beat Robbie up pretty easily but these guys look rougher. And there are almost ten of them,

I try to deescalate and pry my hand out of Tony's grip. "Let me go, Tony. Please. I'm serious."

"Oh, you're serious, huh?" He gets to his feet, still chuckling. "Listen, just because you managed to get this idiot here to see you as something other than a whore doesn't mean shit to me. I remember you. I know who you really are."

The anger flares up in my chest again but before I can say anything, before I even see it coming, Micah's fist smashes into Tony's face.

CHAPTER THIRTY-TWO

M ICAH

If I had a nickel for every time I wanted to talk to Carly and ended up in a fight with some bonehead, I'd have two nickels. Which isn't a lot, but it's strange that it's happened twice in such a short time span.

I guess I can't really be surprised. Carly is beautiful and sexy and has that mysterious grace that just intrigues a soul. When she focuses on someone, it makes you feel like the most important person in the world. And being the focus of that quiet intensity feels electric. Incredible.

It's part of why I walked in here, eager to see her in the first place. She's the first person I want to tell about the deal with Declan, the only one I really want to share this exciting news with. I can already see her eyes light up, glittering with amusement at my excitement, her lips parting to flash those pearly whites at me as she utters something so delightfully snarky.

And then maybe I'll kiss her after she does. Maybe that will lead to more kissing and I'll have to take her to an empty room or a back alley where I can make love to her under the stars.

The idea heated me from the inside when I got out of my car. But when I walk in to find Carly being accosted by yet another asshole with his hand on her, that heat turns into something else entirely.

The bastard has his hand wrapped around her wrist, tugging her closer. And unlike with Robbie, her expression is wholly hostile to this man. She hates him.

Which is good. That just gives the angry red-eyed demon inside more reasons to destroy him.

As I walk to them, my vision is a haze with the only point of focus being her and the bastard.

My heart thumps like a war drum as I stride to them. I hear my voice order him to let her go. He says something stupid back. I don't care about whatever the fuck he says because the whole time, I'm just trying to give him a few seconds to see reason and obey, my blood pounding in my ears, that murderous rage building and building.

But maybe I could have let it go if he let her go at any point during that wait. It's not like I'm a maniac who just likes to go around fighting people all the time. I'm sane and logical for the most part. Maybe I could have somehow suppressed the urge to cave his face in if he'd only listened to Carly's urgent plea for him to let her go, if he'd understood how close to the edge I was seeing him touch my woman, make her uncomfortable.

But then the bastard made it so much worse when he decided to call her that ugly word.

And from that point on, I completely lost it.

So you see, I can't be blamed really for plowing my fist in his face. Neither can I be blamed for grabbing his head after the fact, and slamming it right into the table.

"Micah!" Carly screams but it sounds like it's from far away and it's hard to hear her over the pounding in my ears.

Especially when the man's equally huge but stupid-looking friends roar as they jump to their feet and charge at me. One of them tries to tackle me and I instantly drive my elbows into his back, feeling satisfied when he yelps and falls to the floor. Another one tries to punch me and I duck to avoid it, and then duck again to avoid the third idiot's drop kick. He almost gets me with a second kick to the eye, but I drive my leg up to his crown jewels instead.

He howls as he drops to the floor and I smile in satisfaction.

They keep coming in twos and threes.

I break one's nose with a satisfying crunch but the other one manages to kick me in the stomach. It doesn't take me down though. I barely feel it and I manage to judo-throw him into a table, breaking it in the process.

Now I'm so thankful for all those self-defense classes my father made me take in case I ever got kidnapped. I know how to take a hit and deal an even more painful one.

Three more of the assholes come at me and I hop back over a seat to avoid their blows. Then I kick one in the face and kick another one into the bleeding asshole with a broken nose who was just getting to his feet.

It's going well, but there are still too many of them and in my periphery, I notice one of them grab a seat ready to chuck it at me.

Good thing I'm not alone.

Because as they pick up a seat to throw at me, an older man yells, "Watch out!" and smashes his beer bottle over the asshole's head leading him to drop to the floor.

His eyes meet mine. It's the guy from yoga, Old Man Shoreton. He nods.

I nod back.

And just like that, an all-out bar fight breaks out.

It's total and complete chaos. More chairs are thrown, and more glass is broken. Angry snarls form a cacophony mixing in with the punches and grunts. I manage to take care of myself and also watch out for Old Man Shoreton, who helps me. And he's not the only one doing it too. It seems his entire table of elderly gentlemen is going after the thugs too, ganging up on them.

At first, the thugs don't seem to know what to do with them, but then one of them grabs Shoreton and rears back his fist to punch him.

Oh no, you fucking don't.

I hit him in the back with a chair before he can, and then smash his skull again so he passes out.

Someone breaks a chair against my back and I rear back in time to watch an elderly man tackle him to the ground. And another one is beating people with his walking stick.

"That's my yoga teaching assistant," he says as he fights. "You get your grimy hands off him."

Later maybe, when I have the presence of mind, I'll be touched by the way all of them jumped to my rescue and rallied to fight with me. But right now, I'm still too enraged.

I snatch one up by his collar ready to deal another blow.

And then I get a glimpse of Carly's expression.

She's still standing at the same place, staring straight at me. She doesn't just look pissed. She looks devastated.

My fist stills in the air.

In my hesitation, the thug manages to get me in the eye before I finally complete the punch and lay him out. After he drops, my eyes go back to Carly. A tall, lanky fellow leaps over the counter and stands next to her as her eyes travel around the room in shock.

At the other end, Emma's yelling trying to get everything back under control. Her bodyguards surround her, preventing her from getting involved. The fight still rages on, but I'm not paying attention anymore. I'm still staring at Carly and when her eyes meet mine again, the disappointment in them hurts me on a visceral level. It pierces through my chest and clears my anger.

Why is she looking at me like that? What did I do to deserve that look?

My heart jumps restlessly in my chest and I don't see the punch coming until it crashes into my jaw. I stumble back and I'm about to retaliate when a loud whistle breaks through the atmosphere.

We all turn in unison to see a sheriff standing at the entrance of the bar, his eyes scanning the crowd.

"What in tarnation is going on here?" he says. "I came in here because I heard there was supposed to be a tomahawk special. Didn't expect to find y'all tearing the place apart. And in front of the damn tourists too. Y'all ought to be ashamed of yourself."

My jaw stings as he yells, and I put my hand up to my eye, which smarts like hell. *That's definitely going to leave a mark.*

"Who's responsible for this?" he asks.

I immediately point at the bastard who is currently passed out cold on the floor. "He started it."

Unfortunately for me, about a dozen other people point at me.

"That fella punched out the other fella," one woman says.

"That other fella probably deserved it," Old Man Shoreton counters, but seeing as he's one of the assailants, his account is less trustworthy.

The sheriff shakes his head in consternation. "Well, then that settles it. I suppose you're all coming with me."

And that's how I find myself and about fifteen other people being cuffed and loaded into the back of the two police cars that arrive on the scene. Four of us are squeezed in the back like a pack of sardines and we still don't all fit. A bunch of people are being carted in another truck that's supposed to follow us.

But I'm not even paying attention to the discomfort. Before I left, I noticed that Carly was giving her statement and apologizing profusely to some customers who were all looking stunned at everything that just happened. I willed Carly to look at me, to see her expression, but she didn't turn my way.

"Carly," I called out as they led me out but her shoulders only stiffened. And then I felt it in my gut. She wasn't just mad at me. She was disappointed.

And that does not make me feel good. Not one bit.

Yeah, maybe I shouldn't have done that.

But then I remember that asshole's hand around her wrist, the leer on his face, the ugly word he called her. I recall the satisfaction of knocking him out.

Yeah, I wouldn't take it back, I think. *Given the chance, I would do it the same way all over again.*

If this is what I'm going to jail for then it's a worthy cause.

"Damn, man," Shoreton says when we're in the cop car waiting for the driver. "I don't think I've fought like that in a while. My back is killing me. Can't deny though, it was a lot of fun and a good way to stretch my muscles."

He chortles and I shake my head but can't help but smile despite my sadness at Carly's reaction. "Thanks for having my back. I'll show you some stretches for *your* back when we get out."

"Of course, I have your back," he says. "Here in Laketown, we look out for each other. I saw that asshole bothering Carly and we wanted to step in. Roger was even raring to get his gun from his truck. Right, Roger?"

"Yeah," Roger says. "If Yule hadn't put a stop to it, we would have. But you beat us to it, defended our own and so that makes you one of us now."

"By the way, I'm learning now that you're Carly's fella," a third man says. "Take care of her. That little girl has been through a lot."

I nod, touched on Carly's behalf. "I'll try my hardest too."

Once again, I wonder if Carly hasn't gotten the townspeople all wrong all along. So far, I haven't met anybody who showed outright animosity toward her or even dislike. At worst, they pity her for her situation.

So why does she think everyone in this town detests her?

Or maybe it's her parents who planted that idea in her head? Especially that mother of hers. I could see her telling Carly things like that, to alienate the girl from the people who might have helped her out and separated her from their abuse.

I think about all this on the way to the cell. I also ask the men about Carly and her family.

They tell me the story on the way there, and it continues while we're sitting in the cell. The conversation also veers from that to discussing hunting, and I get invited on a hike the men are going on soon. Also at least one fishing trip. So sitting in a jail cell isn't bad, all things considered.

But I still can't forget the sinking feeling in my chest, when I recall Carly's face.

I hope I haven't screwed things up permanently.

CHAPTER THIRTY-THREE

C ARLY

It's hard to explain the emotions coursing through me as I stare at the wreckage all around.

It's like observing the aftermath of a disaster, like coming out of a warzone but still hearing the blasts in the background. Okay, maybe that last comparison is a little dramatic, but it's hard to get my heart to stop pumping from the leftover adrenaline, and it's even harder to stop hearing the sounds of battle drowning out my screams for everyone to stop. None of them listened. Even though I screamed till my voice was hoarse for Micah to stop what he was doing, he didn't care, smiling in rage as he continued to wreak havoc throughout the room.

I can't believe that just happened. As I glance around the bar, taking in the broken chairs and the glass shards on the floor, along with the disturbed patrons who didn't flee during the fight, devastation tightens my chest. I can't help but think that somehow all of this was my fault. I did something bad that inadvertently led to this.

Even though I can't pinpoint exactly what I did wrong, the guilt remains. I just can't help being a screwup and I attract trouble everywhere I go and now that has brought all this to a head.

It's what my mom used to tell me when I was younger, after all.

You're bad luck, Carly. Her words echo in my ears. Ever since I had you, we haven't had a moment of peace. You mess up everything around you and it's because of you this family can never be happy.

She told me all those vile words when I was six years old and broke a plate. She'd already been annoyed that day at something my father did, and the broken plate just gave her an excuse to unleash her vitriol at me.

I told myself that she didn't mean it and even if she meant it, it wasn't true.

But after today, I might have to reconsider. Tears push the back of my eyelids, bathing me in waves of emotion.

"Carly?"

I jerk around to see Emma approaching me with a concerned look on her face. Her body guards stand back, though they'd leaped in to protect her during the fray.

"Are you okay?"

I nod and swallow my emotions, even as the guilt pushes past my control. "I'm so sorry, Emma," I say and my voice still cracks a little despite my best efforts. "This is all my fault. I can't believe this happened."

Emma frowns and shakes her head. "Carly, it's not your fault. Those assholes probably came in here looking to start trouble, and they did."

"Yes, but Micah attacked them because of me, and that led to all this... obliteration." I gesture around. "The chairs and the drinks... all of it wasted. Destroyed." I've seen how hard Emma and her grandfather worked to keep this place running, especially through all those months where they barely had any customers and we were hemorrhaging money. Still, they kept the doors open and kept things going. They took care of their employees and they worked hard because of how much they love this place. The Tiki Bar is their pride and joy.

And because of me, some assholes just destroyed everything.

"It's okay," Emma says gently, moving to hug me, maybe because she can sense I need it. I hold her tightly, trying my hardest not to cry and not to keep babbling about how sorry I am. "It's fine. Sure, I wish Micah would have controlled his temper and let Yule handle it and toss those assholes out. And I definitely wish Old Man Shoreton and his pals hadn't gotten involved. But none of this is going to break us, alright? We have insurance, and even if we didn't, I have that hot billionaire fiancée, you know?'

She winks at the quip and I manage a weak smile. "Still. I'm sorry. I wouldn't blame you if you wanted to take it out of my check."

"Okay, now you're talking nonsense and you're going to piss me off." Emma sighs. "Look, no one's taking anything out of your check because none of this is your fault. And even if it was, I wouldn't take money from you. And for you to tell me that means you're not in the right state of mind right."

I press my lips together and say nothing. If I do, I might cry.

Emma's gaze gentles even more. "Look, you can go home for the rest of the night. Yule and I are probably going to clean up and then close. Maybe you should bail out Micah. Looks like he's going to need it."

I shake my head. I don't want to see Micah right now. I'm still too angry at him, and also feel guilty because of that anger because I know he did this to defend me. I don't want to hurt him.

At the same time, I'm not happy with how he acted, so I can't stand in front of him and pretend to be okay with it right now.

But I don't want to go home either, or even to Mrs. Peach's right now. If I do, all I'm going to do is cry and torture myself with the thought of Micah sitting in a jail cell somewhere because of me.

Ugh, Emma's right. My mind is a mess.

"I'll help you clean up," I tell Emma instead.

"You sure?" she asks and I nod.

We get to work and as we do, Yule returns from soothing the customers. I apologize to him too. Like Emma, he waves it off and tells me that it wasn't my fault and somehow their easy acceptance only makes me feel worse.

And then to top it all off, Grandpa Crane walks in while we're picking up the broken pieces from the floor and says, "I heard there was some kind of kerfuffle in here. What happened?"

"Nothing major, Grandpa," Emma responds. "Just some asshole who was bugging Carly, and Micah defended her, but then it devolved into a whole bar fight."

"Carly?" Grandpa turns to me and something on my face makes his eyes melt in concern. "You doing okay, Lady Fishy?"

"Yeah, I'm good." My voice is hoarse, but I've managed to fight back the worst of the emotionality by that point. "I'm really sorry about all of this, Grandpa. I feel a little responsible."

"Nonsense." He waves his hand. "You're not any more responsible than I was for the time an ex-girlfriend tried to run me over with her car because she heard another girl at school liked me. Say, did I ever tell you that story?"

"Yes," Emma and Yule deadpan simultaneously.

"Oh?" He rubs his chin. "Well, I'm going to tell you again. It was a cool and rainy afternoon...."

About an hour and a long, convoluted story later, we're finally done cleaning, and Emma, Yule, and Grandpa say their goodbyes at the entrance of the restaurant.

At this point, I'm conflicted. On one hand, I just want to go home and rest and wash the day off of me. On the other hand, I don't feel good about leaving Micah in jail overnight either. I also don't like leaving things unresolved between us.

So I sigh and catch a bus to the police station.

When I get there, from the entrance, I already hear the raucous conversation. I listen to Micah's voice loud and clear, arguing with someone about the dimensions of a building's foundation. I hear Shoreton arguing back and then I hear the sheriff telling them both to shut up or he'll put them in solitary.

"It's a jailhouse, not a prison, Sheriff," Micah counters. "And you can't put me in prison for being right!"

At that point, the sheriff rubs his temple in annoyance and notices me lingering at the doorway. Relief flashes in his face. "Come to get him out of my hair?"

I nod.

"Good. I'm tempted to have him sleep here the whole night, but something tells me he's going to be a pain in my ass."

As I glance at them arguing, Micah's still gesturing wildly as he discusses the jailhouse's lack of proper ventilation.

"This is inhumane," he says, "It smells like piss and donuts in here, and someone could pass out and get their—"

He freezes when he sees me, the words dying on his tongue. "Carly..."

He turns and his hands grip the bars as I walk forward.

My emotions are a mix of several things–relief, gratitude, affection, and sadness. But for some reason, it's the frustration that rushes to the forefront.

I raise my eyebrow as I stare at him. "Really? That's all you have to say to me?"

He gives me a crooked grin. "You still mad at me, huh?"

"Of course, I'm mad at you, Micah." The words rush out of me and for the first time in a long time, I don't care about my tone or who might be watching. I don't care about keeping up my perfect mask. I only see Micah and I need him to see me. "Do you know what I hate more than anything in life? Spectacle. I hate being involved in it. I hate being the subject of discussion and having people look and talk about me all the time. I've lived with that embarrassment my whole life because of my parents. As a teenager, do you know how many times I've had to rescue my dad from a bar brawl? I don't want to do that anymore. I chose you because I thought you wouldn't make me do that, that you were more stable than he was." Micah's face falls at the comparison, and guilt pricks me. That was wrong. He's nothing like my dad.

"I'm sorry, I didn't mean it like that." I take a breath. "I appreciate what you did and why you did it. I know you were just trying to protect my honor, but I don't want you getting in fights because of me anymore. Okay? If we're going to be together, then I need you to act like an adult and not put me in this position–"

I cut off when I realized what I just said, regretting that last sentence as heat fills my face. *Ah, shit. I didn't mean to say that.*

I'm hoping Micah will ignore it, but he doesn't.

"Wait." A slow smile spreads across Micah's cheeks. "Is this you asking to be my girlfriend?"

I blush even more aggressively. Drat. "That's n-not what I was s-saying," I stutter. I'm suddenly hyper-aware of all the men in the jail cell watching. "Micah I–"

"Because if you're asking, the answer is yes," he continues, excitement brimming in his voice.

That stuns me silent again. "What?"

"I want you to be my... girlfriend." He seems a little puzzled as he says it, but confident as well, his smile widening. "I think I've wanted to ask you for a while now but I didn't know how to bring it up."

I gape. "Really?"

He nods and I don't know what to say next. This is... I can't...

Did Micah Landing just ask me out?

I'm too stunned I don't even know how to deal with that. So I go back to the point at hand.

"I'm not going to if you keep ending up in jail," I find myself saying, still shocked that I'm actually going along with this.

"I won't," he says, raising a hand. "Scout's honor."

"I'm serious, Micah."

"I'm serious-er, Carly." He grins. "Now can we kiss on it?"

"No," I say, but it's too late. His hand reaches through the bars and wraps around my uniform, tugging me forward. His face leans in and presses against the iron, his lips pursing.

He waits with his eyes closed.

I roll my eyes. *He's such a goof.*

But I'm smiling as I lean in and kiss him anyway. Clapping and whooping break out over our heads.

After I bail Micah out of jail, he bails all the other men out too. As he does, their wives and girlfriends start showing up to pick them up and give them an earful about what happened. As Micah is helping argue their cases and using his charm to soothe the women, I step out for some air.

Just in time to see my cousin being brought out of a police vehicle in handcuffs.

I freeze on the steps. "Nate?"

He looks up at me. "Oh hey, Carly."

The police officer with him looks between us and then eyes me as he walks Nate up.

"Just going to get some more paperwork done," he says as he passes by me.

"Wait, Nate." I turn and want to ask him about the burned guy he told me about. But the officer is staring closely and looking at us suspiciously and I don't want to say anything that will make him even more suspicious.

So I say, "Never mind."

CHAPTER THIRTY-FOUR

M ICAH

Despite the chaos of the previous night, I start the next day in relatively high spirits. Maybe it's because of Carly and everything we did last night. And this morning before she went to school.

Or maybe it's the breakfast I had at My Fair Lady, which wasn't half bad at all.

Or maybe it's just the fact that I'm starting up a new project with Declan and I'm super excited about it. This deal could change everything. It might even be enough that I no longer need my grandfather's help after all, depending on if more work springs out of it. I've already called my team and informed them, and they're all ecstatic too. So far this will be our largest project yet and it's a great thing to add to our portfolio.

I'm in high spirits by the time I make it to Declan's home that morning.

I arrive earlier than our meeting time, expecting to find Declan having breakfast or something.

Instead, it's Amelia who's emerging from her room as one of her bodyguards, a tall blonde woman with a stern face, opens the door.

"It's you," she says, sounding unenthusiastic about my presence.

"Nice to see you too, princess." I nod at the guards and try to ruffle her hair when I walk in. She slaps my hand away characteristically, giving a very teenage grunt as she turns her heel and walks back in. I step in and glance around the cool hotel suite. "Where's your dad?"

She shrugs. "I think he's off with Emma doing gross adult stuff. And Sandy went to get us breakfast, but I'm pretty sure she met that guy she likes at the coffee shop again and that's why she's taking so long."

Sandy's Amelia's nanny and babysitter who Declan had brought from New York. According to him, she is also settling in town nicely.

"I see." I settle on a couch, opposite Amelia who takes her place on the floor once again. A plethora of books and papers are sprawled in front of her. She also has her iPad propped on a low table and she's peering at it every now and then before hunching over the books once more.

Then the iPad vibrates and she glances at it. She reads whatever it says and then mutters, "Of course."

"What's up?" I ask, halfway not expecting her to answer, at least not without snark. I know how teenage angst can be.

But she must be dying to share the information because with little prompting it starts spilling out.

"It's this guy that my friend Jace found," she says. "Jace is a friend I met online who's helping me solve the case and find the thieves from Madam T's diary."

"Right," I say, recalling the story briefly. "What about them?"

"Well, Jace's dad is a cop in Texas and according to what he said, there was this guy who mentioned long ago that he thought he'd seen them. Madam T and the two other thieves. It was in Texas and he called the police and reported it and everything, but by the time they got there the thieves were gone. Jace managed to get some of the files from that incident and found the guy who made the report. He wanted to meet up with him and ask him a few questions. But guess what? Now the guy's missing."

I frown. "What do you mean he's missing?"

"Well, Jace went over to his house and they said he'd wandered off somewhere. His family thinks he's probably just lost because he has dementia or something and has been saying crazy things about seeing ghosts. But I dunno." She shrugs. "This is like the third dead end we've had in the past two months since we've been searching for clues. It's almost like someone doesn't want us to figure out what happened."

"Or..." I propose, "it was a weird crime that happened fifty years ago before they had the Internet and probably even before most of the forensic knowledge that we have today. All that evidence is probably lost and rotting somewhere."

Amelia thinks about it, but her expression remains stubborn. "People have solved lots of cold cases before, even older than this one. If there's any clue, I'll find it." Her chin goes up. "What if they're still alive? The thieves that is. What if now they know we have it, they come back and try to steal the pearl again?"

"With that much FBI attention on that thing, I don't think they would be that stupid," I say. "'Also, if they're still alive they're going to be what, like eighty? The only things they're looking to steal are dentures and Depends."

Amelia smirks a little at that, but then she says, "Anyway. I'm not going to stop looking. It's what Madam T would have wanted."

"The dead lady?"

"Yup. But we don't know if she really is dead. Remember they never saw her body or Vincent, so she could be alive." Her eyes glitter. "Maybe she's still in hiding because the other thief wants to kill her. Or maybe something supernatural happened to her and Vincent, and they're asleep like vampires waiting to be unearthed."

My eyebrows raise. "Wow." Who would have thought that sensible-to-a-fault Declan would have such a conspiracy theorist for a daughter? "Anyone ever tell you you'd make an amazing writer?"

She lingers on that thought for a second and shrugs. "Maybe. But I think I want to be a detective when I grow up instead. Dad says he won't let me because it's too dangerous. But I'll probably do it anyway."

I shake my head and then a beep signifies that a card was scanned over the keypad. The door opens and Declan walks in looking a bit disheveled without Emma. She probably had to get to work. There's a hickey at the base of his neck and his hair looks like someone was clutching it and pulling. It doesn't take a genius to tell what he's been doing.

I let a smirk spread on my lips. "Well, look what the cat dragged in."

He frowns at me. "Didn't think you would be coming today."

I raise an eyebrow. "We have a meeting, don't we?'

"Yeah, but Emma told me you got locked up last night for starting a riot in the Tiki Bar."

"You went to jail?" Amelia's eyes widen and I nod with a grin.

Hopefully, that gives me some street cred.

"Is that where you got the black eye?"

"Yes," I respond, grinning even more. Carly tried to cover up the bruises with some of her concealer but I guess it didn't work entirely. "I was defending my woman from some thugs, but one of them got in a sneaky hit." Luckily, it didn't hurt too bad and the swelling had gone down considerably after I iced it. Figures that the muscle-bound asshole hit like a total pansy.

"Your Uncle Micah started a riot," an amused Declan repeats.

"I didn't start that riot," I correct. "The asshole who was bothering Carly did."

"But you threw the first punch."

"Well, he threw a symbolic punch when he insulted my woman. What was I supposed to do? Stand there like an idiot twiddling my thumb while he went at her? And the bastard grabbed her arm too? You would have done the same thing if that was Emma."

"No," Declan smirks at me. "I would have done a lot worse."

"Is Carly alright?' Amelia asks, and I nod.

"She's fine. She was pissed at me but we've made up now." I grin to myself thinking, *Boy did we make up*.

"Was Emma mad that I got her place wrecked?" I ask. "I can pay for all the damages if that makes it any better."

"Nah." Declan waves a hand. "They've got insurance. Besides, she wasn't actually mad. She just thought the whole thing was funny. Carly on the other hand was mortified." Declan eyes me for a few seconds, as though deeply considering the words he's about to say. He even goes to pour a coffee for himself from a coffeemaker before he can speak.

"So this thing with you and Carl," he ventures, "it's getting serious, isn't it?"

I cock an eyebrow. Even though Carly and I talked about our relationship last night and this morning, I don't feel comfortable discussing it yet. I don't know why. Maybe I'm not ready to accept all that quite yet, because it just feels so huge. Maybe I don't want to jinx it when it's so new and tentative.

I never thought I would be in a relationship, a real one that is. I always figured that I would either be a scoundrel for the rest of my life, or I would do what my dad did and settle for some type of arranged marriage where we lived in different houses and barely tolerated each other.

A part of me is scared that I'm misreading my own feelings and I'm leading Carly on.

I'm scared I'm going to fuck up.

"I guess," I say to Declan and he frowns at me. That clearly isn't the answer he's looking for.

"You guess?"

I shrug. "I still don't know yet. But I do care about her."

His frown deepens and I can't resist joking. "Is this the part where you play protective brother-in-law and tell me to stay away from her?"

Declan hesitates. "I was going to but now I'm not so sure." He cocks his head. "So what do you feel for her?"

Sigh. He really is going to make me talk about this, isn't he?

"I care about her," I admit. "A lot. But love... I don't even know what that is."

Declan nods like he understands. He takes a sip of his coffee, grimacing slightly.

"I didn't know I was falling in love with Emma either." He gives the window a nostalgic look. "Didn't know what love was until she tried to break up with me and suddenly it was like my world came crashing down. I couldn't eat or sleep or breathe without her." He smiles a little. "Still didn't figure it was love until it knocked me over the head."

"Gross," Amelia says. "If you guys are gonna talk about this stuff don't do it in front of me. I'm a kid."

"Yeah, a kid with a secret online boyfriend," I tease and she blushes.

"He's not my boyfriend. We're just solving mysteries together."

"That's how all the best love stories start," I say, and she makes a face.

"How was jail?" she asks and I have a feeling she's eager for some cool stories full of violence and turf wars and people getting shivved with sharp spoons.

I want to give it to her, just to raise my street cred a little more, but Declan shoots me a warning look.

I sigh.

"Don't ever end up there," I tell her. "It smells like piss and donuts."

Declan's words about love stick with me even after our meeting and after I go pick Carly up from school.

We go for a walk and have lunch by the lake. And

then we go home to take a nap. We do plain old relationship stuff but for some reason it's never boring. I can't be bored with her.

It's a nice, relaxing day.

Until I wake up to the feeling of her tongue circling my cock.

CHAPTER THIRTY-FIVE

CARLY

I wake up a little before Micah does, and see it.

A nice, glorious erection pushing against his chinos. I lick my lips as I stare at it, admiring the large bulge and imagining what his cock looks like underneath. Of course, it's not a total mystery. I've seen it before many times.

But never like this, in the stark light of the day with him lying there defenseless, mouth slack with sleep.

I grin and sit up, running my finger lightly up his thigh.

"Micah," I whisper. "Are you awake?"

He murmurs something but then almost immediately subsides back into slumber. And then I grin and consider my options here.

Micah once told me that one of his fantasies was being woken up with a blow job or someone having sex with him while he was asleep. To be honest, even though I laughed it off, I was more intrigued than disturbed by the concept. He also basically gave me free rein to do just that, winking at me and saying, "Feel free to use me anytime, pretty lady. Even when I'm snoring away. As long as Junior is still working, it's yours for the taking."

And though he'd said it in a casual tone, I saw the hunger in his eyes.

At the time I just snorted and rolled my eyes. *Why on earth would I try to have sex with someone who was sleeping?*

But now I see the appeal.

I reach over, undo his pants and slowly lower the zipper. The glorious man is commando as usual and I reach in to pull out his half-mast cock admiring the beautiful stalk that reaches nearly past his bellybutton.

I can't believe that's all mine. I can't believe it all fits inside me.

I giggle as I stare at it for even longer, running my finger up and down it. He jerks once in a while when I do, his hands squeezing into a fist and his eyebrows furrowing. But he doesn't wake up.

He must be a deep sleeper, huh?

Well, time to test how deep a sleeper he truly is.

I lean down slowly and trace my tongue up the stalk of his cock. A groan tears out of his chest. His hands unclench to grip the sheets underneath him.

"Fuck me, Carly," he whispers and pleasure swells inside me. *Even in sleep, he knows it's me. Or at least he wants it to be me.*

I suck the mushroom tip into my mouth and watch as his eyes fly open. His head immediately tilts down to watch me.

I suck him even deeper and see those eyes roll back.

"Oh, God."

Oh, I feel a rush of delicious heat and power when I make his voice go watery like that. It doesn't take long for his cock to harden into a rod in my mouth, his body growing tight. His thighs are hard underneath my hand, trembling with the effort to control his lust as I bob up and down slowly on his cock. Slurping sounds fill the air and he turns his face to bite his forearm, groaning wetly against it.

I shift to sit astride his shin, and gentleman that he is, he bends his leg to press it against my pussy.

I almost lose track of what I'm doing, shivers racing down my body. He pushes the leg up even more, somehow managing to find my clit without even looking and I cry out.

God, he knows me so well.

I shut my eyes and moan around his cock. My pussy is already wet, just from the thought of teasing him, and this makes it so much worse. I lose myself a little as I ride his leg, sucking faster, dirtier, everything inside me growing more and more desperate.

"Oh, fuck yes. Suck me while you get off."

His harsh whisper drives me higher, but then I pull back, releasing his cock to stare at it bobbing in the air. Micah snarls and tries to get in my mouth again. His hip lifts off the bed but I back off.

Given how many times he's teased me, I figure payback's in order. I want to drive him crazy, the same way he's driven me crazy all those times.

His eyes meet mine again and I can see the tortured

look in them.

"Shh," I say when he starts to make little protesting sounds and harsh rasps, his hips continuously pumping in the air in protest. "Patience."

"Fuck, Carly, *please*."

"I know. I'll give it to you. But in my own time."

I smile and trace my tongue around the base again and again, then follow a vein that climbs to the tip. I flick the underside of the tip with my tongue and he jerks like I shot him. His body is hypersensitive now and so is mine. My skin feels hot, urgency pulsing in my clit, but I don't rush. Because I love seeing him like this. As much as I love the dominant side of him that makes me scream, I love this side too, the one that can accept vulnerability and be under someone else's control for a bit.

It's so fascinating how he can be both, but then again, I should have expected it. Micah's a dichotomy in many ways: playful but surprisingly profound, sweet but also deadly.

And the more I learn about him, the more I like him. The more I...

I don't finish that thought. Instead, I swallow his cock, letting his strangled groans elicit a wash of desire.

This is just for fun. I remind myself as I do it again, and enjoy his hungry shouts. *Just for fun.*

I don't see Micah much the next day, by design. I have an important test in the afternoon, so I spend much of my time at the college library studying for it.

Micah tells me that he is hanging out with his elderly jailbird friends today–his words, not mine–and assures me that he'll be fine without me.

That doesn't stop him from texting me periodically though.

What kind of shoes do you wear when you're going on a hike? He sends first. *Because I've got my loafers and they look better than anything else, but I also don't know if they'll be comfortable enough. So I'm thinking maybe the ONS.*

He sends me pictures of both shoes, one of them black classic sneakers, and the other tan loafers.

I smile.

They're both great, but definitely not the tan ones. Plus, the other ones bring out your eyes.

Yeah, that's what I thought, he says and I chuckle.

My laughter pauses when I realize. *Wait, you're going on a hike with Old Man Shoreton?*

The response is almost instantaneous. *Yeah? Why?*

I wonder if I should warn him that Old Man Shoreton's hikes are somewhat different from regular people's. Perhaps I should mention that the man is a major nudist and likes to explore nature at his most natural state if you know what I mean.

But then I decide to leave that piece of news as a surprise.

Nothing, I respond. *Have fun.*

I'll try. But it's hard sometimes to have fun without you.

I roll my eyes at the cheesiness and then giggle at the smiley faces he tacks onto the end.

And then I try to focus on my reading again, running my calculations. But after thirty minutes, my phone beeps once more and I know it's Micah without even looking at the text that pops up on my screen.

WHY AM I STARING AT A BUNCH OF ELDERLY SCHLONG RIGHT NOW??

I crack up then, laughing so hard that the woman at the next table throws me a dirty look.

"Sorry," I say to her and text Micah an apology too. *My bad. I should have warned you.*

I mean, it's fine, he texts back. *I'm not judgmental, it's just... wow, they really let it all hang out.*

Are you going to join in? I text. *Don't feel pressured to.*

Absolutely not. Not joining in that. No way.

That's good. Remain firm. Just know that they might feel offended if you don't.

Well, then they're going to have to feel offended because ain't no way I'm showing them my nude form. That's for your eyes only.

I smile again.

Another thirty minutes later, Micah sends me another photo of him having stripped down to his briefs with a dry look on his face. *They got me.*

I snort. *Looks like you're halfway down the tourist-to-nudist pipeline.*

Never. How is studying going?

Okay. I'm going to mute you now so I can finish.

No! Don't let the nudists have me!

I almost crack up again but manage to just smile. I

put the phone on mute focusing on the test.

Despite Micah's distractions, I manage to retain most of the information I learn and the test goes well. I walk out of there smiling despite a dull headache on the side of my temple.

As I wait for Micah to pick me up, I decide to head to the pharmacy across the street for some Advil and while there, I browse the aisles for anything else I might need.

It's while I'm standing in front of the feminine hygiene section that it hits me.

Oh boy does it hit me.

It slams into me then, a horrible sinking realization as I stare at the box of tampons in front of me.

My period is two weeks late.

CHAPTER THIRTY-SIX

M ICAH

After spending my day with the nudists, I head back to my hotel room to get ready for Carly's return.

She texted me after she was done with her tests and said she thought she'd passed, which was cause for celebration in my book. She seemed like the kind of person who would like a nice home-cooked meal after something like that. Except I've never made a meal in my life before, but I'm determined to try anyway.

After all, how hard can it be?

Following a quick shower, I go to the grocery store to pick up the ingredients (still no organic kumquats despite my strongly worded email to the branch manager) and head home. And then I spend the next thirty minutes to an hour, squinting at a video on my iPad screen, while trying to slice a variety of vegetables in perfect shapes, while also manning a boiling cauldron of water and somehow missing the fact that I had to put the marinate and simmer throughout this whole process.

So, safe to say that the home-cooking thing is pretty much a botch.

So instead, I order Carly's favorite food from the restaurant in Bayview and pray that it gets here before she does. I pay a small fortune for rush delivery and tidy up the space, laying the table in the center of the room nicely. And then I realize that I missed something. A card.

Shit.

I have someone from the hotel run to the pharmacy to get me two. And then once they arrive, I use my fountain pen to write on the first one: *Congratulations on passing your test!*

And on the second one: *Sorry that test sucked. You'll get the next one.*

Just in case.

And then I wait.

It turns out that the food arrives way before Carly, and the servers even have time to set up some candelabras and flower vases for a romantic candlelit dinner. The rich umami scent of the meat flavors the air, complemented perfectly by the well-spiced buttered asparagus and the milder, gentle smell of the roses. My stomach grumbles already, but I still have a few more hours to wait after that. She's taking her sweet-ass time.

Is everything alright? I can't help but wonder as my worry begins to grow. I call her once and it goes through, but she doesn't answer her phone.

I call Emma next and ask, "Hey, is Carly with you?"

"No," she says. "Why?"

"Never mind." I hang up because I don't want to worry her unnecessarily, but my tension grows. Lakewood is reportedly safe, but just a few months ago there was a kidnapping in this town, which led to a shootout. I can't forget the sound of gunshots as I grabbed Amelia and carried her out of that forest. They kept her in a shed in the woods. And for some reason, I can't stop seeing Carly tied up somewhere crying for my help.

No. Calm down. She's probably with Mrs. Peach right now and lost track of time. Damn it, why didn't I get Mrs. Peach's number?

I'm about to call Emma and ask for Mrs. Peach's number when I hear the door unlock. Relief floods me as I hear the familiar footsteps. She's okay. She's here.

"Carly, why weren't you answering your phone? You scared the crap out of–" I freeze when I catch sight of her face, taking in her reddened eyes and her flushed cheeks. "What's wrong?"

She shakes her head, but there's no way I can accept that when it looks like she's just been crying her eyes out. My mind immediately jumps to the worst-case scenario. *The results came out on her way home and she failed the test, didn't she?*

My poor baby.

I don't say anything. She probably isn't ready to talk about it yet, so I simply go to her arms wide and wait to draw her close into a tight bear hug. She steps right in and hugs me back with her arms around my waist. I feel wetness spread across the front of my shirt, which tells me that she's crying some more. My heart aches. I lift her into my arms and carry her to the couch wrapping her up in my arms as she cries. As we settle in, I stroke her hair, kissing her forehead, trying to give her as much comfort as I can while her cries wrench my heartstrings.

I've never seen her like this before. She sounds like she's suffering so badly that it's hard for me to even think much less talk. All I want to do is make it okay, to make her okay, so she isn't sad anymore. And I'll do anything, promise anything, to take it away.

But I remain silent as I think about the best way to handle this. I don't want to say the wrong thing, make it worse.

I hold her for long enough for the sobs to subside. Then she just rests against my chest, hiccupping away while I rub her back.

"Do you want to talk about it?" I ask and she immediately shakes her head.

Her eyes instead travel to the spread on the dining table and her breath hitches again. "You made me dinner?"

"Yeah," I say instantly and then when she glances at me, I sigh. "No. I was going to lie and say I did it but even I don't think that's believable."

She snorts and says, "Well, it's the thought that counts. Thank you."

I nod, not knowing what else to say. I've never had to comfort a crying woman who wasn't crying because of me before.

As I rub her back, my heart breaking for her and my ears hypersensitive to every gasp and sigh to immediately soothe it, it suddenly hits me.

Holy shit.

Is this what love feels like?

My mind runs through a list of scenarios, every cheesy movie I've ever been forced to watch, everything my friends in love have ever said and done, and it hits me that I must truly love Carly.

Because I'm feeling all the same things. The sexual attraction I could explain away. Even the affection I feel for her could be camaraderie because we both come from messed-up families and it only makes sense that that would bond us together.

But the fact that I'm pretty sure that I would slice my own wrist open if it meant that she didn't have to cry again... well, that kind of psychotic thought can only be love.

I love Carly.

And even more damning, the thought of that doesn't terrify me. I don't feel trapped or angry at myself, or panicked.

I feel... free. Free to let myself feel all the things I've been trying not to feel for her. Free to let myself explore those emotions, voice them out and promise her the world like I've wanted to for a while now....

Except maybe now's not the best time to tell her all this. She's too broken up about the test, and I don't want her to feel like I'm making it about me.

So I just keep holding her in silence.

Eventually, Carly stops crying, mostly because she falls asleep in my arms. I let her rest there for as long as I can and then carry her into bed, laying down with her cradled against my chest.

At a point, I think of maybe returning to pack up the food but, honestly, screw the food. I don't want to leave her, not even for a second.

Yeah, buddy. You're definitely in love.

Now the question is, what the hell am I going to do about it?

I think about my newfound feelings for Carly most of the day. Not that I have a choice, because it pushes itself into my mind when I least expect it. She pushes herself in. When I'm with Declan having a meeting about hotel tiles, I think about what tiles Carly would want for our potential future home. Or when I'm with Hal fixing pipes. Suddenly I think about how much I'd like to fix her pipe. Or when I'm laughing at lunch with Shoreton and Roger, I think of Carly laughing too.

Except she wasn't laughing much this morning.

Carly was still melancholic but she seemed to be making an attempt to cheer herself up, even cracking a few jokes at breakfast. I let her know that she didn't have to pretend to be happy on my behalf. And if she ever wanted to talk about it, I'm here to listen.

She nodded and gave me a watery smile.

In the meantime, I also think about what I can do to make her happy. Maybe an impromptu trip to Paris after her exams are over? Or something more low-key, like attending Fashion Week together?

What would she want?

I'm on the brink of asking Emma for help when, while advising Hal on how to install the pipes, my phone rings.

It's my father.

I sigh. Of course, he would be calling at a time like this. I don't have time for him to destroy my mood today, so I ignore the call, regarding Hal who seems sweatier than usual.

"You okay, buddy?" I ask.

He glances at me. "Yeah," he said. "It's just a little hot, isn't it?"

I raise an eyebrow. It was pretty even temp. Declan

already warned me that he never takes off his jacket, even when he's hot, so I know not to ask.

Still, I can't resist. "That's maybe because you're wearing all those layers. It's not that cold."

"Yeah." He chuckles. "Right."

I shake my head and the phone rings again. I sigh and take it out of my pocket and then realize it's my grandfather this time.

I also don't want to talk to him, but I figure I should.

"Hey, Gramps."

"Micah," he said. "Where are you?"

"Laketown," he said. "I've been exiled here, remember?"

Except it's no longer feeling much like an exile. Maybe like a semi-weird vacation that had nudists and old ladies doing yoga in the church parking lot, one of whom was incredibly well-armed.

"'I would like you to come to New York," he says. "With your fiancée."

"You mean Carly?" I frown. "Why?"

Grandpa sighs. "It occurs to me that maybe I was a bit harsh and hasty with her. And I didn't give her a fair chance with that first impression. I mean it was clear that she defended you so vehemently because she loved you."

I frown. "Right." What's going on? The old man is being far too reasonable right now.

"And it's clear you care about her as well," he says. "Which is why you've rejected every attempt for me to set you up with another. In any case, affection like that is rare, and seeing how your parents' relationship ended up... maybe I was wrong. Maybe I want better for you."

I'm stunned for a few seconds. I don't know what to say genuinely because this is very unusual for my grandfather to, first of all admit that he was wrong, and then second to go back on his staunch belief.

What is going on today?

"I would like to invite the two of you to a formal dinner at my estate in New York," he says. "To start afresh."

I think about it. On one hand, something about this feels off and a tad suspicious. On the other hand, maybe that's just my paranoia talking. I've had a bad feeling all week, but some of it is because I'm scared that I'll mess something up with Carly unintentionally.

But I would like Carly and my grandpa to get along.

Apart from my mother who I cannot contact for legal reasons, he's the most important person in my family.

"Alright," I say. "We'll go to your estate in New York then. Or are you still at Lennox Hill?"

"Yes, I'm at the townhouse. We can meet there," he says. "I look forward to it."

After he hangs up, I stand staring at the phone for a few seconds.

Maybe you can teach an old dog new tricks after all.

CHAPTER THIRTY-SEVEN

C ARLY

Being pregnant isn't the end of the world.

That's been my mantra ever since I sat in that stupid pharmacy bathroom staring at the two lines drawn on the stick. I sat staring for a while, unable to believe what I was seeing.

How on earth could I be pregnant? It makes no sense. I religiously take the pill and only missed it once and it was the night Micah and I had sex for the first time. And the next morning, I made sure to take the–

That thought freezes in my head as horror slams into me. No, I *didn't*, I realize. I was supposed to take the morning-after pill, and was on my way to the pharmacy to do it, but then I got distracted by the email from school telling me I was going to fail the class. So I never took it.

Jesus. How stupid could I be?

And now, I have to face the consequences of my own actions.

I finally have to leave the bathroom because the cashier comes to check on me, but I can't leave the shame, confusion, and depression behind. And then somewhere on the way out, I start crying. I sit on a bench outside and cry some more, and then I cry on the bus too. People throw me odd looks, but luckily, everyone leaves me alone for the most part. I quietly weep while staring out at the city passing me by and, truly, I couldn't tell you why I was crying. Except that, I remembered my mother's words about how getting pregnant with me ruined her life. How she was supposed to be someone and do all these amazing things, but then she got pregnant and got shackled to my father and stuck in this town. I can't help thinking that I've done the same thing to myself.

I don't blame the baby of course. It was my own stupidity that brought this on, and I can't believe I've been pregnant for so long without noticing. It's been over a month. Was I stuck with the baby? Was there nothing I could do about my situation?

I probably need to go to urgent care to be sure. But even if I can have the abortion, I'm not sure that'll be the easier choice either.

I manage to get myself under control before I get home. I wipe my face and even visit the downstairs lobby bathroom to wash it clean of tears and smeared makeup before I head up to see Micah.

But it's no use. He takes one look at me and asks, "What's wrong?" And the tears just start again. But thankfully he doesn't grill me about it. He doesn't do anything but sweetly hug me and order my favorite food. And somehow that makes everything worse.

The tears just continue to pour down my face and choke my throat. I just continue to feel so bad that I can't stand it. And eventually, I fall asleep on his arm and wake up in the middle of the night snuggled into his chest.

I slowly extricate myself to stare at the roof and that's when I start to recite it to myself.

It's not the end of the world.

I run some calculations and find that there's still time for me to get an abortion. And even if I can't, for whatever reason, and I have a child, I'll deal with it. I'm not my mother. I'm not going to turn into a bitter woman who takes out all her problems on an innocent baby. I'll make sure that the child is loved and valued always and that they know that they're the most precious thing in my life.

And they will be. I'll make sure of it. I may not be the mother they deserve right now, but I'll try my hardest. Which means getting my life in order, and getting a job so I can support them even if I have to do it on my own.

I picture it now, a little boy or little girl growing inside me. I lay my hand over my belly. It feels so surreal. Never in a million years did I think that this would be happening to me at this point. This is also not how I thought my day would end.

But it's here now and I have to deal with it. And like I said. It's not the end of the world.

I turn over and observe Micah's face, relaxed in sleep, one muscular arm casually thrown over my body, the other one under his head because he gave me all the pillows. I can't help but smile. He really is a sweet man. But I don't know for how much longer he's going to stick around.

As much as I'm enjoying our relationship so far, I'm also waiting for the other shoe to drop. This isn't forever. In a lot of ways, this is Micah hiding from his family, and taking a vacation from his life. It's why he feels so free here, why he doesn't care what anyone thinks in Laketown. Because to him, Laketown probably isn't a part of his real life. It's simply a stop on his journey to wherever he's going.

But eventually, whenever his business with Declan is over and whenever he gets sick of this small town, he'll have to return to his grandfather who hates me, and to his father who wants him to be something he's not with, and to the rest of the high society where there are women way more suitable for him.

And then it will be just me alone again.

No, not alone, I remind myself.

I have Mrs. Peach and Emma and Yule, and Grandpa Crane. I can even add Poppy and Tate Moon to that list now. I have a solid circle of friends who have become like family to me. I'll be all alright with or without Micah. At least that's what I keep telling myself. My heart will be shattered when he leaves of course. I already know that. A part of me that's in love with him and enjoys the comfort and excitement his presence brings will be devastated to see him go.

But at the end of the day, I'll be fine. I'll make it.

At least that's what I tell myself now.

With a bittersweet ache in my chest, I reach out to caress his cheek, and he doesn't stir except to lightly angle into my touch. He doesn't want a kid. I don't know for sure, but I suspect that Micah isn't the type that wants children, which is a shame because he would make a good father. He's the perfect mix of playful and caring that kids usually love. He's also surprisingly mature and responsible. Well, maybe not entirely responsible seeing as how he was still participating in bar fights but at the very least, he was hardworking and seemed to like taking care of people.

Should I tell him?

Telling him would inevitably face the possibility of losing him. Because if he tells me to get rid of the child, even though I'm 85% sure that's what I think I'm going to do, it'll break my heart. And if I decide not to go through with the abortion, it'll undoubtedly be a huge problem between us.

As I lay there, thinking, Micah's eyes finally flutter open. He blinks the sleepiness out of them and stares at me. That crooked smile I love so much twists his lips as he says, "Hey you. Feeling better now?

I don't answer. I shift forward and kiss him.

The kiss is soft, exploratory on my part, questioning on his.

He's not sure where it's coming from or what I intend with it. And I'm not sure myself. Because the only thing I'm sure about is that I want to feel good for now, and forget about everything that came before. I want to feel his comfort, his love... even if it's not real.

I reach out and grab his shirt, tugging him closer. His body smoothly moves above mine and sinks into me with all that comforting weight.

The scent of his cologne surrounds me, the scent I've come to closely associate with home. He then nudges my thighs open. I welcome him, his hardness, his length as he starts gently grinding against my pussy.

I gasp as the pleasure unfurls and spikes like a wave that grows and grows. He swallows the sound into his mouth, still kissing me slowly, gently, and passionately. Our tongues tangle again and again until I twist my head to catch my breath.

But I can't. The breath remains trapped in my throat as the pleasure climbs to the point where I start shaking with it, shifting desperately against him, my toes curling with the need to explode.

And then he wraps a hand loosely around my throat and nips my earlobe. "Come for me," he says, and that's all it takes to fling me off the edge into a shuddering orgasm.

As I gasp in breaths, coming down from my high, he presses soft kisses all over my face, on my forehead, over my eye, on my cheeks, my pulse.

When I reach for his pants, he shakes his head and kisses my forehead again.

"You're not in the mood for that right now," he says.

"But you are," I can feel his hardness nudging against my thigh.

He smirks. "Hon, I'm always like that when I'm around you. Doesn't mean I want to necessarily do anything about it."

I shake my head. "But-"

"But nothing. What we just did, was just for you. And for me too because I wanted to do it. But that's it. We don't need to do anything else tonight. Alright?"

I stare into his beseeching, sparkling green eyes.

And then I start crying all over again.

"You want me to meet with your grandfather?" I ask, gaping at him the next day at dinner. I spent much of my day today, setting up doctor's appointments and checking on my test, which I passed with flying colors. The earliest the OB-GYN could get me in was three days from now, but they told me I could go to urgent care immediately and meet a PCP. Which is where I was this afternoon. The doctor confirmed that I was pregnant, and the man must have noted my dismay because he very kindly and gently explained my options, as well as the timeline for everything. The meeting was a blur to be honest, but he gave me some pamphlets and scheduled a follow-up in case I couldn't get in with the OB-GYN early enough.

I come to the hotel in a daze, expecting to process all this tonight.

Only to have Micah drop this bomb on me.

"I thought we already agreed that the ruse was over."

"It's not for the ruse," he says. "For real this time. He wants to meet you because he can tell how much I care about you, and while there, I'm going to come clean about everything."

"Are you serious?" I can't help but gape at him. I know how much his grandfather's opinion means to him and coming clean could risk that.

"Yeah," he says and reaches across the table to hold my hand. "I'm serious about this, Carly, serious about you. I want him to know how much you mean to me and who you really are to me."

Emotion rises in my throat, making my eyes misty again. *Oh, God, don't cry.* I don't even know how I still have any tears left in me with the way I've been bawling all of yesterday. Maybe it's the pregnancy hormones.

But I can't help but remember my last meeting with his grandfather and how unpleasant that was. I'm not looking forward to another one.

"I mean..." I linger on the word. "Do I have to?"

He thinks about it. "No, you don't have to. At least not for now, but you should probably meet him eventually before the wedding."

"The wedding?" I squeak.

"Yeah. You *are* my fiancée, remember?" he winks, and something in my chest eases.

Oh, right. He was just joking.

I shake my head. "Alright, but if he starts talking about homeless people again I'm going to say something."

"Please do," he chuckles. "That old dog could learn a thing or two."

Micah takes us there on his private jet the next day, once more it's a thrilling experience. So is the limo ride to his grandfather's brownstone in the Upper East Side.

As we walk in through the classic, luxurious dark oak doors, my first thought is that it looks and smells like old money. Understated colors, ceramic fixtures, a mild rich unidentifiable scent in the atmosphere that just seems to suit the room for some reason, even though I've never smelled anything like it before. Like leather with hints of... spice and lemon? I don't know because I can't really pick apart the different notes. It comes together so seamlessly and it's one of those things where the whole is more sophisticated than the sum of its parts.

I take in the elegant decor, a mix of modern and classic, the high, arched ceilings interrupted by pillars, and the French windows pouring in light.

"Nice to see you again, son."

I freeze at the same time Micah does, peeking from behind to find that it's not Micah's grandfather we meet in the vast space. Sitting in the living room is another man who looks like a bigger, meaner-faced version of his grandfather.

Micah freezes when he sees him and I know who the man is before he even says the word.

"Dad."

CHAPTER THIRTY-EIGHT

M ICAH

"Dad." My father has his scolding face on, meaning he's about to start telling me off in five, four, three...

"What on earth is wrong with you, Micah?" he asks. "You've been ignoring my calls all week. Not giving me any updates. And now your grandfather tells me that you got affianced to a woman you just met, a woman who he says is some kind of imposter."

The minute the word leaves his mouth I feel Carly stiffen behind me. I glance over at my grandfather's unapologetic expression.

My expression hardens. I understand this for what it is. An intervention.

My grandfather likely didn't mean any of what he said on the phone. He just said it to get me here, so they could gang up on me and Carly.

And while I can take it, I hate that I've inadvertently put Carly in this situation once again.

"With all due respect, Dad." My voice is low, silky with my anger. "You don't get to dictate my love life. Neither do you, Grandfather. And the fact the two of you called me and my fiancée here to do... whatever the fuck this is, is total bullshit. And the two of you can frankly fuck off with that for all I care."

Shock reverberates around the room as the two men stiffen. I hear Carly's gasp as well. No one was expecting me to say that, especially while vibrating with as much anger as I was feeling.

But I don't stop there.

"I mean, Jesus, what is wrong with you two? Are you serious? You think I'm going to let you disrespect her in front of me again? And what, I'm just going to fall in line and break up with her because you said so?"

My grandfather's face grows hard. My father just looks shocked and perplexed by everything going on here.

"Micah," he says, "calm down."

"Calm down?" I turn to frown at him. "How do you expect me to calm down when you brought us here to ambush my woman and call her names."

"Micah, that woman is an imposter," my grandfather says, his eyes frosty as they regard Carly. "Probably a social climber too. She's not who she says she is."

Shit. Some guilt presses through the anger and hangs in my stomach. This is mostly my fault. I knew there was a possibility that my grandfather would dig into her deeper after that disastrous dinner. Even if it hadn't gone haywire it was only a matter of time before he searched. At the time, I was just hoping he would give me the money before then.

But I no longer need his money.

And even if I did, I'm done with him talking about Carly and people like her as though they're somehow inferior to him due to circumstances of their birth. I can stomach it when he does it to me, I've lived with that my entire life. But not my Carly.

Not the only woman I've ever loved.

I swore to myself that I'll protect her from anything, including them.

"She's not an imposter," I say. "I'm the one that told her to lie about her origins. I made up that whole story so you would accept her."

My father doesn't look shocked, but my grandfather does for whatever reason. As though he never expected me to have the audacity to do anything that crazy to him. Maybe to my dad, but not to him.

"Why would you do such a foolhardy thing?" he asks.

"Well, because at the time, I wanted you to loan me the money and I thought that was the only way to get it. Because we all know how you feel about people who aren't bluebloods marrying into the family. It's why you saddled Mom and Dad together even though they clearly didn't like each other very much."

"Well..." my dad starts, but I ignore him and keep going.

"I was wrong for lying," I say. "I admit that it was childish and stupid and, most importantly, it put Carly in a position where she had to tolerate being humiliated by you just for my selfish gains. But we're not doing that anymore. Now I'm going to be honest. Carly isn't a blueblood. Her family is an... interesting gaggle of people, but she's not from royalty. She's from Laketown, a funny place filled with a lot of interesting people, and she's the most interesting one there. She's beautiful, smart, unbelievably strong... she's way better than anyone you could ever imagine me with, way better than I deserve. And she's going to be an accountant, a fantastic one." I feel I want to say more, to expound more on Carly's qualities but I can't find the words. And I don't have to. I don't have to explain who she is to anyone, but I want her to know how I feel. "And I love her irrevocably."

I hear Carly gasp again, and I take a chance to look at her. Her eyes are misty, once again, but this time I can tell they're good tears. Or at least I think so, seeing that it's accompanied by a tremulous smile. I lean in and brush my lips against her, but she puts her hand on my cheeks and kisses me back passionately. I taste her tears, her relief, and her love. Even if she hasn't said it to me yet, I know she loves me, just like I love her.

My father clearing his throat has us pulling back. My grandfather is stunned and seems confused.

His expression would actually be funny under different circumstances, because I don't think I've ever seen him look quite like that before. He glances at my father, and says, "Well, do something about this."

My father sighs. "Micah, is it possible that I may talk with you for a second? Alone?"

"There's nothing you can say to me that you can't say in front of my fiancée." I figure since it's settled that we're in love now, there should be no problem with me calling her that. After all, we're going to get married eventually. Why not stay engaged and save ourselves time and effort?

"I need to tell you this alone," he says and he puts on his stern father voice, the one that brooks no refusal. But I'm not in the mood for it. I'm no longer just his son and my duty is no longer to him.

I'm also Micah Landing, Carly's fiancé. My duty is to

her.

"No, Dad," I say. "And I think with that, this meeting is officially over."

I take Carly's hand again and start walking her out, ignoring the calls of my father and grandfather behind me. I catch Elvira's wide-eyed gaze on the way out, and I wink at her. She throws me a thumbs-up in response.

We're soon outside in the crisp air, and that's when my anger recedes enough to realize that Carly is quietly calling me.

"Micah, just wait a second," she gasps out the words running to keep up with me. I stop and then turn.

"Sorry, babe. I was going too fast, wasn't I?"

"A little," she says with a smile. "But that's not why I was calling you. I think maybe you should go back in there and talk to them. Without me."

"Not happening."

"Come on, Micah." She sighs. "At least for your dad. I don't think he has the same problem that your grandfather has with me. I think your dad was more hurt that you were dodging his calls and didn't tell him that you were engaged. You didn't see his face when we were leaving, but he seemed pretty devastated."

"He's devastated that he's losing his second heir, the person who he thinks is going to take over his corporation and he's mad that he can't control me with money anymore," I point out testily. "Even if I have to be dirt poor, I'm not going to kowtow to him. I'll figure out some way to make it. As long as I have you, I'm good."

Carly smiles at me, gently her hands touching my cheek. "That's sweet. And thank you for defending me back there. But I just want to ask, could you possibly be reading your dad wrong in this situation?"

I shake my head. "I've known that man for years. I know what he wants from me."

"Oh yeah? And you've never been wrong about him? Just like you've never been wrong about your grandpa."

"Well..." I hate to admit that I didn't think my grandfather would pull something like this. He's always seemed too straightforward a man.

"Could it also be possible that your negative thoughts about your father might have been at least partially initiated by your grandfather?"

I open my mouth to deny it, but then my mind lingers on a few conversations here and there, where my grandfather would casually mention how my father clearly prefers my brother, and how my brother is better at business than I am, but that I probably had other talents elsewhere.

I thought he was sticking up for me, pointing out the inequality.

Now, I have to think again.

Huh. How come I never saw that before?

Not to say that my father was completely blameless in the deterioration of our relationship and he definitely did enough things to warrant my doubt of him, but maybe... hmm.

"Maybe things aren't exactly the way you think they are," she says.

I smirk. "Is this you turning my words against me?" I said the same thing to her a few days ago, about the townspeople not hating her as much as she thinks they do.

She shrugs. "If the shoe fits."

I shake my head and tweak her nose affectionately. "How did you figure all this out anyway?"

"Just a hunch." She smiles gently. "They kind of remind me of my family, but it's easier to see things clearer from the outside looking in. Go back there. Talk to your father. I'll be right out here waiting for you." She glances behind her, at the fancy neighborhood park. "In fact, I think I'll sit on that bench."

"Alright, but don't talk to any strangers while I'm gone."

"No promises," she quips as I brush my mouth over hers again.

And then I sigh, turn around, and head back into the house to speak to my father.

They're still in the living room, and my grandfather is ranting about something when I arrive, with my father listening on quietly. His eyes flicker to me when I walk in and my grandfather falls silent.

I still can't forget what he said about Carly, so I ignore my grandfather and focus on my father instead.

"You said you want to talk," I say. "Now talk."

He nods. "Dad, please leave us."

My grandfather looks incensed. "This is my home. How dare you make demands on me?"

"Please," my father stresses, throwing him a pleading look.

My father stares at him and digests that. He stands and with all the dignity he can muster, he walks into the adjoining living room.

And then my father says, "Micah..."

"No let me speak first." I hold up my hand. "I'm sorry

that I didn't tell you I got engaged. I'm also sorry that I've been ignoring your calls. It's my petty way of getting back at you for forcing me to stay in Laketown. But I shouldn't have done it. I understand why you did what you did."

"You do?" He looks and sounds surprised.

I shrug. "Well, you need an heir, don't you?" I say it without bitterness this time because I've had plenty of time to accept it. "And that's my job as the adopted son.... A spare."

My father does an odd thing in response. His mouth emits a choked sound. Hurt and pain explode all over his face.

His expression breaks into so many pieces that it's uncomfortable to look at him for a long time. But he can't seem to get a word out. So I continue talking.

"I know you never wanted to adopt me," I say. "Grandfather made it clear that it was always mom's idea. But you lost your first son and now I'm here...."

"Micah, stop." He squeezes his eyes shut and holds his hand up. "Please just stop for now."

I raise an eyebrow. "Did I say something wrong?"

"You said everything wrong." The answer burst out of him in a harsh breath. Then he inhaled deeply. "It doesn't matter what I said or thought before. The minute your mother came home with you, you were my son. Period. I was not very good with kids and still have difficulty expressing my care to you. And your brother will testify that it was the same for him too, may God rest his soul. But I've always made a point to treat the two of you equally so you would know that you were in every way my son as he was."

"You wanted me to be like him."

"No," he says. "I didn't want you to be like him. I wanted you to be a better version of yourself. I became heavy-handed with it because you seemed to lack direction and didn't care about anything. You stubbornly flitted from one thing to the next, aimlessly drifting through life. I didn't want you to continue to waste your life like you've been doing. I thought this was a way to teach you responsibility, so you would put down some roots and wouldn't keep going through life like you were."

Ah. I see it now. So Carly was right. And I'm a little embarrassed that I didn't see it before. Because my father was right. From the outside looking in, it did seem like most of my life, I had no ambition. Even with architecture, I'd given it up at the slightest push back from him.

I love it, but I don't have enough resolve or drive to push through the hard parts.

Or didn't. I do now. And now I see things better from his perspective.

"I get it, Dad," I say. "Truly I do. But what I'm doing now, with my architecture firm, that is something I've wanted for a while. This is not me asking you for permission to do it, or for a handout. This is just me letting you know as my father, that this is what I'm going to do. I'm going to sell my Laketown shares to someone who can manage the place. And I'm going to pursue architecture full time."

He stares at me for a minute, then nods. "If that's what you want, then that's fine."

I nod at him too, and then it feels like an understanding has been reached between us.

"And as for your fiancée," my father continues. "I was only hurt that you didn't tell me Micah. I don't disapprove of her. I don't even know her really. But I would like to. If you would give me that chance."

I bite my lip and then sigh. "That's fine Dad. I think she would like to know you too. In fact..."

I turn and head out to the door, to call for Carly to come back.

But when I glance at the park, Carly's gone.

CHAPTER THIRTY-NINE

C ARLY

My head hurts.

That's the first thought I have as consciousness returns in bits, along with the knowledge that the floor is somehow moving underneath me jaggedly in a rhythm that makes me sick. All my limbs are heavy and my head feels leaden and filled with fog. Eventually, I manage to pry my eyes open and try to make sense of my surroundings. Boxes are propped up in front of me, in front of a window with trees flying across. The ground is moving still. Where the hell am I? A car? I feel metal on my hand, and then a pillow under my head as though someone wants to make sure I am comfortable. It smells like grease and paint back here. The scent of paint is so strong that it worsens my headache and I want to throw up, but I don't want to vomit all over myself.

So, I simply crane my head and peer up at the roof

in wonder.

I'm in a van, I realize. *And it's moving.* And then slowly I start to regain awareness of my body, noting that my hands are tied in front of me and so are my feet.

It takes a second for the alarm to kick, and for me to begin struggling to free my limbs. I groan as the struggle makes my head hurt worse, and then, suddenly, a low voice says, "Relax. You don't want to hurt yourself and I don't want to have to hurt you."

I crane my neck toward the direction of the voice at the front of the van. It's coming from the driver whose face I cannot see but who's wearing familiar-looking boots.

There's another man in the passenger seat. He turns to look at me and the second our eyes meet, recognition flashes.

I gasp.

It all comes rushing back to me.

Of course.

It's Hal's father. Jordan. While I was sitting on the park bench someone walked up and called my name. It was him, and I was shocked to see him here in New York. He told me that he was here for a special surgeon's visit, and he needed help getting something just around the corner. In hindsight, it was all a sketchy excuse, but I didn't think much of it then. I stupidly followed him. The next thing I knew someone was putting a foul-smelling cloth on my nose and the world was going black.

Damn it. I wouldn't have fallen for it if it had been a stranger, but since I knew Jordan through Hal, I let my guard down. But why's Hal's dad kidnapping me? What have I ever done to him?

He grimaces as though he can hear my questions

and says, "Sorry, Carly. This isn't personal. It's just about getting something that should have been mine in the first place."

"What are you talking about?' I keep struggling, giving into my inherent instinct to panic. I try to twist my wrists out of their bindings as I stare up at the man who regards me with a calm and almost apologetic energy. "I never took anything from you."

"You didn't," he admitted. "But someone did very long ago."

"What the hell does that have to do with me?"

He sighs.

"The Pink Pearl," he says. "It was my father that found it in the first place, you know that? No one knows of course. That little bit of history was wiped from the history books and even if they knew they didn't care about that. All anyone cares about is who presented it to the hotel. When my dad found the pearl, he didn't know what it was at the time. He was an old fisherman, a country bumpkin who thought he'd just found a cute little trinket that he could give his wife. At most, he figured the gemstone could act as some kind of family heirloom. And then when the hotel manager, Pierce, offered him a hundred bucks for it, a big deal at that time, he was over the moon and gave it right to him. Not knowing that that very same thing would now be worth millions."

The cable ties aren't budging. Of course, I know they're much tougher than I can handle, but I was hoping to at least get them a little loose.

Oh God. A frustrated sob breaks out of my throat. My wrists are turning red with my effort as I utter helpless cries. My legs still feel very noodlelike and it's hard to move them much less remove the ties from my ankles.

Eventually, I have to accept that they tied me up

too securely, and it doesn't look like I'll be escaping these bonds any time soon.

I have no choice but to listen to what he's saying.

"When the pearl was displayed at the hotel, for all those rich folks to come and salivate over, we finally realized what it was worth. And Dad was pissed that he'd been had. Tried to go to the police, but they didn't care. They said he'd been an idiot to sell it for that price in the first place. Then he went to his good friend Pierce to get more money, but Pierce said 'No can do.' It wasn't happening. And so what choice did he have? He had to get the money somehow. His family was hungry and that hundred bucks didn't stretch as far as millions of dollars. He had to get the pearl back one way or another."

The story starts sweeping away the fog in my mind as I follow it and put two and two together. Suddenly, everything becomes starkly clear.

"You hired the thieves to steal the pearl," I say.

He coughs and then says, "They were supposed to be the best in the business. I thought it would be easy, they get the pearl and then we all split it four ways. But one of them had to go and fall in love and ruin all our plans." He sighs and shakes his head. "We've been trying to find them, or to find the pearl for years but nothing. It disappeared off the face of the Earth. But then your grandpa fished the pearl out of the water again. The same damn water where I go fishing every damn Thursday and yet Crane is the one to get it." He laughs bitterly. "What kind of dumb luck is that?"

"He didn't mean to," I try to reason with Jordan. "Look if it's money you want, I'm sure Declan would be willing to pay you a fair price for the pearl. More than that even. Look, just call Micah and ask for however much you think it's worth and drop me off. I won't tell anyone it was you and you can disappear into the sunset."

But he shakes his head and my heart sinks. A part of me expected it. There's no way it would be that easy, especially since he has no qualms about exposing his face to me.

If he's exposing his identity to me, then it means he probably doesn't plan on my getting out of this alive.

Especially when he gives me another regretful look and says, "I'm afraid it's beyond that, Carly. A lot of people got hurt trying to find that pearl and at least one of them is very angry. And he's out for blood."

"'Oh, God." I start struggling again screaming, fear taking hold. I hope that someone can hear me even though it seems like we're driving through a forest of some kind.

"Stop that hollering," the man in the driver's seat says. "I don't want to have to gag you."

"But I have nothing to do with this!" I say. "Please I don't have anything to do with the pearl."

"You have plenty to do with it. You are Crane's granddaughter's best friend and one of the hotel owners is your boyfriend."

"And I already told you that they'll pay your ransom if you want." At least I'm confident Micah will.

Jordan shakes his head again. "You don't get it." He sighs. "But you will when we get to our destination."

I glance through the windows again wondering where the destination is. Right now, all I see is woods. So we're probably out of New York City. Are we upstate? Are we in a different state? There's no way he drove all the way back to Laketown, right? Surely, I haven't been out of it that long, right?

My brain scrambles for what to do or what to say to get myself out of this situation. I doubt my phone is still on me. It probably got left behind so they couldn't track us. I need to call for help so I'll have to get one of their phones. I don't think screaming will work because we look like we're in a very remote area, if not, they would have gagged me already. But the fact worries me that they're not wearing masks and they're letting me see their faces. So, they almost certainly intend for me to die here.

I think about my child.

I feel so sad for the baby that will never get to see life, never get to take its first breath. It'll never know what a kind and wonderful father it has, a father that will probably love it dearly. And then I think about Micah, who's probably panicking right about now. I was supposed to wait outside for him and now he's probably wondering where I am.

I never should have gone with Jordan. I never should have left that bench.

But it's too late for regrets.

I hope Micah doesn't blame himself if anything happens to me.

I also think about Emma and Mrs. Peach and Grandpa Crane and Nate. I don't really think about my parents because I don't know how sad my parents will be if I die. I know my mom will make a big deal at the funeral, and she might try to convince people that all this is Micah's fault. And she'll try to extort money from him too. But she won't truly grieve me like a mother should.

And it's weird that I'm figuring all this out now when I'm assigned my doom. So why did I waste so much time trying to please them, trying to take care of them? What was all that for, when they've never once shown they cared for me?

Micah is right. They are just vultures using me and I should have figured that out a long time ago.

But I didn't. And now here I am.

The van eventually stops moving, slowly swerving into a park. The two men get out of their seats and a few seconds later the backdoor slides open. Hands reach out for me and I think about struggling but decide it will probably not do me any good. I'm too weak to even fight anyone off right now even if I didn't have my hands and legs tied.

He pulls me out like a sack and heaves me over his shoulder. I bite back a shout and he says, "Good girl. You keep up the behavior and you might get out of this unscathed after all."

Yeah, right. Like I'm going to fall for that.

But I won't fight back now. I just need to lull them into a false sense of security while I wait for an opening, a chance to get out of here. And then once I get that chance, I take it.

Even hanging upside down, I see where they take me– into a drafty mobile home that smells like mildew and old clothes. And dust. Lots and lots of dust. Unfortunately for me, the mobile home isn't surrounded by others. It's on its own in the middle of the woods, and it reminds me of where they reportedly took Amelia after they kidnapped her.

They're such a cliche.

As they set me down on the floor, I finally get to see the face of the man holding me. He's older than I expected, almost as old as Jordan. And his eyes are grim.

But it's the hand that has my heart racing in my chest.

Oh my God. There are gnarled scars on his hand.

He's the burned man.

CHAPTER FORTY

M ICAH

"Carly?" I call out heading around the block. At first, I thought maybe she just went around the corner to do something or check something out. It's a pretty quaint neighborhood so maybe she's just taking in the scenery.

But I circle the block once and she's nowhere to be found.

Odd.

The next thing I do, which I probably should have done in the first place, is to whip out my phone and call her. It rings through my phone but no one picks up. And then I realize that there's a faint ringing coming from outside too. I walk slowly, following the tune down the street, where I turn the corner and see it.

Carly's purse. It's lying on the ground, vibrating from

the ringing of her phone.

But Carly herself is nowhere in sight. She's been taken.

Oh, God.

Instantly my heart begins pounding again, trying to pound out of my chest. Fear douses my entire body as I scream, "Carly!" and jog around like a madman, looking everywhere as though she'll materialize out of thin air smiling at me, and somehow this will turn out to just be some kind of elaborate joke. She'll pop up laughing that I fell for it.

But none of that happens. Only the silent streets of the Upper East Side, and a woman walking her poodle across the street, greet me.

Panic floods my thoughts and I try to breathe through it. I can't panic now. I need to think. Someone has taken Carly and I need to find out who and why.

And then I need to completely destroy them.

I grab the purse from the ground and immediately storm back home. The whole time, a single phrase rings in my head.

I knew it.

I knew something bad was going to happen, maybe not today but sometime this week, or this month. I didn't know what it would be, but there was this feeling this entire week at the pit of my stomach that Carly and I were being watched.

But I ignored it. I thought maybe I was just being paranoid and letting all of Amelia's stories get to my head. I thought maybe I was just seeing ghosts where they weren't.

But now I know how fucking wrong I was.

I storm into my home, startling both my father and grandfather, who were sitting at the living room engaged in a heated discussion. I also startle Elvira who was about to pour them some tea.

I fix my gaze on my grandfather. "Did you do this?"

"Excuse me?" His eyebrows furrowed.

"Carly. Did you fucking take her?" My voice booms across the entire room and the tension trembles in its wake. The two men share a puzzled look before turning back to me.

"Why would I take her?" he says. "And where would I take her?"

He looks genuinely confused and maybe old Micah would have believed him outright. But not this Micah. This Micah has his mind whirling with suspicion and doubt and so much fear and anger is choking out every other emotion.

"You didn't want her to marry me. So you had her kidnapped, is that it?"

"Micah... did you just accuse me of kidnapping your fiancée?"

"Grandpa, I swear to God if you did—"

"I did not." He looks so incensed that his face is totally red as he regards my father. "Has he lost his mind? What on earth does he take me for, some kind of Mafia don or something?"

"Micah, calm down." My father stands holding both hands up as though to ward off my emotions. "Just take a breath. I don't think your grandfather did anything to Carly."

I ignore my dad and continue staring at my grandfather, and he stares back at me just as indignantly. And finally, I have to accept that I don't think my grandfather did anything either.

After all, this all began in Laketown. And something tells me it's about that damn pearl again, which is the reason Amelia got kidnapped in the first place.

And here I thought it was overkill that Declan still has so many bodyguards around even though the case happened months ago. Now I know that I should have done the same. And because I didn't, Carly's missing.

I take a deep breath through my nose and run my hands over my head.

And then my eyes open wide with a realization.

"You still have security cameras that overlook the street, don't you?' My grandfather is nothing if not paranoid, and he had three hundred sixty cameras installed on the deck to circle all around the front of the block. It should catch the park too.

He still looks annoyed at my accusation but he nods. "Yes, we still have the cameras."

"Where can I access the footage?"

"You know where it is, Micah. It's in the security room down the hall."

I don't say another word and jog across the vast living room. At the end of the hall, I open the door and startle the guard sitting there, watching the cameras.

"Move," I order, and he obeys without a word.

I bend over to see the monitor better, identifying the camera that has the best view of the park. Then I maximize that on the screen and rewind it by minutes until Carly appears again. And when she does, my heart catches.

She's talking to a man. I can't see his face, only his back in a long, wool coat and a hat. He's slender and bent, like someone elderly.

And Carly is gesturing and smiling like he's familiar to her. Who on earth is he? She doesn't know anyone in New York as far as I know, so it would have to be someone from Laketown. But who from Laketown would be in the Upper East Side?

Maybe Emma would know.

As I watch Carly and the man walk out of view, I immediately dial Declan's number.

"Your timing is terrible as always, Micah." Declan answers in a roughened voice, which gives me a hint as to what he's doing. What I should be doing with Carly right now, if she weren't missing.

"I don't care," I say tersely. "Someone took Carly."

That gives him pause. "What do you mean someone took Carly? Who?"

"Well, if I knew, I wouldn't be talking to you. Listen, I'm going to send you a video of her going off with some guy. It looks like she knew him. I need you and Emma to watch the video and tell me if you recognize him."

"Um, okay, sure. But this is just… hang on, Emma, I'll explain everything in a second. Micah, are you in New York?"

"Yes. At my grandfather's home. They took her from the park. She followed him somewhere and now she's missing."

"Um… are you sure she's not just busy? Maybe she's helping him out."

"Her purse and her bag were left behind. I'm about to call the police, Declan, but first I need to understand what we're dealing with."

Declan is quiet for a bit before sighing. "Okay. Send the video."

I hang up and do just that, expecting he's probably telling Emma what I just told him. Good. Maybe Emma knows more about what's going on if it's about that damn pearl. Heck, get Amelia on the case. She is more of a detective than anyone.

And then I wait in excruciating silence while I try not to think about what Carly might be going through right now.

Who the fuck took her? And why?

Why her and not me? If they wanted the damn pearl they could have just taken me and I would have given it to them. I'll give it to them now if they ask. Whatever ransom they want for Carly, I'll pay it. I just want her back.

But if they do anything to her, I will not rest until I destroy them all.

CHAPTER FORTY-ONE

CARLY

I don't know how long I've been here.

I stare out the window at the setting sun, fear tightening my stomach. It's been hours at least. The two men have me in a dingy trailer that probably belonged to a hoarder at some point with how much random crap is lying around. There's a coat of dust over everything and mold on the walls, which has me sneezing every couple of minutes. One of those sneezes nearly turns into a sob.

But I refuse to cry. I don't have time to despair. I need to figure out a way out of here.

The men are standing right outside the door. I see their silhouette against the thin wood. I wish I could hear what they're talking about. I wish I at least knew what they wanted from me so that maybe I could negotiate my release. They haven't made any demands of me yet. They've just kept me lying here on the floor with my hands and feet tied behind me and no hope for escape.

No. My breath hitches as panic threatens. *I can't think like that.* There's always hope. I just need to find it.

I have a lot to fight for. For Micah. For my baby. For my family and friends and my damn degree that I worked so hard for. I'm going to get out of this and I'm going to survive and thrive. I won't let them break me, no matter what comes.

When the door creaks open, I hold onto that resolve despite the fear pounding in my heart. Black boots approach me and I stare at them unblinkingly, unflinching. The bile rises in my throat, the stale scent of urine stinging my nostrils. I wonder how many people they've done this to, how many have been in the same position I am right now. I wonder how many of them survived.

You will survive. They won't break you.

The Burned Man reaches down and grabs my shoulders. I flinch then, but he only sits me up and leans me against the wall. I refuse to show my fear. I stare at him dead in his cold eyes.

He grins, and it contorts his face to display cruel satisfaction.

"You know you look just like your cousin?" he says. "He had the same look on his face the first time I met him. When he and Rick decided to get involved in my pearl business with those other assholes. I told him that I liked the look in his eyes, and told him that I had another job for him to do, but he might not be ready for that. But once I told him the job was attached to five hundred thousand dollars, he said he would do it. He didn't even care what it was at that point. He would do it because he wanted the money for two reasons. His mother and you."

I keep staring at him, wondering where this talk is leading to. I suspect he's trying to find my weakness, but I also think that there's something more to it, something that I can't understand yet.

Nate warned me about this man, but for some reason, he never told me the entire reason and never gave me the full story so that I would know why I had to avoid him. Almost as though he were reluctant to. The only reason Nate would be reluctant to share information like that is because he did something worse than what he's in jail for, something he's scared will make me judge him even harsher.

And that's probably what this bastard is about to tell me.

"When I saw how good your cousin was at being resourceful and getting information, I made a deal with him," he continues. "I told him that he won't be able to keep up with the pearl trade forever. They were running out of the very finite resources and eventually, his partner Rick will get greedy and cut him off. In total, he'd be lucky to make a hundred K from that gig. What I was offering would give him five times the money. It would give him enough for you, him, and his mother to go somewhere far away and start a new life. And I didn't care about the money, haven't cared about it for a while. I only wanted one thing. Revenge."

He pauses and the wind whistles against the floorboards. His eyes gleam, his voice a threatening whisper. "You know when they say money doesn't buy happiness? I never understood that until I had it. The pearl business was going well. I had enough that I could stop whenever I wanted and retire somewhere nice. Like Boca. But I couldn't. Because I was still so damn angry. Those pearls took everything from me. It took my father from me after his partner betrayed him that night the Pink Pearl went missing. They were supposed to make off with the loot together, but he got betrayed because that bastard fell in love with a bitch and they ran off together. The pearls took my mama too, because she drank herself into a stupor after it all happened, and the whole town found out that Daddy was a thief. It took my childhood, my future..." He chuckles mirthlessly. "Those damn things are cursed and they cursed me with a life of nothing but pain and suffering. And someone needs to pay for that."

I understand only a little about what he's talking about. Amelia told me about it once, about how she figured out from Madam T's diary that Madam T and her lover Vincent, who was one of the pearl thieves, ran off after someone fatally shot her fiancé Victor. Grandpa told me the story too, in far more elaborate detail. I'm guessing the Burned Man's father was one of the other thieves and he wants revenge for the betrayal.

"Please." I try to reason with him. "I'm sorry about all that, but I have nothing to do with it. Or the Pearl."

"I know," he says and his burned hand caresses the side of my cheek, making me shiver on the inside. "A lot of innocent people got dragged into this hell. Me included. And you too. But you see the ones who should be suffering aren't. They're too busy enjoying a guiltless time, having made off with the loot. My dad's partner and that damn lady didn't die that night. They ran away and disappeared. Vincent was always really good at disappearing when he needed to. It's what he did best. And she did it along with him. My father searched for them his whole life, wanting revenge. He could never go back to his family because of them and died in hiding from the police. And those two lovebirds probably lived the rest of their life happy and in love, while my old man was alone and depressed. Does that sound fair to you, Carly?"

Not knowing what else to do or say, I shake my head.

"Exactly. So here's what I wanted Nate to do. He was supposed to help me find out where those two bastards were, or where their kids were. And he was supposed to help me make them pay." The look in his eyes left no mystery about what he meant by "pay."

"Nate told me before he got caught that he had a lead. But suddenly after the police arrested him, he had a change of heart. Suddenly he didn't have a lead anymore. What do you think made him change his mind?"

Oh, God, Nate. My thoughts are echoing my horror. *What did you get yourself into?*

Now I understand why my cousin was reluctant to tell me this part. Because thievery and smuggling is one thing. But being involved in an elaborate scheme to get revenge on the innocent descendants of a man on behalf of another man who is driven mad with vengeance is a whole other thing altogether. And I can't believe my cousin was actually involved in any of this in the first place, but this man would have no reason to lie to me.

My gut tightens as he keeps talking. "This isn't just about the money or the pearl for me. This is about that lead. I want Nate to come and fulfill his end of the bargain. And the only two things Nate cares about is that mother of his and you." He cocks his head. "The mother might have been an easier catch, but Jordan told me to go with you instead. That way we can kill two birds with one stone. Get Nate and the Pink Pearl from Declan Tudor. And if all goes well, once I have those, you'll be let go."

I swallow. I don't think all will go well. Because I don't think the cops will let Nate give out that information, and I don't think I'll be able to live with the knowledge that my freedom hinges on other people dying. I need to find a way to get out of here by myself.

"Of course," he continues and as though he can read my mind, he gives me a threatening smile. "If you don't play by my rules, I can always just kill you when I get what I want. I don't want to have to do that, but I will if you annoy me enough. So don't be stupid, alright? You're right. This has nothing to do with you. You're innocent here, and as long as you continue to be, I'll make sure you live to see the end of it. Okay?"

I exhale shakily. I have no other choice so I just nod. He straightens. "Good. Now I'm going to call your honey and we're going to tell you exactly what you're going to say, okay?"

I nod again and the door opens, Jordan strolling in. I don't know if he was standing there listening to our entire conversation but I suspect he was. His familiar scent cuts through the stale air as he gets close.

He's holding a phone and he says, "I took your boyfriend's number off your other phone. I'm going to contact him with this burner phone and when I do, you're going to relay the following: You're being held captive by two strangers. These are their demands: We want the Pink Pearl left at an earmarked location that will be sent to them tomorrow. We also want Nate Huntley. Failure to do either of these things will lead to your death. Understood?"

I look into his eyes, finding it hard to believe that this is the same man who I often walked by in the street and waved hello to. The same man who's come to the Tiki Bar on several occasions, the same man that I would have counted amongst the handful of people I can actually stand in this town.

Then again, if someone like Rick could betray Emma, a girl he practically raised, then I suppose it's easy for Jordan to betray me too.

I hold his gaze and, once again, it's almost apologetic. But I know he's not going to help me. He's too blinded by hate and has himself in too deep with this man.

They make the call and hand me the phone.

"Hello?"

Micah's voice sounds so panicked and tense that I want to cry already

"Micah, it's me."

"Carly." His voice is a breath of relief. "Thank God. I've been so worried. Where are you?"

"I can't tell you that."

He's quiet for a second, the tension throbbing in his voice when he asks, "Why?"

"Because, um... I've been kidnapped. And I have to tell you that they want the Pink Pearl to be delivered to a location that they will give you tomorrow. They also want Nate Huntley to be delivered too."

"Nate?" Micah's voice is confused and panicked. "You mean your cousin? What the hell does he have to do with it?"

"I can't tell you that either." And then suddenly emotion washes through me, all the fear I've been trying to hold back trembling to the surface. "I'm scared, Micah."

"Carly, I'll find you." His voice is frantic. "I'll find you, baby, okay? Just hang in there."

"I love you." I want it out there just in case I never get the chance again. I need him to know. "I love you, Micah. "

"I love you too, baby. So much."

And then I get a risky idea and add, "Even if I'm trailer trash?"

Pain explodes across my cheek, and I scream. The phone is ripped from my ears and I stare up into the gleaming eyes of my captor who just slapped me.

"I told you not to try anything stupid," he says. "Now why did you do that?"

"I'm sorry." I didn't think he would realize what I was doing. It was such an innocuous-seeming comment that I thought I could get away with it. But he's smarter than I gave him credit for. And angrier too.

Jordan sighs in disappointment as the Burned Man's stare bores into me.

"You try something like that again and I'm going to kill you."

CHAPTER FORTY-TWO

MICAH

"Carly!" I scream as the line goes dead. Rage and panic course through my body so strong that I see red. One of them hit her. I heard a smack and I heard her cry out. One of those bastards fucking hit her.

Fuck, I have to find her before they hurt her even more.

And I have to find them and make them pay.

"Micah."

I spin around to find my dad standing behind me, with my grandpa beyond him looking worried. It's been hours of stress and phone calls, getting whatever information we can from houses in the neighborhood. We confirmed that Carly was taken and was driven out in a white van. We suspect she was also knocked unconscious, which is why there was no sign of a struggle.

My family members each look uneasy. I probably look like I'm losing my mind right now. But it's only because I am.

Carly, my Carly, has been taken by a maniac who just fucking put his dirty hands on her. Who knows what else they're doing to her right now while I stand here clueless like an idiot?

No, don't let your mind go there or you'll lose it.

Focus on what you just found out.

The kidnappers want the Pink Pearl and Nate Huntley of all things. The demands aren't the problem. I can get them the Pearl and Carly's bastard cousin. Heck, I can even give them an additional million dollars if they want it. Billions.

As long as they don't hurt her. But they already did. And the fact that they won't release her before tomorrow makes me so damn worried it's hard to breathe.

Nate Huntley.

If this is about him, I'm going to kill him once and for all.

I close my eyes and take a deep breath. *Hold it together, Micah.* I can't lose my cool now, because Carly needs me to be calm and collected to get her out of that mess.

"Call the police," I tell my dad. "Have them track the guy on the video and see how far he went. We need all the surveillance cameras, traffic cams, all of it. Take it up as high as you need to go, so they know how fucking serious this is."

My father nods and whips out his phone when my grandfather speaks up.

"I play golf with the commissioner," he says, surprising me. "I'll call him up and have him station officers at the roads going out of state. They'll be on the lookout for whoever has taken her."

I narrow my eyes at him and hearing my unspoken question, he continues, "It doesn't matter how I personally feel about her. You love her and you're determined to marry her, and no piece of shit is going to kidnap a daughter-in-law of mine and get away with it."

"Thank you," I say. I wish I could show my appreciation more, but I'm still too anxious, too uncertain. I don't know what to do now. Do I go back to Laketown and handle the demands myself? Or do I call Declan and make him do it?

Restlessness rifles through me. I can trust Declan with handing over the pearl but the cops might need convincing to let go of Nate Huntley.

I'll convince them.

It's while I'm heading out that Declan finally calls me back.

"Micah," he says. "Where are you?"

"In my car planning how to raze the Earth to the ground if I don't find Carly." It's not an exaggeration. I'm not sure what I'll do, who I'll become, if my Carly doesn't come back to me safe and sound.

Declan hesitates for a few seconds before he keeps talking, "I think we recognize the man in the video. It took Emma some time but she said the gait looked familiar. She had to call her grandfather and he confirmed that it was Jordan Rojas."

"He's related to Hal?"

"Yeah. His dad."

So Hal is also involved in this. Jesus. No wonder he was so damn sweaty and nervous-looking all the time.

Declan continues talking. "We're driving around trying to find Hal right now, but he's nowhere to be found."

"Of course, probably hiding like a rat." But I'll find him. One way or another I will. And I'll make them all pay for Carly getting hurt. "Get me in contact with the security company you got your bodyguards from, and the best damn PI money can buy." Declan has more contacts in that regard than I do. "I'll be there soon."

I hang up and I'm once more conflicted. On one hand, I don't want to leave New York without Carly. On the other hand, she might already be gone from the state. Even if she's not, I'm not going to be of much good to her from over here. The only way of getting her back is by getting to the bottom of this, which I can't do from all the way over here. My father and grandfather already have the situation with the police here handled. So I need to go back to Laketown and figure out what the fuck is going on and why they took my Carly.

"I'll be there in two hours," I tell Declan. "Arrange a meeting between me and Nate Huntley."

The second I touch down in Laketown, I'm on the move. I step out of the airport and the cold night air hits me in the face, mirroring the ice in my heart. At the same time, my body burns with rage.

Driving through Laketown doesn't feel the same as all the other times. Everything feels still, colorless. Scents are muted and colored with a tang of steel. Carly's not here. Nothing feels right.

The first thing I do is head to the sheriff's station to meet with Nate. Declan was able to get him out of prison for this meeting, using his innumerable contacts. He's now at the Laketown station waiting for me.

Thirty minutes later, I walk in there and it immediately quietens.

The sheriff must have had another field day because several people sit in the jail cells, and they were previously arguing with him about something, but they say nothing when I arrive. Even the sheriff doesn't say a single word. I guess that one look at my face gives them a hint of the kind of mood I'm in, and no one wants to mess with me right now.

"Where is he? " I ask the sheriff and he simply points in the direction of a cell at the back of the room. I walk there, my footsteps the only sound clicking in the room, the scent of metal heavy in the air.

I stop right in front of the bars and find Nate Huntley sitting at the table, glaring at me.

I walk in, sitting down across from him despite his defiant gaze. I don't give a fuck what he's mad at. I just need him to help me save Carly.

"What the fuck are you doing here?" he snarls. "You were supposed to protect her."

I raise an eyebrow. "So were you. Especially since something tells me that you're the reason she's in this mess in the first place."

Anguish and guilt squeeze his features. I don't feel a shred of pity for him. He looks away. Silence echoes between us for several tense seconds. A sheen of sweat rolls down the side of his face, and his Adam's apple bobs rhythmically. Meanwhile, I just sit still, steadily staring at him as he tries to find the gumption to talk to me, while I rapidly lose my patience.

"I don't fucking have time for this, Nate," I warn him, my voice quiet but brimming with violence. "I don't give a fuck what you're hiding. Tell me how to save her, because if anything happens to her, I swear to

God you will not escape my wrath."

Nate finally meets my eyes. Something in there convinces him to start talking.

"I didn't know his name," he starts, "only that he had a burn on the side of his face. I think he got it from a fire, the one that killed Emma's parents. He set that fire to burn down the hotel because of everything it had taken from him."

"What the fuck does that mean?"

"I think his dad was one of the thieves who tried to steal the pearl over fifty years ago. And after that, his life went to shit because his dad had to go into hiding, abandoning his family. He blamed his dad's partner for it, the one who ran off with the lady. He wanted them to pay. So he wanted me to find out what I could about where the man and his kids were. He thought I could use Emma's diary and my knowledge of people in this town, my closeness with Poppy and Grandpa who were both alive during the robbery, to figure it out. He said if I did, he would give me a lot of money and I could take Carly and my mom and skip town." Nate's eyes drop as he considers his laced fingers. "That's all I've wanted to do. To get away from here, to start somewhere new where I wasn't Nate the thief and I could give them a fighting chance away from our bullshit family." His voice shakes, as he grips his fingers "After some poking around, I found something. A name, but I couldn't give it to him. I couldn't destroy someone else's life just to save ours. So I told him that the lead didn't pan out. Tried to convince him that it was nothing, but he didn't believe it. I didn't count on how insane he is. And now that he has her, if I don't give him the name, he's going to hurt her to get back at me."

"Fucking damn it, Nate," I snap. "Why didn't you warn us? I could have protected her better if you had told us what was going on."

"I'm sorry." Misery battles with the rage in every line of his face. "I didn't mean for any of this to fucking happen. I just... I didn't want to tell her. She was already so ashamed of me. I didn't want to make her even more disappointed. And I thought... I thought he would stay away because of the FBI and all the media surrounding this case. I thought he would let it go, or at least that he would only come after me. Like I said, I underestimated how crazy he is."

"You did," I say coldly because it's true. Nate fucked up and because of his fuck up, this crazy asshole has my Carly now and there is nothing I can do.

"Take me to him," Nate says. "I'll pretend to give him what he wants in exchange for Carly. By the time he figures out that I've tricked him, we'll be far away and Carly will be safe."

"He'll kill you."

He smiles sadly. "Maybe that's how it needs to end. Maybe I need to do one good thing for once in my miserable life."

I should feel pity for him. I know I should, somewhere in my mind. But right now, my heart is stone. And it will be until I get Carly back.

Nate's plan sounds like a fine one. But there are still too many loopholes and too many ways it could go wrong. What if this madman asks for confirmation of the lead before we can make the exchange? What if he changes his mind and decides to kill Carly anyway? And what the fuck does Jordan and Hal have to do with it?

I need to figure it out.

On my way out of the station, Declan calls me and I answer.

"Hal's here," he says before I can speak. "He wants to talk to you."

I'm filled to the brim with loathing but I smile anyway. "What a coincidence. I want to talk to him too."

The night sky glitters as I break traffic laws getting to the Marriott. I head to Declan's hotel suite and find Hal standing in the middle of his living room.

Rage overpowers my mind and I charge at him but Declan steps between us.

"Let me go," I tell him.

"No," Declan responds. "He's not a part of this, he's here to help."

"I suspected what my father was up to," Hal starts speaking quickly, probably smart given the fury in my face. "He's done this before. With the fire... the one that..." He shoots a quick look at Emma who's sitting on the couch and staring into the air, looking pale like she just received shocking news. "He and Craig, the man who took Carly, they were supposed to meet up at the hotel to talk. But Dad didn't know that Craig planned to burn down the hotel and wanted them to do it together. He made Dad help him, and I was supposed to wait in the car, but I was hiding behind a pillar, watching the whole thing. Craig got burned because he accidentally got a little gasoline on his face and was so crazy for revenge that he didn't notice before he set the fire. I got burned because I ran in there trying to help people." He smiles sardonically. "Obviously, I was a kid so I couldn't do anything, even before my dad dragged me out. I couldn't stop him then. And I couldn't tell anyone that he set the fire because I didn't want my dad to go to jail. Craig disappeared from town after that, and Dad swore to me after that he wouldn't involve himself with him like that again. But recently I caught him talking to Craig again. I knew they were planning something, but I didn't know what it was."

"How the fuck do you think I'm supposed to believe you?" I snarl. "How do I know this isn't just a part of their plan?"

Hal swallows and then he quickly takes off his jacket. He's wearing a white faded vest underneath it, but that's not what he wants to show me. He holds out his arm, revealing a gnarly burn mark on the underside of his forearm.

"Like I said, I was at the fire," he says. "I got hurt when I tried to stop it, but Dad hid that from everyone so no one would know. He thought they would ask questions about what I was doing there in the first place and it would lead back to him. It's why I always wear a jacket, even when it's hot. I thought eventually people would forget and I could take it off but I couldn't take the risk."

His story makes sense, but my mind is still overtaken by suspicion. I can't trust Hal. I don't think I can trust anyone right now.

"Where are they?" I ask him regardless.

"I'm not sure," he says. "They're still in New York I think. I heard them speaking about a cabin in the woods owned by Craig's dad. It's where he hid out all those years ago."

"Do you know how many cabins in the woods are in fucking New York?" I snarl but then another thought occurs to me. I think about what Carly said and why she got hit.

She revealed something. She gave me a hint. *Trailer trash.* She knew that would bother me to hear her say that about herself, but she said it to give me a hint. And they hit her for it.

"It's a trailer," I say. "Not a cabin. A trailer park. Maybe an abandoned one."

"How many abandoned trailer parks are there in New York?" Declan asks.

I shrug, but then suddenly a little girl's voice intrudes. "I know."

We all glance over in unison to where Amelia stands at her room doorway. She's in her pajamas and clearly supposed to be asleep but has probably been listening in on the conversation the whole time.

"I think I know where they are."

CHAPTER FORTY-THREE

CARLY

I get my chance to escape sometime around daybreak.

Both men took turns keeping watch over me throughout the night, but the Burned Man just went outside muttering about needing some air, and Jordan Rojas is asleep on the couch.

Jordan hasn't stirred since his "shift" ended hours ago. And the Burned Man has only gotten more irritable as time passes. Maybe it's because I made a show of softly sobbing into the makeshift pillow, no matter how many times he told me to stop. Eventually, he went to the couch to sit and observe me from there, which was the whole point of my crying in the first place. The couch shielded his view of me just a little, just enough for me to do what I had to do.

Strangely, it's just the two of them keeping watch. I

thought there would be more lackeys arriving, but I guess the rest of the pearl thieves have been rounded up by the FBI so they must be low on manpower. This also doesn't feel like a well-planned operation on their end, more like something they cooked up due to sheer desperation and hatred. It works in my favor because it gives me loopholes to exploit.

I bided my time the whole night, playing up how scared I was and pretending to be spooked by the slap they gave me. My cheeks still sting even though Jordan put some kind of treatment on it. Apparently, they have a first aid kit lying around for whatever reason and Jordan is still playing up the "nice guy without a choice" angle. Nevertheless, I didn't give a single protest for the rest of the night. I simply lay in the corner, on the floor, crying but obedient.

But my sobs were also to hide the fact that I was slowly trying to extricate my hands from the zip ties. They took off the one on my legs when I had to pee, and simply tied them with a rope when we returned. Jordan, who was the one to take me to the bathroom, made a mistake and tied the rope over some of the fabric of my maxi skirt, which gave me some slack to work with. Not a lot, mind you, and I rub myself raw but I don't give up.

I have to get out of here.

I continued working on the zip ties on my wrist too. I tried different angles, scared that I might have to dislocate my finger to get it out. But sometime, during the night, I found out that by tucking my thumb in and pressing down to the point of pain, I can make one of my hands small and flat enough that it just about squeezes out.

But I don't do it until the Burned Man is gone.

Once he leaves that morning, I work as quickly and silently as I can to get those things off.

It takes me about twelve tries and two minutes to

get it right. Too much time. For those heart-pounding minutes, I stare at the door, terrified that he'll come back and catch me before I manage to break free entirely. I swallow the desperate cries as I tug and tug and finally tug my hand free. I don't stop to celebrate, making quick work of the rope around my ankles.

And then I get to my feet quietly and look around. I can't go out the front door. He might be there, waiting for me to escape. Luckily, there's a window in the kitchen, but the metal frame and casing look rusted.

It's going to be a pain to open that without making noise, but I'm going to have to somehow manage it.

I creep there and climb onto the counter by the sink, praying it doesn't break or give off any sound. Then I put both hands under the window, slowly attempting to slide it up. It lets out the littlest of creaks and my heart pounds.

Shit.

I glance back toward the living room. Luckily, Jordan doesn't show signs of stirring.

Relief flows through my body. I don't dare breathe, nor do I lift the window anymore. I can't risk waking him up.

I analyze the opening. It's just enough for me to get out, but I'll have to get creative. I don't have a choice because I can't afford to pull it up anymore and wake Jordan. After a few seconds of serious thought, I bite my lip and bend over, putting my right leg through. Once it gets close enough to the ground, I slowly inch my body along.

A few seconds later, I almost get stuck somewhere with my neck against my left thigh. But I don't panic. I simply breathe and imagine I'm doing yoga or something. Yeah, that's it. This is just an uncomfortable yoga pose, like the one Tate tried to teach me that one time she had Emma and me in her class.

Relax. I hear Tate's voice in my head. *Breathe in and out. Let your body do what it's built to do.*

I twist my head to the side and stick it out first, before pulling the rest of my body.

And just like that I'm free.

I don't take time to savor the victory.

Run, I think, as urgency tightens my muscles. But I temper the impulse to take off blindly. It's still pretty dark out and we're surrounded by woods, but I still need to be on the alert. He could be anywhere.

After my initial scan I immediately run for a tree, hiding behind it. I don't know where I am, or how far I am from the road. I also don't know where the Burned Man is. I know I'm not safe yet, not even close. If anything, things have become much more dangerous.

He already let me know in no uncertain terms, what he would do to me if I tried to mess with him again. And I don't doubt that he'll follow through.

I try to keep an eye out and stay as silent as possible as I creep behind the bushes, dashing from one tree to the next. When I get about a quarter-mile away, I glance behind me to make sure I'm not leaving any obvious track. Then, I continue.

I don't know if I'm moving farther from the road or closer, and I don't have time to even stop and think about it. I just need to get away.

If I were smarter or savvier at this, I probably would have gotten their phone and called 911, but I didn't want to risk getting caught. As I crouch behind another tree, I suddenly hear footsteps crunching on the twigs in the distance. Oh no. My heart scurries away when I peek up and see him. The Burned Man.

He hasn't spotted me yet. He's frowning, his head pivoting from side to side. I shrink back against the stem, overgrown grass brushing against my face. He glances around and calls out, "You know if you surrender now, I'm going to make it easier for you. But if you waste my time looking for you, it's going to get real ugly."

Fear has me pressing my hand over my mouth so I don't accidentally let out a scream.

Even when he pulls his gun from his waistband and takes off the safety.

"I'm a hunter, little girl," he says. "I can smell fear from a mile away. And I smell yours right now."

I try to hide amidst the shadows but then startlingly and suddenly his head snaps to my general vicinity. And then he points the gun.

I manage not to scream as I run.

The gunshot scatters behind me, covering the sound of my escape. It propels me forward even as I keep from screaming. My feet naturally move in a zigzag pattern, my memory randomly pulling up one of the things Emma's grandpa told me about what to do when I'm being shot at. I stay low and hidden, behind trees and bushes. I desperately search for a place to hide.

At the same time, a pessimistic voice inside my head tells me that I'm not going to make it.

He's going to catch me and he's going to kill me for this stupid attempt.

Why did I think I was smart enough to pull this off?

No. My legs pump as I run down the hill. *I'm going to survive.* I don't care how much I have to run, how hard I have to fight. I'm not going to let him get me, because I have way too much to live for now.

I spot another trailer in the distance and run for it. Maybe if I can somehow get inside it, I can hide or find a weapon. Or a phone.

Despite how unrealistic that last one is, the thought keeps me going.

But before I get far, a hand shoots out of nowhere and grabs me, pulling me behind a tree.

Another hand slaps over my mouth to muffle my scream at the same time as another shot rings out.

I freeze, not fighting, or he might hear me.

I look up to the man holding me.

It's Hal.

My heart races with fear again but he shakes his head before I can scream and his eyes plead with me to trust him.

It's not like I have a choice now. I don't know if he's working with his father or not but if he is then I'm doomed either way.

Hal does something else. He points in the distance, and I squint in that direction, but I don't see much. It's too dark.

I glimpse up at him and he points again, meaningfully. Then he mouths a word. *Micah.*

My heart skips a beat. Is he saying Micah is out there? How? How did they find me?

I glance back in that direction and think I see something, a glint in the bushes. And I feel it deep inside.

Oh my Gosh. He really is there.

The crunching twigs let me know that the Burned Man is closer.

Hal's eyebrows ruffle in frustration and then he presses his finger against his lip again, bidding me to stay quiet.

I nod, and then he steps out with his hands up.

"Don't shoot," Hal calls out. "It's me."

The Burned Man doesn't shoot at him instantly. Instead, he sounds contemplative.

"I thought your father said you didn't want to be a part of this."

"Well, I changed my mind," Hal says and walks up out of my view. "I heard Declan mention that Micah caught someone on video taking her. They'll eventually figure out who it is. And the whole town is going to come down on me like they did with Nate Huntley. I can't take that. Micah and Declan are out for blood and they're not going to believe I had nothing to do with it anyway. So I might as well save my ass, and my dad's."

"Smart," he says. "How did you drive up here?"

"Took a bus out of Laketown. When I got close, I rented a bike but ditched it a few miles ago. We should probably move soon." He pauses. "If you're looking for Carly, I think I heard something in that direction."

"Yeah, you're lying. And you're terrible at it."

Bang!

The shot makes me flinch but I still don't scream even as Hal lets out a cry of pain and falls to the ground. Oh, God. I hear the footsteps getting closer, and know at any moment he's going to see me. I can't stay here. I have to run.

I start down when I finally see it. Micah. Before I can react, he springs out of the bushes and rushes for me, throwing me to the ground just as the gun fires again.

And then we're surrounded by a flurry of gunshots, flying out and peppering the atmosphere with steel. Amidst it, I finally scream and sob the way I wanted to.

But the heartbeat above my ear is Micah's. And it smells like Micah. He stares down at me with Micah's eyes too.

"Am I dreaming?" I ask.

"God, I hope not," he says, his hand caressing my face desperately. "I hope not, my Carly."

And then finally, in his arms, surrounded by the cacophony and the faint scent of blood, I finally breathe.

CHAPTER FORTY-FOUR

MICAH

I hold Carly close, pressing her into my body as the breath struggles to push out of me. The pressure builds in my chest even with my ragged exhales. I haven't been able to take a full breath since she's been gone and now it's like all of it tries to enter and exit at the same time.

The terror still floods my mind, the image of watching her run and get shot at.

When I heard the first gunshot, my blood ran cold.

I almost bolted out to get her but Hal and an FBI agent dragged me back. The agent, Silas, reminded me that this is why they didn't want me on the operation in the first place. But there was no way I was going to stay back agonizing while my Carly was in danger.

"You being here puts her in even more danger," the

agent hissed at me. "And if you run out there and jeopardize our plan, then she's as good as dead."

The harsh words got through to me, shocking me back into reality. He was right and as painful as it was, I stayed hidden, knowing that the rest of the agents were stationed around different parts of the forest and at least one of them might see her and save her.

We were able to narrow down what forest Carly was being held in, thanks to Amelia and her investigative online friend. Turned out that they managed to find the man who had seen the thieves and through his demented ramblings, he'd given them a clue that one of the thieves had stayed in a trailer in a forest near Sterling. It took some time to convince the police of our theory and to organize this operation. But I let them know I was going after her with or without them.

By two in the morning, the FBI and Declan's security team began staking out this hill to find her. We've been searching for the past two hours and were communicating via walkie-talkies about how to approach the situation, when we heard the gunshots. That threw everything, especially me, into disarray.

Was it Carly who got shot? Was she dead?

Just the thought of it made terror grip my heart and for the first time in a long time, I prayed. I didn't care about anything that happened to me but nothing could happen to her.

Just as I uttered the prayer, I saw her screaming, breaking out of the clearing. Hal got to her first but the bastard found them. When I saw Hal go down for her, I couldn't hold back anymore. I had to save my Carly.

And thank God, I did.

I squeeze her tight now, the ringing in my ears finally diminishing enough to note that we're surrounded by people. Somewhere, officers are barking out orders and apprehending the suspect. Somewhere else someone is asking me if I'm okay. But the only sound that matters to me right now is Carly. She's crying while she grips me. Her body is shaking. Her soft rosy scent floods my nostrils.

She's mumbling and telling me how scared she was, how she thought she would never see me again. Oh, God, me too. As much as I tried to shepherd my thoughts away from that direction, and as much as I tried to stay positive, there was a big part of me that was terrified that I would never see her again either.

"Micah," she sobs against my chest.

"It's okay," I whisper, kissing her on her hair, all over her face, tasting her tears and savoring them because it means that she's alive. "You're okay."

"Yeah, but you're not." Someone's voice rudely intrudes and I almost tell them to go away but that would mean me stopping the whispering in her hair.

"Micah." The voice is firmer this time. "You were shot."

This breaks Carly out of her stupor and she leans away from me, but I move forward capturing her lips with mine. She groans into the kiss and so do I until she puts a hand on my chest and pushes me away.

"Wait, Micah," she says. "You're bleeding."

"It's a flesh wound," I say even though I have no idea if it is or isn't. It doesn't hurt that bad but maybe it's because I'm focused on other things.

But since Carly won't let it go, I glance down and finally notice the searing pain in my bloodied shoulder. I snort when I see it.

"I guess Declan and I will finally have matching gunshot scars now," I say, and Carly offers me a trembling smile. One that makes me kiss her again.

It's only when Silas threatens to brain me and warns me about the possibility of death by blood loss that I finally let her go and allow them to treat me with the first aid kit they brought along for this mission.

After the ambulance arrives and they stitch up my shoulder, I still keep a grip on Carly's hand. We each give our statements to the officers, and she tells us everything that transpired. We match up her information with ours. It's just as we suspected, but those men sound more insane than I imagined. Jesus. I understand the concept of wanting revenge (I was contemplating it myself if anything happened to Carly), but I can't believe they would go to such lengths and involve innocent people in that. One of them killed Emma's parents. The other one attempted to kill Carly.

And I would kill them for it, except the Burned Man is already dead and Hal's father is in police custody. Luckily, Hal is alive and being held in the ambulance. He didn't watch his father's arrest.

Once we're done, we're asked to visit a hospital, but frankly, I just want to get back home. And I'm shocked to find that home to me is now Laketown. I want to go back there and feel the gentle breeze on my face, and pass by stretches of lake. I want to remember all the great memories Carly and I had there and not the fear that has plagued me for the past twelve or so hours.

Nevertheless, I need Carly to get checked up at least, so I have Declan's security team drive us to the hospital. The four of them will probably be our new bodyguards and I'll get to know them once I have the mental fortitude for it.

After about an hour at the hospital, during which it's confirmed that none of us are gravely injured, we head to my grandfather's townhouse. It's currently teeming with security and it's the only place I'll feel safe.

Carly lies against my chest during the trip. Her hands squeeze mine as we arrive, entering the home.

My father is still there. He and my grandfather are at the dining room table and both look like they haven't slept all night.

They stand as we walk in.

"Micah," my father says.

"I'm fine, Dad," I tell him before he can ask. I wrap my arm around Carly's waist. "We're fine."

A part of me can't believe she's here with me and it feels like this might all be a dream. It's why I haven't been able to let her go. I don't think I'll be able to let her go ever again.

"You were shot," my father says, looking at my shoulder. I'm still wearing my bloody shirt but the shoulder's bandaged underneath.

"It's just a flesh wound. The paramedic and the doctor said that the bullet missed any major ligaments or arteries."

My father doesn't respond. He simply walks to me and draws me into a tight hug, carefully so as not to jostle the shoulder.

And then his other arm wraps around Carly too drawing her in too.

I'm surprised. I'm not used to my father showing such affection. I pat his back awkwardly as he breathes heavily.

"I'm just glad you're both okay," he says shakily.

I smile. "Thank you, Dad. And thank you for all your

help too."

"Of course. You're my son."

As my dad hugs me, my grandfather walks closer with a serious look on his face. When his eyes travel to Carly, I stiffen. His grim faces makes me expect his bullshit again, but

"I think I owe you both an apology," he says. "But I can give it to you once you're both rested up. I'm glad you're safe, Micah. Carly."

As my father pulls away, Carly graciously smiles at him. "Thank you, sir."

Soon, they let us go to my room and there, I pull Carly close again, scenting her hair.

"Thank God, you're okay," I tell her.

She nods.

"Was it horrible?" I ask, then add. "It's okay if you don't want to talk about it."

"It was," she says with a weak smile. "But I knew I would survive. I had to because of you. And because of..." She lays her hand on her belly. "Micah, I have to tell you something. Something I should have probably told you earlier, but I didn't know how to break it to you then."

"What is it, my love?" I ask the question, while I'm kissing her all over her face, powerful emotions rumbling through me.

"I'm pregnant."

It takes a while for the words to sink in because I'm too focused on the kissing.

And then when it does, I freeze and look down at her. Did she just say what I think she said?

She nods and her eyes are once again filled with tears.

"I'm pregnant," she whispers. I found out a few days ago. When you 'cooked' me that dinner. That's why I was so out of it."

"Not because of your test?" A choked sound emits from my throat. "I thought you failed it."

She laughs. "No, I passed my test. Aced it, actually. But the baby... I didn't know if I wanted it back then. But I know now that I do want to keep it. And I know a baby wasn't part of the plan and we haven't even talked about having a family or if we want kids and–"

I cut her off, kissing her so deeply, swallowing the rest of her frantic words. Passion and love and wonder meld together, and I can't believe for a second she thinks I might not want this baby. Of course I do. I mean sure I didn't know it even existed five seconds ago, but I love this baby. Because it's part of her.

I imagine a little boy or girl that looks like her.

"I love you," I whisper against her lips, kissing the tears that have rolled down her cheeks. "And I love this baby too."

She smiles. "I'm glad to hear you say that because I love you, Micah. So much."

The next morning, I wake up to a surprise. Literally.

I open my eyes to see a figure in black standing at the foot of my bed.

"Jesus." I throw my body over Carly's to protect her from the grim reaper, only for my vision to clear enough to recognize the familiar form in a long black gown. "Mom?"

My mother smiles as she says, "Hello, Micah."

I run my hand through my hair, my heart galloping away. "Why the heck are you in my room dressed like that? I thought my time on the earthly plane was up."

She cocks her head, and comes to my side. Her eyes still hold the sadness in them that has been there since my brother's death, but she puts a gentle hand on my forehead. "Your father called me. He told me everything that happened. Why didn't you tell me earlier?

"I didn't want to bother you," I say. "Because I know you're still grieving Tristan."

"Yes, but losing another son isn't going to make me feel any better." She sighs. "My God, Micah, if anything had happened to you, I don't know what I would do."

"Good thing I'm not going anywhere," I grin. "How was the sabbatical?"

"Dull," she says. "Which is kind of the point."

I chuckle, and at that point Carly stirs and her eyes flutter open.

Carly takes one look at my mother and screams too loud and long.

When she catches herself, I say, "Carly, meet my mom."

She gapes for a full minute as though waiting for the punchline that isn't coming.

"It's nice to meet you, Carly," my mother says. "I've heard a lot about you."

"Sorry!" Mortification takes over her expression as she stares at her. "I didn't mean to scream like that."

"It's okay." My mother smiles wanly. "I get that reaction a lot."

Once my mother leaves the room and we get dressed, we go down for a nice breakfast, during which my mother asks Carly a hundred and one questions, my father dotes on her, and my grandfather quietly apologizes to both of us. It's our first family meal in a while and it's quite pleasant and not as awkward as I thought it would be.

But that's nothing compared to the welcome we get back in Laketown that afternoon.

It isn't just Declan, Emma, and Amelia who show up at the airport for our arrival. It's Grandpa Crane, Poppy and Tate Moon, Mrs. Peach, and Yule. Heck, even my nudist buddies show up, clothed this time.

As we greet them all, I realize Declan was right. This town has truly trapped me, giving me all the things I could never find in New York or Paris, or any of the other cities I've flown to. It gave me Carly. And I'm glad I get to be with my family and raise my child in a town like this.

I stare at Carly loving her eyes, the way they glow. And with her, I find my way home, to a place full of endless adventure.

EPILOGUE

CARLY

It's my second time at a grand masquerade ball but I have a feeling it won't be my last.

Once again, it's being held at the Pink Hotel ballroom, which is basically packed to the brim with a line outside of people hoping they get let in. It's the grand opening of the Pink Hotel and paparazzi are camped beside a literal red carpet rolling through the front doors that are guarded by suited-up security. And inside the room holds even more glitz and glamor.

More than just regular aristocrats, this time the place is filled with an interesting combination of people, from actual celebrities, drawn to the spectacle of the Pink Pearl to bluebloods like Micah's grandfather and parents, and just regular old Laketowners. It's an interesting mix of people that shouldn't work but somehow it does.

Declan says his rebrand is about maintaining the rustic charm while still giving the Pink Hotel some prestige. It's a difficult thing to do and something

Micah lets his father and Declan know he has no interest in helping them facilitate. He's too busy on a list of new projects including a new Yacht Club he's building.

Micah succeeded in selling his shares to someone he knew from his fancy boarding school, who he called "kind of a weird guy." To which Declan responded, "If he's weird, then he'll fit right in in Laketown."

I can see the new owner, Toby, standing at the front of the room alone, glowering at everyone. Or at least I think he's glowering. He might just be focusing though. Micah tells me that the man is hard to read, but his eyes are fixed on the room as though trying to scorch everything to the earth at once. He's quite tall, even more so than Declan, and handsome despite his expression. His pitch-black hair sets off nicely against his bronze skin, and matches black eyes that are disconcerting to look into for too long.

His back is straight, broad shoulders sitting back like Micah's posture lessons taught me to do. He oozes good breeding but in a different way than Micah does. While Micah gives off more laid back, spoiled rich-boy vibes, this man has the aura of command that Declan has, but also something else. Something I can't put my finger on, but is undeniably... odd.

I watch him for a few more seconds, noticing his eyes linger on Tate who's arguing with her mother about something. His gaze rests there for a few seconds, before he looks away, frowning and muttering something to himself.

Yeah, definitely an oddball.

"Are you okay, ma'am?" I jerk around and stare at a large man who approaches me cautiously.

"Oh yes. Thank you, Mercer." It's hard to get used to the feeling of being followed around by bodyguards.

I now have two of them with me at all times. Now I understand how Emma feels. A lot of the time, they try their best to blend into the background and once in a while, you may even forget that they're there. But then something happens and they'll jump out to protect you and you'll realize they were right there.

Although they haven't done much jumping lately, since the pearl saga seems to be coming to a close.

I glance aside at where Nate and Hal are speaking. Nate got released on bail with an ankle monitor, thanks to his cooperation and Declan's efforts. He's not free of all the charges yet, but at least he gets to stay home while getting ready for the trial.

Hal, on the other hand, is a new hero in town. Despite the scandal that rocked Laketown, with his father in jail and branded a murderer, Hal's reputation seems to have survived the fallout. Everyone heard how he took a bullet for me–mostly because he won't stop talking about it–and now he gets all sorts of perks.

But I love that for him because he's earned it. It's because of him that I'm alive and I let him know constantly how grateful I am. Micah gave him a handsome reward for it too, and Grandpa Crane now allows him to eat for free at the Tiki Bar for life. It's hard to know which of those things Hal likes more.

As Hal drifts away from Nate, I walk over to my cousin and smile. "That is a real gnarly mask."

"Oh yeah?" His mask is black with puckered scars all over it. "Seemed to fit the occasion. And who are you supposed to be, Cinderella?"

"Something like that," I say. We pause and regard each other.

"I'm sorry," he says.

"Nate, this is like the fiftieth time you've apologized,"

I say. "You don't have to keep doing it."

"I feel like I do. I feel like all this mess is my fault."

"It really isn't. If you hadn't been there, Rick would have found someone else to help him with his scheme. Someone who may not have helped Amelia get saved in time." I nod. "I know you did the wrong thing, but you have a good heart, Nate. Always have and always will."

He smiles weakly. "I just hate that I disappointed you, Lady Fishy."

"Oh, don't you start with that." Nate has been spending a lot of time with Grandpa Crane since he got out and I guess the nickname is rubbing off. He chuckles.

"I love you," I tell him. "You know that, right?"

"Yeah, I know. I love you too. And I'm sorry."

"Fifty-one," I say tiredly, and he laughs.

Then, I spot Micah's grandfather conversing with an equally distinguished-looking man. His eyes meet mine over his companion's shoulder and I wink, smirking when he huffs and looks away.

It's funny the transformation our relationship has undergone in such a short time. Even after his apology, the man still frequently says ignorant stuff about the less fortunate, but I make sure I call him out on it. It surprises Micah and his dad till this day, but they're getting used to it. At this point, I think they might be enjoying it.

Last week, I convinced Micah to help me take his grandfather to a shelter, where we met up with the manager. His grandfather only lasted five minutes before he wanted to leave, but a part of me thinks something got to him that day. He's still a raging snob, but he at least no longer calls the unhoused "riffraff." And I overheard him talking to Micah about possibly funding his affordable housing project.

So, yes, perhaps he's not completely hopeless.

At the other side of the room, I spot Grandpa Crane talking an actress' ear off, and Roger and Shoreton standing not too far off looking a tad suspicious. I walk close by and hear them muttering, "Do you think anyone would notice if we made off with that tray of shrimp cocktail over there?"

"Nah, I think they're all too busy schmoozing," Roger responds. "You can cause a distraction and I'll grab it and hide it in my jacket."

"Both of you, be on your best behavior," Poppy scolds. "We're not savages."

"Nah, just you," Shoreton says and Roger snorts.

I smile, and sail away with the rest of the bodies moving between us.

At the corner of the room, Mrs. Peach sits and talks to another elegantly dressed woman I've never met before. Just like Micah's grandfather, her eyes catch mine and I wink at her too. She beams with so much pride and love that it's palpable.

The only ones who aren't here are my parents, no matter how much they've pleaded and begged. I cut them off a while ago when, after my kidnapping, the only thing they wanted to know was how big Micah's family home was. I mean I realized earlier that they never truly cared about me, but that proved it. I said goodbye, walked away and haven't been back since. Neither has Nate.

I'm not answering their calls either. Sometimes I feel a little guilty, but I don't give into that. At some point, the cycle has to break and we have to sever ties with the ones who try to keep us tangled in them. I've told Nate the same about his mother, but it's going to take some time for that one to sink in.

But it has stuck for me. My only family, in my opinion, are those who have been there for me who I hold dear to my heart: Mrs. Peach, Emma, Grandpa Crane, Poppy and Tate, Yule. And of course, my Micah.

I drift around the party across the smooth burnished wood gleaming under the chandelier lights and search for Micah. In my search, I catch sight of Amelia and her friend, Jace, a tall blonde boy who seems to hang onto her every word.

They would make a cute couple, I think, walking up the sweeping staircase where rows of rooms lead down a hauntingly beautiful hallway with tiny stars embedded in the ceiling washing it with golden light, and gilded windows letting in the moon's haze.

Suddenly, a hand shoots out of an open closet and grabs my arm.

I already know who it is, so I don't panic. I can practically smell him from here even before he drags me close and whispers in my ears, "Did I tell you how beautiful you look?"

"Only about a dozen times."

"Well, you look beautiful," he says, his hand traveling over my ass. "And sexy. And hot."

Desire thrums in my belly. "I think all those things mean roughly the same thing."

"Do they?" He runs his nose down my neck and I shiver.

"Were you just hiding here waiting for me?"

"Nah. I saw you coming and decided to drag you in here to descend upon you like a hungry beast."

"You know there's a bedroom right across from us, right?"

"Yeah, but we've never done it in a coat closet."

I giggle and then sigh as he kisses the nape of my neck.

"Thank you," he whispers.

"For what?"

"For being with me. For having our child. For being the sexiest damn accountant I've ever seen."

"Well..." I wait until his eyes meet mine. "You're welcome." I take a second to soak in the silence, with the faint sound of classical music downstairs triggering memories. "You know this reminds me so much of our first hook up. At a hotel party, fooling around upstairs while the event goes on downstairs."

"Yeah, I remember. I got real nostalgic in this coat closet." He pulls back from my neck so I can stare into his beautiful green eyes. "The best decision I ever made was walking over to talk to the beautiful Athena."

God, he can be so sweet.

I can't help it then. I kiss him.

Please check the other books too from Summer's catalog.
SCAN OR CLICK HERE

Receive a FREE BOOK and join Summer's mailing list.
SCAN OR CLICK HERE

About the author

Summer Hunter writes romantic suspense with bite—where love sizzles, danger lurks, and someone always ends up shirtless.

She calls Hawaii home, which means she's fueled by sunshine, strong coffee, and the occasional plot twist that shows up between bites of fried noodles. Her characters are bold, her banter is sharp, and her happily-ever-afters always come with a little chaos and a lot of heat.

When she's not plotting her next twisty love story, she's probably side-eyeing tourists from behind her sunglasses and pretending it's all "research."

"Spicy Love, Sassy Suspense – Always HEA."

Grab a fan. Things are about to get steamy!

Printed in Great Britain
by Amazon